Crisis in Utopia . . .

Art Bonner began moving off the fast lane again. An elevator was waiting for him, of course, and there were two uniformed men next to it. All through Todos Santos the Security people would be moving quietly into place, just in case there were more to this attack than just three intruders in uninhabited areas.

Maintenance and engineering and the fire department would be on alert, too. If the hydrogen lines went, even if there wasn't a fire, Todos Santos would come grinding to a halt. It took energy to run the city. Less than the same people would need if they were scattered out in hundreds of thousands of buildings, of course, but it took plenty.

He limped off the pedway, acknowledged the guards with a wave, and entered the elevator, twitching while it rose. How's Pres taking it? He's killed two people! The elevator loosed him and he ran for Preston Sanders's office, angling sideways to favor the bad leg.

Most Pocket Books are available at special quantity discounts for bulk purchases for sales promotions, premiums or fund raising. Special books or book excerpts can also be created to fit specific needs.

For details write or telephone the office of the Vice President of Special Markets, Pocket Books, 1230 Avenue of the Americas, New York, New York 10020. (212) 245-6400, ext. 1760.

OATH OF FEALTY

LARRY NIVEN
JERRY POURNELLE

PUBLISHED BY POCKET BOOKS NEW YORK

POCKET BOOKS, a Simon & Schuster division of
GULF & WESTERN CORPORATION
1230 Avenue of the Americas, New York, N.Y. 10020

Copyright © 1981 by Larry Niven and Jerry Pournelle

Library of Congress Catalog Card Number: 81-9222

ISBN: 0-671-82802-9

First Pocket Books printing August, 1982

10 9 8 7 6 5 4 3 2

POCKET and colophon are trademarks of Simon & Schuster.

Printed in the U.S.A.

For Robert A. Heinlein,
who showed us all how.

Contents

the big one came up and I didn't reach you—"

"Yeah?"

"I'm in charge, isn't it nice that—"

Dramatis Personae

Joe Dunhill	Probationary Officer, Todos Santos Security
Isaac Blake	Lieutenant, Todos Santos Security
Preston Sanders	Deputy General Manager, Todos Santos Independency
Tony Rand	Chief Engineer, Todos Santos
Arthur Bonner	General Manager, Todos Santos
Frank Mead	Comptroller, Todos Santos
Delores Martine	Executive Assistant to the General Manager, Todos Santos
Barbara Churchward	Director of Economic Development, Todos Santos
MacLean Stevens	Executive Assistant to the Mayor of the City of Los Angeles
Sir George Reedy	Deputy Minister of Internal Development, Canada
Genevieve Rand	Tony Rand's former wife
Alice Marie Strahler	Executive Assistant to Tony Rand
Allan Thompson	Student
Sandra Wyatt	Assistant General Manager, Todos Santos
James Planchet	City Councilman, Los Angeles
Mrs. Eunice Planchet	James Planchet's wife
George Harris	Businessman and convicted tax evader

Thomas Lunan	Newsman
Amos Cross	Chief, Todos Santos Security
John Shapiro, LL.D.	Counsel, Todos Santos
Samuel Finder, M.D.	Medical Resident, Todos Santos
Hal Donovan	Lieutenant, Robbery/Homicide, Los Angeles Police Department
Cheryl Drinkwater	Todos Santos resident
Armand Drinkwater	Waldo Operator
Glenda Porter	Tattoo Artist
Sidney Blackman	District Attorney, County of Los Angeles
Penelope Norton	Judge, Superior Court, State of California
Phil Lowry	Newsman
Mark Levoy	Publican; former Yippie
Ronald Wolfe	General, American Ecology Army
Arnold Renn, Ph.D.	Professor of Sociology, UCLA
Rachael Lief	Bulldozer operator
Mrs. Carol Donovan	Lt. Donovan's wife
Vito Hamilton	Captain, Todos Santos Security
Vincent Thompson	Subway mugger

OATH OF FEALTY

Prologue

The only thing necessary for the triumph of evil is for good men to do nothing.

—Edmund Burke

THE INVADERS

Elsewhere in Los Angeles it was late afternoon, but here was only twilight. The three invaders peering out of the orange grove were deep in shadow. The sky blazed behind them and sent chinks of blue-white light through the trees to make the shadows darker. There was a fresh smell of fertilizers and crushed orange peel carried on the warm Santa Ana wind.

Close ahead the eastern face of Todos Santos was a black wall across the world. Thousands of balconies and windows in neat array showed in this light as no more than a faceless void seen through gray leaves, a sharp-edged black rectangle blotting out the sky.

The invaders blinked as they searched through uncertain light, and froze at the thunder of wings above. Nobody was about. They had watched the grounds tenders leave. They had seen no guards.

"There." The girl pointed. Her voice was no louder than the leaves' rustle in the wind. "There."

The two boys stared until they made out a square outline, barely visible, at the base of the towering wall. It seemed about man-sized. "The big door," she said. "We're still a good way away. It doesn't look it, but that door is thirty feet high. The little one is to the left of it."

"I can't find it," said one of the boys. He giggled suddenly, and stopped as suddenly. He said, "Nervous? Me?"

The other boy was lean and sketchily bearded, and he carried a black case on a strap. He stared at tiny lights set on its top, then said, "Run for the big door until you see the little one. On the count. Three, two, one, go."

He ran holding the case in front of himself to cushion against shock. The others lagged behind. They were carrying a much larger box between them. The leader was already taking things out of the case when they came puffing up.

"This lousy light," he panted.

"Bad for the guards, too," said the girl. "It's late afternoon everywhere but here. At night they'd *know* they couldn't see. They'd be watching harder."

The other boy grinned. "We'll give 'em a hell of a shock."

There was a sign on the door. Below a large death's head it said:

> IF YOU GO THROUGH THIS DOOR,
> YOU WILL BE KILLED.

It was repeated in Spanish, Japanese, Chinese, and Korean.

"Subtle, aren't they?" the girl said. She stiffened as the bearded boy pushed the door open. There was no sudden wail of alarms and they grinned at each other for a moment of triumph.

They dodged through fast. The bearded boy closed the door behind them.

I

Life in the state of nature is solitary, poor, nasty, brutish, and short.

—Thomas Hobbes, *Leviathan*

THE WATCHERS

Joe Dunhill polished his badge on his sleeve and plucked imaginary lint from the crisp blue of his uniform. The door was still there, still marked CENTRAL SECURITY: Authorized Personnel Only. He took a deep breath and reached for the small button at one side. Before his finger could touch it, there was a faint buzzing sound and the door opened.

The room inside gleamed with steel and chrome and Formica. A policeman with metal sergeant's chevrons on his collar sat at a desk facing the door. There was nothing on the desk but a small TV screen. "Yeah?"

"Officer Dunhill, reporting for duty."

The older man raised an eyebrow. "Bit early for the evening shift."

"Yes, sir. I thought there might be paper work, my first day and all."

The sergeant smiled faintly. "Computers take care of that. Dunhill?" He frowned. "Oh, yeah, you're the new man from Seattle PD. Guess you had a pretty good record up there. Want some coffee?" He turned to a machine on one side of the room.

"Uh, guess so. Light and sweet, please."

The sergeant pushed buttons. The machine thought for a moment, then whined faintly. The sergeant held out a molded plastic mug. "Here you go."

Joe tasted experimentally. "Hey. That's good." The surprise was obvious in his voice.

"Well of course it's—Oh. You're new here. Look, *all* the coffee machines in Todos Santos make good coffee. We wouldn't have 'em here if they didn't. Boss lady bought a thousand of these."

Even clichés die, Joe Dunhill thought.

"Why'd you leave Seattle?"

The question sounded casual, and maybe, Joe thought, maybe it is. And maybe not. "Todos Santos made me an offer I couldn't refuse."

The sergeant's smile was friendly, but knowing. "Dunhill, I wasn't on the board that decided to hire you, but I've heard the story. I think you got a raw deal."

"Thanks."

"Yeah. But I wouldn't have hired you if it was left up to me."

"Oh." Joe didn't know what to say to that.

"Not because you shot that punk. I'd have done the same thing myself."

"Then why not?"

"Because I don't think you can do the job."

"I was a damned good policeman," Joe said.

"I know you were. And probably still are. And that's the trouble. We don't have police here." The sergeant laughed at Joe's blank stare. "We look like police, right? Badges. Uniforms. Guns, some of us. But we aren't police, Dunhill. We're security people, and there's a lot of difference." He came over to put his hand on Joe's shoulder. "Look, I hope you work out. Let's go."

He led Joe out of the reception room and down a long hall to a closed door.

"Did they tell you about the locking system we use here?" the sergeant asked.

"Not really."

"Well, everybody in Todos Santos has an ID badge. There's some kind of electronic magic—well, hell, it might as well be magic for all I know! It opens locks if you've got the right badge for it. Residents' badges open their own doors, that kind of thing. Security badges open a lot of doors." He waved his own badge at the door in front of them. Nothing happened. "But not this one. Security Central's kind of special. What happens is we alert the inside duty officer."

They waited for a few moments, then the door opened into a small, dimly lit room the size of a closet. The door behind them closed, then another door in front of them opened onto a much larger and even more dimly lit room.

There were TV screens around all four walls, banks of them, with uniformed men seated in front of each bank. In the center of the room was a huge circular console with dozens of dials and buttons. More TV screens were built into the console. A uniformed captain wearing a tiny telephone headset-microphone sprawled in a comfortable chair in the middle of the center console.

"Dunhill, Captain," the sergeant said. "First day. Assigned to Blake."

The captain nodded. "Thanks, Adler. Welcome aboard, Dunhill."

Isaac Blake had a square face with roundness shaping under the square chin, a square body also turning round, black-and-white hair with the white winning. He lolled at ease before the bank of TV screens and sipped coffee. Every twenty seconds or so he touched a knob and the pictures shifted.

There seemed no order to the flow of pictures. Now

the camera looked down on the heads of hundreds of shoppers strolling along a Mall, bright-colored clothing that looked strange because the light was artificial but the scene was so large that you expected it to be sunlight. Now a view of a big dining hall. Now a view through the orange groves, looking up at Todos Santos standing a thousand feet tall.

"Whew—this is one big city. Even on a TV screen."

Blake nodded. "Yeah, it still gets to me, sometimes." His fingers moved, and the view shifted to look along one side wall. Seen from that angle, the two-mile length seemed to stretch on forever.

The kaleidoscope continued. Sparse traffic in a subway. Interior halls, stretching far away; people on moving belts, people on escalators, people in elevators. A dizzying view down onto a balcony, where a nude hairy man sprawled in obscene comfort on an air mattress. Thirty men and women seated at a long bench soldering tiny electronic parts onto circuit boards, chatting gaily and working almost without looking at what they were doing.

The camera switched to the greensward beyond Todos Santos's perimeter, where a dozen pickets lethargically marched about with signs. "END THE NEST BEFORE IT ENDS HUMANITY," said one. Blake sniffed and touched buttons. The scene jumped to a pretty girl in a miniskirt carrying a bag of groceries; the camera followed her down a long hall from an escalator, zooming along to keep her in closeup as she walked into a small alcove. When she took her badge out of her purse, the door opened, and she went inside, leaving the door standing open while she set the bag down on an Eames chair. For a moment the screen showed an expensive apartment, meticulously clean, thick rugs, paintings on the walls. The girl was unbuttoning her blouse as she came to the door and closed it.

"Like to watch the rest of that show," Blake muttered. He turned a lazy smile toward Joe Dunhill.

"Of course we aren't supposed to do that," Dunhill said.

"Nope. Can't, either."

"Oh. I've noticed you haven't shown up the inside of any apartment. I guess I wouldn't want cameras in my bathroom either."

"Oh, we've got them there," Blake said. "But they don't go on without authorization—there's one now." He touched his headset. "Captain, I'll take that interior call."

"Right."

The TV screen flicked to show a kitchen. A small boy was pulling things out of cabinets, scattering flour on the floor and carefully mixing in salt preparatory to pouring a bottle of sherry across the mess. Blake reached forward to a button under the screen. He waited a moment, then said into the tiny headset microphone, "Ma'am, this is Central Security. Somebody pushed the panic button in the kitchen, and I think you'd better have a look out there. Yes, Ma'am, it's *safe* but you ought to hurry."

He waited. On the screen above, a woman, mid-thirties, not very attractive at the moment because her hair was partly in curlers and partly in wet strings, came into the kitchen, looked down in horror, and shouted, "Peter!"

Then she looked up with a smile and moved closer to the camera. "Thank you, Officer," she said. Blake smiled back, for no sane reason, and touched a dial. The picture faded.

Joe Dunhill watched in concentration. Sergeant Adler had been right, this was no kind of police work he'd ever seen. He turned to Blake. "I don't get it. You just skip around."

"Sort of. Of course there are exceptions, like when somebody asks us to keep an eye on things. But mostly we watch what we feel like. After a while you get some judgment about the feels."

"But wouldn't it be better to have assigned places? Instead of jumping around—"

"Bosses don't think so. They want us alert. Who can be alert just staring at one scene all the time? The math boys worked it out, how many of us, how many TV screens each, probability of trouble—over my head, but it seems to work."

Joe digested that. "Uh—seems to me I'd be more valuable out on the streets. Responding to calls—"

Blake laughed. "After you've been here a year maybe they'll put you where you interact with stockholders. If you work out." The kaleidoscope above continued. A moving beltway, with some kids walking on a balcony above it. Blake touched controls, and the camera zoomed in on the kids. After a moment the kaleidoscope started up again. "Think about it," Blake said. "In Seattle, you were a cop, and out among the civilians. You worried about making good arrests, right? Best way to get promoted."

"Sure—"

"Well, in here it's different." Blake suddenly frowned and set down his cup.

It took Joe Dunhill a moment to realize that Blake was no longer interested in the conversation, and another to see why he was staring. It wasn't the screen at all. A blue light to the side had lit up.

"On the roof," he said, with a question in his voice. Then, with more confidence, "Visitor. How did he get up there?"

Blake played with the controls. The screen jumped with disconnected pictures, flashing views of four square miles of roof: the curtained windows of the Sky Room night club; golfers on the golf course; a view down onto one of the inverted-pyramid shapes of an air well, plunging down in narrowing steps each one story high and lined with windows. Then a forest of skeletal structures: a children's playground, empty at the moment, then another jungle gym with a dozen kids hanging like bats. The Olympic swimming pool, with a wide, shallow children's wading pool just beyond. Baseball diamond. Football field. On the Todos Santos roof was every kind of playground for child or adult.

Then beyond a low fence, an empty area, bags of concrete and piles of wood for forms, cement mixer idle at the moment. The camera zoomed to the mixer. "ID badge," Blake muttered. "Visitor badge, must be stuffed into the cement mixer. What the hell for? And what's he doing up there?" The TV screen flowed across the roof again, searching—

"There," cried Joe Dunhill.

"Yeah. I see him. Doesn't seem to be carrying anything. Might have been, though. We'll have to search the roof. Detectors would have picked up anything metal, and there's not a lot worth bombing up there, but we'll have to look anyway."

The figure moved rapidly along the twelve-foot fence between him and the edge. He was hunched over, a caricature of a man sneaking. He found a gap in the fence, hesitated, and moved into it.

Blake grinned. "Hah! Maybe we won't have to send anyone up after all. He's found the diving board."

"That's not the pool area."

"I know. Sometimes I wonder about Rand. You know about Tony Rand? He's the chief architect for this place. Rand's high board isn't in the pool area."

"Uh?"

"Watch. If he's really a leaper, we won't have to call anyone." Blake touched another button. "Captain, I have the bandit on the roof area. Looks like he's going to dive." Blake fiddled with the knobs. The picture sharpened.

• • •

He had been following the fence for thirty minutes, looking for a way to reach the edge. The fence seemed endless, and he wondered if he could climb it, and if there were alarms. Todos Santos was said to be very Big Brother . . .

Then he saw the opening. There was a cement mixer nearby and he pushed the visitor badge into it. The badge wasn't his, and told nothing about him, but it was the last possible clue. Maybe they'd find it and maybe not. He moved on, to the gap in the fence.

There was a big sign: WATCH YOUR STEP. He did not smile. His long, unhandsome face was dead calm, as if he had never smiled and never would. He turned into the channel of fencing. It was just wider than his shoulders.

The channel ended in a steel ladder. Through the steps he could see the orange groves and parks far below, then beyond them the tiny shapes of city houses, some with the blue splash of a swimming pool, all looking like miniatures. He pressed his forehead against the cold metal and looked down . . . a fifth of a mile down to the green landscape around Todos Santos. A thousand feet to oblivion.

He climbed the steps. The situation was strange. The steps ended in a long, narrow rectangle. He tested it with his foot. Wood padded with burlap . . . and it shook slightly.

A high-diving board.

He walked out on the board and looked down.

The balconies receded in perspective until they merged with blank wall. The parkland below was a green blur. A view more mathematical than real, parallel lines meeting at infinity. So here was the end of a dull and thwarted life. He was carrying no identification. After a fall like that they would never know who he was. Let them wonder.

The board bounced as he shifted his weight.

"But—but suppose he jumps?" Joe Dunhill asked.

"Well, we don't advertise it, but there's a net that comes out when he passes the spy-eyes. Then we just collect him and eject him. Let him give his bad publicity to someone else," Blake told him.

"Does this happen all the time? You don't look particularly interested."

"Oh, I'm interested. I've got five bucks in the pool. See that chart?" Blake waved at the far wall, where chalk marks said:

LAUGHING 3
BACKED OUT   JUMPED 8
TERRIFIED 7

"That's this quarter's tally. Work it out," said Blake. "The roof of this place is eight miles of sheer cliff. We get every would-be suicide west of the Rockies and some from New England and Japan. But the high-diving board is the only access to the edge, and it does have a funny effect on people." Blake frowned and scratched his neck. "He sure looks like a jumper. If he backs out I stand a fair chance to win."

The man stood straddle-legged at the end of the board, brooding above a thousand-foot drop. The picture of melancholy . . . until a gust of wind slapped across him, and suddenly he was dancing on one leg and waving his arms.

"Maybe not," Blake said. The jumper was reflexively fighting for his life. The gust died suddenly, and he almost went off the other side of the board. He wound up on hands and knees. He stayed there, gripping the board. Presently he began backing toward the ladder. When he reached the steps he stayed stooped and backed down, placing his feet very carefully.

"Leaper's off, Captain," Blake called.

"Right. Got a detail going after him."

Joe asked, "Some of them laugh?"

"Yeah. It's a funny picture, isn't it? You're going to kill yourself. It's the most powerful statement you can make about the way the world has treated you. That's what Rand says, anyway. And when you finally get there, there's a high-diving board to add ten feet to the drop!"

Joe shook his head, grinning.

"They don't all back out. Once I watched a woman stand up there, take off her overcoat—she wasn't wearing anything under it—bounce once, and take off in a really gorgeous swan dive." He smiled, then shook himself. "But the board turns off a lot of them. Rand isn't any dummy. He built Todos Santos, and he's still building it, if you know what I mean. He's always tinkering around."

"I'd like to meet him."

"You will."

Fat chance, Joe thought. "What happens to the leaper?"

"One of the bosses will talk to him. Standing orders. Rand wants to know what makes them tick. Maybe think of ways to discourage them." Blake looked at his watch. "This one may have a wait. There's a bigwig from Canada coming in for a visit and all the brass will be busy."

"Can we hold him?" Joe asked. "I mean, civil rights and all—"

"Sure. Some of us are real live cops," Blake said. "It's a legal thing. Todos Santos is legally a city. Sort of. But the insurance is cheaper if most of us are security officers rather than peace officers. But we are a city. We even have a jail. Judges, too, but they don't get much work. Corporation people take care of civil matters, and felonies go to the LA County District Attorney."

"It sure is different here—" Joe blinked and leaned closer to the screen. "Hey—"

"What?"

"I saw a light flash. That one."

"Um. Tunnel area. We better check, that's critical territory—" He did things to the console, and a row of lights flashed green. "Nobody there who doesn't belong there. You sure you saw something?"

"Almost sure."

"Probably some maintenance troop had his badge

inside a tool box." Blake yawned. "Get me another coffee?"

"Sure."

•   •   •

Preston Sanders ranked high in the Todos Santos hierarchy; high enough to rate the enormous office furnished as he liked it, with abstract paintings and maps of ski slopes. A teak-bordered TV screen nearly covering one wall showed motion pictures of ski events. The flickering motions, shifting from third-person to over-the-shoulder views of an expert taking the world's steepest slopes and jumps, generally drove his visitors to ask for something else, but Preston loved them.

The furniture was mahogany and teak; even the panels of the desk console were covered with teak, and there were dark wood borders on the TV screens on the desk and on the walls. When Sanders had explained the decor he wanted, Tony Rand had characteristically remarked, "Matched set, eh?"

Sanders thought of that sometimes. It was true enough. Sanders was the color of oiled teak. And Tony Rand had meant the remark exactly as it sounded. Sanders looked up at Rand, who was doing his best to ignore the gut-wrenching view of the Olympic jump. "I used to wonder about you," Preston said. "You don't have any racial prejudice."

Raised that suddenly by a black man, the subject would have jarred some whites. Rand said, "Should I?" and still not looking at the TV screen with its instant vertigo finished pouring coffee from the silver samovar. He tipped a dollop of Sanders's brandy—Carlos Primero, and far too good to be put into coffee—into the coffee.

"Certainly. It's normal. So I wondered, and I finally got the answer. You still think of Todos Santos as practice for building a starship, don't you?"

"Sure, Pres. I *built* Todos Santos. Who should know better than me? We could start building the ships right now. The design is straightforward. What we can't do is build a technological society that's self-sufficient with only a few thousand members."

"Did the Directors know you thought that way? I'm surprised they even let you work on this place. They could have picked someone who thought it was an end in itself."

"It isn't. I don't think the Directors think so. They think it's practice for better arcologies. It is, too. We're too dependent on Los Angeles, but we'll learn what we didn't put in the design and the next one will have it. Brandy?"

"Not just now. I've got to see Art before he gets tied up with a visiting fireman—surprised you don't know about him." Sanders reached to the teak panel and turned a dial. The Olympic scene vanished, to be replaced with a view of Los Angeles as seen from the top of Todos Santos.

"I know about him. I convinced Bonner I'd be busy all day. What was your great contribution to race relations?"

"Well, one day I said to myself, here I am, one of a couple of hundred black people in a building the size of a city, and I'm Art Bonner's deputy. And here's Tony Rand, flying a starship in his head, with a single black man in the bridge crew. Then it came to me. I'm the token alien, and you're studying me."

Rand grinned slowly. "Token alien. On the bridge. Interesting . . . listen, if you'll tell me your token skin color, I'll tell you the shape of your token ears."

"Green."

"Pointed."

They grinned at each other. Rand said, "Tell you something. There *are* aliens on the bridge, and you aren't either of them. And yes, I'm studying them. Will you grant me that Art Bonner is a genius?"

"Sure," Preston said without hesitation. "I know what the top job in this place involves. Nobody else could do it."

"Think you'd catch me trying? All right, is Barbara Churchward a genius?"

Sanders frowned for a moment. "I don't work the Economics department much. Art thinks so." He frowned again. "Aha. I think I see what you're driving at."

"Right," Tony Rand said. "Now, they've both got those implants." Rand's face took on a strange look; almost, Sanders thought, one of intense longing, like an exile looking across the sea toward home. "Wonder what it's like to know anything you want to, just by asking? Anyway. We can think of both of them as man-computer interfaces. What I have to decide is, just how important is the computer link? They were both geniuses *before* the implant link went in."

The TV screen showed the phallic shape of the Los Angeles City Hall jutting up through the smog. Sanders tuned the picture more sharply. "And the implants are hideously expensive," Preston said. "I see. You have to decide if the officers of your starship need them anyway."

"Or of my next arcology. So you tell me: are those two just geniuses, or are they now something more?"

"How the devil would I know?"

"Just on the odds, I thought you might be a genius yourself. I mean, the only black man in the command staff of Todos Santos must have had something more than the usual going for him."

"Oh, you idiot."

"Query?"

"It doesn't *take* that. It takes a certain amount of intelligence, plus being willing to take the responsibilities for the orders you give, and—" He stopped, flinching at the word he had been about to use; and he looked to see if Rand had guessed.

But his problem was just the opposite. Rand, without the faintest idea of what he was talking about, was waiting for him to go on.

"All right," Preston said. "We play the politics

game here. It means a lot of interpersonal friction, a lot of compromises, between one guy who thinks he's got the right answer and another guy who thinks *he* does. I get caught in the middle a lot, maybe more than anyone, because I'm more noticeable." Sanders shrugged. "So I put up with it. I give in a lot, even when I know I'm right. There are people who would call that tomming."

"Tomming? Uncle Tom? But you give more orders than you take."

Rand would *never* understand. It was the trait that kept him out of Todos Santos's micropolitics: you tried to manipulate him, and suddenly he was somewhere else, redesigning your closet space while you were trying to get someone fired.

Which was why Sanders generally felt comfortable with Rand. Tony Rand was no threat. Like Art Bonner, he was someone you could trust all the way.

But if he ever does get involved, Sanders thought. If he ever does, he's going to be a dangerous man. True, Maintenance was part of Operations—but the Maintenance supervisors would probably side with the Chief Engineer if it came to a choice. Maybe not openly, but—. Sanders had a mental image of someone trying to lever Rand and ending up with his sink connected to his toilet while his air conditioning poured out eau d' skunk. His face split into a wide grin.

Rand said, "Something?"

"Do the name Sir George Reedy mean anything to you?"

"No."

"He's the chap you ducked out of meeting, the Canadian who's come to study Todos Santos. I've been watching for his helicopter."

"I thought you'd changed the scene to be polite."

"And, Tony—Sir George has an implant."

"Uh. I guess he's worth talking to, then." Rand looked thoughtful.

"More than you know. He got the implant as a

favor someone owed his family. I doubt that he was a genius before the implant went in."

"Oh *ho*." Rand glanced at his new toy, a Bulova Dali watch, as thin and flexible as the sleeve of his shirt. "Uh—I think I ought to see about some details," he said. "Maybe I can get free for the afternoon. Pres? Thanks." Rand left hurrying, followed by that white grin.

The grin slipped away as Sanders followed private thoughts.

His family had never been enslaved. Undoubtedly someone had been, somewhere; but from as early as 1806, the furthest back anyone could trace, the Sanderses had been free Negroes working for the United States government in Washington. His father had been a Public Health Service physician. Sanders himself had gone to the best private schools . . .

. . . where they were so liberal they wouldn't even *think* the word nigger. And how I hated those snotty bastards, Sanders remembered. He looked down at his dark hands and wondered at himself. So why don't I hate Mead and Letterman and the others, the ones who get nervous talking to me?

He straightened, remembering, and used the console controls to change the view on the TV from eastward toward LA to westward toward the ocean. A joystick control moved the camera until he saw a brightly colored shape in the afternoon sky, and he zoomed in on it. Frank Mead, shouting happily as he hung from the double-winged hang glider. Mead wasn't overweight, he was just *big*, and it took a specially designed glider to carry him. Mead was one of them; one who made no secret that he thought Preston Sanders was going to blow it one day.

So why don't I hate him? Preston wondered. He makes me nervous, but I don't hate him. Why?

Because I don't share the black experience? That's what my roommate at Howard would have said.

Or because we're all doing something we believe in? We're running a civilization, something new in this world, and don't bother to tell me how small it is. It's a civilization. The first one in a long time where people can feel *safe*.

If only they believed in me.

He got up from his desk. It was time for his interview with Art Bonner.

II

Management has been the success story of a century which has not been one of the most successful centuries in human history.

In the society which our history books describe, everybody worried constantly about rank and precedence. Nobody today worries about precedence. What all these managers worry about is talking to each other.

—Peter F. Drucker, "Management's New Role" i₂ *The Future of the Corporation*, Herman Kahn (Ed.)

THE MANAGERS

Preston Sanders walked briskly along the corridor called Executive Row, not really noticing the thick carpets and the paneled walls dotted with paintings. He considered what he had to cover, rank ordering priorities for Bonner—who had a million demands to fill, and couldn't possibly give Sanders everything he wanted.

The anteroom to Bonner's office was a study in comfort, designed by psychologists to make waiting to see Bonner, if not pleasant, at least as minimally unpleasant as possible. Delores Martine certainly contributed to that feeling. Sanders knew she was at least as busy as Bonner—possibly even more so—but she always had time to chat with anyone waiting.

"Get your work done, Dee," Preston said. "I've got a couple of things to sort out anyway."

"All right. Mr. Bonner will be free in just a moment. He got a satellite call from Zurich—"

From the big bosses, the money people who owned Todos Santos. "It's all right," Pres assured her. "Really."

She nodded and began shuffling through papers, leaving Sanders to his reverie. He wanted to think about the labor problem in Air Shaft 4, but his thoughts strayed to Delores—and Art Bonner. Wonder what happened to those two? They were obviously having an affair the year after Art's wife left him. Who'd want a casual visitor for a husband and father of her children? But Dee sees him all day. They were at it hot and heavy for a while, and then nothing. Wonder why?

"He's off the phone now," Delores said.

"Thanks." Sanders went into the inner office.

Art Bonner leaned back in the black leather chair and put his heels on the walnut desk. Despite the expensive furniture there was a junkyard look to the office: model sailboats; shelves full of bric-a-brac including the truly horrid souvenirs sold in stalls near the boat landings of a dozen tourist-trap cities; a couple of yachting trophies; and mixed with all the nautical stuff were expensive "executive toys" of every conceivable variety, most of them ridiculous. There were also books opened and left on the credenza, some piled two deep. No one would accuse Art Bonner of compulsive neatness.

The TV screen on the wall showed a holographic view of Todos Santos in all its complexity.

"Zurich problems again?" Sanders asked.

"A few. OPEC's raising prices next month. Thank God we've got our own power sources," Bonner said.

"If we can keep them. That's my top problem," Sanders said.

Bonner sighed. "Yeah. Okay, unload the bag, Pres. But you'll have to make it fast. My visiting fireman is early for the cocktail hour." He frowned slightly, and the hologram faded from the TV screen, replaced by a view from the roof looking toward the Los Angeles City Hall. A dark speck came toward them.

• • •

The building was a thousand feet in height rising
starkly from a square base two miles on a side. It
rested among green parklands and orange groves and
low concrete structures so that it stood in total
isolation, a glittering block of whites and flashing
windows dotted with colors. The sheer bulk dwarfed
everything else in view.

"Magnificent!" Sir George Reedy crowded against
the window of the Los Angeles Fire Department
helicopter, then turned in wonder to his host. He had
to shout above the thrum of the motor. "Mister
Stevens, I've seen it on TV, of course, but I had no
idea—"

MacLean Stevens nodded. Todos Santos Independency affected everyone that way, and Stevens was
long accustomed to the reaction. That didn't make
him feel any better about it. Los Angeles was a great
city too. "If you'll look out there beyond it, Sir
George, you can see the Catalina Island development.
Closer, on the mainland, the city marina is just off to
our right. We think Del Rey and Catalina are significant developments in their own way."

Sir George Reedy dutifully looked off toward the
sea. "Ah, I was going to ask about that. I saw it
when we flew in. The great white mass—"

"The iceberg." I might have known, Stevens
thought. Five hundred billion gallons worth of
Antarctic iceberg had been towed into Santa Monica
Bay. Los Angeles water had never tasted better;
Arizona, San Francisco, and the sea gulls of Mono
Lake had never been happier. The berg sat out there
in a kind of tub. There were teams of climbers going
up two faces, and a dozen Boy Scouts glissading
down snow near the bottom. "Romulus Corporation
tows the icebergs here. They're the ones who built
Todos Santos, too."

"Ah."

There was no way to get off the subject of Todos

Santos. Stevens gave in gracefully and called the pilot. "Captain, if you'll just circle Todos Santos for Sir George—"

The whine of the turbines changed subtly as the big red chopper curled in a tight circle. It traced the perimeter of the parks surrounding the huge building. To their left was Todos Santos and its outlying moat of orange groves and green parklands. Reedy peered down, then exclaimed, "Did I see deer?"

"Likely enough," Stevens said.

Directly below them, where they couldn't see, was a ring of shabby houses and decaying apartments.

MacLean Stevens did not look down but he was acutely aware of what was below. Block after block, a mockery to city government and all of Stevens's hopes, houses filled with families without hope living on welfare—and on the leavings from Todos Santos.

The turbine whines continually changed pitch as the pilot varied the speed, and Stevens hoped his visitor wouldn't notice. Eaters didn't usually shoot at the Fire Department anyway. Not anymore.

"But what is that made of?" Sir George asked. "This is an earthquake area."

"Yes. They tell me it's perfectly safe," Stevens answered. "The contracts require that the architect, contractors, and a lot of the work force have to live inside. They put a lot of design sweat into it."

"Ah."

"As to what it's made of, just about everything. The supporting towers are steel trusses, mostly. The walls don't carry gravity loads, and they can be anything that resists the wind stress. Composites like fiberglass reinforced with carbon filaments. Some of the more advanced compote tuffies. Lot of concrete on the lower levels. See the gaps there? The apartment complexes are assembled down below and hoisted into place as units—"

Sir George wasn't listening. He had lifted his binoculars and was busily staring at the monstrous building. Fifty levels rose out of the parklands and orange groves below. Balconies jutted at each level. At seemingly random intervals, yet with an overall pleasing pattern he couldn't have explained, extra-large balconies protruded, and these were covered with tables and chairs where groups of people in brightly colored clothing ate, or played cards, or did other things not noticeable even with binoculars from a mile away.

"I say, some of those people are naked!"

Stevens nodded. Not the diners and card players, of course. Sir George must be spying on individual apartment balconies. The inhabitants of Todos Santos were fond of sunbathing, and the balconies were completely private from one another. Only airborne peeping toms could watch them—as if anyone cared all that much in Southern California. Evidently, high-ranking Canadians had different standards.

"And what are all those below?" Sir George asked. He pointed to a series of low mounds, obviously the roofs of underground buildings; the mounds were covered with trees and shrubs, but concrete driveways led downward to doors at each one.

Stevens shrugged. "Food factories, mostly. Dairies. Chicken ranches. Processing sheds for the citrus groves. Sir George, I'm not really an expert on Todos Santos. You'll get better information inside."

"Yes, of course." Reedy turned away from his binoculared rubbernecking and looked at Stevens with sympathy. "I forgot, it's not really part of your city at all, is it? Aren't you a bit jealous?"

Stevens controlled his face and the grimace he felt. The question reminded him of the ever-present sour pain he felt in his guts recently. "Of the wealth, yes. Of the money that flows into it and goes out of the country. Of the taxes it evades. I resent those, Sir George, but I am not jealous of the people who live in that termite hill."

"I see."

"No, sir, I doubt if you do." The bitterness was open now and Stevens rushed on, heedless of the consequences. "Termites. When you're inside, notice the similarities. Caste system remarkably well developed. Warriors, Kings, Queens, Workers, Drones, all represented. And a strong tendency toward identical units within each caste."

He checked himself before saying more. It would be better to let this visiting dignitary see for himself. Sir George looked an overweight fool and might be one, but Stevens thought he probably was not. He ranked as a Deputy Minister, and Stevens had noticed that many English-Canadian officials feigned careless buffoonery.

"I saw demonstrators," Reedy said.

"Yeah," Stevens answered. "Several varieties, too. Todos Santos is not exactly popular with the younger generation."

"Why not?"

"Maybe you'll see for yourself." And maybe you won't, Stevens thought. Maybe—ah, to hell with it.

The helicopter had turned again and now cruised above a well-marked flight path across the orange groves toward the building. As the chopper rose, the roof came into view.

The enormous surface was cluttered. It was cut into areas by four huge light wells, each step-shaped with interior balconies.

"They look like the box the Great Pyramid came in," Sir George quipped.

Stevens laughed. "Actually, they're bigger."

Even with the light wells, the remaining area was huge. There were parks, swimming pools, miniature golf and a driving range; heliports, playgrounds with running children; corner towers for penthouse residents, the highest caste of all.

"What powers it all?" Reedy asked.

"Hydrogen," Stevens said. "They've got a complex of nuclear breeder plants in Mexico, with pipelines running up to Todos Santos."

Reedy nodded approval. "Hydrogen. Todos Santos doesn't add much to your LA smog, then."

"No. That was part of their contract with the federal government." Stevens paused. "Some environmentalists are still unhappy, though. They say Todos Santos is simply exporting its pollution—"

He was interrupted by the roar of the helicopter as the pilot let the bright red machine settle gently onto a painted circle at one corner of the massive building. The roof was so large that it was difficult to realize they were hundreds of feet above ground level.

Men waited for them. A brisk wind whipped across the building. The wind was cold in the late afternoon, and they were glad to get inside one of the low rooftop structures.

The heliport reception area was not large. Most of the men in it wore uniforms and carried weapons. The guards very politely photographed them.

"If you'll just put your hands on this identiplate, please, sir," a guard lieutenant prompted. The readout screen was hidden from view of visitors, making it impossible to know what the guard found out.

Machinery hummed and spat out two thick plastic badges. MacLean Stevens, Executive Assistant to the Mayor of the City of Los Angeles; and Sir George Reedy, Deputy Minister for Internal Development and Urban Affairs, Dominion of Canada. Their photographs filled half the badges' faces, and VISITOR was printed in letters of fire across them.

"Please wear these at all times while in the Independency," the lieutenant said. "That's very important."

"What would happen if I lost the badge?" Sir George asked. His voice was very precise and clipped, perfect Oxbridge accent. It held just the right note of incredulity and contempt, and MacLean Stevens envied it.

The guard didn't seem to notice that he had been insulted. "Sir, it would be very serious. Our detectors would indicate someone without identification in the Independency, and officers would be sent. It might be embarrassing to you."

"Might be dangerous, too," Stevens said. "Lieutenant, how many people come in here and never come out?"

"Sir?" The guard was frowning now.

"Skip it." No point in harassing a rent-a-cop. The man might not know. Or, Stevens thought, I might be wrong. "Shall I take Sir George, or do we need an escort?"

"As you choose, sir. Mister Bonner—" the lieutenant lowered his voice, as if in fear, or reverence, or both—"will be expecting you shortly. If you're planning any delay en route, please tell us so that we can notify him."

"We'll probably take a quick tour through the Mall, thank you."

"Very good, sir. I take it you will not need a routing slip."

"No. I've been there before."

"I know you have, Mr. Stevens." The guard glanced down at the invisible screen. "Have a pleasant stay in Todos Santos."

• • •

The holographic view of Todos Santos blinked a blue light, and two small blue dots appeared in the heliport reception area. "My visitors will be here pretty quick, Pres," Art Bonner said. "Anything you can't handle for me?"

"No. But I want to say it again. That hydrogen delivery schedule is *very* tricky, Art. If the FROMATES manage to zap an input line *this* month, we're hip deep in trouble."

"All right, already. You can have the overtime authorization for your cops." Bonner frowned.

Bonner's pause was momentary, almost imperceptible, and Sanders wondered what his boss was listening to. Only it wouldn't exactly be listening, either. What would it be like to have data fed directly into your mind?

"The comptroller won't like you much for it,"

Bonner said. "Mead was screaming about budget overruns just yesterday. But it's your decision."

"He'll scream louder if those yippies shut down our power," Sanders said.

"Right. Have no pity on me. I have to account to Zurich. You don't."

Bonner's contract gave him complete authority within Todos Santos. He was responsible to the money people who'd built the city, but they had no right to interfere with how he ran it. Of course they could always fire him.

"Take it as easy as you can," Bonner said. His voice became serious. "It isn't just Frank Mead. Zurich's going through cash-flow problems just now. The orbital construction shack eats money like mad. But damn it, do what you have to do. It's my problem, and Barbara's. Maybe she can pass a money miracle." He turned to the TV screen and pointed. The blue dots were moving rapidly downward. "Here they come. Look, we've settled the labor situation in central air control. We've promoted three policemen. We've got your memo blowing smoke up that vendor's arse. You're authorized overtime for your patrolmen, which is what you came in here for in the first place. Enough, already. Back to the cotton mines, Rastus."

"Yes, baas." It was easy to talk that way to Bonner. It hadn't always been—which was probably why Bonner did it, Pres thought. Art Bonner was damned if he'd have a thin-skinned deputy.

"You know how to sort the crap," Bonner said. "Well, my people will be here shortly. Drinking and carousing at all hours, no doubt. The wild and happy life. So, guess who'll be on duty tonight?"

"Yes, sir," Sanders said.

Bonner eyed him critically. Then he thumbed a button in the arm of the big chair. "Delores."

"Yes, sir," the intercom responded.

"Dee, if Mac Stevens and that Canadian get here

before I'm ready, give them the Number 2 Stall, will you?"

"Yes, Mister Bonner."

"Thanks." He cut the intercom. "Okay, Pres, what's eating you?"

"Nothing—"

"The hell there isn't. Talk."

"All right. I don't like being in the worry seat, Chief." If you've got to know, he thought. "I like my job. It isn't the work, and it isn't the responsibility. You've never given me anything I can't handle—"

"Precisely. So what's the problem?"

"The people out there don't like me as Number One. Number Two to you, sure. I'm *their* black man because I'm *your* deputy. But not in that seat."

Bonner frowned. "You been getting static? Who from? I'll—"

"No." Sanders spread his hands hopelessly. "Don't you understand, Art, you'll only make it worse if you have one of your famous talks with—with anybody, about this. It's nobody in particular anyway. They *all* resent having me in top charge. A lot of them may not even know they resent it. The ones that do work like hell at hiding it. *But I can't make a mistake!* Not even one."

"Neither can I—"

"Bull puckey. You can't make a *big* one. I can't make one at all."

"You're telling me to replace you because you can't handle the job?"

"If you think that, do it."

"I do not think that. If I thought it, I'd have replaced you a long time ago." Bonner sighed and shook his head. "Okay. You know how to find me. But for God's sake, see if you can't buy me a couple of hours, anyway."

"Sure. I can always do that," Sanders said. "And if the big one comes up and I can't reach you—"

"Yeah?"

"I'm in charge, Art. I know that."

"Good. Now can I see my visiting Canadian? We finished?"

"Sure."

"For now. We'll have lunch on this," Bonner said. "See Delores about when." He looked at the array of screens around him. They were all bordered nicely in green. "I'm giving you a clean board. Call me when you reach your office. As of then, you're in charge."

As Sanders left, he noticed that the blue dots had moved to a level far below Executive Row.

• • •

"We can talk here if we keep it down." The bearded boy sounded uncertain, but there were no alarms, and he grinned.

The others nodded and opened one of the boxes. The girl took out a gas mask. It was warm in the tunnel, and she wiped sweat from above her eyes before she put it on.

III

Custom reconciles us to everything.

—Edmund Burke

A TOUR OF TERMITE HILL

The reception lobby opened onto a roomful of elevators.

"The Executive Suites are below," Stevens told Sir George. "We can go straight down, or we can take a quick look at this anthill before they assign you a guide."

"But I thought we were expected."

"Don't worry about it. Bonner has plenty to keep him busy, and he knows exactly where we are."

"Really? Then there is some means of tracking these badges."

Stevens nodded. "We'll take a quick swing past some of the outside corridors. It wouldn't be fair to take you to the Mall first thing."

"Whyever not?"

"Too much to see. There's every kind of store in the world, and it's pretty crowded."

Reedy frowned. "If it's so big, why is it crowded? Surely there aren't enough people living here to—"

"Not the residents," Stevens said. His face held a sour expression. "Angelinos. A lot of them come here to shop. Hell, I can't really blame them. It's convenient. All the stores in one place, and the subway system to get them here. But the money comes in, and it never goes back out, not back to LA anyway."

"But—" Reedy gasped as the floor dropped from under him. "I say, that was abrupt." He watched the floor indicator blink rapidly. "I don't suppose you can restrict your people? Keep them from coming here?"

"How?" Stevens asked. "We tried that once. Courts threw out the ordinance—and the voters wouldn't have put up with it anyway. Didn't matter, though. Todos Santos owns the subway system. This place is the hub—and it's easier to get from San Pedro to the San Fernando Valley by coming through here than it is to drive. A *lot* easier than riding the bus."

The elevator door opened onto a broad corridor. "We're on Level 15," Stevens said. "Mostly small industry. Electronics assembly, waldo operators—"

"Waldo operators?"

"Yeah." Stevens looked as if he were swallowing a live mouse. "It's the latest way Todos Santos drains off money from LA. Skilled machine operators are scarce. A lot of them want to live in Todos Santos, but there aren't enough jobs for them here. So they live here, and work here—the lathes and milling machines are out in LA, and controlled by TV and a telephone-computer hookup. The technical name is 'teleoperated systems.'"

Stevens led the way to a moving pedway. "Watch your step." They walked onto the moving black slideway. "This one's slower than some. If you want to get to the other side of the building, you go to another floor and catch a fast strip."

The ceiling was high, and the entrances to the chambers off the corridor were no more than a series

of closed doors; at infrequent intervals there was a
split-second view of the outside. Tubs of growing
plants stood along some of the walls, but there was
never any illusion of being anywhere but in a
building.

"Todos Santos built the Los Angeles subway?"
Reedy asked.

"Sure. They have the capital. Middle East oil
money funneled through Zurich. Also the equipment,
big semiautomatic tunneling machines. Matter of fact,
they're digging a new one right under my office in
City Hall. With their stuff they can dig for about 10
percent of what it would cost us."

The inward side of the corridor was another jumble:
neat signs on the doors announcing electronic shops,
repair services, light industries of one kind or another,
interspersed with small convenience shops. Sometimes
there was a long series of doors blocked off, each
with a single sign: Westinghouse, Teledyne, Inter-
national Security Systems, Oerlikon, Barclay-Yama-
shito Ltd., stood out as some of the largest.

They ended at an elevator bank. "Well, now that
you've seen the drab parts, you're ready for the
Mall," Stevens said. "That's a sight not to miss."

The elevator dropped like a falling safe. Stevens
watched Reedy's face as the doors opened.

Reedy knew what to expect, of course. Most visitors
did. And they still took several seconds to make sense
of what they were seeing.

They were looking down a broad corridor that
stretched diagonally through the ground floor of
Todos Santos. It was almost three miles long. Moving
pedways in the center were a blur of human figures
approaching and receding, though they stood
motionless. Lines met at infinity. The pedways were
flanked on both sides by walks, and people strolled
along these, looking into shop windows, going in and
out of stores, clumping to hold animated discussions
where they would block the passage of others. Tiers
of balconies rose high above them. Residents strolled

along the balconies or idly leaned over to look down. Glass-sided elevators clung to walls and moved at impossibly high speeds. Gigantic spaces, and walls and a roof enclosing all; that was what confused the mind; but the real shock was to see all these shoppers taking it so lightly.

Stevens chuckled. "Tell yourself you can get used to anything." He led the way out onto the floor.

They passed under an enormous sign:

PRIVATE PROPERTY
PERMISSION TO PASS REVOCABLE
AT ANY TIME

"Which means?" Sir George asked.

"Exactly what it says," Stevens answered. They stood looking for another moment, then Mac escorted his visitor onto the pedway strip. Sir George seemed accustomed to them. Most new shopping centers and airports had them, although not as elaborate as these.

The outer strip was broad and had seats. A series of much narrower strips separated it from another broad seat-laden belt in the center. Each strip moved faster and faster until the inner one flashed past at fifty kilometers an hour. They moved progressively across strips until they reached the fast one, and sat next to the transparent windscreen partition that moved with them.

Parallel lines converged ahead at the vanishing point. There was a medium-sized city poised over their heads. Mac knew it, but he had never been able to sense it, not even here, in this tremendous . . . room.

Through the Plexiglas they could see the flicker of faces and bright clothing of passengers coming in the opposite direction, a blur of humanity. Both sides of the barrier were lined with shops, all doing a brisk business. Reedy noticed a branch of Dream Masters, the chain of fantasy art galleries. They swept past a side corridor that led upward to another level with more walkways and conversation areas. More changes of level; balconies overhanging the pedway itself, with more shops.

There was no special order to the shops, but the signs . . . Reedy frowned, puzzled. What was it about the signs on the shops?

"See it? The Corporation permits advertising," Mac Stevens said, "but they regulate the size of the signs, and they've got an aesthetics committee that sets up standards. If Art Bonner doesn't like something, it'll probably be found to be unaesthetic."

Sporting-goods shops, stationery, clothing, bicycles, restaurants, banks, electronics, music, bookstores. People moved in and out in random patterns. The buildings had a fragile look: not made to withstand weather. Sir George grinned at the sudden incongruous sight of a tobacconist's shop, built apparently of brick, and as solid-looking as a Mayan pyramid.

"Does anyone buy?" Reedy asked. "No one seems to carry packages."

"Security," Stevens said. "Visitors have their purchases delivered. Either to the exit plaza, or directly to their homes. Residents don't usually carry much around either. The guards don't like it."

"I should think Americans have a long tradition of telling the police off," Reedy said.

"Sure. But the residents of Todos Santos are different. I didn't say the guards won't put up with residents carrying packages. They just don't like it. And the residents don't deliberately annoy the guards. They'd rather cooperate." They had reached the opposite corner of the building, and Stevens led the way across the slow strips and finally to the corridor.

"I don't see badges on everyone," Reedy said. "In fact, not more than half."

Stevens nodded and led the Canadian to the end of the diagonal. A series of exits funneled the traffic and they went through. "If we hadn't had unrestricted visiting badges, we'd have been stopped back there," he said. "The Mall is an open area. They let in nearly anyone. They only watch for known criminals and terrorists." His lips tightened. "With their fast transportation system they siphon off a lot of business from the city."

He pointed down a long corridor. "East perimeter, Mall level. Mostly apartments, of course. The outside view is a first choice for living quarters."

"Totally? That seems a poor design—"

"No, not totally. There's a mix here, as everywhere. Night clubs, restaurants, private clubs, even some exclusive shops. Of course any business out here draws only customers from inside, except for favorite customers with permanent Visitor badges."

"Strange," said Reedy. "I'd think they'd want visitors. Why all the restrictions?"

"Oh, there're reasons." Stevens indicated a door. As they approached it, it slid open. A red-and-blue-uniformed guard stood inside. The rent-a-cop smiled pleasantly as they passed and headed for another bank of elevators.

About fifty people were waiting for elevators with them. All had badges, and very few bore the bright VISITOR label. Reedy looked at the badges and people, saying nothing.

There was no way to characterize them. Pick fifty random citizens from any major city and you would find as much variety. What was it about them that made them seem like a gathering of distant cousins? Reedy couldn't put his finger on it.

The elevator rose swiftly and deposited them at another moving pedway. They were on the outside periphery, and they passed apartments, open areas leading to outside enclosed decks; it was obvious that this was an affluent area.

"All right," Sir George said. "I've been unable to work it out. What is it about the people—the sameness? They don't dress as flashily as one expects of Southern Californians, but it can't be merely that."

Stevens grinned. "Termites. No? Well, I admit I

don't know either, not completely. But did you notice how quiet it was, even in the Mall, among those people?"

"Why—yes. Not at all the noise level I'd have expected. Is it some regulation?"

"Custom. Customs are very powerful here. By the way, I wouldn't be surprised if some Company policeman were listening to us through those badges."

Sir George looked at his badge as if he had discovered a poisonous spider on it. "Do the residents put up with this?"

Stevens shrugged. "Resident badges are different. Or so they're told. But, Sir George, the residents *want* surveillance. It's another custom. The Law and Order tradition is very strong in here. A kind of siege mentality—"

"Paranoia?"

"Oh, they've got their reasons. Paranoids have enemies too," Stevens said. "Here, that's where we're going, the exit up ahead. Have you been following the news? The FROMATES, the Friends of Man and The Earth Society, keep trying to sabotage Todos Santos. Not to mention various other hate groups. And just plain gangsters out to extort money. Stink bombs. Hornet nests. That kind of thing, mostly, but sometimes the terrorists come up with something really nasty, like the grenade that killed a dozen people in the Crown Center Arcology in Kansas." He shrugged helplessly. "My police haven't had much luck at catching them outside, so the Company has its own police."

"But doesn't that play into the terrorists' hands?" Reedy asked. "One purpose of terror is to provoke a reaction. Make things so bad that people welcome any change—"

"Any change that will protect them," Stevens said.

The journey ended at another elevator plaza, and they took an Up car to the Executive Suite. They emerged into thick carpets and walnut paneling. It came to Sir George that he was lost.

Every resident of Todos Santos had known that moment of shock, save only the children and Tony Rand. One can lose one's way among city streets, but being lost in Todos Santos was like being lost in Carlsbad Caverns. Lost in three dimensions, in a maze almost a cubic mile in extent!

The moment passed. It didn't matter that Sir George had followed an impossibly twisted path. He had guides; he wasn't trapped. But there was always that moment.

MacLean Stevens was in his mid-thirties, and very athletic, while Art Bonner was ten years older and walked with a limp he'd picked up in the Army. Stevens's hair was light tan, Bonner's dark and thinning on top, with a bare spot his hair stylist had more and more trouble covering. Both were tall men, over six feet, Bonner perhaps an inch higher and twenty pounds heavier than Stevens.

Put that way the two men didn't look alike at all; yet those who knew them, and sometimes even visitors who met both casually, were more impressed with their similarities than their differences. It wasn't anything you could put your finger on. Certainly you would never mistake one man for the other. But both looked at people in the same way, and both spoke in the same tone: the tone of command, of a man so thoroughly accustomed to being obeyed that he did not have to raise his voice or resort to threats.

"Good to see you again, Mac," Bonner was saying.

"Been a while," Stevens responded automatically. "Art, this is the Honorable Sir George Reedy, Deputy Minister for Development and Urban Affairs for the Canadian government. Sorry we're a touch late, but I took the liberty of showing Sir George the shopping mall—"

"Sure, I know," Bonner said. "Come in, please,

have a seat. Drink? We've got nearly anything you
could possibly want, and a lot you wouldn't."

"You sound as if you're showing off," Reedy said.
He smiled broadly. "Pimm's Cup, if you please."

"Certainly. Mac? The usual?"

"Yes, please."

Bonner waved them to leather chairs and took
another in the conversation group with them, leaving
his desk in the background. The office lighting
adjusted subtly so that only the conference area stood
out.

There was a low hum in the background. Otherwise
the office was silent. "Quite a place you have here,"
the Canadian said. "I'm very impressed." But he
looked uneasy. Too much of the touch of strange here
. . . and the moment of being *lost* was still with him.

"Thank you," Bonner said. "Would you like to see
more of it? Let me show you around." He gestured
toward the wall and the decorative art works
vanished to be replaced by an enormous cutaway view
of Todos Santos in three dimensions. Colored dots
seemed to crawl through the holographic presentation;
it was all diagrammatic, with the too-realistic lines of
an architect's drawing. That vanished to show a
montage of color pictures, each a blur of motion:
shops, people getting onto a moving pedway, a riot of
color.

Sir George frowned. "Why, that's the route we
came here by—"

Bonner smiled. "That's right." The diagram
reappeared. "You see the moving dots? Those are
members of my staff that we want to keep track of.
Your badges are tagged VIP so I was able to see
where you went. Not that I paid a lot of attention,
but the route is recorded anyway—"

There was a slightly louder hum. "Here we are,"
said Bonner. He was having fun. The solid black
rectangle of a coffee table in the conversation group
opened to reveal three glasses. Bonner reached down
and lifted the tray. "Pimm's Cup. Talisker. And

Mac's Royal Gin Fizz. Don't know how he can drink that mess. Cheers."

Sir George laughed, and was joined by the others. "Well done. I will admit I thought you had forgotten—" The smile faded into something else. "Just whom do you have listening to us?" he demanded.

"Nobody," Art said. "Oh—my apologies, Sir George. I like doing this with drinks and food orders, but believe me, nobody is listening to us. I used my implant to tell MILLIE what we wanted and she took care of it."

"I see." Sir George's eyes focused on nothing for a moment.

Bonner grinned. "Try again. Use your last name for the key."

"Ah. Thank you."

"You're welcome. I've given you a visiting VIP access clearance. Mac, have they made any progress on swinging an implant for you?"

"Think the city's got an extra million bucks?" Stevens asked. "Hell, we haven't got an extra five hours' overtime for a sanitary engineer." Stevens eyed Sir George warily. "I hadn't known you were one of the elite."

Reedy looked sympathetically at Stevens. "Don't rate it, actually. Family helped PSYCHIC LTD. once and they paid off with this." He paused, searching for words. "Very useful gadget, but you know, you can communicate with a computer about as well with a good briefcase console."

Reedy and Bonner looked knowingly at each other. It was a look that left MacLean Stevens out. It was the look that sighted men might give each other in the presence of the blind.

"Well, what would you like to see, Sir George?" Bonner asked. "As you've gathered, we're rather proud of Todos Santos. I have us scheduled for dinner a bit early, 1900, but we've plenty of time before then. Oh, and Mr. Rand, our Chief Engineer, will be joining us."

"Will we be eating in the Commons?" Stevens asked.

"I thought Schramm's. Best Hungarian food in the country."

"Um."

"Hell, Mac, I'm not trying to hide anything," Bonner said. He grinned. "There's nothing alcoholic to drink there, and the food's nothing special in Commons, but there's plenty of it. Shall I cancel out Schramm's?"

"Commons by all means," Reedy said. It was obvious to him that Stevens thought he had scored a point in some complex game.

There was an awkward silence, and Sir George said into it, "As you know, we're thinking of building units like this one. We must construct the housing at any event, and the Government is wondering if we should not do it rationally as you have. There are a quarter of a million people here, as I understand."

"About that," Bonner said. "MILLIE could tell you. But we ought to let Mac listen in, and we can't." He looked thoughtful for an instant, and words flowed on the wall screen.

Total Present:	243,782
Unrestricted Visitors in Mall:	31,293
Visitors with Special Passes:	18,811
Non-resident Workers:	114
Unauthorized Visitors:	7
Detained Prisoners:	1

"Who's the prisoner?" Stevens demanded.

Bonner looked thoughtful, then said, "A leaper. They've got him in Central Security. He's been under arrest for three hours. They'll let him go by midnight if nobody's free to interview him before that. Afraid we're holding one of your people in durance vile, Mac?"

"No."

Words crawled on the screen again. How many residents are accommodated here?

Design Goal:	275,000
Now Resident:	247,453
Resident in Outbuildings:	976

"Roughly a quarter of a million, then," Sir George said.

Bonner nodded. "In four square miles of building, or about ten square miles of buildings and grounds. That's about the highest population density ever achieved on Earth *anywhere*. Remember the studies a few years ago that proved that if you pack a lot of people into a small area they'd all go insane? Doesn't seem to have happened."

MacLean Stevens chuckled. Bonner threw him a threatening look, then grinned.

"Where did you have in mind building, Sir George?" Bonner asked.

Reedy shrugged. "There are a number of possible sites. We have so much undeveloped land—"

"Won't work," Stevens muttered. Bonner said nothing, and the two executives exchanged significant glances.

Bonner is laughing about this, Reedy thought. Why? I'd expect Stevens to be negative about the whole idea, Lord knows he hates this whole complex—do all Angelinos think that way?—but what is this joke they share?

And why, when three of these arcologies have been more or less failures, is Todos Santos apparently so successful despite being packed in among ten million enemies in Greater Los Angeles?

IV

KINGS AND WIZARDS

The guard turned with a puzzled expression. "Seems to be a glitch in Tunnel 0-8, Captain."

"What kind of glitch?"

"No visual."

The duty captain frowned. "In *8?* That's a critical area. Don't need intruders in 8 . . ." He typed furiously on his console, then looked relieved. "MILLIE shows maintenance in that," he said. "With overtime authorized yet, the lucky beggars. Punch in an immediate repair request for the visuals."

"Hell, it's near dinner time. They'll never get it fixed tonight."

The captain shrugged. "If they don't, we'll send in a patrolman. Give 'em a chance, though. They're in there already, maybe they can take care of it." He looked at his readout screen again and nodded. "Looks all right. Nobody's opened any doors to the outside. Let me know when the visual comes on again."

"Sure." The guard settled back and sipped coffee as the kaleidoscope began again.

• • •

Anthony Rand put down the telephone with a grimace. It was always an unpleasant experience when Genevieve called, and he wasn't sure whether it was worse when they fought or when she tried to make up. Why the hell didn't she marry and get out of his life? She was no bloody use when he was trying to make a career; and when he hadn't risen fast enough to suit her, she'd walked out taking Zachary and two-thirds of his inadequate income with her. Now, of course, she wanted to come back.

She doesn't want to live with me, she wants to live in Todos Santos, Tony thought. And I will be damned if she's going to come here and live like a goddam princess off my status.

Of course she had a bribe to offer: Zach, aged eleven. And she had some good arguments. The boy needed his father, but Tony Rand didn't have time to raise a son—he barely had time to have the boy in for visits—and someone should take care of Zach, why not his mother? And maybe their breakup hadn't been quite so simple and one sided. She did have her side to the story—

He squirmed a bit as his body remembered Genevieve, suddenly, against his will. Djinn had been wonderful in bed. It had been too long since he'd had a satisfying affair. No time for that; no time to make friends. Too bad you couldn't rent mistresses. He'd heard that was possible: that there were women who'd gladly pretend affection, be attentive when you wanted them to be and self-reliant when you had no time for them. He wished he knew where to find someone like that. It wasn't so much that he was afraid to ask, as that he hadn't any idea of *whom* to ask.

Why not Genevieve? She was offering almost the same thing—no, I'll be damned first.

His apartment was nothing like the others in Todos Santos. It was large, because his status rated a large place; but much of the space was concentrated in one enormous room. There was a small bedroom, but he seldom used it because it was too far from the drafting table; he'd forgotten a good idea once while stumbling from bedroom to drafting table, and that wasn't ever going to happen again.

The drafting table dominated a whole side of the big room: a vast expanse of metal surface littered with drafting instruments and bordered by switches and buttons; when he drew on it, an image went into his computer files and was accessible in his office, or on a job site. Another wall held awards, framed scrolls and trophies. Books took up another. There wasn't room for all the books he needed—and where should he keep them, here or in his office suite? Better to get them read into the electronic brains of Todos Santos. Somehow, though, storing his books in computer memory hadn't conquered the mess: the room was still littered with letter trays full of papers, magazines (mostly unread but full of important articles he didn't want to miss) in half a dozen mahogany rack tables, unanswered letters spilling out of drawers. He was drowning in paper.

He envied the quiet efficiency of Preston Sanders or Art Bonner or Frank Mead. Their assistants almost invisibly took care of details. Tony had never been able to manage that. It wasn't that he didn't have good people. Alice Strahler was a good engineer and executive assistant, and Tom Golden ran the procurement division, and—

But good as his staff people were, it wasn't enough. They might protect him from mere details—but far too often he'd found that details were the key to the problem. He had to follow the minutiae, because he didn't know what would turn out to be vital.

That led to his development of robot probes; small

devices with cameras and sound equipment which could move freely through Todos Santos under Rand's direct control. If he sent out two or three of the small teleoperated devices (he called them Arr-twos after the small droid in *Star Wars*), Rand could effectively be in several places at once, see machinery and construction details in real time from both above and below, and generally explore without leaving his bedroom.

Good as the Arr-twos were, with their full two-way communications and their TV screen to show Rand's face, he'd found it necessary to get out and talk to the technicians and carpenters and pipe fitters and maintenance people; talk to them himself, because most construction people didn't like talking to an Arr-two even with Rand's TV image.

And he had to go himself. His subordinates, even the best ones, didn't seem able to recognize an important point when they heard it. And getting around Todos Santos took time, which meant that the journals and magazines and letters piled up until he was hopelessly behind—

The phone rang. Genevieve again? he wondered. What in hell does she want this time? "Hello," he barked at the empty room.

"Strahler here, Chief," the phone speaker said.

Uh oh. Alice wouldn't call about something trivial. "Oh, ah, yeah, hello."

"Sorry to bother you at dinner time. We have a problem on that carbon filament reinforcing lattice. Medland can't deliver on time."

"Grrrr—"

"Sir?"

"Nothing. We need that stuff." Boy do we ever need it, and it's completely out of our control, damn it all to hell! How would we handle this if we were a space colony? Or a starship? "Alice, the schedule's godawful tricky, and—"

"That's why I called," Strahler said. "I tried alternate sources. Farbenwerke has the best delivery schedule, but it's still a four-week delay. But I did find a condominium going up in Diamond Bar that has enough to take care of us for a month, and they've got a strike so they don't need it right now. We can buy theirs and have Farbenwerke ship ours to Diamond Bar—but they'll want a premium."

"Sounds like you've done your homework," Tony said.

"Yeah. But it'll cost us," she said. "Rescheduling around a four-week delay costs one point six million. The Diamond Bar deal costs nine hundred thousand. I can't find any other choices."

"Pretty clear what we have to do," Rand said.

"Yes. Shall I talk to the comptroller?"

"Yeah. Do that. Say, this is Tom's job, not yours."

"Mr. Golden has an anniversary party," Strahler said. "His wife would leave him if he missed it. So I took it."

"Thanks, Alice. Okay, make the deal."

"Sure will. Good night."

"Good night," Rand said. "Finished with phone." An expensive call, he thought. Nine hundred thousand bucks, no small sum. Oh, well. Alice and Tom would take care of it. That was the kind of thing he thought of as a detail, no matter how much money might be involved; somebody else could handle it. But if he hadn't got his hands dirty working on the sewage treatment system, he'd never have found out that the instrumentation pathway wasn't workable until the system was finished. He shuddered at the memory. They'd have had to tear out a concrete wall and delay completion of the new residential wing . . .

It was only by accumulating details that you found something like that—and the way the details fit together wasn't at all obvious, which meant there was no rational filing system for them, resulting in the mess in his apartment (his office was kept relatively neat) because you never knew when you'd need an old memo or an article . . .

Maybe, Rand thought; maybe if I had an implant?

Is that how Bonner keeps track of everything? But Pres manages without one, and so does Mead.

He put on a clean shirt. It was time to meet Bonner and Stevens and, what was his name? Reedy. Time to meet them for dinner.

• • •

The dining hall was large enough for six thousand people and served an entire level. Holographic panels along one entire wall gave the impression that it looked out over the sea; sailboats moved on the Bay, and lights winked as sunset shadowed Catalina Island in the distance. The great bulk of the iceberg in the Santa Monica harbor was outlined against the dying sunlight, a mountainous island that shone too brightly to be stone.

"That's lovely," Sir George said. "And quite realistic."

"It ought to be," MacLean Stevens told him. "They've piped the view inside."

"Yep. Real time," Rand said proudly. "Cost less than moving the dining hall. There's never enough outside view area, and—" He cut himself off. He hadn't come to talk, but to listen. That was going to take careful control; he'd been told he talked too much, and he supposed it was true, although he never said anything he wouldn't have wanted said to him if he didn't know the information.

And certainly he had reason to be pleased at Reedy's response: appreciative silence, and another close look at the holographs. "Pity the ceiling is so low," Reedy observed finally. "But even so the illusion is nearly perfect."

Art Bonner laughed, a short polite sound. Tony Rand had no trouble reading Bonner's mind: the cost of the holographic walls had been high enough without using up valuable space to give high ceilings to the Common rooms. Rand had suggested it and got nowhere.

Art hadn't wanted the holographs, either, but Tony

insisted—and brought them in under budget, too. He was proud of that. The Commons wouldn't be nearly so nice without that illusion of looking out—

The room was filled with the buzz of conversation and clicking plates. There were the random sounds of people in motion. "A good bit less noise than I'd have imagined for this many diners," Reedy said.

Rand was about to tell him about the acoustic design: walls subtly not parallel, indentations at key places, and the rest, but Reedy wasn't listening.

"Custom again," MacLean Stevens said. "Deeply ingrained custom. Developed pretty rapidly, too."

"Doubtless there is selectivity," Reedy said. "Those who can't adapt won't stay long."

"The idea is to adapt the habitat to the inhabitants' needs," Art Bonner said.

"You seem to have done well," Reedy replied.

The tables were long and narrow, with a pair of moving beltways down the center. Dirty dishes came from their right, and a continuous stream of food and beverages and clean utensils poured from some cornucopia to the left. "Take a place," Art Bonner said. "You can choose your own company, or wait for someone to choose you."

"No reservations?" Reedy asked.

"No. It's a random proposition." Bonner led them to an empty stretch at a long table. "Scheduling's going to catch hell for this if it doesn't fill up." He paused for a moment to stare at nothing.

That's the value of that implant, Rand thought. He's just made a note, with all the details, and tomorrow MILLIE will remind him to think about schedules.

Reedy waited until he saw Bonner was attentive again. Then he said, "How can you plan without reservations?"

Bonner shrugged. "We manage."

Stevens's voice was carefully controlled as he said,

"Residents *must* take a certain number of meals in the Commons. They're not only charged for them as part of the services, but they pay extra if they skip out too many times. With that incentive it's a simple matter of queuing theory mathematics."

"Not all that simple," Rand said.

Reedy frowned. "That doesn't seem very pleasant."

They took seats, Reedy and Bonner on one side of the table, Rand and Stevens on the other. The moving dishes and foods seemed to distract Reedy and made it hard for him to talk across the table. Bonner didn't seem to notice.

"You'll find clean plates coming along any second," Bonner said. "I think you'll like the meal, and certainly it's efficient." Pause. "Tonight's was only seven dollars twenty-eight cents per person that we'll serve, assuming the projection's right. If you see something you like, just take it. When you've served yourself, put the rest back on the conveyor."

"Is that sanitary?" Reedy asked.

"Certainly." Bonner snared a covered dish of chicken fricassee. "There are no more than four portions in a dish to begin with. And we've empirical evidence, too. Check our absenteeism due to minor illness—"

Reedy looked thoughtful. "Quite low," he said.

"Check the LA rate for comparison. Not that they have as good data as we have, but it gives you an idea."

Rand watched them carefully. In his office he could have got the same data just as quickly, but here he would have to take out his pocket communications terminal, type in the question, and read the answer. Reedy and Bonner simply thought the question and got the answer piped into their heads without interrupting the conversation.

"There's another reason for no more than four portions to a dish," Rand said. "If the FROMATES do get in and poison some dishes they won't kill many people—"

"Oh dear. Is there much chance of that?" Reedy asked. He seemed to have lost his appetite.

"Almost none," Rand assured him. "The security agents watch all the time." He waved toward the low ceiling.

Reedy glanced around nervously, as if feeling eyes on the back of his neck. Then plates and silver came past and he took them. Bonner handed him Hungarian goulash, and vegetables and bread quickly followed. There was tea and coffee, and milk, and water, and fruit juice. The goulash was hot and smelled deliciously of paprika.

Rand ate eagerly, but Reedy was still hesitant.

"Gets to you, doesn't it?" MacLean Stevens said gently. He began to eat. "Not much you can do about it, so enjoy your meal."

"About what?" Rand asked.

"Being watched all the time."

"But we're not watched all the time," Rand said. "The guards follow a random surveillance pattern."

"What do you do if you catch them?" Reedy asked. "Saboteurs. Or even just pickpockets."

Bonner snorted. "That's a sore subject. What happens is, we turn them over to Mac's police, and they let them go."

Sir George lifted an eyebrow. "Really, Mr. Stevens?"

"Not quite—"

"Close enough," Bonner said. "Let's suppose we catch an Angelino with his hand in a stockholder's pocket. Suppose we've got him dead to rights, a dozen witnesses. We call the LA police. They come get him. One of the District Attorney's people comes out and takes statements. So far so good.

"But now the Public Defender gets in the act. It'll be some bright youngster just out of law school, anxious to make a reputation. So we get delays. Continuances. Every time the victim and our witnesses show up, the Public Defender isn't available. Schedule conflict. Something. Until the day the victim isn't available, and wham! That's the day they insist on a speedy trial."

"Now, damn it, that's not fair," Mac Stevens insisted.

"It's close enough, Mac, and you know it. If we want a conviction, we have to spend hours and days in courtrooms, and for what? Even if we do it, the yo-yo gets bail and probation."

"So what do you do, Mr. Bonner?" Reedy asked.

"We grit our teeth and play the game," Bonner said. "And try to see that no repeat offenders get in here. We do have the right to keep the bums away from our people."

And how would we do that on a starship? Tony Rand wondered. Hmmm. We'd have to have criminal law. Justice, if you will. Which is hard to automate . . . and not my department.

The food was good, and they ate in silence for a few minutes. Most had second helpings. Rand started to tell them about some of the problems he'd had in getting the conveyor belt system working properly, but he saw they weren't interested.

Finally Sir George looked up and said, "Surely there's a lot of wastage? You can't possibly predict how much will be eaten."

"We do better than you think," Bonner said.

"Yes, and they sell the leftovers to Los Angeles welfare institutions," Stevens said grimly. "Churches, skid row missions, that sort of thing. There's no waste because the Los Angeles poor live on Todos Santos's garbage."

"Now, that's not true," Rand said. "The garbage goes to the pig farms—"

"He means that only the untouched portions are sold for human consumption," Bonner said. "And he's right, the real garbage feeds animals. And, Mac, you may not like feeding your welfare people on our leftovers, but I notice you don't complain about the water we supply."

The sun fell into the sea and the iceberg offshore

winked with navigation lights. The darkness of the holograph was lovely, but it made the low ceiling press down even more heavily. Sir George glanced around again. "I shouldn't think Americans would like surveillance while they eat."

"The Corporation doesn't much like the expense of providing it, either," Bonner said. "Now tell me what I should do? Despite everything the FROMATES do get into Todos Santos. And they *do* try to poison people—"

"They don't think it's poison," Stevens said.

"LSD is poison," Bonner said. "If my people want to turn on, they'll do it themselves. They don't need help from eaters. And slipping acid into the food isn't all the honorable Friends of Man and the Earth do. They've also tried blowing up the kitchens, as well as other parts of Todos Santos. They tried—well, their diseased minds come up with pretty ingenious stunts.

"So we have to watch for them, and we can't abandon the Commons. Wouldn't if we could. Most of our residents like the Commons. Some never eat anywhere else. After all, it's our most democratic institution."

"Why do these criminals dislike you so much?" Sir George asked. "Surely they know your people are not unhappy here—"

Bonner and Stevens laughed together, a shared joke, which Rand could have joined if he wanted to, but the memory was too painful. Genevieve had lived with an eco-freak after she left Tony's bed. Tony tried to be objective, but he found it difficult.

"The FROMATES claim to be ecologists," Bonner said. "As if I didn't have some of the best ecological talent in the world available to my staff. Only they can save the Earth—"

"Art's not being quite fair," Stevens said. "I've got no use for terrorists, but the FROMATES have a point. They claim that if Todos Santos succeeds, there'll be no barrier to population growth. Not even famine and overcrowding can stop the population bomb, until it's too late for everyone and everything. Actually their best arguments are fiction. They're backing a movie made from an old science fiction novel, *The Godwhale,* about how the human race crowds itself until no humans are left."

"I take it you agree with them," Sir George asked.

"No. But they do have their share of truth. Todos Santos uses enormous resources to produce an elite that enjoys—" He clamped his lips firmly together. "I'd rather you saw everything for yourself."

Saw what? Rand wondered. Something not working right? Where?

"I saw the demonstrators outside," Sir George said. "Do you often have serious attempts at sabotage? Bombs, that sort of thing?"

"More than I like," Bonner said. "But they don't often get past Security. Setting off a bomb's pretty hard when the guards are looking over your shoulder."

"Isn't there anywhere the guards don't watch?"

"Not many places."

A young family came over to their part of the table and sat next to Art Bonner. The man was about thirty, and his wife considerably younger. There were two boys with them, about six and eight years old. All wore the neat slacks and wrinkle-free shirts that seemed to be standard dress, and all four wore resident badges. Like most resident badges these were personalized. The parents' had color drawings with their names in stylized calligraphy; the children's had cartoons. The shirts had complementary patterns of wild color, designed so that you could see from a distance that they were a family, although each shirt was different.

The man sat next to Bonner and examined Art's badge with care before he spoke. "I thought I recognized you, Mr. Bonner."

"Good evening," Bonner said pleasantly. He looked at their badges: Cal and Judy Phillips. The color had already told him they were resident stockholders, and the badge identified his business: Executive Row Clothing Rental, 25th Level Mall.

Bonner gestured to his companions. "Mister Phillips, this is Tony Rand, the Chief Engineer. Our visitors are Mr. Stevens of the Los Angeles Mayor's Office, and Sir George Reedy of the Canadian government."

Phillips's eyes widened slightly. He nodded pleasantly to the others, then began to gather dishes for himself and his family. He spoke in a low voice that they could just make out if they listened hard enough.

The newcomers talked only to each other for a while, but when Cal Phillips was certain that Bonner was finished with his meal, he said, "Mister Bonner, my shower is not delivering enough water."

Bonner frowned. "You've had Maintenance in to check?"

"Yes, sir. They say everything's fine."

"But it isn't," Judy Phillips said. "I used to be able to rinse off completely, and now I can't. And there's been no water allowance reduction in our neighborhood."

"Where?" Rand asked.

"Forty-four, West, R-ring," Judy answered.

"Hmm. Could be the computer. I don't think there's—"

"Leave it to Maintenance, Tony," Bonner said. He frowned for a moment. "All right, someone will look into it."

"Thank you," Cal Phillips said. "If you've a few minutes—"

"Not tonight," Bonner said pleasantly. "I have to show my guests around. If you'll excuse us—"

"Certainly," Cal and Judy Phillips chorused.

"We'll have coffee at my place," Bonner said to his guests when they were away from the table. "And we can discuss the economics of the situation, Sir George. Expect that will bore you to tears, Tony—"

Was Bonner trying to get rid of him? Rand wondered. Why would he do that? But it had happened before, when there was diplomacy to discuss.

Before they reached the outside of the Common Room, Bonner had heard five more complaints, been given three separate solutions to problems in garbage disposal—one interesting enough that Rand took out a notebook and wrote it down—and had been encouraged not to give in to outside pressures from the Teamsters.

When they reached the corridor, people obviously recognized Bonner, but they didn't speak to him, except to wish him a pleasant evening.

"We'll head on up to my place," Bonner said. "Sure you can't join us, Tony?"

Definitely a hint, Rand decided. "Thanks, Art, but I think I'd better turn in early," Rand said.

He watched them get onto an elevator.

• • •

There were other residents in the elevators, and they didn't speak to Bonner either as he led his guests to a corner of the 47th floor. An apartment door opened as they approached. He ushered them into a large carpeted room. The view of the city was magnificent on two sides of them.

Long lines of light that were streets overflowing with traffic; dotted lines of empty lighted streets; tall buildings with more patterns of light; a bank of fog rolling in from the bay, shrouding the iceberg, its top far below them; Los Angeles lay in splendor around them.

MacLean Stevens stood at the windows basking in the light. "Now *that's* a city," he said. "Alive and lovely and free."

"Splendid," Sir George said. "Really lovely."

"Especially from here," Bonner added. "Pimm's Cup again, Sir George?"

"Thank you, I'll have brandy—"

"Carlos Primera be all right?"

"Splendid. Thank you."

They took seats. They watched the solid coffee table for a moment, a duplicate of the one in Bonner's office.

"Customs again," Reedy said.

Bonner looked puzzled.

"The residents. They are permitted to speak to you in the Commons, but not in the corridors."

"More or less," Bonner said. "Not so much *permitted* as—well, as you say, a custom."

MacLean Stevens started to say something, but caught himself.

"Actually," Bonner said, "anyone can speak to *anyone* in the Commons. If you hadn't been along they'd have talked my arm off. They were being polite to outside visitors."

"And why was everyone so interested in garbage disposal?" Reedy asked.

"It's the 'Problem of the Week'," Bonner said. "Every week we have something the residents are asked to think about. If they come up with a good idea, we use it. Works more often than you think."

"I see. And you eat in the Commons regularly?"

"Reasonably so. I'm exempt from the requirement, of course, although I'm not so certain that's wise. Getting out and meeting the residents is just plain good politics. If Nixon had gone drinking in bars once in a while, he'd have served two full terms as President. For that matter, Mac, your Mayor would benefit by getting out and meeting some random citizens."

"Sure. With fifty bodyguards."

"See?" Bonner said. "I don't need bodyguards. Not in Todos Santos. I can go meet anyone I like. Ah. Here are our drinks."

The coffee table opened to reveal three large snifters of brandy.

Reedy asked, "Is an automatic bartender standard in all apartments?"

"It's not automated," MacLean Stevens said.

"Somewhere in this building a very human bartender poured those drinks."

Bonner nodded agreement. "Most places get deliveries by jitney to their outside door. Executive and luxury suites have direct conveyors."

"A service reserved for the higher castes," Stevens said. "Kings, Queens, and Drones." He lifted his glass. "Cheers."

"That's a very old image, Mac." Bonner lifted his own glass in reply. "Cheers. I suppose you could call the executives kings and queens, and the major stockholders drones, but what's the sense of it? Sir George, Mac doesn't like Todos Santos—but his wife wants to live here. Doesn't she, Mac?"

Stevens nodded sourly.

"You'll notice he doesn't say he can't afford to bring her here, either," Bonner said. "I've offered him nearly every job in my department."

Stevens fidgeted nervously, then glanced at his watch. "Sir George, I really must be leaving soon."

"Good heavens, yes, of course you'll have to get back to your family. I'm very sorry—"

"You needn't leave," Bonner said. "We have guest suites. Please stay on, Sir George. What time is your first appointment in the morning?"

"Well, actually I had expected to return here—"

"That's settled, then. I'll have a guest suite with some toilet articles laid out for you. You've no family with you in Los Angeles."

He didn't say it as a question. Stevens wondered for a moment, then nodded. Bonner would have had MILLIE check airline and hotel reservations.

"I would enjoy staying over, if Mr. Stevens doesn't mind," Reedy said.

"No, of course not. I can find my way out, Art. Can you have my chopper meet me?"

"Sure."

Stevens downed the last of his brandy and stood. "Be seeing you. I'll come by for Sir George in the morning. Call City Hall about an hour before you're ready to leave, if you please."

"We'll get him back to you," Bonner assured him. He walked with Stevens across the thick carpets to the entryway. "Bring Janice with you next time. Sometime when you're not showing the Commons—"

Stevens nodded. "Thanks." The door slid open for him, then closed.

"Poor Mac," Bonner said as he came back to his seat. "His wife really enjoys this place, and Mac thinks coming here is a chore. Excuse me a moment, please?" He frowned in concentration.

Reedy could hear the instructions: That is, he could hear MILLIE listening to them. MacLean Stevens leaving 47–001 now. Full Protection. Call LAFD for his helicopter.

ACKNOWLEDGED.

Bonner said, "I expect you've got a few more questions."

"Millions," Reedy agreed. "I don't know where to begin. Uh—I say, Mr. Bonner, I can't help noticing that your relationship with Mr. Stevens is rather peculiar."

Bonner grinned broadly. "That's not the way I'd put it, but yes. Mac is convinced that this place couldn't exist without Los Angeles. To him we're no more than a vampire sucking up sustenance from his city. And since he's got an ungovernable mess out there, naturally he resents our order and tranquility even more."

"I see. And yet you're friends."

"I wish we were closer friends. He's a very good man, Sir George. But then you've seen that."

"Yes. Is his theory correct, by the way?"

Bonner hesitated for only a second. "Certainly. In a way. There have been several experiments in arcologies, Sir George. This is the only one that has succeeded."

"You're quite the largest and best financed."

Bonner nodded. "True. But that isn't all of it, I

think. We have had a lot of success. Not just avoiding deterioration, we've had growth and improvement and we make a profit for the stockholders and financiers. The earlier arcologies need massive tax subsidies, Todos Santos *pays* taxes. As few as possible, but we pay."

Sir George nodded agreement. "I know. It's the purpose of my visit. Why?"

"Our independence and lack of tax strangulation," Bonner said quickly. "We make our own laws, and no one outside bothers us. Dictatorial efficiency. 'The first bloom of fascism.' I make the trains run on time. I even build trains."

"Seriously—"

"I am being serious. We do have efficient administration. Simply getting out from under the dead hand of government, chopping out bureaucratic deadwood—that's worth a *lot.*"

Reedy nodded again. "That's the standard explanation, but I am not at all certain that I accept the standard theories, else I'd not be here. I am looking for what the sociologists and economists may have missed. Most of them hate you from theoretical principles. Or love you from others."

"Something else you've seen," Bonner said. "Security. Nobody has to be afraid in Todos Santos. Everyone in this place can talk to everyone else, and not be afraid. I think that's worth something, too."

"But what of Stevens's theory?"

Bonner smiled. "I'll jump Mac's gun, since he'll tell you all about it tomorrow anyway. But do keep in mind what I said. Without our communications, upwards and downwards and sideways, the rest wouldn't matter.

"Now, Mac Stevens believes that without the resources of a big city to draw on we'd never make Todos Santos anything like self-sufficient. We'd forget something vital, and it would take time and effort to correct. That's why he said you couldn't build an arcology out in your undeveloped lands."

"I see. But there was an experiment like that. In India." Reedy leaned back in the comfortable chair and sniffed brandy. "Back when the United States was sending aid to India. The Rockefeller Foundation tried to build an instant industrial complex in an undeveloped village and farming region."

Bonner nodded. "MILLIE has the details, if you're interested. Yes. And the project failed dismally, for precisely the reasons I've mentioned. Sure. Sir George, I won't try to hide from you just how much we depend on Los Angeles. I *know,* because MILLIE monitors everything coming into this place. I know where every dollar goes out of here, too. I think Mac's absolutely right, you have to be near a big city, near enough to draw on its resources, or your arcology's going to flop. Economically, socially, in every way."

"But certainly that's not enough by itself. It can't explain your economic successes."

"Right," Bonner said. "But you saw some of that tonight."

"Did I?"

"The Phillips boy. Clothing rental. Obviously there was a need for that service. We weren't providing it, but our people like to dress up for parties and weddings and such. So we were importing rental clothing and exporting money. Now Phillips does it, and the money stays right here. More than that, he's buying stock with his profits."

"And he brought in the capital to start the business," Reedy mused. "Of course, I can see why people with no capital resent you."

"And you're wrong," Bonner said. "I admit I checked on Phillips so I know in advance, but his story's typical. He came in with nothing. We loaned him the money to build up his business."

Reedy thought that over. "Do you do that often? It seems risky."

"Win a few, lose a few. We do pretty well. Our

Director for Capital Development is *very* seldom wrong."

"Ah." Reedy smiled. He wondered if Arthur Bonner realized just how much he was revealing. Or cared. "And how would we go about locating such a magician?"

Bonner grinned. "That's your problem. We've *got* Barbara Churchward."

V

Then conquer we must, for our cause it is just . . .
— Francis Scott Key

COMMAND DECISIONS

Tony Rand was at loose ends. There would be movies, either in Commons or on his TV . . . or he could read some of the technical articles now cluttering up his working space . . . but he wasn't sleepy and he didn't feel like working.

He had wanted to watch Art Bonner and Sir George together; but Art had made it clear that he would be in the way. Business. Fine. Art was no engineer, but he had a way of smoothing things out, so that the real work of Todos Santos could go on. Tony was still annoyed.

He punched for his own level, 100, and braced for the thrust. There were slow and fast elevators; you learned which were which. Art polled the residents regularly. Some hated waiting for elevators; some hated the accelerations. It wasn't hard to change the operating speeds to suit the users.

Hmm. Delores had seemed glad to see him when he

was in Bonner's office earlier. She'd be up, it was early. Could he drop by her place? But on what excuse? Damn it, why couldn't he learn how to pick up girls? Even with women he knew, like Delores, he couldn't seem to change the relationship from business to social. Did other men have this problem?

He decided that Delores wouldn't want to see him, not at this hour, without an appointment. Who would?

Genevieve. She'd be glad . . .

He'd been in love with her once. He was still in love with her when she left. And to be fair, he hadn't been much of a husband. Too wrapped up in work, irritable when interrupted, unwilling to go places with her, rude to her friends, and glad enough when she decided not to go to conventions with him because she was always bored . . .

There'd been plenty of danger signals. He could see that now, looking back at the last year they were married; but he hadn't seen them then.

If I had, he thought. If I'd noticed how unhappy she was, could I have done anything about it? I'd have tried. But tried what?

She'd be glad if I called. I could invite her to come visit. Bring Zach and come stay a few days. She'd like that, and, dammit, she used to be fun to have around. Am I still in love with her?

The elevator stopped at his floor. Somehow the idea of his empty apartment was unpleasant; too unpleasant to face. Instead he took his pocket electronics box—calculator, phone, computer terminal, alarm clock, and calendar, an invention of his own that someday he'd market when he had time to perfect it—and plugged it into a jack in a panel near the elevator call box.

Genevieve's number didn't answer after twelve rings.

So now what? The apartment was still empty. Dammit, there had to be someone who'd be glad to see him—

Sanders. Pres would be on duty, and he could use

some company. Pres didn't like night duty on the worry desk. Rand entered the elevator again and punched for the Operations level.

The Olympic ski jumps were back on the screen in Preston Sanders's office. "Evening," Tony said. "Why can't you be addicted to reruns of the Mary Tyler Moore show? Or at least watch the evening news?"

"I do watch the news," Sanders said. "And I generally get some work done when I've got night duty on the worry desk."

"Quiet tonight," Rand said. "Oh—there's some kind of problem with water deliveries in 44-West. Could you have Maintenance check it out?"

Sanders laughed. "I logged that one in an hour ago. How did your dinner go? Any conclusions about implants and genius?"

"Haven't made up my mind. Best way to find out would be to get my own."

"Sure. Tomorrow morning."

A shrill tone shattered their conversation. Red flashed above the screen, and the skier disappeared in mid-jump, replaced by a red-bearded guard captain. "Break-in. Intruder on C-ring, 18-North."

Tony stopped breathing. *Burglars in the house?*

Sanders looked automatically at the holographic model. Tony Rand didn't bother. The north side was unfinished in large part: nothing but girders and framework and the thin curtain wall that had been erected for appearances and environmental control. But two main hydrogen intake lines and a fastube to Santa Barbara came in near ground level on the north side.

A red pinpoint winked on in the holographic display. Level 18, and definitely out in the unfinished area. "Visual," Sanders demanded.

"Getting it, sir," the guard said. Another screen swam, then showed a dim figure on a narrow catwalk. "He won't know we've spotted him."

Rand went around behind the desk to look over Sanders's shoulder, careful not to distract Pres. There wasn't enough light for details.

"Keep it that way a minute, Fleming. What's he carrying?" Sanders demanded.

"Can't make it out," Captain Fleming answered. "No history on him. He had a badge at one time, or he wouldn't be here."

"And he ditched it before he went into that area. Right," Sanders said.

Rand felt beads of sweat pop out on his forehead, and a cold knot began to grow under his belt. This was no lost child. And if he felt the tension, what must Sanders be feeling? The black man looked calm enough. "A teener resident out to have fun?" Rand suggested.

"Possibly," Sanders muttered. He continued to stare at the screen. "But not likely. Not out there. Keep on it, Fleming. You've sent men down there?"

"Yes, sir."

"Maybe you ought to call Bonner," Rand suggested.

That got him a scowl. "Art's been drinking with the Canadian," Sanders said. "Afraid I can't handle the situation?"

"You know better," Tony protested. Was that what I was thinking?

"Two more," Fleming said excitedly. "Two bandits, Accessway 9. They've got some kind of interference gear. Don't know what it is, but we can't get an exact location."

"Interference?" Rand shouted. "What in hell could they—" He fell silent, thinking furiously, recalling the details of the security system. Accessway 9? That was a main hydrogen input tunnel!

A bright band sprang into view on the model: the indeterminate location of two intruders, deep underground. The southwest pipeline complex that ran parallel to the tunnel showed up as a series of thick purple lines.

"It makes a pattern," Pres said uneasily. "Opposite

sides. Both aimed at hydrogen intake lines. That's our weakest spot. We've got to get visual on those new bogies!"

"Yes, sir," Fleming said from the screen. "Trying. I can send men into the tunnel—"

"And alarm them. Hold that." He looked up helplessly at Rand. "Christ, if they've got explosives, they can make one hell of a mess."

Tony could only nod agreement. "Pres! My Arr-two's. I've got one near Tunnel 9. Maybe they wouldn't be suspicious of a robot—"

"Maybe worth a try," Sanders said absently. "Use that console over there to fire it up, but don't do anything else without letting me know. Now let me think."

"Sure, Pres." Tony went to the console. It wouldn't be easy controlling the robot with this standard input; Tony usually used joysticks and gloves with special sensors, and other devices, but there weren't any of those closer than Tony's office—and by the time he could get there, this might all be over.

Sanders came to a decision. He pushed another button on the desk console. "Cut the hydrogen in those lines. All the lines next to Tunnel Niner, and the northside lines too. MILLIE, what does that do to us?"

"WE WILL GO TO FLYWHEEL DRAIN. NO ESSENTIAL POWER LOSS FOR SEVENTEEN MINUTES. AFTER FOURTEEN MINUTES WE MUST BEGIN PHASEDOWN POWER CUTS TO PREPARE FOR INEVITABLE POWER LOSSES. DO YOU WISH MORE DETAILS?" The contralto voice spoke in impassive block capitals; at least that was how Rand always visualized them.

Power cuts would—

"Negative phasedowns," Sanders said. "Carry out previous order and use flywheel storage."

"DONE."

"Not enough!" Rand said. "We need those—"

"Tony, shut up," Sanders said. "Fleming, are you

certain they've got something that intentionally fouls up the detectors? That's not an accident?"

"Not bloody likely, sir."

"MILLIE?"

"PROBABILITY INSIGNIFICANT."

He turned to Rand. "Tony?"

Rand shrugged. "I don't know how they did it, but I can't see *that* happening by accident." He pointed at the fuzzy band on the hologram. "We ought to have intruders located to the decimeter."

"I'm getting an infra-red image now," Fleming said. "Tunnel Niner."

The screen showed a dim shadow of two figures, each carrying something heavy. The faces bulged like the snouts of pigs.

"Gas masks," Sanders said grimly. "MILLIE, do the images match anything in your memory?"

"PROBABILITY OF GAS MASK OR DE-LIBERATE SIMULATION OF GAS MASK, 76 PERCENT. OXYGEN MASK, 21 PERCENT PROBABLE. IF OXYGEN MASK, THE TANKS ARE VERY SMALL."

"Simulation? What's the chance of that?" Sanders demanded.

"INSUFFICIENT DATA."

"Jesus. Tony, get that damned robot of yours in there. Fast."

"I can't, Pres. Whatever they're using to interfere with our detectors is jamming my comm links with the Arr-two. I can't help you a bit."

• • •

It had happened at last. Preston Sanders had always known it would. It was the reason he hated the worry desk. Sitting here always involved political decisions; nothing else would be bucked up to the top duty officer. That was hard enough.

And now the big one had happened while he was on duty.

I've got about thirty seconds to dither. Should I call

the boss? It'd take him at least that long to get up to speed. Maybe I should have called him earlier. Probably would if Tony hadn't suggested it. Oh, damn it—

And what if Art's not sober? That LA man has left, but the Canadian is still here—

One of the shadows in the tunnel bent over. Possibly to tie his shoes. Possibly to set off a bomb that would wreck the lines. Sanders made his decision.

His voice was calm as he said, "Big one. Tunnel Niner. Big stuff. No drill. Execute."

His voice was calm, but sweat dripped from his chin. He'd never been in the Army.

And he had just killed two men, deliberately, in cold blood.

"Now we take care of the one on the north side," Sanders said. "Stand by lights and snipers. He doesn't look to be carrying anything heavy enough to do much damage. Right?"

"Right," said Fleming.

"Make sure he's got nothing to penetrate the intakes. And no bomb. Then catch the son of a bitch. Catch him alive, and no alarms."

"Roger, Mister Sanders." Captain Fleming turned away from the screens, and Preston Sanders sank back into his chair.

• • •

Art Bonner drank a final nightcap with Sir George Reedy and left the Canadian in the guest suite. The perimeter corridor was dark and deserted as Art limped slowly toward his empty apartment, but he paid it no attention.

He almost turned to the elevator that would take him to Delores's apartment. But . . . no. She'd made it clear that whatever they'd been, it was all over now. She'd be glad to see him, but for what?

What do I want? he wondered. For the apartment not to be empty when I get there. And that's impossible, because who wants to live with a man who lets a city set his schedule—and loves it. It was a wonder Grace stayed five years.

Actually . . . Delores will be glad to see me. We can talk about next week's schedule, and she'll make some tea, and—

Not fair. She must have men friends. One of them might be with her right now.

It would be literally no effort to find out; he had only to think the question. Why not? But—

There was a rising and falling note in his head. It wasn't quite sound; the implanted receiver fed directly into the auditory nerve, and he could sense the difference from true sound. For one thing, there was no vibration. But it was loud enough to startle him no matter how often he had heard it before.

He thought, MILLIE?

INTRUDER ALERT. SINGLE INTRUDER NORTHSIDE LEVEL 18 CORRIDOR 128 RING C. INTRUDER APPARENTLY UNARMED CARRYING NOTHING LARGE. TWO INTRUDERS CARRYING SURVEILLANCE INTERFERENCE EQUIPMENT AND GAS MASKS AND OTHER HEAVY EQUIPMENT EXTENT AND NATURE UNKNOWN IN ACCESS TUNNEL OH–NINER LOCATION IMPOSSIBLE TO DETERMINE.

More information poured into his head: everything MILLIE knew about the situation, the computer's probability estimates, the probable consequences of explosions in the penetrated areas; all happening so quickly that Bonner was hardly aware of it.

"Lord God," Bonner said to himself. He moved toward the fast lane of the pedway.

Sanders has it?

AFFIRMATIVE.

He's in charge.

ACKNOWLEDGED.

He was automatically going toward the Operations Center. And what do I do when I get there? he wondered. I left Pres in charge. He'll think I don't trust him if I come in and take over. He hasn't asked for help.

And there's the little matter of the brandy, too. Am I competent to make decisions?

SANDERS HAS ORDERED LETHAL GAS ACTION IN ACCESSWAY NINER, MILLIE told him.

"Christ Almighty," Bonner muttered. He had seconds only to interfere, if he were going to. And he had no information.

Pres is a good man, he thought. Another part of his mind answered: "He'd damned well better be." Bonner walked rapidly along the pedway. It was silly, it wouldn't get him to the control offices more than a few seconds earlier, but he did it.

VX RELEASED IN ACCESSWAY NINER. SECURITY IS MOVING IN ON THE INTRUDER IN NORTHSIDE AREA.

Well. That's that.

He was past his own apartment now; not far to the elevator to the top floor. That location was silly, Bonner thought. Administrators ought to be either next to their own apartments or somewhere in the middle of the building; but the designers had their own ideas. What was happening to Pres?

He began moving off the fast lane again. An elevator was waiting for him, of course, and there were two uniformed men next to it. All through Todos Santos the Security people would be moving quietly into place, just in case there were more to this attack than just three intruders in uninhabited areas.

Maintenance and engineering and the fire department would be on alert, too. If the hydrogen lines went, even if there wasn't a fire, Todos Santos would come grinding to a halt. It took energy to run the city. Less than the same people would need if they were scattered out in hundreds of thousands of buildings, of course, but it took plenty.

He limped off the pedway, acknowledged the guards with a wave, and entered the elevator, twitching while it rose. How's Pres taking it? He's killed two people!

The elevator loosed him and he ran for Preston Sanders's office, angling sideways to favor the bad leg.

• • •

Tony Rand watched the black man with awe. How can he be so damned calm about it? he wondered.

Maybe he's not. He's smoking like a chimney—have I ever seen him smoke before? He's usually so fussy about emptying ashtrays, and that one's half-full already.

He went to the shelf and poured a shot of brandy, tossing it off, almost laughing at the absurdity of his thoughts: it came unbidden that he'd put Sanders's prize brandy in coffee this afternoon, now he was drinking it like medicine. "Brandy?"

"I'm still on duty," Sanders said. "Fleming, what's the status on that northside intruder?"

"He's spotted us. He's hiding."

"Thank you."

"Maybe you ought to call Bonner now," Rand said.

"MILLIE already told him," Sanders said absently. "Standing orders on anything this big. He'll be here in a moment." He pointed at the holograph, where a blue star moved rapidly upward toward the operations suite. "I'd go easy on that brandy. Art will want you in on the conference."

Two dead, Rand thought. What the hell did they use to interfere with the surveillance?

Art Bonner came in. He took in the situation at a glance, his eyes resting momentarily on the full ashtray. "Status?" he asked.

"You already know," Sanders said. "I gassed Niner. They're getting men into survival gear to go inspect. And—"

"INTRUDER CAPTURED," MILLIE announced. She used audio to speak to all of them.

Fleming appeared on the screen. "Got him." Another image formed: a young man, early twenties at most, long hair in back but cut short at the sides and in front; scraggly beard, which wasn't unusual; cotton denim pants and jacket.

"No weapons," Fleming reported. "We fluoroscoped him. Nothing. And Medical says no drugs. He tried to put on he was high, but we've got him convinced we know better."

"That may have been a mistake," Sanders said. "Mister Bonner's here. Take over, Mister Bonner?"

"I relieve you. Get Delores up here, will you? And Sandra. I'm going to have to have some sleep before this night's over, and you will too. Fleming, send that intruder up here."

"Yes, sir." The images faded.

Bonner put his hand on Sanders's shoulder. "Relax."

Sanders tried to smile. It didn't work. "I killed them, Art. Both. In cold blood."

"Sure. Tony, get Pres a drink."

"It happened so *fast*. All over in a minute. Art, what if it's nothing? Like that kid, no weapons, nothing? Just trying to throw a scare into us? They never had a chance!"

Tony Rand brought over a brandy. "If they were trying to scare us, they made it nicely," he said. "Here."

Bonner nodded agreement. "You made the right decision. Same as I would. What if it wasn't nothing? What if they had bombs all set to take out the hydrogen lines? Set off the hydrogen with a big whoosh. Big bonfire, right in the park."

"I wish it hadn't been me."

"It was. And I'll back you all the way."

"It isn't Zurich I'm worried about. Or the Angelino police. It's me."

"Sure."

•   •   •

The boy was grinning. That was the first thing Tony Rand noticed when Lieutenant Blake ushered him into Sanders's office: a wide, triumphant grin.

"We got an ID on this one," Blake said.

"Sure. I'm Allan Thompson," the youth said. His voice was pleasant and sounded educated. "My father's a real estate broker in Hollywood. Where are the others?"

"What others?" Bonner asked.

"Aw, come on," Thompson said. He was still grinning. "You gotta have them by now—" He shrugged. "Maybe you don't." That seemed to amuse him even more.

Preston Sanders had ignored his brandy, and sat staring at the youth, his eyes a study of misery. The grin got to Tony Rand. "What's so damned funny?" Rand demanded.

Bonner raised a hand in warning. Rand subsided.

"We found a VIP Visitor badge outside the crawlway entrance to the unfinished section," Blake reported. "A Mr. Roland Thompson, who's a favored customer for a number of places."

"Sure, that's my Dad's badge," Allan Thompson said. "Okay, so now you call him and tell him the prodigal's in trouble again."

"Please sit down, Allan," Bonner said carefully. "And tell us why you were crawling around on a catwalk a hundred meters above ground level this late at night."

"It was fun, man." Thompson sat with the attitude of an important visitor. "We thought, what the hell, they're always talking about the security system at Todos Santos, we'll just show 'em it's not as good as they think—"

"We?" Bonner demanded. "Who are the others?"

Thompson grinned slyly. "So you really haven't caught them yet! That's choice. Well, I better tell you, 'cause it's getting pretty late and sitting here's a bummer. I don't guess you'll let me loose until you round 'em up. There are two, Diana and Jimmy, and they stayed in the stupid tunnel we got in from."

There was a sharp hiss as Preston Sanders took in a quick breath. Lieutenant Blake looked grim.

"Hey, what's the matter?" Thompson demanded. "Look, they aren't going to hurt anything!"

"Allan, were your friends carrying anything? Special equipment or anything like that?" Bonner asked casually. It was difficult to keep the strain from his voice.

Tony Rand leaned forward to listen. He felt the same thrill of horror that Bonner did; but he also wanted to know, how did they do it?

"Oh, some big boxes full of sand. Had 'dynamite' painted on the outside, you know? Just to show you. And Jimmy, that's Jim Planchet, he's an electronics genius. He made something that he thought would really give your detection stuff fits—"

"What? How did it work?" Rand demanded.

"Hell, I'm no electronics type," Thompson said. "But it must have worked if you haven't got 'em yet!"

Art Bonner was posed in the characteristic way he used to talk to MILLIE with his implant. His face looked—strange. Rand got up and went behind the desk so that he could see the TV screen that Sanders was watching. What had Bonner found out?

The screen showed:

JIM PLANCHET. IDENTIFICATION.

COUNCILMAN JAMES PLANCHET OF LOS ANGELES HAS A SON AGE TWENTY NAMED JAMES EVERETT JR.

"Lord God," Tony said involuntarily.

"What?" Allan Thompson squinted at Rand. "Did you say something?"

"No," Bonner said. "Who is Diana?"

"Aw, Diana Lauder. Kind of engaged to Jimmy, you know? Rooms in the dorm with us."

"I see. Well, I hope the automatic systems haven't harmed your friends," Bonner said evenly. "Lieutenant, please take Mr. Thompson to Central Security. We'll have to hang on to you for a while, Allan. What you did was highly illegal, didn't you know that?"

"You mean unlawful. Illegal's a sick bird," Thompson said. "We didn't mean any harm. Might even have done you a favor. Suppose we'd been somebody really out to get you? Wasn't my idea anyway. Jimmy's father kept spouting off about this place, and—there's something wrong, isn't there?" The boy's grin faded. "Jesus, they weren't hurt, were they? Look, Mister, they didn't mean any harm, they didn't have any weapons or anything! You didn't hurt them, did you? Jesus, Councilman Planchet will kill me if anything's happened to Jimmy!"

"So it was your idea," Bonner said evenly.

How can he be so calm? Rand wondered. And Pres just sits there staring at the brandy.

"Take him out, Blake," Bonner said. "We'll talk to him later."

"Hey, wait a minute, tell me, what's happened to Jimmy and Diana? Let me go, you goddam rent-a-cop! What did you bastards do? You can't handle me this way—"

* * *

The door closed behind the guard and the struggling youth. So that's that, Art Bonner thought.

"Kids out playing," Sanders said. "I don't want to believe it! Boxes full of sand. Art, they're as dead as—they're *dead!* I killed them, and they were just kids!"

"Yeah. Get hold of yourself. You did the right thing, given what you knew. Suppose it'd been FROMATES with a bomb?"

Sanders sat unmoving, staring at a wall he couldn't see.

"Come on, Pres, it's all right," Rand said. "Look, they tried their best to make you think they were FROMATES, right? I thought so, watching over your shoulder. What else could you do?"

Medical. Get someone in here to take care of Mister Sanders, Bonner thought.

ACKNOWLEDGED.

And get Sandra on duty. For everything except this. I don't want to be bothered with trivia.

MS. WYATT IS JUST REACHING HER OFFICE.

Tell her she's in charge as soon as she sits down. And Medical can give Pres a shot to get him through the night, but what the hell are we going to do tomorrow?

An LA City Councilman's kid and his girlfriend. Planchet—Jesus, why did it have to be him? He spouts off a lot, but he's not really an enemy. Wasn't an enemy. He will be now.

Can we keep it a secret? No. Thompson knew where the others were. Others might. Maybe not. Unwanted, a thought crept into the darker part of his mind. *Sorry, kid, you know too much*—Bonner pushed it away.

Get me legal. Roust out Johnny Shapiro, right now, and get him up to my office.

ACKNOWLEDGED.

Status?

SECURITY TEAM NOT READY TO ENTER. DETOXIFICATION ALMOST COMPLETED. ESTIMATE TEN MINUTES UNTIL SAFE TO ENTER.

We'll just have to wait.

• • •

Rand watched impatiently: Bonner giving orders and getting reports through his implant, while Tony knew nothing. Bonner could have had the decency to put it all on the TV screen! "What's happening?"

"They're flushing out the last traces of nerve gas," Bonner said. "Not important enough to send guards in there with protective suits, not until it's safer. Is it?"

"Don't think so. I tried to get a robot in, but the comm link is still jammed."

"Why the hell can't your people develop something better than nerve gas? Something to knock a man over instantly but not kill him?"

"Tall order," Rand said. "You've got one, but it

has to be inhaled. These were wearing gas masks. If you want something that works on skin contact and knocks them over before they know what hit them, war gasses are all there is."

"I suppose."

"Here's the route they must have taken," Bonner said. A thin line moved through the holograph; a second screen showed what someone traveling that route would see. Twice the stark words appeared:

IF YOU GO THROUGH THIS DOOR
YOU WILL DIE

SI USTED POR ESTA PUERTA
HABRIA PASADO, USTED HABRIA MUERTO!
MUY PELIGROSO

"Subtle we aren't," Rand said. "And those were good locks on those doors. Anything more and we couldn't get through them ourselves. Maybe if I—"

"You too?" Bonner said irritably. "Look. We took precautions. At great expense. Dammit, we aren't morally obligated to design this place so that idiot geniuses can't hurt themselves! What are we supposed to do, sit back and let a pack of crummy bastards shoot our police, poison our people, burn the city, put our people out of work—and never fight back?"

"Sure," Tony said; but he couldn't help wondering if there wasn't something else he could have done. A more foolproof design. But these kids were anything but fools!

A young medical resident came in and gave Preston Sanders a shot. Later, a security team brought out the bodies of Jimmy Planchet, age twenty, and Diana Lauder, nineteen. They had nothing dangerous with them; only dummy bombs with garish cartoons, a box of sophisticated electronic gear that Rand thirsted to study, and masks connected to Scuba gear.

There were no weapons at all.

VI

Knowledge of human nature is the beginning and end
of political education.

—Henry Brooks Adams

EYE OF THE STORM

Lying on a strange bed in a strange city in a foreign
country, Sir George Reedy gradually realized that he
wasn't going to sleep.

It was jet lag, of course. Sir George had always
suffered from biorhythm upset. It was a pity, because
his work involved a good deal of traveling. He would
not have survived had he not learned to sleep on
airplanes.

But, having slept through the flight to Los Angeles,
Reedy was now wide awake at midnight. He was
tired but not sleepy. If he closed his eyes tight and
clenched his fists and *willed* himself to sleep, he'd still
be doing it come the dawn. He'd tried to force sleep
often enough. The trick (he thought, as he sat up and
reached for his contact lenses) was to take the
additional awake-time as a gift, and *do* something
with it.

The day was full of undigested data . . . . Anthony

Rand had mentioned stockholders who worked outside without ever leaving Todos Santos. An intriguing possibility in a world running out of fuel. What had Rand called them? Waldos. And a technical term he'd forgotten.

MILLIE, Sir George said in his throat. Reedy.

READY, SIR GEORGE.

What have you got on waldos?

WALDO: A SYSTEM IN WHICH THE MOTIONS OF A HUMAN HAND OR HANDS ARE IMITATED BY A MECHANICAL HAND OR HANDS LOCATED ELSE-WHERE. THE IDEA WAS FIRST CONCEIVED BY ROBERT HEINLEIN FOR A SHORT SCIENCE FICTION STORY, WALDO, PUBLISHED IN 1940. WALDOS, OR TELEOPERATED DEVICES, WERE LATER DEVELOPED FOR USE IN HANDLING RADIOACTIVES, THEN FOR ANY DANGEROUS PROFESSION: THE MINING OF URANIUM OR COAL, MANIPULATION OF DAN-GEROUS CHEMICALS, WORK IN VACUUM ON THE MOON. THE TELEOPERATED TOOL MAY BE OF ANY SIZE, AND MAY BE MITTEN-SHAPED RATHER THAN HAND-SHAPED. A ROUTINE MAY BE RECORDED ONCE USING AN OPERATOR, THEN THE PROGRAM MAY BE REPLAYED INDEFINITELY.

How many waldo operators presently reside here?

FOUR HUNDRED AND TEN.

Reedy was at the window now, looking out at a glowing carpet of light. Indeed, Los Angeles *was* beautiful . . . from here. Does the Todos Santos air conditioning system filter smog?

YES, WITH 80% EFFICIENCY.

Cost?

RESTRICTED.

Sir George paced. Order me a large mug of chocolate and two ounces of bourbon.

DONE.

This science fiction writer. What else did he invent? Did he make any money at it?

ROBERT HEINLEIN IS CREDITED WITH THE IDEAS BEHIND THE LINEAR ACCELERATOR LAUNCHER,

THE MOVING WALKWAY, AND THE WATER BED.
NO PATENTS ARE ON FILE.

Reedy shook his head, grinning. Typical. But
waldos, now: that would have a strong bearing on
how much parking place Canada must allot to a
projected arcology. What else should he be checking,
before he started digging for real information,
tomorrow?

An arcology wouldn't work without a city nearby?
If true, it was crucial. What kind of city? How near?
Todos Santos and Los Angeles were perhaps too
close; relations between the two seemed strained. The
kind of tension he'd already seen couldn't hold
forever, Reedy thought. Something would snap.

Perhaps the Canadian host city, or its citizens,
should be given concessions of some kind?

That family in the Commons: they had been
financed by Todos Santos itself. Bonner had said so.
How would that work?

Millie.

READY.

What data have you on a Phillips family, man and
wife and at least two children?

PHILLIPS, CALVIN RAYMOND, AND JUDY NEE
CAMPBELL. INDEPENDENT STOCKHOLDER RESI-
DENTS. MARRIED ONE TIME NINE YEARS TO
PRESENT. CHILDREN CALVIN RAYMOND JUNIOR
PRESENT AGE EIGHT YEARS, PATRICK LAFAYETTE
AGE SIX YEARS. COOPERATIVE OWNER UNIT
18–4578. PERCENTAGE OF OWNERSHIP RESTRICTED
INFORMATION.

Omit personal details, Reedy instructed. How was
his business financed interrogative.

DIRECTOR FOR CAPITAL DEVELOPMENT AD-
VANCED CORPORATE LOAN FUNDS IN EXCHANGE
FOR ONE QUARTER INTEREST IN THE BUSINESS
ENTERPRISE.

What security was given for the loan? Sir George
scratched his ear. The tiny voice in his head tickled.

NOTE OF HAND ON RECOMMENDATION OF MISS CHURCHWARD.

He'd heard that name . . . from Bonner? Who is Churchward?

DIRECTOR FOR CAPITAL DEVELOPMENT.

"My word," Reedy said aloud.

QUERY?

Glitch. Is this kind of financial arrangement normal?

443 STOCKHOLDERS HAVE OPENED BUSINESSES IN TODOS SANTOS USING LOANS RECOMMENDED BY BARBARA CHURCHWARD. 27 HAVE SINCE DE-CLARED BANKRUPTCY.

That was quite a good record, Reedy decided. Tell me about Barbara Churchward.

PERMISSION FROM CHURCHWARD REQUIRED. CHURCHWARD HAS PRESENT STATUS NO DIS-TURBANCES FOR ROUTINE MATTERS. IS THIS AN EMERGENCY?

No. That will be all, thank you.

The table opened to deliver Sir George's hot chocolate. He sipped enough to make room, then added the bourbon. The mix had put him to sleep on other occasions.

Sipping, he smiled out at the carpet of light. No wonder the Angelinos were bitter. Every previous arcology had begun its life as a hopefully self-sufficient entity. Todos Santos had begun as a symbiote on Los Angeles. Now, by searching out the people it needed, by luring them inside with loans and concessions, the city-in-a-building was making every attempt to *become* self-sufficient, within Los Angeles's borders.

Just how necessary was Churchward to the process?

Might she be looking for a new career, with a hefty rise in salary? Reedy made a mental note to find out.

• • •

That a man could be so lost in despair that he was prepared to destroy himself, and that other men could mock him in the very act! He would never have believed it. The last of his illusions had burned out of him while he danced in the wind on the high board. His anger was deep inside him, too deep to show, and turned against itself.

His face wasn't even sullen. It was dead calm, as he sat, waiting, waiting; for what he didn't know, and didn't care. He had walked where the guards had led him and sat where they pointed.

The guards had found him leaning against the fence, looking outward, with tears running down his calm face. He had felt the stubby fingers on his arm, had followed the pull. The guard had spoken in reassuring tones; he had not heard the words. They led him into an elevator. Down, like a falling stone. Out. To this room, where he waited.

The door opened.

He did not bother to look up. But people were talking.

"I don't know, Tony. I don't know what's going to happen now. But I swear they looked like they were going to blow up the hydrogen lines."

"I was there. I came down to see the equipment they carried. It's not in here? Oh. Who's he?" Voices grew clearer as heads looked into the room.

"Him? Oh, he's a leaper we pulled off your high board."

"Jeez, Patterson, we've got worse problems than him! They've got Mr. Sanders doped to the eyes. Mr. Rand, what do we do if the Angelino cops come for him?"

"Nothing. Pres killed two saboteurs and captured a third. That third one was lucky. Pres had every right to kill him too. Los Angeles isn't going to do a thing to him."

"Yes, sir—but the kids weren't carrying dynamite, dammit! It was just a box of sand. How will that look to a Grand Jury?"

He looked up to see "Tony" shrug and say, "Blake, those three did their damndest to convince us they were ready to wreck Todos Santos. I'd say they succeeded beyond their wildest dreams. Think of it as evolution in action."

A bark of laughter, and a sober voice: "It won't stop there, Tony. God, I'm glad I'm not Bonner."

Answering laughter. "So is everyone else tonight."

They closed the door. They had forgotten him again. He resented it. He resented their laughter; it mocked his coming death.

They remembered him an hour later. The stubby-fingered guard led him back to the elevator and took him down and put him in a subway car and said things he didn't bother to hear. He had already made his decision.

• • •

Thomas Lunan zapped the electronic gizmo and drove the Jaguar into its garage. He wrestled two bags of groceries out and set them down, then busied himself with locks: an enormous metal bar across the steel garage door, then the police lock and two deadbolts to let himself out the smaller door for humans. Once outside with his packages he had to set them down and lock up.

His apartment was three blocks away, and he had to carry the groceries. The streets were well lighted, though, and busily traveled; it was one reason he'd selected that garage.

The apartment building had been a house before it became old and run-down; dilapidated wouldn't have been too strong a word. The hall carpet was threadbare, and the walls hadn't been painted in years. There were only two apartments in the ancient house. He climbed one flight to his own and unlocked it. The locks were not new and didn't appear particularly good, although in fact they were recommended by a firm of security consultants he'd interviewed.

Inside, everything was different. His apartment was tastefully furnished, and everything was bright and clean. His stereo and TV were expensive and new. Some of the paintings on the wall were originals.

But from the outside you'd never know there was anything worth stealing; which was the idea. Lunan was rather proud of the method he'd hit on. He wanted to live near the beach, and couldn't afford the expensive beach communities; therefore it had to be Venice with its old houses built in the 1920s. But Venice was a high-crime area, so how could he enjoy his expensive possessions without being ripped off? Obviously he had to live in a way that kept anyone from knowing he had anything worth stealing.

The car was the toughest part; if he parked the Jag near the building someone was bound to get the idea that its owner had good loot. They'd follow him home and rip him off. Lunan lived alone, and his job kept him away for week-long intervals; that was bad enough, but worse would be for a street gang to come when he was home. Which was why he was careful going from his car to his apartment, and so far it had worked perfectly.

He turned on the news, but paid little attention to it, keeping an ear tuned to alert him to anything unusual. Unusual *for* him meant a lead on a hot story.

Lunan was in trouble. Not, he told himself, *big* trouble, but trouble just the same. He hadn't had a big story in months, and the station director was breathing down his neck.

If he didn't find something pretty quick, they'd assign him something; and he'd worked too long and hard for his high status as a roving investigator to go back on assignment. Worse, the associate producer who handled assignments didn't like him, and neither did most of his reporter colleagues. They'd give him dull crap. Not all dull crap, of course; he was too good for that. But any dull crap was too much.

The trouble was, he hadn't had an idea in a long time. And he lived on ideas. Lunan didn't do stories the way others did: didn't chase ambulances, or go to fires, or hang around the police station. He didn't do what the others would call *news* at all. His specialty was in-depth interviews, digging out big human-interest stories that explained the world.

So what to do now? He estimated that he had about two weeks before they called him in and put him back in the pool. Not very long. How in hell was he to find something big in two weeks?

He decided to fall back on a technique that had worked for him in the past: go fishing. Wander out, people-watch, talk with anyone he could find, and let matters develop. It sounded haphazard, and it was; but luck had been with him in the past. He'd gotten two Pulitzer nominations that way.

So where to go? He put on a classic, the Beatles, and relaxed with a glass of Chivas Regal, and after a while he remembered that he hadn't visited the Santa Monica Mall in quite a while. Why not? Maybe something good would come of it.

• • •

The leaper left the subway at the Flower Street exit in central Los Angeles. There were buildings here: not high by Todos Santos standards, but high enough. The men who had mocked him in Todos Santos would read of his death, and they would be sorry.

But would they know?

It was important. He was carrying no identification and no suicide note. He had only the money the Todos Santos guard had thrust into his pocket. He had decided to die anonymously. Now that was not enough. He must leave something. He stood between the empty track and the walls scrawled with obscene messages and gang symbols, while half-thoughts formed in his mind . . .

He searched his pockets for a Magic Marker until he found it. He stood before the wall (not caring if anyone was watching) and presently inspiration came. He printed in large letters, over a message that had almost been washed away:

THINK OF IT AS EVOLUTION IN ACTION

Now, that was good. It was not too proud. It was the statement of a man who had done one last service to the human race, by ridding it of a chronic loser. He would scrawl it on the parapet, or wherever, just before he jumped. And this man, Tony, would recognize it for his own words . . .

He turned and walked briskly toward the exit stairway.

• • •

Big Jim Planchet poured himself another bourbon and settled back into his study chair. He thought that his visitor was finally getting to the point. George Harris had spent a lot of time talking about nothing, and it was late; time for Planchet to rejoin his other guests on the patio.

"You know I go to jail every week," Harris said.

Councilman Planchet frowned. "I guess I'd heard about it."

In fact, he knew almost as much as Harris did; he'd had to check it out, because he wanted to be sure that having Harris on his campaign finance committee wouldn't cause him trouble with his Los Angeles constituents.

George Harris had falsified his income tax returns, been caught, and convicted of tax fraud. At his trial he'd said he'd done it in protest against Washington policies that he refused to continue paying for. That may not have helped him get the judge's sympathy; in addition to his fines, Harris had to spend four dozen weekends in the county jail. They let him out on Sunday nights so he could conduct his business, but every Saturday morning he had to go back.

Not many knew where Harris went on weekends, and most of those who did felt sorry for him. Doesn't everybody cut his tax return as close as possible? There were some who thought Harris deserved a medal. So there wasn't any problem about remaining friends with George, which was just as well, since Planchet had known him for years.

"I need help," Harris said.

Big Jim Planchet frowned. "Look, George, that was a federal court. If your lawyers can't get you out, I sure can't—"

"I know that," Harris said impatiently. "Most people think I got off easy. I guess I did, compared to what it would be like if they kept me inside all week. But Jim, I can't stand much more of it."

This was going to be embarrassing. Planchet could tell. Harris, tough old George Harris, was about to break down and cry. And that wouldn't do at all. They weren't *that* good friends. Harris would regret it later, and—"Look, George, I know it's not pleasant, but—"

"Not pleasant? Jim, it's sheer hell! No human dignity at all. The jailers are sadists. Every week it's the same speech from one of the fat slobs. 'I'm real easy to get along with. Real easy. But you give me trouble and I'll make you regret it. Just remember that. Them rules you see posted on the wall got nothing to do with what really goes on in here. Remember that and we'll get along fine.' Every week he says that.

"And he means every word of it. They *enjoy* their work, Jim. They like waking us up at four-thirty in the morning. They like herding us to the showers in lockstep. They like rousting us into a holding tank and keeping forty men crowded into a cell meant for six. I come in every Saturday at eight in the morning. I have to be there at eight. They don't even let me in until nine, but God help me if I'm not there at eight to sit out front for an hour. Then jammed into a holding cell for processing. Every damn week. They know I'm coming, so what's all this processing? But I don't dare ask, and you wouldn't either."

"Yeah, well—"

"And that's not the half of it." Harris had broken

the barrier of reluctance to talk. Now the words rushed out in a flood. "Breakfast at five, and it's not edible. Soggy bread. Eggs cooked in fish oil. At five A.M.! On Sunday. They say breakfast has to be early, because most of the inmates have court appearances and need to be ready by eight. Maybe that's so, but on Sunday? And for lunch there's the same damned bread, and greasy meat, sausage wrapped in rubber with rubber potatoes. They are. They *bounce* when you drop one."

"Jail isn't supposed to be fun, George."

"I know that! But do they have to take away every last shred of dignity? Are they 'reforming' me? How? I'm not a criminal."

"No. The judge thought you were something more dangerous. A rebel."

"Damn it, Hitler was treated better when they jailed him after the Munich *Putsch.*"

Sure, and if they'd treated him worse, maybe he wouldn't have tried it again, Planchet thought. Make it easy on tax evaders, and there'd be a tax rebellion all over the country, and what would happen to the poor then? George was protesting nuclear power plants, but the same logic could be used to protest welfare—and welfare was a lot less popular than power plants. He really didn't have a lot of sympathy for George Harris. On the other hand, there were those campaign donations, and Harris seemed to have influence with some heavy people in real estate. A good man to be friends with.

"And the people they put me in with! Jim, one weekend I had a cell by myself. The toilet didn't work, it had overflowed all over the floor, but that was the best weekend I had yet. The animals they throw me in with—"

"I guess that could get pretty bad," Planchet said. "What do you want me to do? The jail's county, not city. I don't have any control over it. That's the sheriff's department."

"But can't you do *something?*"

"We try. Every now and then a judge declares that jail 'cruel and inhuman' and there's a big brouhaha about 'reforms,' but it never amounts to anything."

"Yeah, but what can *I* do? I'm at the end of my rope, Jim."

"I suppose," Planchet said. He lifted a microphone from a desk drawer. "Emil, see if you can get Mr. George Harris—spelled like it sounds—set up for VIP treatment at county jail. He's on one of those weekend detention work furlough programs. Reports on Saturday morning and gets out Sunday night. At least try to get him a better class of cell mate. County owes us a couple, call in one of our favors." He put the microphone back in the desk. "There. My assistant will get on it in the morning."

Harris looked genuinely relieved.

"Can't promise," Planchet warned. "But I think things will change for the better. A little better, anyway."

"Thanks. Thanks a hell of a lot." He drained his glass. "Oh. About your fund raiser. I think I can get some of the guys at the Athletic Club to buy tables. It'd be easier, though, if you'd show up once in a while." He looked accusingly at Planchet's middle, which was beginning to hang over the Councilman's belt. "If you'd been that out of shape, you wouldn't even have made the team at USC."

"Suppose you're right," Planchet said. That had been a long time ago, when Jim Planchet was a star running back. That hadn't hurt his political career, either.

George patted his own flat stomach. "You ought to keep in shape, Jim. Work out sometimes."

"Weekends in the pokey don't seem to have hurt you that way," Planchet said.

"Hell they don't. The only way to exercise is *regularly*. Every damned day. And can you see me doing exercises in a cell with a screaming queen? But leave out how flabby you're getting, you ought to get to the club to meet the boys. Play a little poker once in a while. You'd be surprised how many friends you can make losing a couple of hundred bucks."

Planchet nodded. "Good advice. Now when do I do it? I don't even have time to see my own son."

"What's the problem?"

Planchet shrugged. "Todos Santos, mostly. Lot of businesses in my district losing customers to that termite hill. Not much I can do, but they sure want me to try."

Harris nodded in sympathy. "Yeah. They bring in their own construction people too. Buy everything from their favorites. For a while I thought I had a deal lined up selling them some electrical supplies, but they found somebody inside their shop to take care of it for them. Your constituents have a legitimate complaint. Todos Santos is exempt from most of the regulations that drive our businesses under."

"Sure. But that was the only way they'd build the place," Planchet said.

Fifteen years ago, Los Angeles had been glad to get Todos Santos. Terrorists had tried to start riots by starting fires in one of the ghetto areas. It had worked fine. They threw so many firebombs that they started a firestorm and burned down square miles of city, leaving a hideous, angry scar, a lot of people homeless, and unemployment soaring. When the consortium that owned Todos Santos offered to rebuild and create a hundred thousand jobs, and solve the fresh-water problem in the bargain, Congress and the state legislature and everybody else had fallen all over themselves to give the money people the incentives they demanded.

Probably a mistake, Planchet thought. But it looked like a good idea at the time.

"You ever have to talk money with Todos Santos?" Harris asked.

"Not too often." Planchet got up and put his glass on the bar.

Harris continued to talk as he followed Planchet to the party. "Be glad you never did. They've got a female shark you'd have to do business with. Beautiful woman, but cold as that iceberg they have out in the harbor. Hard as nails."

• • •

When the waiter brought the check, Barbara Churchward took it before the young man across the table from her could protest. His look of dismay was interesting, and idly she wondered if he were worried about the deal he was trying to swing, or if he simply couldn't accept the idea of a woman paying for dinner.

It never hurt to be nice, she thought. "It's all right, Ted," she said. "We own half of this place. I get a good discount."

Not that it mattered a lot. Mr. Binghampton was in for a disappointment. Possibly several, if she'd correctly read his intentions for the rest of the evening. Not that it would be particularly unpleasant to let him show her his earnings report or whatever he was likely to use to induce her to his guest suite on Level 96. He was handsome, he was intelligent, he was personable . . . but she never mixed business with pleasure, as he was about to find out.

And for that matter, she wasn't going to do any business with him tomorrow either. It had looked like a good deal, if a trifle complicated. She'd recently acquired a company that had an excellent outside sales force; in fact, the salesmen were better than the production staff. If she had a good home product line to add to their wares they could handle it fine.

And Mr. Ted Binghampton represented an undercapitalized company that made excellent low-cost vacuum cleaners that her sales force could peddle door to door with very little retraining. The only problem was the "iceberg."

Tennaha Electric had a generous pension policy. How many of its employees were overage? If there were a lot of them, the initial profits would be high, but after a few years things would come apart.

Millie, she thought. Has Sam come up with the figures on the age structure of Tennaha yet?

Data flowed into her mind. Age of employees, pension entitlement, average turnover, average age when hired. When the stream was finished she examined what she'd learned. From long experience she controlled her expression, but inwardly she frowned. Tennaha was an oldsters' outfit; old craftsmen. They weren't hiring new people, and they had a lot of elderly craftsmen who wouldn't be around more than a decade.

No good. As she'd suspected, the iceberg was just too big. She toyed with the idea of buying Tennaha out, skimming the cream, and unloading; but that involved the risk of finding a sucker. She could probably do that. The inflated downstream cost load was well hidden, and it had taken a lot of investigation to nail it down. But she couldn't be sure of a sucker when she needed one.

Besides, she had a better use for the sales force. There was another company, CMC Inc., small, located right here in Los Angeles, that was vulnerable to a stock takeover, and that looked like a much better deal. She had two of her people out talking to the employees; if the key ones were willing, the whole outfit could be moved into Todos Santos, adding to TS capabilities; the money would stay in TS banks and credit unions, available for additional investment, rather than moving outward to Columbus where Tennaha had its plant.

There were a lot of advantages to that. Todos Santos was exempted from most of the stupid regulations that businesses outside had to live with. If they bought Tennaha they'd have a hell of a time streamlining the place, what with equal opportunity and anti-age discrimination and all. Far better to import the capability than acquire an outside firm.

Of course the management of CMC wouldn't want to sell out to Todos Santos, but that was a technical problem only. The right offer to the stockholders at the right time and the directors wouldn't know what hit them. They were a pretty naive bunch anyway. A couple of the directors weren't so bad, and those she'd keep on, but most would have to go—

"Hey, come back," Ted Binghampton said. "You're a million miles away."

"Oh. Sorry," Barbara said. "I guess I was."

"I can never tell what you're thinking."

She gave him her best smile, which she knew was pretty good. "There's luck." Until she found out if the key CMC people would move to Todos Santos, it would be best to keep the Tennaha deal alive.

She listened idly as he said something about what a pleasure it was to do business with a lovely woman. She'd heard that before, and she could respond with the proper smile without listening.

She didn't have to listen. She had a totally objective appreciation of her attractiveness: high. After all, *Playboy* had once offered to do a spread on her when she was just getting started in business. Now *that* was flattery. Thank God she'd had sense enough to refuse, although at the time she sure could have used the money. Back then she was young enough and naive enough to think that physical attractiveness was terribly important. All the evidence said it was. She'd made plenty of money by modeling.

Enough that she'd had to pay some attention to what was done with the money, and discovered that she liked business. It was the most exciting game in town. It hadn't hurt to be a pretty young thing who could talk like an ingenue, either. Not then. She was popular at parties, where she met a lot of other young women with money. Models, movie and TV stars, the whole panoply of Hollywood society, and after a while she was managing their investments; before that phase of her life ended she'd built a multimillion-dollar investment counseling firm, in which she still owned a 20 percent non-voting interest. She'd also earned enough to pay for her implant, and *that* was invaluable. While the people she negotiated with fumbled with papers and tried to remember figures, she had all the data available simply by wanting it.

"And we have some new production figures," Ted was saying. "I didn't bring them down to dinner, but if you'd like to go over them now I can show you."

She was considering how to refuse politely when the warbling began inside her head, and she knew she had real trouble.

VII

Those who would treat politics and morality apart will
never understand the one or the other.
          —John, Viscount Morley of Blackburn

NIGHT MEETINGS

The conference had started when Tony Rand came
back to Executive Row. He entered quietly and took
his seat at the big mahogany table.

Most of the rulers of Todos Santos were there. Art
Bonner at the end of the table, with Preston Sanders
next to him. Sanders wore a strange expression:
haunted eyes in a face relaxed by tranquilizers.

Barbara Churchward, even more beautiful than
usual, in a gold lamé gown that probably cost two
thousand dollars, her red hair swept up into a
sculptured helmet, her eyes focused on nothing.

Next to her was Frank Mead, his buttocks
overflowing the comfortable chair, his face in a
perpetual scowl. As Comptroller, Mead worked for
Bonner and Churchward, but he also reported directly
to the Board in Zurich. Rumor had it that Mead was
almost as powerful as Bonner. Certainly no one
wanted to annoy him needlessly.

There were others. Colonel Amos Cross, Chief of Security, a thin, dapper man going bald in a handsomely distinguished way. The young medical resident who'd given Sanders the shot, looking very out of place among the mighty. And John Shapiro, the head of the legal staff, self-conscious in a shirt open at the collar; usually he wore a full-vested suit and conservative necktie.

They were all looking at Tony Rand. Bonner frowned. "Learn anything?"

"Some. They had one signal generator that put out a code MILLIE interprets as routine maintenance, another that bollixed up the capacitance detectors, and a couple of others I won't understand without a few hours work."

"Any conclusions from that?" Bonner asked.

"Good brains at work. How could anyone that smart be that stupid?"

"Tony, how did they know what they'd need?"

Tony shook his head. "Some of it's logical, but they couldn't have guessed the frequencies, and they'd never have guessed the codes to open locks."

"Meaning they had an inside source?" Frank Mead asked.

"It's likely," Tony said. "Probably somebody who has access to MILLIE. But I've no idea who."

"I don't either," Bonner said. "I hate to think of anyone as disloyal—"

Mead asked, "Whose staff would he be on?"

"Yours?" Rand asked.

Mead shook his head. "None of my people know a damn thing about electronics. I don't myself. Look, if we've got a goddam traitor in here, we have to get rid of him."

"Certainly," Bonner said. "We'll see what we can do in the morning. But for now, we don't need another penetration. Colonel, are your troops on alert?"

"Yes, sir," Cross said. He smoothed down his nearly invisible pencil mustache, then put his hands together and laid them carefully on the table where he could watch them. "I've doubled the watch in Central, and we've got teams with dogs out walking the perimeter. Also, with your permission, I'd like to see just who's had access to MILLIE."

Bonner nodded agreement. "I've already got MILLIE working up a report for me. Tony, is it possible they've got a way to get information out of MILLIE without leaving any record?"

"Sure. You do it all the time. So does Barbara. And your deputies, and Delores. Anyone with an implant, or with a terminal and unrestricted access."

"Aren't there records of who's called up what file, and when?" Barbara Churchward asked.

"Sure," Tony said. "But the accession records aren't secure. Almost anyone could alter them."

"Why is that?" Mead demanded. "Seems awfully loose to me."

"Well," Tony said, "every time you put in closed files, you complicate the programs. Complex programs are hard to maintain. We can do it, but it will get expensive."

Bonner's lips tightened. "Okay. That's another problem that'll have to wait until morning." He took in a deep breath. "Planchet's kid, of all people. He's more powerful than the Mayor! He can really hurt us, and we've got to assume he'll try."

"Scapegoat," Sanders said. "He'll want a scapegoat. Me."

"Well, he won't get you," Bonner said. "Johnny, what's the legal situation?"

"Not good," Shapiro said. "For the moment we're all right. We're a police department, and we've notified ourselves. But it's been an hour, and by now we should already have called the County Coroner's office. Once we do that, the D.A.'s men will take jurisdiction away from us."

"Can we fight that?"

Shapiro shook his head decisively. "No, sir, no way. Todos Santos has a lot of legal immunities, but we're still a part of LA County and the state of California. Nothing we can do about that."

"I'd like to ignore it," Frank Mead said. "Bury 'em deep and say the hell with LA County."

"Be serious, Frank," Bonner said. "A hundred people know about the break-in. Not to mention the Thompson boy."

Mead raised hands the size of small hams. "Yeah, I know. It was just a thought." He brought his hands down flat on the table in a gesture of helpless rage. "But damn all, Planchet's going to *hurt* us, just now when the cash flow's a mess. It's just a bloody lousy time to fight LA."

"There's never a really good time for economic warfare," Churchward said to no one in particular.

"John, what happens when we do report this?" Bonner asked. "Will they try to arrest Mr. Sanders?"

"Probably. They don't have to, but given the political situation they will if Planchet insists on it."

"I don't like that much," Frank Mead muttered.

Preston Sanders laughed. It was a horrible sound. "But Mr. Mead, you've always been so certain I'd screw up. Now it's happened."

Mead was shocked. "Hey, Sanders, I don't deserve that!"

"There's no need for that, Pres," Barbara Churchward said. Her voice was smoothly professional. "Art, we know what happened here. Do we need Pres any longer?"

Bonner frowned. "He's my deputy—"

"And doped to the eyes," Churchward said. "I suggest you let him get a good night's sleep."

"I suppose you're right. One thing we make clear, though. Los Angeles does not put Sanders in jail. They can interview him all they want to, but right here. Are we agreed?"

There was a chorus of assents, except for Shapiro. The lawyer looked worried. "Not going to be easy to do, Art. If they decide to arrest him, how do we stop them?"

"For the moment, he's too ill to be moved. Dr. Finder, you take care of that. Take Pres down to your hospital and keep him there. No visitors without my approval, only don't say it's my approval, say it's Dr. Weintraub's. Won't that do it, Johnny?"

Shapiro nodded slowly. "I suppose. Best get a couple of shrinks into the act. We have to have a plausible reason for this."

"I'm not crazy," Sanders protested. "Damn it, I am not crazy!"

"Nobody says you are," Bonner snapped. "But it's best if we say you're 'emotionally upset.'"

Which he certainly is, Tony Rand thought. "Pres, it's all right. Just go down and babble once in a while. You know, think up some good stories for the city shrinks. Like you see green snakes crawling out of the air vents, and flying purple people eaters in the bathtub. If you lack imagination, I'll come help you."

Sanders giggled. Bonner nodded to the medical resident and Dr. Finder stood. After a moment, Sanders got up and let Finder lead him out of the room.

"He said it, not me," Frank Mead said after the door closed behind Sanders. "And he did screw it up."

"What would you have done?" Bonner demanded.

"Waited for Security to catch the upstairs intruder," Mead said. "And tried knockout gas."

"Letting them blow up the hydrogen input lines," Tony Rand said. "That's not too bright."

"Better than starting a war with Los Angeles!"

"That's enough from both of you," Bonner said. "We are not here to go over what happened. We're here to decide what we do *now*. Understood?"

"The first thing we'd better do is call the coroner's office," Shapiro said. "The longer we put that off, the worse we look."

"All right," Bonner agreed. "I'll have Sandra do

that now." He paused for a moment with his head tilted to one side. "There. Now we've got less than an hour before it hits the fan.

"Next. Who should tell Councilman Planchet? If he has any special friends in Todos Santos, MILLIE doesn't know about it."

"MacLean Stevens," Barbara Churchward said. "Call him and let him notify the Councilman."

"Good thinking. I suppose I'd better do that now. Excuse me." Bonner left the room to go to an adjoining office.

"We'll need statements for the press," Churchward said. "I suppose Sandra can get the PR people on that. I'll check with Art."

Now she's doing it, Rand thought. Telepathy. Well, not quite. She tells MILLIE, MILLIE tells Bonner, and vice versa; but it's as close to reliable telepathy as I'm ever going to see.

"And there will be all kinds of economic impact," Churchward said. "Sales of TS products in the LA area will fall like a falcon. I wonder if we'll have food shortages? Before this breaks it wouldn't be a bad idea to lay in supplies."

"You sound as if you're preparing for a siege," Frank Mead said.

"Not a bad analogy," John Shapiro said. "And not a bad idea, either."

• • •

The man lay sprawled across the concrete stairs, a dozen steps below the subway exit. Beneath the bruises his long face had never been handsome, and the wrinkles formed a permanent sulk. His skull was distorted; it had been pounded repeatedly against one of the steps. His clothes were worn and dirty, but they had been expensive.

The rookie who had discovered him walked away, wobbling a little and looking greenish. Lieutenant Donovan politely ignored him. He watched as a lab man turned out the pockets.

Nothing. The muggers who'd killed him picked him clean. There was nothing in his pockets but a pocket pack of Kleenex and a Magic Marker pen. Donovan wondered why they had left those.

Solving muggings is like bailing out a lifeboat with a teaspoon, he thought. He wouldn't waste much time with this one. He'd been on his way home when he saw the meat wagon pull up and had come over to look, otherwise he'd never have come to the scene. Muggings were for lower-grade detectives, not homicide lieutenants.

Wonder what he was doing here? Damn fool. Of all the places to get off the subway. The trains are safe enough, but not this station. Damn fool. Donovan had given up crying for them.

But he had to go through the motions. It was still a murder.

No witnesses. No way to find anyone who'd been riding the train. They'd either come forward or they wouldn't. But there was another possibility. There was an access way into the uncompleted tunnel system right here in this station. The Todos Santos crews were working back there—if he stood very quietly he could hear it, the humming roar of their big digging machine burning its way under City Hall. Maybe one of their crews had come out to use the can or something. Not likely, but it was possible. He made a note to call the TS tunnel foreman.

Or, he thought, I could go in there now and talk to their people. That would be interesting. I've never seen one of those big machines working, and I'd like to, and this is as good a chance as any.

"Sir?" The rookie cop was back, still looking a bit greenish. His eyes avoided the dead man. "I've found something. If you'll bring that pen that was in his pocket." He led the way downstairs.

Broad lines in blue ink, a freshly printed message among the other messages, less obscene than most:

THINK OF IT AS EVOLUTION IN ACTION

"If that's a dying message, it's not likely to name his murderer," said Donovan. "You're right, though. It matches the marker. He probably wrote it." Another reason to talk to the TS tunnel crew. Maybe they saw him writing on their door.

"I wonder what he meant?"

"We can't ask him," said Donovan, and forgot it. Or thought he had.

* * *

MacLean Stevens kept his emergency phone on a fifty-foot cord rooted in the central hall. That way he could move around the house while tied up on the phone. In particular, he could reach the coffee cup and the liquor cabinet, and when he got calls on that phone he often needed to.

This time he needed both. During a marathon bargaining session on the costs of digging new subways, Art Bonner and Tony Rand had introduced Stevens to the habit of lacing strong coffee with brandy. Now, as he listened to Bonner, he padded barefoot out to the kitchen to put on the coffee, then to the front room for brandy. Then he decided not to wait for the coffee.

"All right, Art. I'll tell him," Stevens said. "God damn it—Oh, hell. I'll tell him." He put down the phone and poured two fingers of Christian Brothers. He was tossing it off when Jeanine came in in her lumpy flannel nightgown.

As usual when she was disturbed at night, she looked both irritated and wide awake. "You'll tell whom?" she asked.

"Councilman Planchet. His son's been killed."

"Oh, no! Mac—Mac, it will kill Eunice."

Stevens nodded. "Yeah."

"Who was that, one of your police?"

"Art Bonner."

Her face showed surprise, then shock, then went blank. "But—Art, what happened to Jimmy?"

"He was killed breaking into Todos Santos. And now I've got to call Mr. Planchet."

She came over and held him for a moment, her head buried against his shoulder. Then she was all business again. "I'll get your coffee. And your slippers, no need for you to catch cold."

Which was the way she handled any emergency, and why Mac couldn't conceive of life without her.

He held the telephone without dialing. This was going to hurt. Big Jim Planchet was in many ways more powerful than the Mayor. Mayors lasted two or three terms at most, but a City Councilman could be reelected forever. This was Planchet's fourth term, and his second as Council President.

He made himself dial the number. It buzzed four times, then a thick sleepy voice said, "Yeah?"

"Mac Stevens."

There was a significant pause. Stevens wouldn't call without a damned good reason. "Yes, Mac, what is it?"

"There's been an accident at Todos Santos," Stevens said. "Your son was involved." He paused just long enough to let that sink in, to let Planchet guess there was worse coming. "He's dead, Mr. Planchet."

"Dead? Did you say dead? But I just saw him at dinner—" The voice lowered, spoke conspirationally. "Accident, you said. What kind of accident?"

"Jimmy and Diana Lauder—"

"Yeah, I know her, nice kid—"

"—broke into Todos Santos. They were both killed by Todos Santos guards."

"Broke in? Killed by guards? Mac, that doesn't make sense! My kid wouldn't have hurt anybody, why would the guards kill him?"

"The Todos Santos people say they were carrying a lot of complicated electronic equipment, and boxes of what looked like dynamite. The guards thought it was a real attack by FROMATES."

Another long pause. Then, "I'll be out as soon as I

get my clothes on. Meet me at the East main
entrance of the Box."

"I wouldn't advise it, Mr. Planchet. There's nothing
to see. Your son and Diana aren't there any longer,
and the area where it happened is—is contaminated."

"Contaminated how?"

"With poison gas."

"They gassed my kid? Gassed him?" Planchet was
shouting in rage. Then his voice fell again. "Where is
he?"

"They're taking him to the coroner's labs."

"To the morgue. Jesus, I don't want—I can't take
Eunice to the morgue! What—what can I do?"

"Stay there," Mac advised. "Get some friends over.
Your clergyman. I'll look into this for you . . ."

"Yeah. Do that." There was another long pause.
"They gassed him. Mac—Mac, I want to see justice
done here. Justice."

• • •

"I'm assuming the District Attorney will decide to
prosecute," Shapiro said. "That's a fairly safe bet.
And assuming that, the first step is a preliminary
hearing. The D.A. will try to convince the judge that
a crime has been committed, and that they have a
prima facie case against Sanders."

He looked thoughtful for a moment. "It's not
customary to put on a defense at a preliminary
hearing, but my immediate thought is that we ought
to. Our defense will be that there's been no crime at
all, only a justified action."

"What are the chances of winning?" Bonner asked.

"Not good. The judge will be under a lot of
pressure. Here are two dead bodies. Unarmed.
Harmless kids. Were we justified in using deadly
force? It's going to be a sticky decision, and most of
the precedents are against us. We could win, but I
doubt it."

"Suppose we do," Barbara Churchward said. "What
do we do with Sanders?"

"Put him back to work," Bonner snapped.

"It would be costly," Churchward said. "I think you ought to consider it carefully."

"She's right," Mead said. "Planchet isn't going to forget this. His kid's been killed. And as long as Sanders is here to remind him, he'll be coming at us."

"He's my deputy. I need him."

"We need sales, too," Churchward said. "I don't mean to suggest that we dump him out, but the Romulus Corporation has a lot more enterprises than Todos Santos. And will we be doing Pres any favors by keeping him here where he'll be surrounded by people who'll call him a murderer every chance they get? Romulus is a big company, Art. They can find Pres a good post somewhere else."

"Prisoner chasers," Bonner muttered.

"Sir?" Shapiro prompted.

"Old Army story. Never knew if it was true, but we all believed it. That if a soldier assigned to guard prisoners ever shot one, they fined him the cost of the cartridges, gave him a carton of cigarettes, and transferred him to another post. What we're proposing to do with Pres. Johnny, suppose we lose this hearing?"

"Then he'll be bound over to the state for trial," Shapiro said. "And we'll try to convince a jury that he acted properly. I think we've got a fairly good chance of that. And we can always play legal games to get it declared a mistrial. And there are appeals, and—"

"And meanwhile, Pres is in jail."

"Well, probably out on bail."

"And spending his life in courtrooms," Bonner said. "I'd like to think we can take better care of our people than that."

"How?" Shapiro asked.

Bonner shrugged.

"That's not all the bad news," Shapiro said.

"What now?"

"You can bet that within a week, someone's going

to file for an injunction to make us dismantle our defenses. Make us get rid of the lethal gasses. And they're very likely to get that, Art. Very likely. We've always been on shaky ground with that stuff."

"Shit fire. Colonel?"

Cross looked sad. "We can increase the physical security. Try to keep intruders out of the system in the first place. But it's hard to see just what more we can do. The VX was a backup, in case physical security failed. Turned out we needed it—"

"Or thought we did," Churchward said.

"Same thing," Colonel Cross said. "Uh—in this preliminary hearing, how much of our system do you have to make public?"

"A lot," Shapiro said. "I have to establish just how tough it is to get into that tunnel. Show that these weren't just casual trespassers—and that Sanders had good reason to *know* they weren't."

"I thought so. Tony, we're going to have to rework the system again."

Rand nodded agreement. He had already thought of that, and was mulling over ideas. "It will take time."

"I can delay the preliminary hearing," Shapiro said. "For months, if you'd like."

"*I* don't like," Barbara Churchward said. "This thing is a financial disaster anyway. Keep it hanging fire and it's worse."

"What about this injunction?" Bonner demanded. "How long can you delay hearings on that?"

"A week. Maybe two," Shapiro said. "No guarantee of longer."

"Not long enough, but it will have to do," Rand said.

"I don't like to be crass about things," Frank Mead said, "but there's this problem I have. How much is all this going to cost?"

"A lot," Bonner said. "And I can't think of one thing we can do about it."

"Me either," Mead said. "Look, Art, I'm on your side."

Sure you are, Tony Rand thought. Support Bonner all the way. Like you did Pres.

"But it's not up to me," Mead said. "It's up to Zurich, and they're bottom-line people."

"We're fighting for our lives," Art Bonner said. "This whole project could go down in bureaucratic regulations. The way the rest of the country's going. So. Barbara, you're going to have to live with delays, and Frank, you'll sign some big checks with a smile, and I'll talk to Zurich."

Frank Mead's jaw tightened, but he didn't say anything.

"No choices," Bonner said. "Rand needs time to redesign the defense system, and until that's done we don't dare show a court the system we use now. We've *got* to delay. Johnny, buy us time. As much as you can. Tony, you and the colonel get to work."

"Shouldn't somebody ask Pres?" Rand asked.

"Sure. We'll talk to him in the morning," Bonnner said. "Okay. We all know what we're supposed to do. Let's get to it."

VIII

Justice consists of an enduring and unalterable
intention to render to each what that person deserves.
—Aristotle

SERENDIPITY

Thomas Lunan relaxed on one of the circular benches
in the Santa Monica Mall, smiling, looking about
himself, sometimes sipping a small Coke.

Thomas Lunan had presence. He carried a tangible
self-satisfaction and a nice smile. Passersby usually
smiled back. He was too well dressed to be a bum,
too sedentary to be doing anything but goofing off. In
a minute or so he'd move on, perhaps to a drugstore,
perhaps to another bench a block down.

Every other reporter would be out at Todos Santos,
or in the LA City Hall. Two kids dead, one a pretty
girl, one a City Councilman's boy, both unarmed,
both harmless. The story of the year! and Thomas
Lunan was in the Santa Monica Mall.

It wouldn't make sense to the City Editor. It didn't
make sense to Lunan, except that he trusted his
instincts, his luck, his *moira*.

The crowd meandered past. Some struggled with

bulky clusters of paper bags. Isolated shoppers swung wide of half-a-dozen college-age boys and a girl. Mostly Lunan was ignored. Others shared his bench; they generally refused his offer of conversation. When nobody was watching, he sometimes talked to himself.

Lunan called it legwork.

A young girl came past . . .

Even Lunan wasn't sure what made her stand out; but she did. She was vivid in a crowd of blurred faces. Her walk. Her hair. Her style of dress. The curious way she treated the people around her: moving obstacles to be avoided, or objects of curiosity.

A Todos Santos girl.

He stepped briskly forward. "Pardon me, Miz—"

Her reaction was curious: she looked around the Mall. Then she looked over Thomas Lunan. "Yes?"

"I'm a reporter for the *Los Angeles Trib*. You've heard about the murders last night?"

She almost walked away. "I've heard," she spat. Her anger showed.

"What do you think about it?"

She debated with herself. To speak, perchance to be misquoted—Lunan knew that reaction. But she was young, probably under twenty. She would speak.

"They were not murders," she said, her voice very much under control now.

"But the District Attorney is going to charge, uh, Sanders with murder," Lunan said.

"Mister Sanders was doing his duty. The Angelinos have no right to interfere in our internal affairs."

He was diffident. "I wonder, did the situation require such drastic action?"

"Yes."

"How can you be so certain? I mean, you can't know much about what happened. There was very little in the news this morning—"

"I know exactly what happened, and I don't need to read it in Angelino papers, either. Mister Bonner showed us this morning." She saw his puzzled frown.

"On the TV. Our cable station. Mister Bonner. The General Manager of Todos Santos. This morning he showed us exactly where the invaders were, and what would've happened if they'd set off a bomb."

He would have hated losing her, but he risked it. "They didn't have a bomb."

"Your Angelino children did their best to pretend they were Fromate saboteurs carrying a bomb," she said. "How can they complain when they were treated like saboteurs? Think of it as evolution in action."

I've heard that before, Lunan thought. In the City Room. Unidentified mugging victim wrote it just before somebody pounded his head into jelly. "Where did you hear that phrase? From Mr. Bonner?"

She frowned, trying to remember. "No. I don't know where I heard it. From one of the guards when I was leaving this morning?"

Too bad it wasn't Bonner, Lunan thought. It would make a better story if it had been said by a high official of Todos Santos. *Think of it as evolution in action*—"Well. It's certainly true that two of them aren't complaining. I notice you name the Fromates directly—" Lunan's microphone, projecting from his shirt collar, stood just beyond and below his chin like a hatpin. Tiny as it was, it made some people nervous.

But not this girl. "Who else?" she asked. "They broke up a concert with wasps only last week. They tried to put LSD in our water. They're *proud* of doing things like that."

"Not bombs—"

"No. There's another group that takes credit for bombs and grenades," she said. "The Ecology Army? Something like that. But they're all Fromates. Who else hates us that much?"

She had more to say, about atrocities real and fancied against Todos Santos. Some Lunan knew about. Others he would have to look up in the files. And of course she knew all about the Kansas City incident where terrorists had killed a dozen arcology dwellers. When she stopped for breath he offered to buy her some iced tea. He was beginning to think he'd struck gold.

Let the other reporters dig for facts. The key to this affair was the conflict between two cultures. How had Todos Santos become so paranoid? Why did they react so strongly? Their official statement on the news this morning said they "regretted the necessity" of Sanders's action. Sorry they'd killed two kids, sure, but stressed the necessity of defending themselves.

And that was what Lunan wanted. The key. Two cultures, so different that Lunan could spot a Todos Santos girl in a milling crowd of shoppers, although he wasn't sure how he'd known. She was about eighteen; she could have spent most of her life inside the towering balconied walls.

He wanted the flavor of Todos Santos: the life, the attitudes, the philosophy. "Your Angelino children—" Like that. He let the conversation drift away from the murders, drift where it would. He asked questions. Listening is a fine art, and Lunan had mastered it.

Her name was Cheryl Drinkwater. She was a student at Todos Santos University, where she was a sophomore in engineering. Her father was a waldo operator. Lunan had found out quite a lot about her, and it wasn't hard to get her talking about life in Todos Santos.

". . . and we used to jump just as the elevator was starting down," she said. "If you're careful you can touch the ceiling, then get back before there's weight."

"Sounds too bloody fast for me. Like a roller coaster."

Cheryl was amused. "If we slowed them down, it'd take twice as long to get anywhere, wouldn't it? We've got a hundred levels to get around in."

Narrow chin, upturned nose, brunette hair streaked

with blond; she was lovely. Not beautiful in the sense of classic beauty, but lovely just the same. When she laughed Lunan wished for a photographer. Maybe later . . .

She knew little of the Fromates beyond their constant sabotage attacks. When he spoke of their work in preserving the ecology of America's wild places, she laughed. "We live in a nearly closed ecology," she said. "We know exactly what comes in and goes out. We grow up knowing what your Fromates have to go to college to learn."

"Not my Fromates."

"Sorry. Not mine either." She frowned. "We never had any trouble from the Fromates *or* the Angelinos when I was growing up. Say, do you remember a movie, a feature-length cartoon? Called, uh, *The Nest,* I think."

"Yah. Ten years ago?"

"Well, my parents say the Fromates made that film, and all the hassle has come since. I don't remember." She looked a question at him.

He *had* heard that, from another source, but he couldn't say so, not in his present role. He changed the subject.

When he asked her how she liked living in a walled fort, she said that a walled fort didn't have balconies.

"You could be getting a bit inbred," Lunan said. "Your university—are all the students residents in TS?"

"Just about. We have a few exchange students. Some of my friends go to schools Outside. I like it where I am. We get real working engineers for instructors. And real managers. Miss Churchward teaches economics. Mister Rand lectures on city design."

And so on. She wasn't exactly defensive, but she wasn't going to admit that life might hold more than a promise of a place in Todos Santos or some other arcology.

"You're watched every minute of the day," he said.

That's why she doesn't freeze up in front of a microphone. "Isn't that a bit much of a good thing?"

She smiled up at him across her second iced tea. "Maybe we don't have a lot to hide."

Touché, dammit. "Well . . . dating? They tell me the automobile revolutionized dating. It meant that couples could find privacy. Any people, so long as they could get to a car. You've taken a giant step backward, haven't you?"

"I wouldn't know. I didn't grow up then."

"But the—" He almost said *rent-a-cops.* "Security would know every boy you dated. Where you went. I suppose they can even spy on the rooms."

She thought it through, frowning. Then, "We don't have cars, and we don't have much privacy. We ball, but we tell our parents."

"You b-b-"

"After all, they'll find out anyway," she said briskly. "'Go ahead and ball, but tell Mom and Dad.' That's what my brother Andy told me when I was growing up. And the schools teach us how not to get pregnant if we don't want to. I wouldn't ball with a boy my parents didn't like, but that still leaves me plenty of leeway. Of course marriage is a lot more serious thing." She noticed his expression, which must have been interesting. "What's wrong? Did I use the wrong word?"

"No. We use it too." *Jackpot.* Talk about serendipity—

• • •

The alleyway smelled of urine and stale garbage. It was bounded on one side by a blank wooden wall, on the other by a chain-link fence opaquely overgrown with ivy. The blacktop surface was marked with crystalline smears of dried urine. Homicide Lieutenant Donovan wanted to hold his nose, but he didn't dare. There was a growing crowd of chanting blacks near the alley entrance.

"PO-LEECE MURDERERS!" The voice was female, but not feminine.

"Metro squad's coming," Sergeant Ortiz said softly. "The local precinct commander's worried he can't hold them."

Donovan nodded and went back to the body that lay crumpled behind an overflowing garbage can. It had been a young black man. There wasn't a lot left of the face beneath the thick Afro. There wouldn't be after a charge of number-four buck fired from the twenty-inch barrel of a Remington Model 870 twelve-gauge riot gun had done its work.

There was also a large hole in the chest.

A dozen police stood near the body. Two stood just apart from the others, not quite part of the group but not yet separated from it either. Donovan motioned to one of them and led him a few steps farther away from the others. He kept his voice low as he said, "Okay, Patterson, let's go over it once more."

"Yes, sir. We got a call at oh-nine sixteen this morning. Householder heard noises at the back door. When we arrived at the address of complainant, we drove to the back of the house. At that moment, without warning, an unidentified black male broke and ran for the alley. I pursued on foot while Officer Farrer took the cruiser to the other end of the alleyway.

"Before entering the alley I drew my service pistol, and observed Officer Farrer with the riot gun at the other end of the alley. On entering the alley I heard at least two gunshots. The shots came from behind a garbage can. I shouted 'Police,' and heard an additional gunshot. The flash attracted my attention, and I saw an armed suspect crouched behind the garbage can. I aimed for the can at chest height and fired one shot. As I fired I heard my partner's shotgun discharge.

"The suspect fell from behind the can. When we approached we found a .45-caliber Colt Commander automatic pistol near the suspect. We then reported an officer-involved shooting to the dispatcher."

And after he's rehearsed that a few more times he'll have it down perfectly, Donovan thought. Now for Farrer—

He looked up in annoyance as a black Imperial came into the far end of the alley. The police line holding back the crowd parted briefly to let the car through. Donovan saw batons uplifted and swinging.

"JUSTICE!" someone shouted.

"Hope Metro gets here soon," Patterson said. "Can I go now, sir?"

Donovan nodded, and stood waiting for the Imperial. When it got closer he recognized MacLean Stevens, and felt relieved. The Mayor kept some strange ones on his personal staff, but Stevens was all right.

The Imperial's window rolled down. Stevens looked at Donovan and raised an eyebrow. Donovan went over. "Looks righteous," he said. "Some crazy kid with a forty-five blazed away at two patrolmen, and they blew him up."

Stevens scowled distaste. "The crowd thinks differently. Why?"

"Hell, they always turn out when there's a shooting," Donovan said. "You know that, sir." He frowned. Something was wrong. Stevens wasn't reacting properly. Why? What was going—Holy shit! No wonder Stevens was looking funny. He wasn't alone in the car.

Donovan recognized the man in the back seat. The Reverend Ebenezer Clay, an old-time civil rights activist and leader. What the hell was he doing here? Frantically Donovan tried to remember what he'd said. Not a lot. No real harm done. He'd said 'they,' meaning blacks in Watts, but what the hell, it was true. They did turn out whenever there was a shooting.

"Reverend Clay had an appointment with the

Mayor," Stevens said. "Then we heard about the shooting and came down to see."

"Nothing much to see," Donovan said. "Uh—the body's not very pretty, sir, you wouldn't want to look—"

"I can stand it," Reverend Clay said. He got out of the car, a tall thin man with skin the color of weak tea. He had cotton-tuft white hair that might have come right out of an old movie. Clay wore a gray suit and clerical collar, but he had put a lavender handkerchief in the breast pocket. He looked around the alley and curled his lip in distate, then went over to the body.

"It *was* a good shooting," Donovan said. "Suspect fired three times at the officers."

"Witnesses?" Stevens asked.

Donovan shrugged. "Only the officers—"

"Only the officers. Nobody heard shots? Nobody saw anything?"

"Nobody who'll admit it," Donovan said. "And believe me, Mr. Stevens, we're looking. Hell, I know what'll happen. As soon as the officers tell their story for the papers, there'll be a dozen witnesses, all saying it didn't happen that way. Then we'll start running them down. Half of them couldn't possibly have been within miles of here when it happened. Some more will tell stories that don't make sense. But one or two could have been here, and will tell stories that fit the evidence they know about, and then we'll have good cops in trouble."

Reverend Clay came back to join them. He gestured toward the crowd. "I will talk with them—"

"To say what?" Stevens asked. "To calm them, or—"

"Calm? What is calm?" Clay demanded. "A brother lies dead, and you speak of calm! A youth, a mere boy—"

"That mere boy tried to shoot two police officers," Donovan said quietly. *Think of it as evolution in action*. Got to be careful about that. Say that here and my ass is grass.

"So they say," Clay said. "Yet why would he do that? He was guilty of no crime."

"None we know of," Donovan admitted. At least the officers sent to look at the house where they first saw the kid couldn't find anything. "But he did have a gun we haven't been able to trace. It may have been stolen—"

"You accuse him, but he cannot defend himself," Clay said.

"Reverend, you're not making sense," Stevens said quietly. "Neither you nor I know enough to have an opinion. You wanted to see the scene for yourself, and you've done that. I think we should leave."

"While my people cry for justice," Clay said.

"Not much we can do to get it for them," Stevens said.

"There never has been. All right, Mr. Stevens, I'll come with you. I have missed my appointment with the Mayor, but there is a matter of importance we must discuss." He got into the car.

As they drove away, the first three units of the Metro Squad arrived, and Donovan felt a lot better.

• • •

Eleven years earlier Thomas Lunan had come here with a girl.

With apartments ready for tenancy in the west wall, the managers had been looking for publicity. There had been refreshments and guides and a hang glider floating around inside the Mall itself. Thomas Lunan had been a fledgling newsman then, but he hadn't come for news. Todos Santos had been publicized to within an inch of its life. The world's television audiences knew all there was to know about the half-finished city-in-a-building.

But it was a fine excuse to bring . . . what was her

name? Marion Something. A fine way to get Marion's attention. She'd loved the way the hang glider floated around in all that empty space, diving down to buzz her, then riding the updrafts from the air conditioning fans. ("Making a pass," she'd said, and in fact the pilot had done so, later.) They had sampled the smorgasbord and shopped the Todos Santos Mall, and then Thomas Lunan had used his press card to get them up on the roof.

The roof of the Mall, that was. The Mall had been finished and two-thirds occupied, with the over-hanging balconies partially completed. The city's outer walls had been finished too, and some of the interior. Lunan and Marion had stood on the roof of the Mall and looked up into a tremendous lidless box crisscrossed with girders, girders to shape the inverted pyramids that would be the air/light wells. The tips of the inverted pyramids stood on four pillars as big as small apartment buildings.

Eleven years later. Marion Something was probably fat and married now, and Lunan had never got around to coming back. The great box had been sitting on the skyline for eleven years, while pressures from within the box had reached out into Los Angeles itself. The thing was too big to notice, and Angelinos didn't like to think about it. It was Sunday supplement material, but not news.

Not until now.

Thomas Lunan and a different girl looked down on the Mall from a small balcony just under the roof. Cheryl was finishing her dessert. Lunan itched to talk to his microphone, but the girl became restive when he did that. Still, the mike was live, and he had a good memory.

"Thanks for bringing me," he said.

Cheryl Drinkwater smiled up at him. There was chocolate syrup at the corner of her mouth. "Has it changed much? It was already finished when we moved in, and I don't remember much anyway."

"It's changed. I like what they've done with the pillars. Last time I was here they were just—pillars."

"You really should see the day-care center. I spent a lot of time there."

They were most of the way up the northwest pillar. Shops wound upward in a spiral, narrowing as they rose, culminating in a series of small balconies with restaurant tables. Cheryl was certainly giving him his lunch money's worth. The whole of Todos Santos was spread below him.

The view was staggering: the vast expanse of the Mall with its bewildering game board of shops, beltways carrying people, the balconies tiered below them, others across from him glimpsed through a maze of pillars and conveyor tubes. You wouldn't dare try hang gliding in here now. Apartments, shops, restaurants, even factories overlooked the Mall, and Lunan thought it must be wonderful to live with a view like this; so many people to watch. But he was getting more than scenery.

Again he wished he could dictate. There was a lot to remember.

The guards. They were not police. They were not obtrusive, unless they were deciding whether to let you in; but they were not invisible. Todos Santos citizens didn't ignore them, any more than Lunan would really ignore a waiter. They were there, and they were convenient.

Cheryl had stopped at the gate to have a guard locate her father. Drinkwater had been just leaving a dentist's office. He had agreed to meet Lunan for drinks when his tour at the waldo transceiver ended at five. And a boy younger than Cheryl had been asking another guard to track down his missing date, and he knew the guard's name. And the drunk businessman. He'd gotten off the subway looking apprehensive, and weaved his way up to the entryway, and his relief at getting into Todos Santos was so evident that Lunan had spoken to Cheryl about him.

"Sure he's relieved," Cheryl said. "Angelino police would arrest him, wouldn't they?"

It hadn't even occurred to her that Todos Santos police might arrest a citizen for being drunk in public, and they hadn't. Instead, one had helped him to an elevator.

He had to remember it all, because it might be the biggest story he'd ever done. The murders/regrettable incident (choose one) had triggered a renewed interest in Todos Santos, and the city-in-a-box was going to get a lot of headlines and prime time; but that wasn't Lunan's kind of story, not by itself. The new culture that had developed unnoticed here; the impact of Todos Santos on its inhabitants; that could be Pulitzer Prize material.

A city at peace with its police force. *Our* guards, *our* police, holding *our* civilization together. And it was a civilization. That showed in the very structures. The seeming frailty of shops not built to resist weather . . . or vandalism.

It showed in the people, too. The stout lady in her underwear—

They had stopped in a clothing shop halfway up the northwest pillar. While Cheryl was buying tennis shoes, a fortyish, matronly woman had realized that the dress she was trying on was too small. She had stepped out to the counter in her bra and support pantyhose to trade the dress for another. Nodded cheerfully to the other customers and went back in. Just before she disappeared, her eye had caught Lunan's.

Clothes weren't needed for protection here, unless on the roof. A constant awareness of the guards' eyes might make concealment seem futile. If the nudity taboo disappeared in Todos Santos, would it be surprising? But that look. She'd *known* he was an Angelino; and *then* she was embarrassed.

Meanwhile, Cheryl had said—? "Day-care center? Sure, let's go see it. Where is it, on the roof?"

Cheryl pointed. Lunan didn't understand, at first. She meant the vast artificial tree enveloping the southwest pillar.

A fence ran beneath the tips of the lowest branches of that great tree. There were many children and few adults within the fence. When Cheryl and Lunan were close enough, the illusion of a tree broke down; the cone of greenery was hollow. Lunan could look up into what the branches had concealed. Not just schoolrooms, but jungle gyms, seesaws, a merry-go-round; and a vast three-dimensional steel grid for climbing, with netting beneath. A score of children were playing what had to be a team sport within the grid.

"You liked it," Lunan said. For just that moment he wanted to be a child again. This was wealth.

Cheryl nodded happily.

"Do all the Todos Santos kids come here?" Lunan asked.

"Sure. Well, we have neighborhood parks too," Cheryl said. "But they aren't used much. Some of them are being closed down. Mr. Rand talked about it in class last month. The original idea was to have small neighborhood parks because that's what the people were used to when they lived outside. But when everybody realized that it was safe for the children to go anywhere, the designers decided to build the tree because it could be better than a lot of small places."

"But you still have small parks?"

"Sure," Cheryl said. "For adults and babies, mostly, though. And we use them for ball games if it's raining on the roof."

Another thing to think about. Would Todos Santos be different if the outside weather were worse? Or would they simply put a dome over the roof? "There are four pillars," Lunan said. "The shops, and this tree—what are the others?"

"Come see."

She led him to the Mall pedway. They edged inward toward the fast strip, Cheryl always ahead of him, Lunan pushing himself and feeling clumsy. They stood upright, hurtling through the Mall at fifty kilometers an hour, while Cheryl tried to explain the rules of the game she'd played as a girl on that three-dimensional grid in the nursery tree. Everybody around him seemed perfectly at ease.

Another datum. They must really trust the Todos Santos engineers, Lunan thought. He was filing other impressions in his head:

Quiet. The machinery was nearly silent, and voices didn't batter the ears. Lunan considered the sound-baffling effect of all those balconies, and the two pillars that had been turned into trees, and the high ceilings. Not enough; there must be soundproofing in the ceilings. Have to ask someone. But that still didn't explain it. Lunan made himself listen . . . and knew that the loudest voices he heard were all Angelinos. Even the children. And he could hear the difference.

Todos Santos children weren't loud, but they were agile. This was their turf (all of it! No wonder the designers had built that nursery tree. Why would you want to play in your own neighborhood when you could go there? And that promoted loyalty to the city as a whole, not just to your own block!) and they moved through it like streaks, never bumping anyone. Even here, where there were a lot of Angelino visitors, clumsy moving objects to avoid.

They came to a wide arch spanning the pedway. Above was an arcade with shops, but for a moment they were passing through a tunnel, stationary walks but no shops on either side of the swift-moving pedway. There were boys on the walks. One slipped a coil of rope off his shoulder. Lunan watched in horror as he flung it high in the air. It floated down, unrolling, across the fast pedway ahead of Lunan. Boys on the other side caught it. They pulled it taut, leaning back with the effort.

"Duck!" Lunan roared. He dropped to the belt and tried to sweep Cheryl's legs from under her. She danced back, laughing, fending him off. The rope caught her across the chest, and disintegrated. It was toilet paper.

Lunan got up. "Swell. What if it was a real rope?"

Cheryl was still laughing. "It can't be. The guards would stop them. Did you see anyone else duck?"

He hadn't. He thought: Even Angelinos learn better. It *can't* be real rope. Security wouldn't let it be. Are they crazy or are they right?

• • •

Stevens drove the Imperial back toward City Hall. They passed through block after block of low, wood-frame houses, structurally sound (mostly) but usually in need of paint; houses that weren't really squalid, but were officially classed as substandard, and looked it.

Some would call them slums, but MacLean Stevens resisted that. Watts and the surrounding areas had open space. There were a few apartments, but mostly there were single-unit houses and duplexes. Most of them had yards, some scattered with occasional blowing paper, some meticulously clean. A few of the yards were filthy, littered with discarded furniture and decaying mattresses, but those were exceptions.

Not a slum, Stevens thought. Los Angeles doesn't really have slums. Not like Harlem, or—

"What I needed to see you about was the Price Memorial Project," Clay said. "They say we need more tests. First the EPA. Now HUD. Mr. Stevens, my people need housing. This is a good project, an excellent project. It can turn that whole area around, if only they will let us build it! And we cannot continue testing and studying. We will soon lose our contractors. They say rightly that they cannot keep their equipment idle longer."

"We saw the report," Stevens said. "The Mayor made a strong protest. I know it was strong, because I wrote it. I could show you the file if you like—"

"I believe you," Clay said. "But protests don't hire people or build housing. We need that housing now! And the jobs. Jobs! You know what that means? Do you know what the unemployment rate is down here? What are the young people supposed to do? They have no jobs. There is no one to work for. The result is that they run in gangs, like that young man today—"

"You saw the gang tattoos, then?" Stevens asked.

Clay nodded slowly. "Yes, Mr. Stevens."

They turned onto a main north-south thoroughfare. It was lined with bars and liquor stores, all looking like fortresses with iron grill window guards and steel cagework to cover the doors. At the corner stood a supermarket, one of a major chain. Stevens noticed the prices. At least 20 percent higher than in his neighborhood.

They have to, he told himself. It costs more to do business. Insurance alone. And security against shoplifting, and—And the higher prices help keep people chained down to this miserable block . . .

"Yes, I saw the gang symbols," Clay repeated. "Could they have a bearing on his actions this morning?"

"I don't know," Clay admitted. "It's possible. Or he may have been high on something. Without jobs, without hope, they join gangs. They use drugs. They also steal. At the moment they steal from their neighbors. Someday the neighbors will have nothing worth stealing. Then they will come out and steal from *your* neighbors, and perhaps you will pay some attention—"

That won't happen, Stevens thought. As long as welfare and food stamps and aid to dependent children and social security and all the other benefit programs pump in money, there'll be something to steal. And we already paid too much attention to Watts anyway. Every department of every government at every level is involved, and all those expensive people think they have to contribute to justify their salaries, and every contribution is another delay.

"Reverend, I know how you feel, but what can I do? The federal government is putting up 84 percent of the cost, and their inspectors have to be satisfied that it's safe. After all, there *was* a chemical plant on that site."

"Thirty years ago!"

"Yes, but they might have buried some toxic wastes," Stevens said.

"The Del Rio Company states that they did not."

Stevens shrugged. "HUD won't take their word for it. They insist on taking their own soil samples and making their own tests." And for that matter, when did Ebenezer Clay start taking a corporation's word for anything?

"The developer will quit while they are testing."

"We'll find another one," Stevens said.

"It took more than a year for Jacobsen and Myers to qualify," Clay said. "A new firm must start completely anew—" He sniffed and wrinkled his nose. "Or perhaps not? Perhaps that is the plan. To delay and delay until we can delay no longer, then obtain an emergency ruling relaxing the affirmative action program? And then a nice lily-white company will come—"

"That won't happen," Stevens said wearily.

"It has happened in the past."

Mac Stevens had nothing to say to that. Of course Clay was right.

"All we want is justice," Clay said.

Justice, Stevens thought. A line from the hymnal ran through his head. "Thy justice like mountains, high soaring above, Thy clouds which are fountains of goodness and love." But what soared above off to the left was neither justice nor mountains. It was the blank wall of Todos Santos.

"Does anybody *really* want justice?" Stevens asked. "If justice is getting what you deserve—"

"A fair chance, that is all we want. Why can't we have it?"

Because nobody gives a damn anymore, Stevens thought. Nobody but you and your friends, and you don't have many of those left. The glorious old days of the civil rights movement are gone, long gone and not many lament them.

We did care, once. A lot of us did. But something happened. Maybe it was the sheer size of the problem. Or watching while everybody who could afford it ran to the suburbs and left the cities to drift, and complained about taxes going to the cities, and—Or maybe it was having to listen to my police explain why they'll only go into Watts in pairs with cocked shotguns and if the Mayor doesn't like it he can damned well police that precinct himself.

People think they've done enough.

What's enough? It *isn't* enough. If we'd done enough, we wouldn't have the problems—

"I'll do my best to speed things up," Stevens said. "We'll call Washington."

"Do you think that will help?"

"It can't hurt." And probably can't help, although you never knew. The problem was that Washington didn't *have* to listen. They might, but they don't have to.

He remembered the chanting crowd outside the alleyway. They demanded justice. And the Reverend Clay wants justice. Mr. Planchet wants justice. The Mayor wants them all kept happy, meaning I'm supposed to deliver what they want. Justice. Hell, I don't even know what it is.

Not that it matters. We'll get Clay his development, but it won't bring justice to the ghetto. It'll just be another project.

And whatever justice is, Jim Planchet doesn't want it. What Big Jim wants is vengeance.

• • •

The northeast pillar had become another tree; but this was no Christmas tree. There was a glass-walled ballroom nestled in its topmost branches. In its sprawling, knotted roots was the red-lit entrance to Lucifer's, the gambling hall. Halfway up the thick trunk were three levels of Dream Masters, the gallery of fantasy art.

Lunan stared, searching for old memories. "And there's a serpent gnawing at the roots, right?" he asked. "And an old one-eyed god comes to impale himself in order to learn the runes?"

"We've got a hologram serpent. I don't think anybody's had the nerve to play Odin yet. Thomas, would you like to get a sculpted bust of yourself? Or a tattoo?"

"Ah . . . why?"

Cheryl laughed. "I'll show you." She led him to an outside elevator shaped like a rocket ship out of a 1930s *Amazing*: baroque fins guiding a pointed glass tube, glow of orange lights in rockets clustered underneath. "You should see this anyway."

Fantasy art had come a long way since the art shows at early science fiction conventions. Dream Masters still displayed paintings: creatures foreign to Earth, and "artists' concepts" of interstellar spacecraft and structures that would have dwarfed the Earth itself. But there were also window-sized holograms that looked out on alien worlds; a gun with a double stock, for use by something with two right arms; tiny landscapes for use as game boards in role-playing games, and dragons and trolls and elves for markers; ornately carved rings, cups, belt buckles.

There were two small shops within Dream Masters itself.

In the solid-photography shop Lunan sat with parallel bands of light and dark demarking his head and shoulders, while a score of photographs were taken from pre-set angles. "It's absolutely accurate," the clerk told him. "The markings guide the computer that guides the tools that carve the bust. We do have to add the eyes; they come out blank. And we can fiddle with the texture of the hair, and make the bust bigger or smaller." Lunan's bust would be the size of a fist, carved in synthetic malachite.

The walls of the tattoo parlor were covered with designs. Line cartoons, very simple and very expressive. Slogans in ornate Gothic script. Photographs of astronomical scenery, suns and glowing interstellar gas clouds, tattooed on human backs; a white comet running down a suntanned arm.

The tattooist was in her twenties, with wild black hair and somewhat protuberant eyes. She caught Lunan staring at a pair of photographs and said, "They were both from the Red Plush Onion."

One was a color photo of a woman's ass—not bad, Lunan thought—with a cluster of vertical lines tattooed on one cheek. Product identification markings. The other, a puffy red giant star losing a stream of flame into the blue-white accretion disk around a black hole, tattooed across a black woman's chest.

The tattooist had a vivid smile, and her eyes danced. Damn, they were almost hypnotic, almost too big for her face. Lunan said, "I didn't know the Onion ran to astronomy buffs."

"You'd be surprised."

Her voice was louder than Los Angeles traffic noises—absent here—and beneath the vivaciousness was a self-consciousness that the Saints eventually lost. *Angelino.* Lunan said, "You haven't been here long."

She admitted it. She had moved in last April, right after making out her income tax form.

"Where were you before? What were you doing?"

"I lived in Westwood. And I did a little of everything . . . including a movie. They had me playing a zombie—" and she widened her eyes and grinned a death-rictus at him, so that Lunan recoiled even while he was laughing.

"Are you glad you moved?"

"Oh, I love it here. I was a little worried, you know, about making new friends, but it wasn't bad at all. There's the Commons; you can't help meeting people. And then, Saints seem to trust each other. As if just being here means you're okay. And I get plenty of customers."

"Angelinos? And the Onion?"

"No, mostly Saints. I think it's like ego plates: you know, personalized car license plates? Nobody wants to be exactly like everybody else. You'll see a lot of my designs floating around . . . that is, you would if you could make friends fast enough. I put some of them in fairly private places."

"I've got one myself," Cheryl said demurely.

There was a buzzing in Lunan's ear. "My master's voice," he said with genuine regret. "I've got to call in." As Cheryl led him to a guard station, Thomas Lunan wondered what could be so important that the City Editor would beep him.

IX

White shall not neutralize the black, nor good
Compensate bad in man, absolve him so: Life's
business being just the terrible choice.

—Robert Browning

THE FURIES

Tony Rand wasn't happy. For one thing, it was lunch
time, but instead of eating he was standing in Art
Bonner's office. "I found out how they did it," he
said. "We've got maintenance people in those tunnels
all the time. Security used to watch them, but that
got too expensive, so we set up a system to have
MILLIE track everyone in there and call Security
only if something unusual happened." He shrugged.
"So the kids fed MILLIE the right signals."

"How about getting in to begin with?" Art Bonner
asked.

"Same thing. As far as the computer was
concerned, one of our own work crews went in for
unscheduled maintenance. Happens often enough. Art,
it bugs me that someone can do that to MILLIE."

"Bugs *you*, does it? Tony, how would you feel if
you knew someone could fiddle with your memory?"

Tony turned, startled. "Oh. I hadn't thought of that aspect."

"I rather hope nobody else does. Don't mention it to Miss Churchward, okay? We'll have to work out some safeguards for MILLIE's memory. I'd say a man could make himself very wealthy by tampering with what MILLIE tells Barbara. And that's not the worst that could happen."

Rand looked thoughtful. "I'll need a couple of specialists in programming. High-priced ones."

"You'll have them. Now, in future I want everyone going into a critical area to check in with Security. At least be looked at," Bonner said. "It won't be as convenient, but we have to do something. Meanwhile, life goes on."

"Maybe," Tony said.

"You still worried about the carbon filament deliveries?"

"Some. That condominium outfit's holding us up for more than Mead likes to pay."

"Like it or not, we've got to keep expanding. He'll pay it," Bonner said. There was a low tone from his phone. Bonner lifted the instrument. "Excuse me, Tony. Yes, Dee?" He listened a moment. "Put him on. She says it's John Shapiro with something urgent."

Bonner listened again. "He *what?* I don't believe it."

"Who what?" Rand asked.

Bonner ignored Tony's question. "That tears it," he told the telephone. "I guess we'd better have another strategy meeting. Ten minutes, in the board room."

There were more people in the conference room this time. John Shapiro had brought a legal assistant, a big competent-looking woman dressed as conservatively as Shapiro was. Colonel Cross, dark suit, narrow club-striped tie, was flanked on either side by uniformed majors. Jim Bowen, Rand's administrative assistant. There were others Tony Rand knew only vaguely, people from Mead's section, an athletic young man whose main job seemed to be fetching coffee for Barbara Churchward. (Did he have other duties? Tony wondered. The way she dressed would be enough to drive most men nuts if they had to work closely with her, and she must know that.)

They listened, some patiently, some not so, while Major Devins talked. "Who was going to stop him?" Devins asked. "Not any of our people. He's our *boss*, dammit. He went down to the subway lobby and caught a train. Nobody had orders to keep him inside."

"Not your fault," Art Bonner said. "I should have told MILLIE to let me know where Pres was at all times."

"How could you know he'd do something like this?" Shapiro asked. "Hardly anyone's fault."

"He must be off his rocker," Frank Mead said. "Why the *hell* would he turn himself in? Messes up all our plans, too."

"That it does," Art Bonner said. "Johnny, what's next?"

Shapiro looked more at ease: he had his vested suit and his briefcase. He spread his hands elaborately. "As I said last night, preliminary hearing. Whenever you want it. I can delay, or start next week, as you'd like."

"Can you get Sanders out on bail?" Barbara Churchward asked.

"I doubt it. Not in a capital case," Shapiro said.

That shook all of them. "Capital case? Death penalty?" Mead asked.

"It's possible. I doubt they can win an appeal, though," Shapiro said. "But Murder One is what Big Jim Planchet insists on, and he's got the clout to make it stick with the D.A.'s office. Besides, it looks better for the politicians if Sanders is in jail. Lets them look much tougher than if he were walking around free waiting for trial. Of course we ask for bail, and if it's turned down we appeal, but that all takes time."

"And meanwhile one of our people is in their bucket," Mead said.

"I am not sure I understand your position," Churchward said. "You don't like Sanders—"

"What's that got to do with anything? He's ours," Mead protested. "We can talk over this damn fool stunt when he's out. Meantime, the Angelinos have one of our people, and I don't like it."

"I see. Art, why did he turn himself in?" Churchward asked.

"Guilt. He wants absolution," Bonner said. "And you know, it's our fault. In all we said while he was here last night, we didn't really make it clear that we're behind him. We talked a lot about strategy and what we ought to be doing, but we didn't just flat out say 'You done good, Pres'."

"You did," Tony Rand said. "When you first came into his office."

"I didn't make it strong enough," Bonner said. "And we should all have said it. Here in this conference room, with every one of us backing him up, and a parade of people to say the same thing this morning. My fault."

"He might have thought he was helping us," Tony Rand said.

"How's that?" Bonner demanded.

"The morning news was full of threats by Planchet," Tony said. "How he'd wreck Todos Santos. It could be that Pres thinks he's saving us a lot of grief."

"It won't help," Frank Mead insisted. "Makes us look like idiots—"

"What do we do now?" Churchward asked. "We didn't talk to Pres about strategy, and we weren't supportive enough. We'll fix all that. But what do we do this afternoon?"

"Prepare for siege," Art Bonner said. "Tony, you and Cross will have to speed up the new security

system installations. Meanwhile, we'll try Angelino
justice. I don't have any faith in it, but we'll give it a
try."

• • •

Alice Strahler waited nervously in the comptroller's
office. Why was he late for his appointment with her?
His secretary had said something about an emergency
meeting in the board room. Some new development
from the Fromate raid.

Could they have found out? Alice wondered. Maybe
I ought to run—

She took a deep breath and laughed nervously, then
glanced up to see if the receptionist had noticed. She
needn't have worried. The receptionist was talking in
low tones on the telephone.

The guilty flee when no man pursueth, Alice
thought. The best way to be certain they know is to
act scared. They don't know. They don't even
suspect. Tony Rand trusts me with everything—

He sure does, Alice Marie, another part of her mind
said. Ain't you proud?

And that was just the trouble. She wasn't proud.
Tony Rand had trusted her, promoted her to an
important position, and she had betrayed him.

I had to. The Movement put me here. And it's
important. We're rushing toward the eco-spasm, we
have to act before it's too late—

But it's already too late for those kids. They're
dead, and they wouldn't have tried it without your
information, Alice Marie. And now the Movement
will want more. Everything about the new security
systems, the guards, everything—and you know why
they'll want it.

Damn, people are complicated. It's so much easier
to work with computers. I should have stayed a
programmer, never taken that promotion, then I
wouldn't have—

Frank Mead came in, charging ahead as if he were
hitting the line for Princeton again. He glanced at

Alice. "Oh. Sorry to keep you waiting. Should have phoned. Come on in."

She followed him into his big corner office. It was elaborately furnished—more so than Art Bonner's, she thought. And that has to mean something. She took a seat and waited for the inevitable inquisition: Frank Mead trying to learn more about Tony Rand's department.

"I have a right to know," Mead had told her the first time he'd summoned her. "And asking Tony is a waste of time. So you're not betraying him, you're doing him a favor."

Which might even have been true. Tony Rand would hate having to explain himself to the comptroller, but since he went over—or outside of— his budget quite often, *somebody* had to come down here and defend what Rand's department did. So she wasn't really being disloyal in talking to Mead— which was a joke, because what Mead learned was legitimate company business.

And what I tell Wolfe is legitimate human business, she told herself. The survival of the human race is far more important than petty bourgeois morals.

Which doesn't explain why I feel so cheap sometimes . . .

"So. Here's the check, all approved," Mead was saying. He held out a slip of paper. "Hope your friends in Diamond Bar appreciate it. Easiest profit they ever turned. They don't really have anything at all coming to them—"

She took the check and waited for the questions, but Mead seemed preoccupied, and after a while she left his office.

• • •

Homicide Lieutenant Donovan drank quietly and alone.

That is not to say that he was not enjoying himself. There could have been drinking buddies if he'd wanted them. He could have gone to a cop bar. He wasn't in the mood this afternoon. Instead, he was in a mood to get quietly buzzed, watching the thoughts that played through his head, enjoying some of the life that surged around him. This very skillful pickup, that clumsy approach that worked anyway. The endless political discussion between the two who didn't know what they were talking about.

He also had memories to savor. The Todos Santos tunnel crew knew nothing about the mugging victim, but they'd enjoyed telling him about their job, and showing off the enormous machine that chewed into dirt and rock, fused the detritus to line the tunnel walls, and crawled inexorably onward. It had been something to see, and there wasn't another machine like that in the western hemisphere. And then came the news that their high mucky-muck Sanders had turned himself in. The work crew hadn't been happy about that at all. Interesting, workmen who worried about their boss—

But the argument at a nearby table threatened to ruin his mood.

Three of them. Men younger than Donovan, getting excited. The youngest sat quietly, happily, letting the others lecture each other. *He* wasn't going to stop the developing fight.

"Don't tell me about those Todos Santos bastards." That one had small features and very pale blond hair. He leaned forward, forearms braced on the table, to emphasize his words.

"They got a right to live," said the third man. He was small and lean, with a face like a hatchet and a tension in him that showed even when he relaxed.

"Yeah? Listen, do you know the Red Plush Onion? Right in the shadow of that big fucking building?"

"I've heard about it. Never been there."

"It's a whorehouse. I thought I'd try it. You know how it is. I got lonely one night." The blond man relaxed, looked into his beer, drank. Donovan watched in the mirror. Donovan's pleasantly melancholy mood had faded somewhat.

It was a pity he couldn't take off his reflexes with his badge. Then he could let them work themselves up, punch each other out, get thrown into the street, incident finished. None of his business anyway. But he'd been a street cop a long time before making detective. He reached into his pocket.

"So I drove out there and tried to get in. You know, they wouldn't let me in? I wasn't drunk. Not *drunk*. The big bouncer said they didn't want my kind." The blond man's lips crawled away from his teeth. "I was going back to my car when a guy went past me. A tall, thin guy with lots of teeth. I knew him. The bouncer let him in. Said 'hello.' Called him by his name. Know who he was? The Todos Santos undertaker!"

"Well, you can see their point," said the other. "They get most of their customers from Todos Santos."

"Yeah. Yeah. And the Hivers won't go in if the Angelinos do. That's what they call us. Angelinos. I hope they put that Sanders bastard in the gas chamber."

If the little guy could have let it lie . . . nope. "Why? Because he killed two kids, or because he's from Todos Santos?"

"Yes," said the blond man. Then, "What are you defending him for? He gassed 'em. *Gassed* 'em. Nerve gas! What the fuck, they were only Angelinos."

"Maybe they won't dare try it again," the smaller man taunted him. "Why don't you try sneaking inside some night with a box labeled *Dynamite?*"

Donovan was there as the blond man tried to surge across the table. "Think of it as evolution in action," he said, because it seemed to fit and had been on his mind.

They froze and looked at him, all three. It was a good stopper, that phrase: just cryptic enough. He held his badge low, cupped, so that only those three could see it. "Forget it," he told them.

Their eyes dropped.

Donovan went back to his own table. His eyes found theirs in the mirror. They left very soon.

• • •

The interview room in the new Los Angeles County Jail had not intentionally been designed to be intimidating. The furniture was heavy and nearly immobile, of course, and the windows were barred; but the designers had tried to make the room comfortable. They hadn't succeeded.

Big Jim Planchet tried to keep his voice under control as he eyed Allan Thompson with distate. Why hadn't he paid more attention to the kind of companions his son had? And yet—what could he have done? This boy wasn't any criminal. Good family, real estate people, good upper middle-class family. Just like Diana Lauder. The Lauders were blaming *him*.

He didn't want to think about it, but he had to. And he didn't have a lot of time. He wasn't supposed to be here, of course. It had taken pulling strings. But Jim Planchet *was* a lawyer, and if Ben Costello (good thing the Thompson family lawyer was an old friend) insisted on having Planchet as an associate, the D.A.'s office wasn't going to object.

"Why?" Planchet demanded. "What did you think you were doing?"

"Easy," Ben Costello cautioned. "Mr. Planchet's right, though, Allan. If I'm going to defend you, I've got to know everything."

For a moment the boy's face held defiance. He even started to say it. "It seemed like a good—" But his reserve broke. "My God, Mr. Planchet, I'm sorry. Really sorry."

"Lot of good that does. Why?" Planchet said again.

"Easy, dammit," Costello said. "Can't you see Allan doesn't like this any more than you do? Why, Allan?"

"Well—Mr. Planchet had said a lot about Todos Santos. Jimmy really respected you, Mr. Planchet. He thought—he thought he was helping you."

It hit Planchet like a blow. And it was probably true. I did, he thought. I did spout off a lot about Todos Santos. Termite Hill. The Box. Graveyard of freedom. Picture of an ugly future.

He remembered it all, public statements and what he'd said at home at the breakfast table (would Eunice ever sit across a table from him again? They had her in Queen of Angels under sedation, and they were talking about nursing homes) and Junior making wisecracks but listening, listening—

"All right. I can see that," he said when he'd got his voice under control. "But—you went past those doors." There'd been a special on Channel 7 showing that door and its ominous warnings. "It was said plainly. 'IF YOU GO THROUGH THIS DOOR, YOU WILL BE KILLED.' It said it."

"We didn't believe it," Allan said. "We just didn't. I mean, everyone's always telling you what horrible things are going to happen to you, but they never do."

Only this time they did, Planchet thought. Oh my God.

He sat down and put his head in his hands. Unwanted pictures came to his mind. Jim Junior with his chemistry lab. Jim getting his ham radio license at age thirteen and getting a home computer for his next birthday. Eunice bragging to their friends about her son the genius. And I guess he was.

Ben Costello took out a yellow legal pad and a dozen pencils. "I'd better get as many details as I can," he said. "This isn't going to be easy."

Allan Thompson looked puzzled. "So what? What's the worst they can do for trespassing?"

"The charge isn't trespassing," Costello said. He tried to keep his voice as calm and gentle as possible. It was obvious that the boy was torn up with guilt. He talked defiantly, but he was ready to collapse—and what Costello had to tell him wasn't going to help, either. "The charge is murder."

"Murder! But I didn't kill anybody! Those termites, they did the killing, with war gas—"

"You were committing a felony. When there's a death resulting during the commission of a felony, the law says it's murder," Costello said. "Same as if you were holding up a liquor store and the police shot your partner."

"Jesus." Allan's eyes darted around the interview room. "Maybe it's right. Maybe I did kill them. But I didn't mean to! I didn't mean any harm!"

May as well hit him with all of it, Costello thought. He'd better know how serious this is. "I can't plea bargain, either. Not with Todos Santos involved," Costello said. "Look, they turned you over to the Los Angeles D.A., but they'll go to the state Attorney General if they have to. They want your arse, Allan. And if you don't help me, they're going to get it. Now. You went to Todos Santos carrying the gear that James had built. You waited until there was no one around, and you went to the access-way door. Was it unlocked?"

"No. Jim unlocked it."

"With what?"

Allan shrugged. "It was an electronic lock system. Jimmy had the combination."

Costello wrote rapidly. "So you unlocked the door. How did you know the combination?"

"I don't know. Jimmy had it."

"He had quite a lot of information about the Todos Santos security system," Costello said. "Where did James get all these data?"

"Arnie, I guess."

"Who is Arnie?"

"Arnold Renn. He's one of the sociology professors at UCLA. Real friendly guy."

"Did Mr. Renn suggest this expedition?" Costello asked.

Allan looked puzzled. "Dr. Renn," he said automatically. "Uh—well, he didn't exactly suggest it."

"But you had discussed it with him?"

"Yes."

Councilman Planchet raised his head and looked at the boy. Arnold Renn? He'd seen that name somewhere—where? On a report his assistant had prepared. Dr. Renn was a spokesman for the ecology group. Had offered to speak at a fund raiser for Planchet. It hadn't been easy to find a way to turn him down—why had he been turned down? Something Ginny had dug up, some kind of connection Dr. Renn had that might be embarrassing—

Good God. Renn was a FROMATE.

*   *   *

They wouldn't let Tony Rand see Sanders in an interview room. That was for lawyers only. Friends had to use a different—and degrading, Tony thought—system.

Rand and Sanders sat at tables facing each other. They were separated by a doubled glass screen, thick. They talked by telephone.

What do you say in a situation like this? Rand wondered. "Hi, Pres."

"Hi, Tony."

Awkward silence. "Now that you've had a week to get used to it, how do you like the accommodations?"

"Not too bad. Are you going to tell me I'm crazy too?"

"Do you want me to?"

"What? The thick glass tended to distort Sanders's expression. "What?"

"If you want me to, I'll tell you you're crazy," Rand said.

"Look, I had to," Sanders said. "I can't get Shapiro to understand that. I had to. I killed—"

"Whoa," Rand said urgently.

"Eh?"

"The Sheriff swears blind these visiting phones

aren't tapped," Tony Rand said. "You can believe as much of that as you want to."

"So what? I don't have any secrets. The whole English-speaking world knows what I did."

Uncomfortable subject. "How are they treating you?"

"All right." He smiled. Almost. "They don't know how to treat me. All that publicity. So I got VIP status."

"That figures. They give you a roommate?"

"Yeah."

"What's he in for? Anything interesting?"

"Tony, he's in for tax evasion. He wants to sell us construction supplies. He does exercises in the cell, and he wants me to do push-ups and jumping jacks with him. He'd really like to cheer me up. Want more?"

"You know, you're a real wet blanket today."

Pres said nothing.

"Why'd you do it, Pres? Why didn't you at least talk to someone first? The first we heard about you turning yourself in was off a television set!"

"It was no good, Tony. Hiding out. Making like I was crazy. No good, dammit."

"Yeah, I can see that wouldn't sit well," Rand said.

"It wasn't right, either. Art was taking a hell of a chance. I could see that Shapiro was worried. Tony, the last damn thing I need is to have Art Bonner in jail because of me. How is he?"

"He was fit to be tied." Rand saw the effect of that, and quickly added, "He wasn't mad at you. At himself."

"Why?"

"He thought he hadn't made it clear enough that you did the right thing. The only thing you could do."

"Sure, he'd say that—"

"Not just him. Pres, you're a bloody hero! It's all they talked about in Commons for days, ever since it happened. Savior of the city and all that."

"They really say that?"

"That's right. Oh, and I've got a message from Art. He says, all right, it's your life, and if you want to try Los Angeles justice that's what you'll get. Johnny Shapiro will be down soon to talk strategy. I gather he's going to ask for a change of venue, what with all the publicity."

"No."

"What?"

"I said no." Sanders was adamant. "No change of venue. No legal tricks. Tell him that, Tony. I don't want to get off on a technicality. I'd rather leave it to a jury."

"A Los Angeles jury? The kids were Angelinos. You aren't."

"Angelinos. Tony, I saw them when they were being carried out. They were dead people, dead human beings."

Tony sighed raggedly. "So did I, on the screen. Pres, could I have designed it differently?"

"What?"

"They got in. They put themselves where we had to kill them, or else let them burn up some of our city and some of our citizens. They had to go to enormous trouble to do that, but Pres, they shouldn't have been able to do it at all. How could I have stopped them? How do I stop the next ones, the ones with the real bombs?"

"Tony, this is silly—"

"The hell it is! Pres, do you think you're the only one with nightmares? You did the right thing. You did the *only* thing. It's not your fault you didn't have any choices. You should never have *been* in that situation. But what could *I* do?

"It looks like a computer problem," Tony Rand brooded. "They knew too much about MILLIE, and MILLIE may be too vulnerable anyway. Too many people with access. They *have* to have access. Okay, maybe I can't deal with that, but suppose there's something else? One more door, or another set of locks, or a trapdoor somewhere—"

"Tony, you're doing it again." Preston Sanders looked as if he were trying to reach through the glass. "You're putting people in boxes. They don't fit. You can't stop *everyone*. It's like trying not to offend anyone. Remember what TV was like in the seventies? Even your high-diving board doesn't work on everyone, does it? A clever, determined suicide brings wire cutters and goes through the fence."

"Yeah. I used to wonder if that was a murder. Why would a suicide go to that much *trouble?*" Tony brooded for a moment. "Skip it. Is there anything I can bring you?"

"Yeah. My roommate brings westerns and is eager to loan them to me. So pick me a good thick science fiction novel with lots of obscure technical terms."

It was perfectly clear to Tony that Pres had said that to cheer up Tony Rand. "That'll fix him," Tony said.

Rand left the jail with a feeling of relief, but he continued to brood. What could he have done differently? And what should he do now? There'd be a next time. He was sure of it. And next time, there would be real bombs.

X

Justice, I think, is the tolerable accommodation of the conflicting interests of society, and I don't believe there is any royal road to attain such accommodations concretely.

—Learned Hand

JUDGMENT

Tony Rand fidgeted uncomfortably on the courtroom chair. From time to time he tried to catch Preston Sanders's eye, but Pres was sitting rigidly upright, his eyes fastened on the witness, and never looked back. He didn't look too bad, considering that he'd been jailed for nearly three weeks.

The courtroom looked like a TV set. It was the special courtroom, with a big Plexiglas panel between the spectators and the area where the action went on. Rand had been told that Judge Penny Norton's bench had armor plate built into it as well. Marshals searched everyone who entered the room. When they were satisfied, they let the judge and defendant in.

Judge Norton looked very stern in her black robes. It was a big case for her, the biggest she'd ever been involved in. In the strategy meetings back at Todos Santos, John Shapiro had described her as "up-and-coming," a judge who'd likely end up on the

California Supreme Court once she had more experience; he'd known her in law school. He also thought she'd pay more attention to the political situation than to the law, but he had no way to challenge her. "And," he'd said, "at least she's smart enough to understand the arguments. I don't think we'd get a better one, and it would take a long time to try."

That had been the deciding factor for Art Bonner. He wanted the trial over and done with, as soon as possible. No delays. There'd been argument over that, with Shapiro protesting that he had to work in Sanders's best interest, not the corporation's, and the best thing for Sanders would be to delay. That was when Bonner had taken Shapiro into his office, and Tony didn't know what Art had said to the lawyer, but certainly the legal proceedings had been surprisingly swift after that.

Tony was no lawyer; actually, he disliked the breed. For Tony Rand the world was a relatively simple place, and there was no need for people whose profession was to get rich by making it complex. However, he had to admire John Shapiro, who had carefully and patiently built his case, not merely in common sense, but in the strange convolutions required by the law. He had wrung Tony Rand dry of information, and at the same time kept a lot of the Todos Santos security system secret. Now he was cross-examining Allan Thompson.

"Allan," Shapiro said, "you told the District Attorney that you carried no weapons, and nothing harmful."

"Yes, sir."

"What did you carry?"

"Well, some electronics gear."

"Anything else?" Shapiro's manner was entirely friendly, matter-of-fact; he seemed almost uninterested in the answers.

"Gas masks."

"Gee. That's a strange kind of thing to carry, isn't it? Why gas masks?"

"Objection." District Attorney Sid Blackman was a tall, thin man with black hair cut to a fashionable length, and good but not expensive clothes: which made him a liar in Tony Rand's opinion, because Blackman was one of the heirs to a department store fortune, although he tried to give the impression of a man of the people. "Your Honor, this witness was not present when the gas masks were worn."

"Let's phrase it differently," John Shapiro said. "Did James Planchet or Diana Lauder tell you why they brought gas masks to Todos Santos?"

"Yes, sir. They were worried about knockout gas. We'd heard that Todos Santos used gas to defend the tunnels."

"Lethal gas?"

"No, sir, we didn't know they used poison gas! We thought they just used something to knock people out."

"Hmm. I see." Shapiro's manner didn't change. "Who did you hear that from, Allan?"

"I don't know."

"But you had all kinds of information about Todos Santos security systems. You were able to open locked doors and defeat the alarm system, weren't you?"

"Yes."

"And surely you learned that from someone. We've heard Mr. Rand and Colonel Cross testify that such information is very carefully guarded. It wasn't published anywhere. Where did you learn how to gain entry to Todos Santos?"

"I guess somebody told Jimmy," Allan said. He squirmed uncomfortably in the witness chair. "But I don't know who."

"You're sure you don't know who told Jimmy Planchet."

"Yes, sir. I'm sure."

John Shapiro looked away from the sweating boy

for a moment. Tony thought the lawyer was disappointed, but it wasn't easy to tell. Shapiro came back, his voice again friendly. "All right. Now, you were carrying other things, too, weren't you? What were they?"

"Some boxes of sand."

"Sand. Did those boxes of sand have anything painted on them?"

"Yes, sir—"

"What?"

"Well, uh—uh—"

Shapiro let him stammer. He waited expectantly, and finally Allan said, "They said *dynamite*."

"Dynamite. The word *dynamite* was painted on the boxes of sand. Is that correct?"

"On two of them. The other one said *bomb*," Allan said. There was a titter of laughter in the courtroom.

Judge Norton looked stern and lifted her gavel, but she didn't have to say anything.

"So. If you hadn't known those were boxes of sand, would you have thought they were dangerous explosives?"

"Yes—"

"Capable of setting fires?"

"Objection," Blackman said. "Calls for a conclusion from the witness."

"Did you want people to think those were dangerous explosives?"

"No, not really. We were going to leave them, and when the guards found them they'd know we *could* have left real explosives—"

"I see," Shapiro said. "And why did you choose Tunnel Nine?"

"Because that's where the hydrogen lines come in—"

"And what's special about hydrogen lines?" Shapiro seemed a little more eager, a little more interested than he'd been before.

"Well, they need it to run that anthill—"

"Anything else?"

"Well, gee, if it had caught on fire it would have been pretty spectacular," Thompson said.

District Attorney Blackman cursed under his breath. Tony Rand saw it, and wondered why.

"If it had caught fire. In other words, the managers at Todos Santos would have legitimate cause to worry about fires if there were an explosion in Tunnel 9?"

"Objection—"

"Excuse me," Shapiro said. "Allan, did you think the managers would have legitimate cause to worry about fires from an explosion in Tunnel 9?"

"Yes, sir."

"Did Jimmy or Diana?"

"Objection—"

"Did either of them tell you they thought the managers of Todos Santos would be worried about fires from an explosion in Tunnel 9?"

"Sure. Jimmy said they'd be scared shitless."

Shapiro smiled in triumph. "And of course you knew that Todos Santos is inhabited. That there were people living there when you entered that tunnel."

"Well sure—"

"Thank you." Shapiro turned away, looking satisfied.

• • •

Thomas Lunan thought it a rather strange bar. For one thing, the bartender was lonely. He never saw most of his customers: orders came up on a television screen, the drinks were mixed, and then put through a pass-through, and from there they went to various places in Todos Santos.

The bar itself was wood with a Formica top. There were barstools, and a television set, and a few tables; but almost no customers. Two Todos Santos men— Lunan wasn't sure how he knew they were Saints, but he did—sat on barstools drinking beer and talking about the unfairness of their wives. Otherwise the place was empty.

Lunan had taken a seat as near the customers as he

could. He'd told Phil Lowry to meet him here, and he had to wait, although he'd have preferred a place with more people to watch. After a few moments he'd struck up a conversation with the bartender, which was how he knew the man was lonely.

He'd never met such a friendly bartender. Or one who knew so little about what was going on. It was typical of Todos Santos people, though; none of them cared much about what went on outside their fortress. Except for the Sanders hearings. They knew all about those.

The bartender's name was Mark Levoy, and he liked to talk. Lunan knew that as soon as he admired the Old Fashioned.

"Yeah," Levoy said. "My drinks, now they're popular. I get more business than the Blackbird, more than Dreamland. But it's all remote. Drinks are popular, but my place isn't. Don't know why."

"Too bad. You own this place, then?"

"Well, me and the Todos Santos bank."

"Ms. Churchward loaned you the money," Lunan guessed.

"Miss Churchward. Yeah. Thanks to her, I got my own business. But it sure gets lonesome in here. Don't like being alone. Didn't like it in my underground days—" Levoy paused, hesitantly.

"Underground?" Lunan prompted.

Levoy's smile was broad. "Yeah. I was in the Weather Underground. Way back when. Had to hide out from the law—"

The two Todos Santos customers picked up their drinks and moved to a table. Levoy watched them with a frown. They didn't seem unfriendly. They just left.

"Regulars?" Lunan asked. He nodded toward the two.

"Yeah. How'd you know? Anyway, I didn't like being alone then either. After a while the statute of limitations ran out. But it started going sour a long time before that."

"How so?"

"Chicago, 1968, the Democratic National Convention. It's not *smart* to put shit in Baggies and throw it at armed men. It's not even smart to be standing *next* to that kind of yo-yo. And three of my buddies were trying to make a bomb to blow up the Statue of Liberty, and one day they blew themselves all over the basement walls."

Lunan considered responses, and chose, "Tough luck."

The bartender snorted. "Luck? My poker buddies would call that a run of bad playing! I'm sorry they got killed, of course. Not so sorry we didn't blow up the Lady. But you know what really got me out of the Movement? You'll never guess."

"I'm sure I can't," Lunan said. The two regulars glanced his way, then grinned at each other.

Levoy had to go mix more drinks. He made a shaker of martinis and put it onto the conveyor, then spent more time on a tall, complicated rum drink. He came back with another Old Fashioned for Lunan. "I wish that damned Canadian would go away," he said. "I've made enough Pimm's Cups to last me the rest of my life."

"Say, I've never tasted—"

Levoy rode him down. "You know, we used to tell each other about how stupid politicians are. You know, so dumb that they passsed a law making *pi* equal to three, exactly?"

"I heard about that," Lunan said. "Pretty stupid all right—"

"Well, it didn't happen," Levoy said belligerently, and waited for Lunan to call him a liar. When Lunan didn't, he said, "I looked it up. I was going to use it in a pamphlet. Didn't happen. What did happen was that some joker in Indiana offered the royalties on his math text to the state of Indiana if they'd pass a law with a lot of complicated mathematical language in it. Turns out the law would have made pi equal to nine, but the—"

"Nine?"

"Nine. But the legislature didn't know that because they couldn't read it. So they referred it to the Committee on Swamps."

"Did you say Swamps?" Lunan was laughing.

"Swamps. Somebody must have been having fun. The Committee on Swamps recommended that they pass it, so they did. The other house figured out what was happening and sent it to the Committee on Temperance. It died there."

"And that's all?"

"That's all," Levoy said. He sniffed. "And here I'd believed all that, you know—"

"Well, hell, so did I! And it's a much better story the other way." The two regulars were grinning at him. Lunan surmised that the bartender had told this tale before. Often.

"Got a question," he said. "Maybe you know. Those pillars in the Mall downstairs. Three of them bring in money. Shops, restaurants, the gambling hall, day-care center, and so forth. But the waterfall—"

"Yeah. Someday Bonner'll sell that waterfall and it'll be something else. He's just never gotten an offer that had enough money in it and would be as pretty as the waterfall."

"That counts?"

"It counts for a lot. Shouldn't it? We could pile a lot more money-makers around the Yggdrasil pillar, but it'd look cluttered."

"Is that why you moved into Todos Santos?"

The bartender grinned. "It was eleven years ago, and coming up on April fifteenth. The word was out that nobody'd be making out their own taxes in Todos Santos. The taxes'd be part of our rent. It came to me that I didn't *like* being an accountant for the government on no pay."

"Nobody does," Lunan muttered. "That's a hell of a deal you people have."

"Sure," Levoy said. "But look at it this way. After the fire, there was this fucking great hole in Los

Angeles. You could see it from orbit! And everybody wanted to forget it as fast as possible, only the city's finances were in horrible shape, and people needed housing—some of the same people who were shooting at the firemen, but how could you pick them out? Anyway, nobody could afford to fill that hole with buildings. It looked like they were going to have to put in temporary housing, you know, the kind that lasts longer than any skyscraper, instant slums." The bartender shrugged. "So, in exchange for leaving us alone, they got this place put up over that big scarred gap, and it's not like we don't pay a *lot* of taxes—"

"There's my assistant," Lunan said. "He'll want Teachers and soda. Nice to have met you." Thankfully Lunan took a table.

Lowry was a regular reporter, and he didn't much like being assigned to help Lunan get a big story. He wasn't much younger than Lunan, and he wanted off assignments, but so far he hadn't had any big breaks, and Lunan didn't think he ever would. Too much of a plodder.

"How'd the trial go?" Lunan asked.

"Dull. Only good part was when the Thompson kid told about the boxes of sand with *dynamite* and *bomb* painted on them. Kid's a liar, though."

"Liar? I've seen the boxes—"

"Not about that," Lowry said. He sipped his Scotch and soda. "Naw, earlier. He said he didn't know who'd given the dead kids the info about TS. Said it right in court, and he's lying."

"He does know?"

"Sure." Phil Lowry looked smug.

"This is straight?" Lunan had a feeling in the pit of his stomach. This could be it, the lever he needed to get some exclusives with the Todos Santos top brass.

"Absolutely."

"All right, I bite," Lunan said. "How do you know?"

"I've got sources," Phil Lowry said. "As many and as good as you, you lucky bastard."

"Sure you do, Phil," Lunan said. Now how can I con him out of the information? I can't. He knows I'm interested. "Look, this place isn't your beat. Are you still interested in that Long Beach harbor scandal?"

"Sure—"

"Trade you," Lunan said. "I'll give you a line on the whole scam. Exclusive. Two commissioners on the take. It'll take a lot of leg work, but you can get it all."

"For what?"

"For everything you know, source and all, about the Thompson kid and the raid on Todos Santos."

Lowry thought it over. "Yeah, that's fair," he said. "You can do more with the Todos Santos story than me." He spoke grudgingly. "That was a good article you did on the two cultures."

Better than you think, Lunan thought. Better than you think. The *Trib*'s publisher also owned a TV station, and he'd liked Lunan's articles so much he'd assigned a camera crew and a director to work with Lunan on a TV documentary, and that was going to make Lunan's career. "So who's your source?"

"You can't use her, Tom," Lowry said. "It's Councilman Planchet's aide. Ginny Bernard. Lonely chick. Not a very good lay, either. And so damned hung up that it took me six weeks to get in her pants, and another month to get any information out of her. But that's my source. Now what about the Long Beach scam?"

"In a minute. Okay, it'll take awhile to use your source. But you can at least tell me what she told you. Who put the kids up to the raid?"

"Professor Arnold Renn of UCLA. He's Fromate, and Ginny thinks he's got ties to the American Ecology Army too. Now what about our bargain?"

"You'll get it." Lunan took out a notebook and began writing names for Lowry, but his mind was somewhere else. Fromates! And Councilman Planchet knew it. That ought to be worth a lot to Art Bonner.

Maybe enough to get some exclusive interviews! Lunan turned a page and jotted a note, rapidly, in neat square printed letters.

"Dear Mr. Bonner:
   I've found out something that I think you would be very interested in knowing. I would appreciate an appointment at your earliest convenience."

That ought to get him, Lunan thought. Now how do I send it?

• • •

Tony Rand brought his drink into the board room. Art Bonner and Barbara Churchward were already there with John Shapiro.

"How are we doing?" Bonner asked.

Shapiro shrugged. "If this was a quiet little hearing out in some hick town with no political implications, we'd have it won," he said. "As it is, I'm pretty sure we can win on appeal."

"But you won't get a justifiable homicide judgment in this trial?" Barbara Churchward asked.

Shapiro shook his head. "I doubt it. Judge Norton only has to rule that the state has enough of a case to go to trial. She can say that most of it hinges on facts, and that's for a jury to decide. We can appeal that—"

"Will Pres be out on bail during the appeal?" Bonner asked.

"Unlikely. The D.A. will fight it. Of course when they deny bail we can appeal. I'd be doing that now only you said get it over—"

"I did indeed," Bonner said. "Tony, please sit down. I don't like people hovering over me. Thanks. Look, Johnny, what's so complicated about it?"

"It just is," Shapiro said. "Look, we've got some tricky points of law here, and Penny Norton doesn't want to rule for us. It'd cost her like crazy. She says she wants on the state supreme court, but I'm betting she'd like to run for state Attorney General in a couple years—" He shrugged again. "But I got the grounds for appeal into the transcript today."

"What, that the kids actually committed suicide?" Barbara Churchward asked.

Shapiro looked thoughtful. "Not a bad argument." He frowned. "But it's no good here."

"Why not?" Tony asked. "That door was marked plainly enough. It practically said that you'd commit suicide if you went through it."

"Good argument for a jury," Shapiro said. "But it won't affect Penny a damn bit. No, I've got another plan."

"Tell us," Churchward said.

"Well, our defense is that there wasn't any crime. In my final argument I'll show that Sanders had good reason to suppose a felony arson was about to be committed—"

"That's why all that about fires this afternoon," Rand said.

Shapiro grinned. "Yep. Blackman hated that. He could see where I was headed. See, one of the key cases in homicide defense came up when an IRS agent shot a man resisting arrest. The courts held that it was justified—"

"But Pres is not a policeman," Tony said.

"Right, and Blackman will try to make a lot out of that. But it doesn't matter," Shapiro said, "because in U.S. against Rice the judge went on to say that the law requires private citizens to prevent felonies from being committed in their presence. Requires it." He chuckled. "And then the judge said that when any person is performing a public duty required of him by the law, he's under the law's protection. And there's another case that says you're not justified in using deadly force to prevent just any felony, but you can to prevent atrocious crimes—such as first-degree arson, that's setting fire to an inhabited building. And we've shown that Sanders had every reason to believe they were trying to commit an atrocious crime."

"Well, I should think so," Churchward said.

"So why aren't we going to win?" Bonner asked.

"Well, there are other cases," Shapiro said. "Mainly ones that say that a peace officer takes his chances when he kills a suspect. It's okay if the suspect was committing a felony, or resists arrest—by the way, I'm going to try to show that those gas masks were a way of resisting arrest—anyway, it's all right if the suspect is running away from an atrocious felony, but not if it's a misdemeanor. And Blackman will show that the kids weren't committing a felony, only misdemeanor trespass."

"But it looked like arson," Churchward said. "They were trying their best to make it look that way."

"And it hasn't always been just trespassing," Rand said. "There've been real bombs. There'll probably be more."

"Now you're trying to use common sense on the law," Art Bonner said. "And I don't think that works. All right. We lose. What then?"

"Appeal. Or let it go to trial and argue it before a jury. We might win with a jury. And if we don't, we can appeal again."

"Meanwhile Pres is in jail."

"Well, until the trial's over," Shapiro said. "I'd bet the worst we'd get would be manslaughter. Then we could get Pres out on bail."

"But you're talking weeks. Months, maybe," Bonner said.

"Sure—"

"That's not justice. Sanders didn't do a damn thing wrong, but he gets locked up anyway." Bonner's lips tightened. "Damn it, I don't like this. I don't like it at all."

"Johnny's doing the best he can. Don't discourage him." The voice was MILLIE's, but it had the subtle differences indicating the words were Barbara's. The computer/medical experts who'd

inserted the implant in Bonner's head had explained
how it worked, that MILLIE was programmed to
transmit non-verbal impulses which implant wearers
learned to interpret as tones and emotional subtleties,
but that didn't make it less miraculous.

"You're right, as usual," Art thought. Then he
said, aloud, "Keep trying, Johnny." He put his hand
on Shapiro's shoulder. "We'll all keep plugging away
at it. One thing more. This just came. An offer from
a newsman, guy named Lunan, to trade information
for our cooperation in his documentary. I think we
ought to discuss it."

"Can't hurt," Churchward said. "We could use
some sympathic news coverage. Let's talk to him."

• • •

There was mist over San Pedro. It couldn't quite be
called a fog. You could see through it, out across the
yacht basin and into the Los Angeles harbor, but the
sun couldn't penetrate it. Early Morning Low Clouds
and Fog, the weather reports said. A better term
would be "gloomy before noon."

Alice Strahler walked along the Los Angeles fishing
pier to Ports o' Call's gaily painted shops. There were
restaurants and ice cream bars and artists' displays,
antique shops and confectionary stores, all painted to
look more like Cape Cod than Pueblo de Los
Angeles. There were not many tourists around; they
would come when the fog burned away.

She strolled through the shopping area, pausing now
and again to look back the way she came, going
through the shops, in one door and out another, until
she was certain that no one was interested in her
movements. Finally she went through a parking lot
and under a highway viaduct.

It was like coming to another world. Instead of
chintz and new paint and new rental cars, this was a
region of run-down buildings and battered old trucks,
marine engine repair shops, warehouses, and cheap
cafes. The road led along the waterfront to a drab

building on a pier. It had once been painted, but years of salt-laden wind had faded it until no one knew what color it had been. Large saltwater tanks of crabs and Pacific lobster stood against the building. There was no one else on the pier. Inside, there was a fat man in a stained apron behind the counter. At first Alice thought he was alone. Then she saw the solitary customer, a thin bearded man watching her from a corner booth where he sat breaking crackers into a bowl of soup. The customer winked at her, and she went over to his table.

He grinned widely. "Good to see you again." He swept his hand to indicate the seat across the carved and marked booth table. "Coffee? And the clam chowder's the best in the city."

"Okay."

He got up and went to the counter to order for her. She sat in silence, biting her lip, wanting to get this over with. After what seemed like ages, he came back with her food and coffee. The coffee mug was old and chipped, and so was the shallow chowder bowl, but the chowder smelled delicious. She automatically ate a spoonful, then another.

"Gets to you, doesn't it?" he asked with a grin. Then his face became serious. "We haven't a lot of time. What's this all about?"

"What I told Phil," she said. "Ron, I can't take it any longer. I quit."

He shrugged. "Okay. So you quit."

She looked at him without saying anything, but he wouldn't meet her eyes. "Damn it, you could say something—"

"Sure. What do you want me to say?" he asked. "That the work's important and we need you? Hell, you know that already. If I could think of anything to say that would keep you with us, I'd say it, but you told Phil your mind's made up. I'm not sure why you wanted to see me."

"Maybe you shouldn't have bothered."

"Come off it. We owed you that much, and more. So I'm here." He shrugged. "Tell me what to say."

"You might ask why—"

"I presume you've lost faith in the Movement."

"I don't know," Alice said. "I—Ron, why can't I work openly? It's this sneaking around—they trust me, and I'm betraying that trust—"

"I know it's hard, but we need the information—"

"Not from me. We killed Diana and Jimmy, and for nothing—"

"It wasn't for nothing." His eyes narrowed and his voice hardened. He spoke so intensely that it came across like shouting, although he never raised his voice at all. "Never say it was for nothing! Because of them, we're closer, much closer, to shutting down that termite hill. People are asking questions, wondering about Todos Santos and all of the arcologies, wondering why they have to defend themselves with war gas, and who they'll kill next. We're showing the world that humanity can't live like that. So you can have all the second thoughts you want, but don't try to take anything away from Diana and Jimmy!"

"But it's my fault they're dead—"

"Bull shit," he said. "Because you didn't know about nerve gas? That was the hive's best-kept secret, and you didn't find out, so now it's your fault?"

"They wouldn't even have got in without me," she said.

He nodded. "That's true enough."

"So it was my fault."

"And now you've got the guilts?" he asked. "You want to atone. Turn us all in—"

"No! I'd never do that—"

"Why not?" he asked. "We're nothing better than murderers."

"But we are—"

"Why? How are we better than some petty crook?"

"Because the Movement is important, it's *right.*

Because Todos Santos is the beginning of a horrible future, and it has to be stopped *now*."

"I believe that," he said. "But you don't—"

"I do, too."

"Then why are you quitting?"

"Because—"

"Because it's hard?" he asked. His voice was full of contempt. "You've got it hard? You don't have to look over your shoulder all the time. You've got a bed to sleep in and plenty to eat. You're not mucking around with explosives, and you don't have to jump every time you see a cop, but you think you've got it hard."

"It isn't that!" she insisted.

"Then what is it?"

"Oh I don't know, you get me all confused—"

"I'm sorry," he said. "It just seems so simple to me. We've got to work for humanity because there's nothing else worth doing. What else is there? Their bourgeois God with his thunderings and mumblings and petty jealousies? *Alle Menschen müssen sterben.* We'll all die. All of us. Poof. Gone, out like a light. Well, it has to mean something. There has to be a reason for living, and keeping mankind human is a damned good one!"

"I don't know—sometimes, watching them in Todos Santos—Ron, they're happy. They like it."

His voice dropped low, and became more intense. "Happy? Of course they're happy. Aristocrats usually are happy. But how many of those places can the Earth support? And there'll be more hives, hives everywhere—you're the one who told us about that Canadian. Hives in Canada, hives in Mexico, hives all over the United States . . . they've got to be stopped, now, before they spread. And you know it."

Do I? she wondered. I guess I do.

"Alice, if you quit now, then you really did something evil. If we don't succeed, then Jimmy and Diana were killed for nothing, nothing at all, and you helped kill them."

He reached across the table and took her hand. "I know. It *is* hard, being inside there, never seeing your friends, having to be on guard all the time. But hang on. It won't be long now. Get us their new defense setup. This time we'll shut that place down. For good."

XI

It is easier for a man to be loyal to his club than to
his planet; the bylaws are shorter, and he is personally
acquainted with the other members.

—E. B. White

CONSPIRACIES

Tony Rand's Videobeam television screen covered
most of a wall. It was big enough to watch reruns of
2001: A Space Odyssey, which was true of damned
few TV sets. He never used it to watch war movies or
rock shows. They seemed just too intimidating on
that huge screen.

Tony was on his bed, with the headboard panel
pulled out to support his back. The huge face
looming above him had a lean and hungry look, like
Cassius.

"What I found," it said, "is a feudal society. Now,
when I speak of feudalism, I don't mean plate armor
and crossbows. Todos Santos isn't just modern, it's at
the forefront of technology. The carbon fibers in those
compote walls were precipitated in an orbital
laboratory, and couldn't have been made except in
free fall. The very concept of an arcology is only a
few decades old. When Paolo Soleri first began to

write about arcologies it seemed like science fiction, even though Soleri was a student of Frank Lloyd Wright."

Tony Rand nodded agreement. When Paolo Soleri began construction of Arcosanti, his new model city in the Arizona desert, the news writers had been intrigued—but they hadn't taken him seriously. Even after it was obvious that Soleri was building his city, that it was growing year by year, most writers thought Soleri a pleasant eccentric, brilliant but dotty. Certainly Genevieve thought so! Tony's decision to spend an unpaid summer working with Soleri ("He can't last much longer, he's been working out there twenty years, Djinn, this is my last chance . . .") had finished their marriage . . .

"Certainly Todos Santos is modern," Lunan continued. "The Romulus Corporation which built the Box has for years been towing icebergs from Antarctica to supply Los Angeles with water." The scene flicked from Lunan to the Los Angeles harbor, panning across to the iceberg, zooming in for a closeup of skiers, then zooming right past and on to Catalina Island, closeup of the Isthmus Harbor with sandy beaches and palm trees.

"Perhaps beyond modern," Lunan said. "Hundreds of Todos Santos residents work in Los Angeles—two work as far away as Houston, Texas, and one works machinery on the Moon!—without ever leaving their homes."

The scene shifted again, to a smiling, burly, black-haired man. Rand recognized him, but couldn't remember the name. Lunan's voice continued, "Mr. Armand Drinkwater is a master milling-machine operator—"

"Experimental mechanic," Drinkwater corrected. His voice boomed.

"—for the Konigsberg Medical Instrument Company. The instruments he works on didn't exist five years ago. Armand, I'm told you generally work stark naked."

"Right. Maybe I'm overreacting. But I used to have to wear white coats and a cap to work in the clean rooms, and I got damned sick of it. Got sick of freeways, too."

"And now?"

"I smile a lot. Oh, you mean working days? My contract says I have to be at work at nine. Fine. I get up at ten of nine. That gives me time for coffee. Harriet generally makes me a bacon and egg sandwich around half past, and I eat it while I'm working. When I take a lunch hour, I get the whole hour. Do a little sun bathing out on the balcony. I knock off at five, and I'm home at five. I can have a drink if I want, and it won't be to wind down from fighting traffic."

The scene faded into a shot of Drinkwater at a combination desk and work table. A bank of TV screens curved in a horseshoe shape along one edge. In the center was a pair of thick gloves suspended from universal-jointed trusses something like an old-fashioned dentist's drill. Cables led from the gloves to plugs on the desk.

"In deference to our video audience, Armand dressed for work this morning," Lunan's voice said over the scene. Drinkwater, wearing a black bathing suit that blended invisibly with his thick pelt, put on the gloves. His hands made precise motions. A complex shape took form on one of the TV screens in front of him.

"I mostly make one-of-a-kind items," Drinkwater said. "But this happens to be the prototype for a production run. Everything I do is recorded, and when I get it right, the computers will take over and make a hundred just like this by doing what I did. I get a royalty." He lifted a micrometer and applied it to nothing; a similar instrument appeared on the TV screen, and another screen lit up with measurements. Drinkwater nodded in satisfaction.

"What are you making?" Lunan asked.

"Pump for a heart-lung machine," Drinkwater said.

"I think this lot's for export to Africa." The gloves moved slightly and the shape on the TV screen rotated. "Pretty tricky work. I doubt if I could do it if I'd had to drive all day just to get to work." He grinned. "I know I wouldn't enjoy it as much."

The scene moved back to real time, Lunan interviewing Drinkwater. "I take it you like it here," Lunan said.

"Nope. I love it."

Tony Rand smiled.

The scene shifted. "Meet Rachael Lief," Lunan said. "Ms. Lief is a bulldozer driver." Lunan paused for effect. "As you see, Rachael doesn't look like your typical tractor driver."

She certainly didn't. Tony remembered meeting her once: a short woman, not particularly pretty, but very delicately built, with small features and piercing dark brown eyes, and a voice so raucously loud that you expected to hear glass shattering when she spoke.

"But then," Lunan said, "not every bulldozer operator works on the Moon." The cameras followed the trim woman into another room, where there was a replica of a large tractor. It was surrounded by TV screens. One screen showed an astronaut seated in the driver's seat, staring impatiently into the screen. A bleak, nearly colorless pit showed over his left shoulder.

"About time you got here," the astronaut said.

"We were busy." Rachael sat down in the driver's seat and took hold of the controls. "I relieve you."

There was a pause. "Busy hell—all right, I stand relieved. Thank you."

The bulldozer moved through the lunar strip mine. Lunan alternated views: inside Todos Santos watching Lief move the controls; the scene that she saw in her control screen; and a composite from over her shoulder looking into her monitor. "As you can see," Lunan's disembodied voice said, "this is no easy job. When Rachael gives a command, it takes over a second for the signal to get to the Moon, and another second for the information to get back to her. It takes a lot of computer power to work this trick, but it's worth it. Meet Colonel Robert Boyd, commander of Moon Base.

"Colonel Boyd, does it help to have Earth-based machine operators?"

"Sure. It costs a *lot* to keep people on the Moon. Now it's like I have four or five times as many people up here, and I don't have to feed them or find air for them."

"High technology applications," Lunan said. "You see a lot of them in Todos Santos." The TV scene changed to show other Todos Santos people: electronic assemblers, an elaborate chemistry laboratory, a man making intricate drawings using a computerized drafting table, more waldo operators. Then it changed again to show children in the jungle tree, people playing on the roof, swimming in rooftop pools.

"There's more than work," Lunan said. "They play hard too. Industrial feudalism can be fun, as we've seen. But *why* are Todos Santos residents so exuberant? It isn't just freedom from freeways—"

The TV came back to Lunan standing in front of a bank of TV screens. They showed a bewildering variety: people sprawled on balconies, people working, people walking in corridors. Uniformed police watched the screens, some lolling back in comfort, others peering intently at the TV monitors.

"Security technology in Todos Santos is modern, too," Lunan said.

Tony Rand cursed. Whatever Lunan's information was, it couldn't have been worth this! "Who the hell let him in—" He looked closer at the screen. "Son of a bitch. It's a fake. Damned good one, though. Wonder who described the security room for him?" They'd even got the chart showing the leaper results.

"The only place Todos Santos residents are not under full surveillance is in their apartments. The security guards have the equipment to look even there, although they're not supposed to do it except when asked to, or if there's good reason to suspect a resident is in danger," Lunan said. The scene cut back to Drinkwater.

"Do you ever worry that the police might be watching you when they're not supposed to?" Lunan asked.

"Should I?" Drinkwater shrugged. "Maybe I do think about it sometimes. We've got jokes about what the guards know, what they've seen us doing. Thing is, though, they're *our* guards. Our friends."

"You love it here," Lunan said. "Doesn't all the constant surveillance ever bother you?"

"Bothers hell out of me if it fails," Drinkwater said. "Goddam FROMATES got LSD into our food once. Put four residents into the giggle ward. If it hadn't been we had a bartender who'd been through that stuff to talk them down, we'd have lost some stockholders."

"You said FROMATES. Are you sure of that?" Lunan asked.

"Who else would it be? *Bleep*ing *bleep* keep trying, too."

The scene shifted to the Mall, with a guard post conspicuous in the foreground. Lunan's voice asked, "Did you always feel that way about police?"

"Nope." Drinkwater laughed. "When I was a kid, my folks gave me that 'the policeman is your best friend' jazz, but it didn't take long to find out what a crock that was. You may get friendly with cops, but that's mostly to talk them out of giving you a ticket, right? You don't *like* them. Look, suppose you're a solid citizen. Never been in trouble. You go out with your buddies and you have one too many, and you're trying to get home. No accidents, but maybe you weave just a little, and the cops see you. What happens?"

"You get a ticket—"

"You talk fast. And you still get busted," Drinkwater said. "Not here. In here the police work for *us*. I get drunk on top level and get lost, the guards bring me to my apartment."

A pretty girl came onto the screen from the right. She went up to the guard station.

"We recorded this yesterday," Lunan said. "Meet Cheryl Drinkwater, Armand's daughter. Unlike Armand, Cheryl grew up in Todos Santos."

She smiled pleasantly at the guard. "I had an appointment with my father, but I'm going to be late," Cheryl told him. "I'm not sure where he is." She held out her Todos Santos identity badge. The guard returned her smile and nodded in understanding while he put the badge into a slot in his console.

"Mr. Drinkwater is in the 40th Level Hideaway," he said. "Do you want to telephone?"

"No." Cheryl's grin widened. "Just let him know I'll be an hour or so late—"

"Sure thing. Have a nice day."

The camera zoomed back, a long way back, to show Thomas Lunan standing on a balcony overlooking the kaleidoscopic Mall. Cheryl Drinkwater and the guard booth were almost invisible dots far below. The scene dissolved to a street in Los Angeles: a dozen police cars deployed around a house, police with rifles, pistols, and shotguns draped over the cruisers while an officer with a bullhorn shouted instructions. The guns erupted in a blaze of fire. The scene dissolved again to a hijacked airliner, to the Zapruder films of John F. Kennedy in the Dealy Plaza. It changed to Reagan leaving the Washington Hilton, ending with a federal agent holding a submachine gun. Then to a montage of scenes showing confrontations between police and citizens; thence to another series showing burglarized houses, muggings, armed robberies. Finally the camera zoomed into Todos Santos, through the wall, and back to Thomas Lunan overlooking the Mall.

"Of course we've been unfair," Lunan said. "Not all police encounters outside Todos Santos are unpleasant, and there have been murders in the Box. Last year a man used a kitchen knife on his wife and two children."

Sure, Tony Rand thought. But Marlene Higgins had lived long enough to push the panic button, and the TS guards got there in time to save the third kid who'd been hiding in a closet.

But those kids with the boxes of sand . . . how could I have saved those kids? Tony wondered. And Pres. Judge Norton had given her decision very quickly after the evidence was presented, sooner than anyone had expected; Preston Sanders would stand trial for murder. Damn, Tony thought. Double damn . . .

Tony got up and went to the icebox for a beer. When he came back, Lunan was lecturing.

"Feudal societies are always complex: everyone in such a society enjoys rights, but few have the same rights. There is not even a pretense of equality—of rights, nor of duties and responsibilities.

"There is, however, loyalty, and it runs both ways. The Todos Santos resident is expected and required to be loyal, but in return, Todos Santos gives protection. Todos Santos accountants negotiate income taxes for the Box. Committees test consumer products—"

Sure do, Tony Rand thought. I still get burned up about those damned paper towels, good quality, but they put the perforations so far apart you used up two when you only needed one, and I could never remember which brand it was until the evaluation committee gave them the "Ripoff" rating sticker . . .

"Loyalties in Todos Santos tend to be personal," Lunan said. The scene faded in to show Art Bonner's office. Lunan spoke feelingly about the luxuries Todos Santos provided for its General Manager. Then back to Armand Drinkwater.

"Armand, are you jealous of Mr. Bonner's position?" Lunan asked.

"Great Ghu no! I only have one boss. Mr. Bonner works for *everybody*."

"Loyalty and protection," Lunan said. "The ties of the Oath of Fealty run in both directions. The trend in the United States has been to cut all ties, so that individuals are alone. The citizen against the bureaucracy, against 'them,' only nobody is really in control and you can't say who 'they' are. In Todos Santos, 'they' is Art Bonner, and if you don't like what he's doing you have a chance to tell him so."

The scene shifted to Commons. There were a dozen residents clustered around Art Bonner, but Tony was looking at the low ceilings, which looked even lower on television. They ought to be higher, dammit—

The telephone rang. Tony's phone turned down the TV's sound as he picked up the phone. "Rand—"

"Art Bonner. Has Sir George Reedy called you lately?"

"No. I wish he would, I need to talk to him."

"I've set it up for him to tour Security and the power plants. Tony, if he asks you to show him around those areas, beg off, will you?"

"Sure. Why?"

"Hell, Tony, how much do we want an outsider to know about our defenses?"

Sir George Reedy, a Fromate spy? That was laughable. Still . . . paranoids have enemies too. "Okay, Art. Is that all?"

"No. Did—" Bonner interrupted himself; stopped to consider. That was odd. Art *never* did that. Then, "You know about the court decision today."

"Sure."

"Have you been watching Lunan's documentary?"

"Yeah—"

"He got me to thinking," Bonner said. "I never thought of this place as a feudal society, but maybe he's right. Tony, we haven't delivered what we promised. Not to Sanders."

Tony didn't say anything.

"So it's time we did," Bonner said. "Tony, I don't think our legal people can get Pres off. Johnny

Shapiro told me today the best legal tactic would be to plead guilty to a lesser charge—"

"Pres won't do that," Rand said.

"I know. Even if he would, I couldn't let him. And even if we can get a not guilty verdict, Pres will have paid too high a price. It's not justice."

"No, it's not," Tony said. "But it is the law."

"Also it's bad advertising," Bonner said. "I don't mean for profits. I mean the message it gives to anyone else out there who's thinking of trying a repeat with real bombs. We need to let the world know we take care of our own. So. I want you to think of a way to break Pres out of jail."

"Huh?"

"You heard me. Plan us a jailbreak. I don't want anybody to get hurt, and I don't want LAPD to be able to *prove* we did it. But I don't at all mind them knowing it was us."

"Art, you have lost your mind—"

"Could be," Bonner said. "But it won't hurt you to look at the problem." The phone went dead. Bonner sometimes forgot to let people know when he was through talking.

Ye gods, Tony thought. He went out to the kitchen for another beer, thought better of it, and dialed for a Scotch. When he looked back at the screen he saw his own face. Lunan was saying something about the "court magician."

Court magician. Tony wasn't sure he liked that. His drink came, and he tossed it off. He decided not to order a second. Jailbreak. Was Bonner serious? He had to be. Art knew how much work Rand had to do. A whole new security system to install. The new wing under construction, and the expansion unit designs to finalize and—

Lunan was going on about feudalism again. Now he was talking about the siege mentality, and the fortress appearance of the Box. Interesting stuff, and Tony wished he had time to think about it more. Ideas buzzed in his head. Jailbreaks. Feudalism. If Lunan was right, how much did the design have to do with it? Corporations were feudal; hell, they were invented in feudal times. The Lord Mayor and Corporation of London—

And Todos Santos certainly did resemble a fort. An arcology always would. True, Paolo's Arcosanti had a light and airy look to it, but that had been the first stage, the tiny little centerpiece that Soleri could afford. The full model of Arcosanti included an immense thirty-level ring city surrounding what actually got built, and despite Soleri's use of glass and open beams and flying buttresses and balconies, if the whole thing had ever been built it would have looked like a fortress.

Of course Soleri hadn't built it all. He hadn't wanted to, because he wanted the design to evolve, and it hadn't, not far enough to construct. He never did do a final design. But Tony Rand, with degrees in architecture and engineering and experience working with Soleri, and considerable fame from building the new Imperial County government-university complex, didn't have the luxury of waiting for evolution. Tony had to *build* Todos Santos, and get it open for occupancy, and do it with real materials and a strict budget that didn't allow for a lot of the frills.

Maybe, just maybe, he thought, I could have got away from those vertical walls? But how? We wanted as much park area as possible. And there was always the budget. And it had to be *built*, with available labor and—

Did Angelinos really read rejection into those high walls, as Lunan claimed? Give them a different shape, and maybe two innocents wouldn't have died.

And maybe we couldn't have defended the place at all? The FROMATES didn't much care for Soleri, either.

Commercial time. Tony shook his head. "Be a nice girl," he said aloud.

"READY," MILLIE's contralto answered. "YOU

HAVE A MESSAGE FROM SIR GEORGE REEDY."

"Later. Tell me about CONSPIRACY."

"CONTEXT?"

"Law."

"CONSPIRACY. CRIMINAL LAW. A COMBINATION OR CONFEDERACY BETWEEN TWO OR MORE PERSONS FORMED FOR THE PURPOSE OF COMMITTING, BY THEIR JOINT EFFORTS, SOME UNLAWFUL OR CRIMINAL ACT, OR SOME ACT WHICH IS INNOCENT IN ITSELF, BUT BECOMES UNLAWFUL WHEN DONE BY THE CONCERTED ACTION OF THE CONSPIRATORS, OR FOR THE PURPOSE OF USING CRIMINAL OR UNLAWFUL MEANS TO THE COMMISSION OF AN ACT NOT IN ITSELF UNLAWFUL.

"THE ESSENCE OF A CONSPIRACY IS AN AGREEMENT, TOGETHER WITH AT LEAST ONE OVERT ACT, TO DO AN UNLAWFUL ACT—"

"Enough. Thank you."

"ANYTIME."

Well, we haven't conspired yet, Tony thought. Not yet. But—

Damn, I need to talk this over with someone. Security problem there—it would have to be someone who'd be told Bonner wanted him to plan a jailbreak. Who? The trouble with being a loner is you're alone—

He thought for another moment, then lifted the phone. The TV considerately muted its sound. He tapped in half a number and hung up, thought about it, punched again. The phone rang six times and he was about to hang up again—

"Hello?"

"Delores? Tony Rand."

"Hi, Tony." There was a question in her voice. What the devil did Rand want.

"Did you see Lunan's broadcast?" Tony asked.

"Some of it—"

"Good. Look, your boss has gone nuts, and I have to talk to somebody," Rand said with a rush. Got that out, he thought.

There was a long pause. "Um. Tony, I'm dripping bathwater. Come down in twenty minutes, okay? We'll talk about it. I'm sure Mr. Bonner knows what he's doing—"

"I used to think so too."

"Oh, come on. Anyway, shall I have coffee waiting, or a drink?"

"Thanks. Uh—both. Irish coffee."

A tiny pause in which Rand suddenly realized that the bartender would be sending drinks in pairs to Delores's room. And the guards would know he was there. No privacy at all in Todos Santos. Tony had stopped noticing years ago, but Lunan's broadcast . . .

"Done," she said, and hung up.

Twenty minutes. "Be a nice girl and call me in fifteen minutes," Tony said aloud, using the voice shift that MILLIE recognized.

"SURE THING, BOSS. I HAVE MESSAGES—"

"Give them to me."

"FROM SIR GEORGE REEDY. 'I WOULD LIKE TO SEE YOU AGAIN TO DISCUSS DETAILS OF MY NEW ARCOLOGY. I UNDERSTAND HOW BUSY YOU ARE DUE TO EMERGENCIES. ARE YOU FREE FOR DINNER TOMORROW NIGHT?' "

Rand scowled. Everything happened at once . . . but he *had* to find a chance to pick Reedy's brain. "Tell Sir George six o'clock, Schramm's, if it's convenient. Phrase it better."

"WILL DO."

"Thank you."

"ANYTIME."

Lunan was taking a camera through his own apartment in Santa Monica. This was the damndest documentary Rand had ever seen. But it made sense

in context, because Lunan was talking about fear and
the siege mentality. He showed good locks, and cheap
stereo equipment visible from a window, and
expensive equipment hidden, and the cheap place
where he stashed his car. Jesus, Rand thought. If
things were really that bad outside, why would he be
showing all his secrets? Lunan must be planning to
move tomorrow!

And what of Zach? My boy's growing up in that,
instead of here where he belongs. And does Genevieve
deserve that? Oh, damn—

Lunan was back with the Drinkwaters again. Cheryl
was saying, "I don't see how you can live like that. I
don't see how anyone could." And now back to an
Angelino woman saying, "I don't see how they can
live like that. Eyes on the back of your neck, all the
time. Sure, I shop there—" Cut back to the Shopping
Mall again, view down a fast pedway, another
kaleidoscope; boys with toilet paper rope (Tony
smiled; it happened to him at least twice a year);
Cheryl again, laughing. "No, of course not," she
giggled. "Nobody ducks. Well, Angelinos duck—"

Not bad, Tony thought. Not bad at all. He dressed
hurriedly, trying to ignore the knot in his stomach.
He wanted to *talk*, dammit; but his glands told him
he wanted something more, and he might, just
might—

". . . siege mentality," Lunan was saying. "Todos
Santos has always seen itself as apart from Los
Angeles. Although not everyone thinks so—"

Cut to Barbara Churchward, neatly tailored skirt
suit and bright silk scarf, radiating both femininity
and competence. "A large part of our development
loans go to outsiders," she was saying. "Of course,
most are to let outsiders come inside. But yes, we
depend on Los Angeles for a lot of goods and services
that it wouldn't make sense to do in-house." She
paused, as if in thought; Lunan's audience would
assume it *was* thought. Would Lunan? "Example: in
one Todos Santos laboratory recently, within a week

they needed Plexiglas sheets, several sizes of O rings, three sizes of drill bits, silicone glue, glass tubing, a dry cell battery, some insulated wire, three lenses, two highly polished mirrors—I could go on, but surely the point is made? Only a *big* city would have all those things in stock and readily available."

"So you do depend on Los Angeles," Lunan said.

Churchward laughed. "Let's just say we spend a lot of money in Los Angeles, probably more than most Angelinos realize. After all, we *could* have our goods shipped in from some other city. But we'd rather not." She said more, but Tony wasn't listening. Twenty minutes, Delores had said. And waiting was tough. Would a cold shower help? Damn—

". . . and an ugly mood has developed lately," Lunan said. "Typified by a phrase that seems to have caught on in Todos Santos." The camera zoomed down on a sticker attached to an elevator door. "THINK OF IT AS EVOLUTION IN ACTION."

"Since nothing happens in Todos Santos without at least tacit approval by Bonner and his people," Lunan said, "we may assume that the TS managers agree with this sentiment. I haven't been able to trace the origin of the phrase—"

Ye gods, Tony thought. I *have* seen that stuck up here and there. Lunan makes it look universal, but it's not, not really. And dammit, where did I hear it first? Somewhere. The night Pres had to kill those kids—Yeah, that night, but not then, earlier. The leaper. Hell, *I* said it! How'd it get out to the public?

"I'M CALLING YOU-OOO-OOO-OOO," MILLIE warbled. "TEN FIFTY P.M."

"Thanks, sweetheart," Tony said. "Be a nice girl."

"READY."

"Rand in 234 Level 28," Tony said.

"HOW LONG, BOSS?"

"Indefinite," Tony said, and felt his stomach knot again. Ah, hell.

XII

Make no little plans; they have no magic to stir men's blood.

—Daniel Hudson Burnham

VISITING HOURS

The Irish coffee was waiting, still hot, the whipped cream half-melted. Rand had been picturing Delores in negligee, half-transparent; but she was in what were probably called hostess pajamas, loose, flowing, violent orange, and quite opaque. She also wore a welcoming smile, which was reassuring.

"So Mr. Bonner has gone out of his mind," she said.

"Yeah. He wants me to—"

"I know what he wants," Delores said.

Hmm. Did Bonner call her, or had she called Bonner to report the court magician's misgivings? Good question. I can find out who called whom from MILLIE. Or I can if Art doesn't mind my knowing. MILLIE was one of the few systems in Todos Santos that Tony Rand didn't control. At least not completely. His mind toyed briefly with an idea, a way to get MILLIE to tell him things Bonner didn't want known—

"Well?" Delores asked. She gave him a half smile, an indication that she understood his preoccupations but she was damned if she'd be ignored when he was in her apartment.

"Delores, you've known Art a long time. Is he serious?" Tony asked.

She looked at him. "Tony, we can't leave Pres with the Angelinos."

Oops. Carefully, Tony said, "That's not Pres's opinion. I think he wants absolution. He wants to be acquitted in court."

"No matter what it costs us?"

Tony shrugged. "Maybe he hasn't thought of it that way. He thinks it's his life."

"And it isn't," Delores said.

Rand looked away. Suddenly, he didn't want to look at Delores.

She lived in dark colors and soft curves. Deep brown rug, a couple of bean bag chairs, tables with no corners, a king-sized water bed piled with huge pillows. Delores was high in the hierarchy. Her apartment was at least half the size of Tony's, and none of it was work space.

"Put it this way, Tony," she said. "We—well, Johnny Shapiro—claimed no crime was committed. That Pres was doing his duty. And now Judge Norton has ruled against us. What does *that* mean?"

"Well—"

"It means that the County of Los Angeles, and the State of California, consider that a crime has been committed. There's no doubt as to *who* did what; so just what is a trial going to be about?"

"Legal maneuvers—"

"Sure. So if we're lucky we get Pres off on technicalities. Won't he just love that?"

"No. But a *jailbreak?*"

"It's not impossible, is it?"

"I don't know. I haven't thought that far." Tony

looked at Delores and saw she was in dead earnest. "It'd be a felony whether it worked or not. Even talking about it is felony conspiracy—"

That didn't faze her either. Of course it wouldn't. Tony giggled.

"What?"

"Well, I suppose Art could always find someone to break *us* out of jail—"

"He would, you know." Delores was dead serious. "You haven't touched your Irish coffee."

"Thanks." He sipped, then gulped. A bit too cool, but strong, bitter and sweet. Irish coffee tastes like a black magic healing spell.

"How do we break him out?" Delores asked.

Trapped. But he couldn't be jailed just for talking about it. Conspiracy requires an overt act—"I guess I'd tackle the computer system."

"How? I've got a terminal—"

Of course she did. And voice pickups too. Tony finished his Irish coffee, then took the chair. It didn't take him long to summon up plans of the new Los Angeles County Jail. He ran through all twelve floors, then returned to the plan for the ground floor. It was about half cells and half administrative offices and waiting rooms. "Pres is a VIP," Tony said. "Ground floor. Mmm . . . he said he got sunrise on the wall. Say southeast side. And the computer's on the top floor, but we don't really need to know that."

"What do you need to know?"

"MILLIE knows a lot already. We *could* fool with the computers. We might even just issue orders to transfer Preston Sanders to the Todos Santos jail."

"If anyone noticed—"

"We'd be up shit creek. We have to fool a computer and some human jailors, and they're likely to notice anything that happens to Sanders. He's their star guest. Thanks," he said, as Delores handed him a second Irish coffee. "Maybe we walk someone in, someone who looks vaguely like Pres. Switch them, and switch Pres's description in the computer. He's got a cell mate," Tony remembered suddenly.

"That's bad."

"Maybe not. The cell mate wants to sell us plumbing." Tony pulled thoughtfully at his drink. Below conscious thought he was aware of a woman's hand resting lightly on his shoulder; but his mind had forgotten Delores, the room, everything but the screen before him. "I don't like it. Everyone in that jail, from the warden to the garbage collector, knows Sanders's face by heart. You know why? Not because they've seen him. Because they watch television."

"Can't we get sneakier than that? Make our stooge look exactly like Pres?"

"We've got a problem there. This is a felony, remember? We'll be leaving someone else in the pickle. And there aren't too many individuals of the black persuasion in the upper ranks here. Of course we don't have to be sneaky—"

She laughed. "Whyever not?"

"Art doesn't care who knows we did it. Prefers they know. All he cares about is whether they can prove it in a Los Angeles court."

"That should make things easier."

"Maybe." He stared at the screen again. "Maybe we just tell the courthouse computer to open all the doors at once. Just a minute." Tony played with the keyboard. He had to give three different security identifications, but eventually MILLIE agreed that he was authorized to have the information.

"Yep. MILLIE can do that. So. But we can't count on Pres cooperating. Otherwise, we could just send a visitor in, and when all the lights go out, he walks Pres out through a horde of escaping convicts. With sirens going off, and fake messages of mayhem on the fifth floor, and like that. Look, it *might* work."

Delores sat down on the day bed. She was on her own second Irish coffee. "Tony, none of these ideas are foolproof, are they? And if we get caught, we're caught for keeps."

"I don't think there is any safe way. Anyway, we're just talking, right?"

"For the moment."

"It'd be nice if we had a plan where we could back out halfway, wouldn't it? So we could try something else."

"Yes?" Delores looked—wary.

"You think I'm trying to back out myself. Not so. What we can do is get them to move Pres outside. The whole cell block goes funny, right? The lights go on and off. The caterers aren't delivering anything but *escargot*. The hot water shuts down. The fire alarms go off."

"The doors between the men's and women's wings open—"

"Yeah! The orgy begins, and the guardroom doors lock. The air conditioning system goes on, then the heating system—"

"—With disinfectant smells—"

"Then air conditioning again. Ruining the orgy. All the prisoners have to be transferred out. We get someone else's computer system to send Pres anywhere we want, and break him out on the way."

"Do you think it'd work?"

"I dunno. I've given you four separate plans. What do you want from the court magician?"

"Aha! I saw that too."

Tony had noticed that her TV was on with the sound muted. "I saw it," he said. "I wonder if he wasn't right. We're a new feudalism. That's what we're doing now, isn't it? Snatching our man out of the king's hands."

Dolores nodded, and she didn't smile. She said, "Tony, what do they do at the courthouse if the power goes off?"

"I don't know. Let's see. No lights . . . no computer. They must have procedures for when the computer goes haywire."

"I'd think so."

"Then *none* of this will work. Sooner or later you

come up against human beings. That's the thing about people who think they hate computers. What they really hate is lazy programmers."

"Don't give me philosophy lessons, Tony! How do we get Pres out?"

"Brute force? How rough do we want to get? We could send Shapiro in with a briefcase full of shaped charges. Blow the wall and go. You don't need me for that. Or take thirty of the security force through . . . hold it a second." Tony summoned up the ground floor plan for the County Jail. "Through the kitchen, it looks like. So we send thirty men in through the kitchen and they shoot anyone who gets in the way. The trouble is, if it doesn't work we've got to bust thirty-one men out next time."

Delores was looking at him with active dislike. Lamely, Tony said, "Maybe we don't have to use bullets? Gas? Or . . . I could rig something sonic. A friend of mine came up with something for a novel. A jet engine running in a truck, with baffles behind the engine to put out sonic waves at terrific amplitude and . . ."

He paused a moment. "Be a nice girl."

"RIGHT HERE, BOSS," MILLIE said.

"Human Factors. Physiology. Sonic effects."

"TOO MUCH TO TALK ABOUT, BOSS."

"Show it to me."

Data flashed across the screen. Tony nodded. "Enough. Thanks."

"ANYTIME."

"At nine kilocycles," Tony said. "It kills everyone within a couple of blocks by ripping the walls of the capillaries apart. We'd want something else, a frequency to stun without killing. Don't know if—"

Her expression hadn't changed.

"Delores, this kind of thing isn't *done* any more. We can't just tie a rope to the bars of a window and whip up the horse."

"So you'll invent a whole new technology for the purpose? Tell me more, Dr. Zarkov."

Tony looked down at his empty mug, then up. "Turn on the sound," he said.

"What?"

"The TV, dammit! Be a nice girl. Television audio on." He was looking at a door on a concrete wall. The legend carefully printed on the door in magic marker said: "THINK OF IT AS EVOLUTION IN ACTION."

"Beaten to death at the foot of the stairs," Lunan's voice said. "The victim has not been identified, but it is established that he wrote the phrase not long before he was killed. No one knows why, but it seems to be the earliest appearance." There was a long shot of a pathetic bundle huddled on subway stairs. Tony recognized the clothing.

"Be a nice girl. Television audio off."

His eyes were still on the screen, and he was grieving. Delores asked, "What is it?"

"He died anyway. He didn't go off the high board, but we pulled him in and sent him off in the subway, and he got off at Flower Street and some muggers killed him. Him too. Dammit. The same night. Dammit."

"Tony?"

"We can bust Pres loose. One way or another. Did you know there's a cable from the Mayor's office to the White House? It's for Civil Defense. We can give the Emergency Alert and they'll have to evacuate the city. We snatch Pres in the confusion. But what do we tell him? Shall we tell him it's my fault? I designed it wrong. I shouldn't have let them talk me into flat walls."

"Tony, I don't know what you're talking about."

"Flat walls. The flat walls make Todos Santos look like a fort. Or a prison. Or a school. I could have done something else. Different shapes. It would have been as easy to defend, because you only have to defend the ground-floor level anyway. A pyramid, maybe. The damn leapers wouldn't have come flocking to a pyramid. Why should they?"

"Build a pyramid and we have no greensward," Delores said. "I remember that argument. Tony, you *wanted* a pyramid."

"Yeah. I should have fought harder."

"Why? Are you trying to bar Death from Todos Santos?"

Rand let out a great gust of a sigh. "Maybe. Maybe I am. But I put an undertaker in here . . . no, I didn't. It's one of the things I forgot. Barbara Churchward put an undertaker in a month after we opened. Financed him."

She had him by the shoulders and was trying to shake him. "People die, Tony. They die."

He laughed. "Do you know what Pres would say? He'd say I'm flying a starship in my head. He'd say I just planned to drop the deceased out of the airlocks."

"Would a Civil Defense Alert break Pres out?"

"Oh . . ." It was getting hard to think. In theory an Irish coffee was the perfect drink for this kind of work. It released your imagination without letting you sleep. "I'd think the rest of the United States would get really irritated if we did that. Besides, how would we get to him in the traffic jam? No, scratch that one."

She studied him for a moment. Then she stepped to the phone to order more drinks. They waited, and she watched him.

"Nothing up my sleeves," Tony said. "I'm out of ideas, Delores. Sorry."

"I didn't mean to shoot you down," she said.

Tony shrugged.

The drinks came. She handed him his, sipped from her own. Then she moved behind him and began to knead his neck and shoulders. She had strong hands. "You're all knotted up," she said. It felt good. His tension started to melt beneath her fingers. "Did I do that to you?"

"No."

"We've got to think of something. Maybe I

shouldn't have shot you down every time. Tony, what if I just ask for a dozen ways to get Pres out of the damned jail. And no remarks from me."

"It isn't that."

"Well, what is it, then?"

The edges of Delores' hands drummed on his shoulder muscles, almost viciously, but it felt good. It put a vibrato in Tony's voice. "I almost got seduced by my wife."

The rhythm broke. "What did you say?"

"Ex-wife. I went to see Pres, but visiting hours weren't until four o'clock. So I set it up with Genevieve to drop by and visit my son. I got there and Zachary wasn't home yet, it says here. I don't know what kind of a damned fool she thinks I am, but she could prove it in court. She had me taking off my clothes before she asked for any promises."

Delores said, "Take off your shirt and lie down on your belly. On the floor."

He did. She knelt above his hips and went to work on his lower back. Tony sprawled out with a long sigh. "I bet I impressed her, though," he said. "I not only walked out of her bedroom, I waited in the living room and drank coffee and made conversation until Zach came home. I think he saw some tension, though. He's eleven, and he's bright. He knows there's something wrong."

Delores was running her thumbs along the edges of his scapulae and on up to the base of his skull, digging in hard. "What does she want?"

"She wants to move in *here*. Over my dead body she will. When I wasn't getting rich and famous fast enough, she walked out on me, taking my son and custody of the money. Now there's no place safe outside . . . umph . . . except the place I built, you should pardon my natural egotism."

"She's not after more money?"

"She'd better not be! She had a sharp lawyer for the divorce. Claimed that since she put me through architecture and engineering school, she had a right to a percentage of my income forever. Got some kind of sliding-scale alimony deal. She lives damn well. Doesn't work. Well, to be fair about it, she's on a dozen civic committees and things. Toyed around with the FROMATES back when we were first building Todos Santos—"

"I wouldn't think an ecosimp would want to live here." Delores kneaded the shoulder muscles, working from outside in, then back out again.

"Ah, give her credit. She didn't stay with that crowd very long."

"Tony, it doesn't add up—"

"What doesn't?"

"If Zach is eleven—haven't you been here longer than that?"

"Yeah. What happened was I got through engineering school and wanted to study architecture. She didn't like that much. Wanted to quit work, start moving up in the world. But she put up with it for a while, until I got the chance to spend a year at Arcosanti—"

"That didn't pay enough?" Delores guessed.

"Didn't pay at all. I had to pay to go there. Paolo never did have a lot of money. So Genevieve walked out and started the divorce. While that was dragging through the courts I got lucky on the Orange County job. You may have heard about that. I was a new associate when the firm's senior people bought it in a plane crash, and I was able to convince the clients that I could finish the project, and I did, and Art Bonner liked the work and he talked to the Romulus Board . . ." His voice trailed off sleepily, and he yawned. "A week after the divorce was final, I ran into Genevieve at a cocktail party and one thing led to another." He writhed at the memory. "We had a lot of problems, but incompatibility wasn't one of them."

She let him chatter on while she pounded on his back.

"Zach isn't even mine," Tony said. "Well, I mean

he *is* mine. The blood types match, and you'd know it just looking at him anyway. But legally he was conceived out of wedlock, and I don't have any claim on him at all."

"I'm surprised you didn't remarry."

"Delores, the morning after Zach was conceived, a dozen Sierra Club people came to her apartment for an emergency strategy meeting. The emergency was Todos Santos. The goddam chapter president had a key to her apartment! I walked out screaming, and didn't take any phone calls. Zach was six months old before I knew he existed. Hey, that feels wonderful."

But talking about Djinn is *not* relaxing, he thought. Not at all. Damn, she almost had me today. I wonder if she's still as . . . oh, crap.

"Take off your pants."

He craned to look over his shoulder. "My *legs* are tense? Or—" He didn't bother to finish. Delores had taken off the tops of her hostess pajamas and was taking off the bottoms.

Tony rolled over. "I hope I remember how to do this," he said.

There was no pale skin on Delores, no mark of a bathing suit. Either she sunbathed nude on her porch, or not at all. Her skin was smooth and hot to the touch. "Now, that can hardly be called premature ejaculation," Tony said, "considering I've been thinking about it for several years now."

She laughed softly. "It's always better the second time. Do you feel like scratching my back?"

Any excuse to touch you, he thought. Should he say that? "Any excuse to touch you," and he ran his fingernails in large, luxurious circles, gradually descending. Djinn had always liked that. Bloody hell, what a time to think of her. But she's the only woman I've ever been really intimate with. Intimate, as opposed to—what? Is this intimacy?

She moved and made purring sounds when he

reached the swell of her buttocks. "Erogenous zone, mark," he said.

"Check. I bet I can find yours."

They made love again, and it *was* better. Good the first time, better the second, and how long could they keep that up? She left him flat on his back, checked their Irish coffees and found them cold, and ordered fresh.

One more datum for the bartender, Tony thought. He rolled on one elbow to watch her as she walked about the apartment, naked. She was as he had imagined her when she wore the orange hostess pajamas, except that she had been wearing a bra and panties. She came back, found him ready, spread him flat on his back to reverse their positions. They were at climax when the Irish coffees arrived, and the table *dinged* to announce the fact, and Tony started laughing and couldn't stop. Would Todos Santos be pleased that Rand and Delores—the court magician and the keeper of the privy seal—were in love? Likely they would.

He sipped Irish coffee and contemplated her back and the world was a nice place to live in.

"Where did you meet her?" Delores asked softly.

"Tenth grade algebra class—uh, who?"

"Never mind."

The sky was gray with dawn, and they'd finished another round of drinks, and she still hadn't mentioned Preston Sanders, and Tony Rand wasn't sleepy at all. "Let's lay down some rules," he said. "First, we want something we can back out of. Second, we don't mind using Todos Santos equipment, if that's what it takes, and if we can say it was stolen. Third, we involve as few people as possible. We use only people near the top."

She nodded. At no time did she seem puzzled at what he might be talking about. And then he knew. Their love affair was several hours old now, and it

was going just fine. But it had started when Delores
decided that Tony Rand had to be jarred loose from
his depression . . . somehow.

And it's still felony conspiracy.

Damn Lunan. Resident magician? Everyone who
saw that show would know who planned the
jailbreak. But if I stop planning now . . . or just keep
my mouth shut?

He was kneeling cross-legged on the bed, looking
down at his feet. He didn't have to look up. He knew
that Delores was waiting, cross-legged herself, the
mingled sweat drying on her, her expression serious,
waiting.

Dammit, nobody can command a genius to make
new inventions. Nader tried that on General Motors.
General Motors made a car that wouldn't start unless
the seat belt was fastened, and sometimes not even
then, and some woman got raped by four big men
because she couldn't start her car fast enough to drive
away from them, and it almost happened to Djinn
that time the purse snatcher chased her except she
had the spray can of toilet bowl cleaner—fah.

All I've got to say is—

"I've got part of an answer," he said, and now he
was committed. The dawn light showed her joy, and
she was beautiful. "I've got to talk about it with
someone. And I've got to know where they're holding
Pres. To the centimeter. My problem is, do I involve
you? You'd be a co-conspirator."

"Come *on*, Tony!" Her hands on his hands. "I'm in.
What are we going to do?"

He told her. She started laughing, and he joined
her.

XIII

'Tis not what man does which exalts him, but what man would do!

—Robert Browning, Saul

SCHEMES

Genevieve Rand woke to the realization that there was a man in her bed. It took her a moment to remember who it was, and she almost laughed aloud, because it wasn't all that usual. A woman with an eleven-year-old boy didn't get too many opportunities to begin with, and although Genevieve had—in her view anyway—far more than her share of sexual drive, she was also rather particular about her bed partners.

Arnold Renn had looked better in the dark. This morning his mouth was open and he snored gently. Genevieve tried to sit up, and her head pounded. Another unusual situation. Slowly it came back to her. Tony's visit. Damn. I almost had him. So close. Then that goddam pride, his and mine both, that always got in our way when what we both wanted to do was hop in the sack and make believe it was an old Chevrolet van stuck in a snowdrift in Minnesota

and we thought we'd better share blankets or we'd
freeze and neither one of us knew anything about
how to do it but we managed damned nicely anyway
thank you, and—

A long time ago.

But it wasn't Minnesota and we weren't in twelfth
grade, and yesterday wasn't an accident. Yesterday
would have been the most deliberate seduction in
history. If it had worked. And I almost had him. If I
could have kept my goddam mouth shut! Who was
the idiot who said honesty was the best policy? But—

But would it have been any good to get Tony in the
sack for a fast lay? Maybe it was better this way. I
didn't get him, but do I want him for a half-hour
stand with Zach coming home—

Arnold had showed up the morning after Zach was
conceived. If it hadn't been for Arnold Renn and his
goddam key to the apartment, Zach would have a
father.

Not fair. Arnold picked up the pieces when Tony
walked out. And he's never demanded anything, and
he was here to pick up the pieces last night, too. I
am a desirable woman. I am, dammit! I know I am.
But Tony sure didn't let me think so. He didn't say I
was a scheming old witch, but he might as well have.

Tony left, and Zach got an invitation to an all-night
camp-out treasure hunt, and the bottle of bourbon
was half-empty when Arnold dropped by for the first
time in a year, and even then he wouldn't have got
anywhere except that documentary came on and there
was Tony looking so flipping smug.

Under her breath she said, "Court magician,
forsooth!" and got up and went to the kitchen. Her
thoughts ran on: Court magician, and what am I?
And what is Zach? And even if Tony doesn't care for
me anymore (and he does, he does, damn it, I can
feel it, I know he does) he sure as hell ought to feel
something for Zach.

Nine A.M. Zach wouldn't be home before noon, so
there was time. She was damned if she'd let Zach find

Professor Arnold Renn in their apartment. Or anybody else, for that matter, but especially Renn. Zach would probably get out that pellet gun Tony gave him for his last birthday if he thought he could get at Dr. Renn. Zach tended to worship his father (and I've never tried to change that, it's not like a lot of divorced couples where there's competition for affection, I want Zach to like his father, but Tony's never thought about that and never will).

She began breakfast, and the smell of eggs Benedict brought Arnold sleepy eyed and unshaven to the table in an old dressing gown that he'd brought over a dozen years before and she'd never quite got around to throwing out even after Arnold married. He'd never looked less attractive, but Genevieve didn't resist when he kissed her. He was dutiful, not passionate, so there wasn't a fight, although she wouldn't have minded having a fight and getting him out of her life forever, except—

Except what? she wondered as she sat across the table from him. Except that he can make me feel wanted? There are other men who can do that, why keep this one around? He's persistent, I'll say that—

"Arnold, why did you come over yesterday?" she asked.

He looked puzzled. "I hadn't seen you in a while and I missed you. Why?" His puzzled look seemed genuine enough.

"Oh—I don't know. Tony was over yesterday."

"Was he, now? To see Zach?"

"Unfortunately."

Renn looked pained. "Genevieve, I have never understood your infantile infatuation with that man. You're worth a hundred of him."

She giggled. "You've made it clear you think he's got a negative worth. What's a hundred times a minus number?"

He shared her laugh. "You know what I meant." He was silent for a moment. "Genevieve—"

He'd tried to call her "Ginn" once, and it sounded like Tony's "Djinn," and she couldn't stand that.

"Genevieve, for God's sake, if you feel that way, why don't you take him back?"

"Take him back!" She laughed and felt rising hysteria and choked that off so that her voice was calm when she said, "What, and live in the termite hill?"

"If need be."

"I thought you Fromates hated that place."

"I'm not a Fromate. But yes, I disapprove of Todos Santos. For a lot of reasons which I'm sure you're tired of hearing me repeat. I was thinking of you. And your son. I've always loved both of you—"

I guess you have, she thought. At least enough to ask me to marry you. Several times, in fact.

And she'd often wondered: did Renn think Zach was his? He could have been. She'd slept with Renn the night before Zach was conceived. And again after Tony walked out. The blood tests made it certain, but Arnold didn't know about them. Was he still wondering?

"Are you going to see him again?" Renn asked.

"I doubt it."

"You ought to. Look, if there's anything I can do to help—"

"Greater love and all that? You'll help me trap my ex-husband? Regretfully, of course—"

"Something like that," he said. "I really do want you to be happy."

"What does Tina think of all this?"

Renn shrugged. "Tina doesn't interfere."

He'd tried to speak in a tone of indifference, but his voice was full of irony all the same. Genevieve wondered if the stories she'd heard were true, that Tina slept around, with Arnold's associates and sometimes even with students. She didn't know Arnold's friends anymore; not for years, since she'd quit the Movement. Open marriages were said to be quite common now, but Genevieve didn't know anyone who admitted living that way.

"Maybe if you moved into Todos Santos," Arnold said. "You'd be closer to him. Ah—if it's money, I think I could help you."

"Sure you could. Give me enough to become a stockholder in the Box." Her laugh was bitter. "What's the matter, Arnold? Giving up the crusades?"

"Damn it, I am trying to put you ahead of ideologies."

"I guess you are. That's sweet." Also just a little unbelievable, she thought. What has come over him? "Arnold, it's not money. Between what Tony sends and my aunt's legacy I probably could buy enough shares to live in Todos Santos. But Tony doesn't want me there. He'd see me as a threat. And, my friend, you don't know what trouble is until you've triggered Anthony Rand's paranoia! No, thanks."

"So you have to make him want you there," Renn said. "And you have something he wants—I presume he does want Zach? He believes Zach to be his?"

"Yes." Dammit, he knows Zach is his. Why didn't I say that?

"Then negotiate. Tell him you don't like it in Los Angeles. You're going a long way off, so far he'll never see Zachary again, unless you've got a better alternative. It's worth a try—"

"I've thought of that," she said, more to herself than to Renn. "Tony doesn't blackmail—"

"If you say it right, it isn't blackmail, it's an opportunity for him to talk you out of something." He stood. "If you'll excuse me a moment—"

"Sure."

Renn left the room. Genevieve drummed her fingers against the dinette table. It might work, it just might. I never wanted to put that kind of pressure on Tony, but why not? I'm not getting any younger. And if Zach is ever going to live in an arcology, he ought to grow up in one.

Might as well get dressed. She started toward the bedroom. Arnold was in the hall. "What in the world are you doing?" she asked.

"Oh, I dropped the telephone. Just checking to see that I didn't break anything. Looks all right." He tightened the earpiece cover and set the phone down.

"I will talk to Tony," Genevieve said. "And—I think you're more right than you know. If I can't bring him around, it probably would be better to leave Los Angeles."

"Hate to see you go," Arnold said. "But I can understand. Main thing is, whatever you do I'm on your side. Just don't forget that."

"I won't. You're sweet, Arnold. Thanks."

• • •

Tony Rand got off the elevator and went to the balcony edge. Midgard was a sight he always stopped for, even if it did trigger acrophobia.

Too bad Delores couldn't be here with him. But there'd be time . . . and they both had work to do, and always would. But being in love was a new experience (well, new again; he'd felt this way when he was married to Genevieve) and he didn't want to be parted from her even for a little while, even for this men-only luncheon . . .

He stood halfway between the floor of the Mall and the top of the pillar. Midgard was egg shaped, with view windows all around, and the bar at the small end. It was packed with men in three-piece suits.

They tended to form groups, small clumps of stability while others circulated with grim determination, maneuvering to be introduced. The older (and probably wealthier) men would find themselves in conversation with the younger newcomers, conversation punctuated with quick turns to greet old friends. Tony shook his head. There wouldn't be any real business conversation here.

A dozen hostesses circulated through the crowd; long-legged, pretty girls in their best party dresses, obviously models hired for the luncheon. There'd been a time when Tony would have looked at them wistfully and wondered how he could get to know one of them. Now he could be amused at the other men's efforts, which, when you came down to it, were futile anyway. These girls weren't for sale (although they certainly were interested in furthering their careers—).

His new-found objectivity was enlightening and wonderful.

But the room was far too crowded. There were elbows everywhere. The transparent walls helped dispel feelings of claustrophobia, but they did nothing to alleviate bruises and spilled drinks. Conversations flowed around him, none interesting enough to catch his attention, although it made Tony feel good to find that he could understand what the people next to him were saying. The sound-absorbent cones in the ceiling worked perfectly, keeping down echoes and the general noise level despite the overcrowding.

In fact, he thought, maybe they work too well: There was a chap yelling his head off at a friend not more than five meters away, and the friend was ignoring him. Deaf? Rude, as the yeller obviously thought? Tony went over to find out, fighting his way to a place next to the man being yelled at. He turned and listened.

"Sam, goddammit, I know bloody well you can hear me!"

Tony could just make out the words. He shouted back, "No, he can't hear you." To make it more effective he made it look as if he were screaming at the top of his lungs, knowing the shouter wasn't going to catch on. Then he pushed his way across again. "See? You can't get his attention from that far away. It always surprises Angelinos on their first visit to Midgard."

"Ah. Okay." He looked at Tony, puzzled, then in comprehension. "Rand. The court magician. You design this place?"

"Some of it. The sound absorbers. Not the rest of Midgard, although I wish I had."

"It's nice," the man agreed. He put out his hand. "Joe Adler. I'm with Disney Studios. I was admiring the holos." He pointed up to the center of the ceiling, where a probe's-eye view of Saturn hung in splendor. The view changed as the probe moved toward the Rings, wide-angle views of the Saturnian system alternating with closeups of the intricate Ring structure, panning over to the twisted streamers of the F-ring, then back to wide angle. "That's damned nice."

"Thanks. That part's mine too. When the probe gets past, the lunch is officially over."

"Good work. You ever think of consulting for the studios? You could make a bundle."

Tony grinned. "In my copious free time. I take it this is your first visit?"

Adler nodded. "Yeah, I just got promoted. One of the studio brass suggested I should contribute to Big Brothers. Suggested it strong enough that I called in and reserved a ticket the same day." He gestured at the crowd. "How do we get a drink?"

"Allow me," Tony said. He waved toward a waitress to get her attention and to let her see his gold-edged badge. She wriggled through the crowd like an exotic dancer, never touching anyone, took their drink orders, and vanished. In an astonishingly short time she reappeared with a tray.

"Guess you are a magician," Adler said. "There—My God!"

"What?" Tony demanded.

"Someone just fell past the window!" There were a lot of people clustered around the windows now. They chattered excitedly, but there was no aura of panic.

Damned strange, Tony thought. He pushed his way through the crowd, heedless of custom or good manners or anything else. *Another leaper? Or Fromates—*

"There goes another one," one of the businessmen shouted. "Wow!"

A human-sized Golden Plover with irridescent feathers fell past in a headlong swan dive. Tony reached the window just in time to see the diver brought up short by the cables that trailed out behind. He—no, she—had almost hit the Mall deck before the cables had completely stretched. Now the girl bounced through the air, arms widespread, held by a pair of enormous shock cords, a riot of brilliant color. Seconds later she was joined by a boy dressed as a California condor.

"Bungee divers," someone said.

Aha, Tony thought. They do that—where? Mexico? South Seas? Somewhere. Dive off tree platforms and use vines to stop themselves. He looked up to see that Adler had followed him to the window. "They ought to warn us about entertainment like that!" Adler said.

"Damned right. I nearly had a heart attack." But it was damned interesting. Wonder why we never had anyone do that before? Maybe it'll catch on.

Adler drained his glass. "There sure are a lot of prizes."

Tony nodded. The luncheon included a raffle. The biggest prize sat in the middle of the room, roped off, crowding the bar area even further. Everyone was crowding to the window, so Tony made his way to the center area and examined the machine: a floatcycle. He'd never seen one of the two-person ground effect vehicles up close, but the ads said it would go over any land or swamp terrain as well as calm water. There were other prizes around the walls: portable televisions, expensive clothing, a hang glider, jewelry, and half a dozen kinds of home computers. He turned back to see that he'd lost Joe Adler to one of the hostesses. She was an Angelino, Tony noticed. She'd probably seen the Disney Studio label on his badge . . .

* * *

As usual there were too many at the table, so that Tony's elbows were jammed into his sides. He didn't catch the names as people were introduced (or if he did he didn't remember them) so he had no idea of whom he was talking to, but they did seem to admire the decor, particularly the holograms.

"I'm surprised to find somebody like you sitting with us," the beefy man across the table said. "I saw Art Bonner in the bar."

Tony smiled and tried to be friendly. "Corporate policy. When we have outside guests, they like us to mingle."

"Makes sense."

Generally does, Tony thought. Of course I'm not the world's best ambassador, but what the hell. And it was fun talking about the holograms . . .

A couple of radio comics had been imported to raffle off the prizes. They also told jokes. Fairly rough ones—

"I wasn't too sure about our welcome. I don't know if Floyd noticed, but they brought us in through Accessway 9, Level 18, past the hydrogen pipe—"

"—and the big sign that says, 'Do your bit for human evolution.' I haven't been so nervous since the Reverend Jones invited me to Guyana for a cool drink."

"*Another* example of evolution in action, I suppose. Neverthestill, here we are, once again, to help redistribute the wealth—"

"Taking from the rich to give to the rich."

"But first, these updates for those of you who like to keep posted on what's happening outside these walls." The comics whipped sheets of notes from inside pockets.

"We're still paying taxes."

"We're still *complaining* about paying taxes."

"Death and taxes and a word from our sponsor. Hey, you people seem to have *solved* taxes, how're you doing on—"

"*Jake!*"

Uncomfortable laughter.

"—Sponsors? Hey, speaking of sponsors, James Shapiro would like to update you on another aspect of the outside world: the great work being done by Big Brothers of . . ."

"Those birds have been retired for years," Tony said.

The man to his left chuckled. "Sure. And who do you suggest we get?"

Tony frowned. "Ah. Yeah, I see. Jake and Floyd have been retired long enough that we remember them from before we built Todos Santos—"

"Exactly. While modern radio people are known mostly to freeway drivers. Look, I'm Louis Charp—" Quick handshake. "I did a lot of the work setting this up. Jake and Floyd have been good to us, we'd probably bring them as guests, but how *can* we get a little more current?"

Jake and Floyd began raffling off prizes, with the assistance of some of the ladies. Tony mulled over the problem. What stars would Angelinos and Saints have in common?

Louis Charp asked, "Do you still watch TV? Soaps, situation comedies?"

"Not those, no. They don't seem to make much sense. News . . . well, mostly in-house news, actually. Even the *Tonight Show* monologue was pretty cryptic last time I watched. We get movies on the cable," Tony realized suddenly. "That new guy in *Star Wars Eight,* the sarcastic one who keeps poking holes in Han Solo's physics?"

"Rip Mendez. Mmm . . . maybe. He might go for it. He's got an adopted son."

The table emptied, and Tony was able to move again. He stretched with a sigh of gratitude and ordered another cognac. For the moment his mind was clear of problems. He'd half finished the cognac when he became aware of a man standing expectantly near his chair. Tony didn't recognize him.

"You're Tony Rand, aren't you?" the man asked. "I recognize you fron Lunan's documentary."

Tony sighed. It was flattering to be recognized, but there was a price to that. "Yeah, I'm the court magician."

The man grinned and put out his hand. "George Harris," he said. "We've got a mutual friend—"

Tony frowned. He was sure he'd heard the name before.

"Preston Sanders," Harris said. "My cell mate on weekends."

"Have you escaped from the jail?" Tony asked.

"In a manner of speaking—"

Tony's mood was completely shattered now. "How?"

"I just walked out—they let me out, Sunday night to dawn Saturday. Except for holidays. Holidays I go back in." He explained the work furlough program. "But weekends I room with Pres."

Like a bloody omen, Tony thought. "How are they treating you?"

"Not too bad, now. Mind if I join you?" Harris didn't wait for an answer. He sat next to Tony and caught the waiter's eye. "Two brandies. Anyway, it was pretty rough before they moved me in with Sanders, but now it's all right."

"Could you take something to Pres for me?"

"Nothing you couldn't send him through the Sheriff's office," Harris said. He grimaced. "They search us going in. Why, did you want to send something? I'd be glad to help, anything I could do to help that fine young man—"

It wasn't hard to draw Harris out. He liked to talk. He wanted to tell Tony about his electrical supply business in between stories about the jail, but after a while Tony had a good picture of the jail schedule.

The weekend schedule, he reminded himself. They might do things differently the rest of the time. *So it'll be a weekend,* he thought, and his heart thudded once, hard.

"I try to cheer him up," Harris was saying. "These things don't last. Look at Watergate. Forgotten. And all those big Mafia scandals. Same thing. People don't remember after a while. Of course that was pretty drastic, killing those kids, and Jim Planchet keeps things stirred up good, but I don't talk to Pres about that. Mostly I try to get him to keep in shape. Exercise. If he'd work out good every day, he could leave that place in better shape than he went in. Look at the bright side, that's what I tell him."

"Pres gets pretty moody," Tony said.

"Boy, and how, it's all I can do to get him talking—"

"He's also polite."

"Yeah, he sure is—hey, it was great meeting you. I've got to get back to the office now. Could I come see you sometime? I'd sure like to show you those new computerized light switch units. I can make you a hell of a price in the quantities you'd buy—"

"I'll call you sometime," Tony said. "Thanks for telling me about them." They shook hands and Tony waited until Harris had left, then picked up the untouched brandy that Harris had ordered for him.

His hands were shaking as he drained the glass.

XIV

There is *nothing*—absolutely nothing—half so much
worth doing—as simply messing about in boats.

—Water Rat in *The Wind in the Willows*

PERCEPTIONS

Barbara Churchward smiled at the couple across the
table from her. "Then it's settled," she said. "I don't
think you've made a mistake."

"I hope not," Rebecca Flan said. She seemed
nervous.

Which, Barbara thought, she had every right to be.
Ted and Rebecca Flan had just bet everything they
owned on a long shot. Of course it was a long shot
for Barbara Churchward, too, but she was used to
that sort of thing. Not all her gambles had to
succeed. Just enough to cover the rest and make a
bottom line profit. It was different for Ted and
Rebecca.

"We'll have the equipment installed by next
Monday," Barbara said. "I've found space for you not
far from your apartment."

"When could we move in?" Rebecca asked.

Barbara stared thoughtfully at the ceiling for a

moment. "Tomorrow after four," she said. "The Services people will have everything ready then."

"You make things happen so fast," Ted Flan said. "I wouldn't have believed it—"

Barbara shrugged. "If it's worth doing at all, there's no point in being slow about it. Quite the opposite. The sooner you get into the market, the bigger your share will be." She gave him her best smile. "And I'm certain it will be a large share."

"I think so, too," Rebecca said. "I always thought Ted could be rich, if he just had a chance—" .

Which just might be true, Barbara thought. Ted Flan was a brilliant man with insufficient confidence in himself. It wasn't that he didn't have the drive. He worked himself silly. With his energy properly directed—

Just now, though, the problem was to get rid of them. The deal was made, the papers signed, and there was more work to do. But of course the Flans weren't the kind of people who could leave drinks half-finished in an expensive place like this. Normally she'd never have brought them. The Inferno Bar was hardly the place to do business. Midgard was much better. You could leave people to enjoy Midgard and they'd never notice you'd gone. But Midgard was taken up by the Big Brothers' fund raiser, and Rebecca had wanted to see Inferno.

It was worth seeing. One whole wall was a looped hologram tape of Antarctica: icy crags eroded by winds laced with fine snow, all in glare white. Another showed holograms of volcanos: rivers of lava cascading down into the sea, fiery eruptions of flame and smoke into the night, then pan downward to towns and farms and fields covered with gray ash. (And in the midst of death there is life, Barbara noticed: Among the ruins of a forest there were tiny green shoots peeking above the thick layers of gray.)

"Great place if you dig bleak," Ted said.

"There are those who like it," Barbara said. She nodded to acknowledge a greeting from a gathering of men in three-piece suits grouped around a table near the bar. Two had shed their jackets and were arm wrestling.

Others came to join them.

"When does anyone get their work done?" Rebecca asked. "It looks like the whole business community—"

Barbara laughed. "It very nearly is. The Big Brothers' lunch was today. Annual event. They figure they'll never get any work done because they're half-looped. So why not finish the job? Including, I see, the General Manager of this place. Uh—if you could manage to excuse me, I think I'd better join him."

"Oh, sure, not at all," Ted said. He stood quickly.

Rebecca joined him reluctantly. "We haven't seen the casino—"

"Plenty of chances for that," Ted said. "We'll be living here."

Yes, Barbara thought. And I wonder just how much interest in the casino Rebecca has? MILLIE. Monitor financial activities at Inferno for new residents Ted and Rebecca Flan. Notify me of any activity over two hundred dollars.

"After all," Ted was saying, "we wouldn't want to see everything in one day—"

"I suppose not," Rebecca said.

Barbara stood and offered her hand. "I think you'll be very happy here. Good luck."

They shook hands, and Ted turned away. Then he stopped. "Oh. I forgot." He fished in his coat pocket and came up with a key which he held out to Barbara. "You will take care of Katie, won't you? She's something special—"

"We'll find her a good home," Barbara said. She put the key in her purse and watched them leave the bar. When they were gone, she turned to go back to her office.

"Barbara—"

Nuts, she thought. No escape now. Tony Rand had

seen her, and he looked a good bit more than half-looped. "Hi, Tony."

"Hi. I'd like to ask you a favor."

"Oh? Sure, if I can—"

"It's kind of complicated," Tony said.

"Well, I was planning on working—"

"It's important," Tony said. He led her toward a table.

Barbara watched analytically as she followed. He's part drunk and damned nervous, she thought. I'd better see what he wants.

Rand waved at the waitress, and moments later she brought him a Scotch and a Pink Lady for Barbara.

"Sometimes this place is just a little too efficient," Barbara said. "I didn't really need a drink." Nor, for that matter, did you.

"Relax," Rand said. "You can't work today. Nobody sober to interact with."

"You've a point there," she said. The arm wrestling game was continuing loudly—an Angelino deputy district attorney against one of Shapiro's assistants. "What's your problem, Tony?"

"Hah. I've got a dozen problems. Including Art's latest idiocy—"

"Yes?"

"Oh, you know—"

"No, I don't, Tony," Barbara said.

"But you have to know. You're on the management council. He has to tell you. It's in his charter." He gave her a wink. "You know—"

She let her voice show impatience. "Tony, I don't have the least idea of what you're talking about, and I don't have time to play games."

"But—" He looked up at the ceiling. "The cones work. I don't think anyone can hear us—"

"Tony, if you're about to say something Art wants kept secret, I'd advise you not to. There are Angelinos all over."

"Yeah. I know." He tossed off the Scotch and

waved at the waitress. "That wasn't the favor I wanted anyway."

"Good." MILLIE. Link me to Bonner. "Art, your court magician is in his cups and wants to babble all our secrets."

"I have another problem. I'm afraid of my wife."

"What?"

"Ex-wife. She called me. Wants to talk seriously with me. If I don't give in to her demands, she moves to New York and takes our son with her."

"Barbara, I see you. Want me to come over?"

"Not just yet. But you better think of a way to get him out of here."

"That's easy. Give me ten minutes and he'll be gone."

"What are her demands, Tony?"

"She wants to live here, for starters," Tony said. "And I think she wants me."

"And you don't want her."

"No. Good Lord no. Not now."

"But you don't want her to move to New York."

"No."

"Why not?"

"I don't—I just don't."

Tell me about Genevieve Rand.

Data poured into her mind. She hadn't time to digest it all, but one thing was obvious. "I suppose it's the boy?"

"Yes—"

"Are you being fair to him, Tony?" Barbara asked. "You're building your starship, and you're leaving your son behind—"

"You didn't have to be so damned blunt about it."

"Sure I did. That's what's bothering you, isn't it?"

"Yes, but I don't know what to do about it. Barbara, the only way he could live here is to have Djinn live here too. He's legally hers, not mine."

"Yes, Tony, I know. But I don't know why you're so dead set against her being here."

Tony was quiet for a long time. Barbara shook her

head. She'd never understood Rand, but he seemed stranger than usual today.

"If—" he hesitated. "If I had to see her every damn day I'd probably be married to her in a year."

"But if—Tony, if you think you'd marry her again, why would that be so bad?"

"Because she's lived off me for all these damn years," Tony said. "And she never did a damn thing for me all that time. Where was she when I needed her? Now it's the other way around."

"So you're making her pay, but you get no satisfaction from it because it hurts your son."

"You sure have a way with words," Tony said. He brooded for a moment. "But I guess it's true."

"Then it's simple enough. Bring her here and put her on the other side of the building. Todos Santos is a big place."

"What would she do here?"

Barbara digested more information. "She seems to have done all right as a civic leader. Quite a natural organizer. I expect she'd do well. Probably be a neighborhood representative within a couple of years—oh. That's the problem, isn't it? You think she'd do too well."

"I'm not that petty."

Oh yes you are, my friend, Barbara thought. I wonder just how long that little dilemma has been eating away at you. "Art, I really think you should get Tony out of here soon."

"I've sent for reinforcements. Shall I join you now?"

"One moment more." "Tony, what do you want me to do?"

"I want you to talk to her. Negotiate for me. You're the sharpest negotiator I know."

"Sure," Barbara said. "I expect I am. But for all my fabulous skills, Tony, what can I do? You don't know what you want, so how could I get it for you?"

"I don't know. You could do something. Better than I can." He hunched his shoulders forward and stared into his drink. "Let her in. I won't be here anyway."

"Tony, what in the world are you talking about?"

"Nothing—Hello, Art. Enter the Grand High Executioner."

"Art, what in the devil is wrong with him?"

"I told him to plan a jailbreak. He's scared."

"!"

"Contingency plan."

"Sorry I couldn't be with you earlier," Bonner said. "Big powwow with MacLean Stevens." He shrugged. "Nothing we could really talk about, of course. The situation's cut and dried. Planchet wants blood, and Mac's got to supply some."

"Ours," Tony said. "Maybe he'll get more than he expects. I've been looking up the law on conspiracy—"

"That will do." Bonner's voice was edged with ice. "You're drunk. Take the afternoon off."

"Oh, yass, baas. Take the day off. Shuffle off, shuckin' and jivin' all the way—"

"This won't do at all," Barbara thought. "Rough and smooth?"

"Right."

She put her hand on Tony's arm. "Art's right, we've all had too much." She pointed to the low table by the bar. The arm wrestlers were still at it, and there was a five-way conversation over their heads, with no one listening to anyone. "And we're the soberest people here!"

"Hi, Tony. Mr. Bonner." Delores came to the table. Bonner stood.

"Hell, you sent for her, too," Rand said. "Christ, no more privacy than a goldfish. There's something wrong with the whole idea of this place. People can't live like this."

"Oh, hush," Delores said. She sat next to Rand. "What did you expect Mr. Bonner to do, send you home alone?" She grinned. "I've got the afternoon off, too. Can we think of something to do?"

Rand rubbed his head. "Maybe we could—"

"That's the spirit. Let's go." Delores stood and dragged Tony up. "Gee whillikers, Mr. Wizard, you walk funny—"

"Oh, shut up," Rand said, but he walked with her out of the room.

"Whew."

"Yeah."

"What did he want from you? He spent long enough telling you."

"He wants me to negotiate with his ex-wife. He wants—"

"STOP!"

The command was a shout in Barbara's head. Involuntarily she put her hands over her ears. "My God, Art, don't *do* that!"

"Sorry." Bonner looked nervously around the room.

"Are you all right? Has everyone gone insane here?"

"No."

He was looking at her but not seeing her. She'd never seen Art Bonner like that. Indecisive. Something really strange was happening—

"Let's go somewhere," Art said. "And—keep the conversation verbal and trivial for a while."

"Sure—where do you want to go? Your office? Mine?" My place or yours. Hah. That'll be the day. I wonder what it would be like? She felt his hand on her arm, and she stood, letting him guide her past an erupting Mount St. Helens. His grip was firm. She couldn't remember if he'd ever touched her before. They'd always been wary of each other, two executives with something like telepathy, guarding their thoughts when they were together, never a man and a woman . . .

He led her onto a crowded pedway. Todos Santos people automatically moved aside to make room for them, but the Angelinos either didn't recognize them or didn't care. No one spoke to them, and they rode in silence.

Strange. Weird, Barbara thought. We could talk without being overheard, only he doesn't want to talk through MILLIE. Something of his sense of urgency kept her from using MILLIE at all, and she rode through the crowded Mall, silent, feeling cut off from the world and alone for the first time in years.

• • •

The guard at the exit gate stared in surprise. "Don't you want someone to go with you, Mr. Bonner?"

"Thanks, Riley, we'll be all right. Going to look at some property. MILLIE can find us if we're needed," Bonner said. He led Barbara out to the subway platform.

"Art, what in hell are we doing?" she asked when they were away from the gate.

"Getting out of Todos Santos for a while."

"Where are we going? I have to tell my staff—"

"No. Please. Not this time. We won't be gone long."

She looked at him intently. "Are you drunk?"

"A little. Has nothing to do with this."

"All right. But where are we going?"

"Anywhere. Restaurant. Coffee shop. Someplace random—"

"Boy, when you flip out, you really do it, don't you?" A train rushed into the station and stopped. They hopped on it and found seats. Bonner's face was a deadpan, no visible emotion, a study in self-control, and that was a little frightening too. "Any preference on where we get off?" she asked.

"No, but let's make it a couple of stops more."

"Sure." She looked thoughtful for a second. "I know where we can go."

"Fine. Lead the way."

Meaning don't say it out loud? she wondered. Well, I won't. The train pulled into the Marina station, and she waited until the last moment, then grabbed Art's hand and pulled him. "Let's go," she said. They ran out just as the car doors closed.

She was laughing as they went up the steps. "Were you really worried about someone following us? Because I think I took care of that—"

"You sure did. But no, I wasn't especially worried about that."

They came out to bright daylight a hundred yards from the ocean. To their right was a long stretch of beach, with dozens of Angelinos playing in the surf, doing exercises on swings and jungle gyms, or just lying around on the beach.

"Nice idea," Art said. "I haven't been for a walk on the beach in ages."

"Actually I had something else in mind," Barbara said. She led him off to the left, into the maze of slips and piers and docks, through a forest of sailboat masts, searching for a slip number. "This way," she said. They walked out a long pier and stopped in front of a big single-masted boat. The name painted across the stern was *Katherine III*.

"What's this?"

"I just bought it," Barbara said. "Well, for the company, but I've got the keys. Want to help me aboard? My skirt's a little tight to climb that rail—"

"Sure," he said. "Uh—those heels aren't going to work so well on teak decks."

"Right." She took them off, then let Art lift her over the plastic-coated wire guard rail. "Pretty boat," she said.

Art nodded. "Forty-foot motor sailor. You could sail around the world in this. You *bought* it?"

"More or less. I took over the payments." She took out the key and unlocked the companionway. A ladder led down to a large saloon cabin fitted out with wide padded berths that served as seats along both sides of a cockpit table. Art followed her down.

She looked around in the mahogany lockers. "Aha. JTS Brown," she said, holding up a bottle of bourbon. "Or should I make coffee?"

"A little bourbon won't hurt," Bonner said. He found glasses in a fitted locker, and a small refrigerator below supplied cold water. They sat at the table and Barbara poured.

"Typical story," Barbara said. "Young couple, bright guy doing well writing software for a computer company. Making lots of money, but they got in over their heads. Cars, fancy apartment, furniture, this boat—so when his boss reneges on promotions, what can the poor bastard do? He can't go start his own company, not owing all that money." She grinned. "So I surprised hell out of the boss and set them up in business."

"And the boat?"

"Distraction," Barbara said. "Look, we set them up, and we're only taking 40 percent of the company. The rest is his. We're risking a lot of capital—so I damned well insist that he risks everything he's got. And I do mean everything. Gives him a powerful incentive."

"Lot of pressure on a young family," Bonner said. He twisted his face into what might have been a grin and might have been something else. "I know what pressure can do. To a person, and to a marriage."

"No pressures," Barbara said. "He's got his office, a DEC computer, some lab space, a C3 apartment, and six months in Commons. He doesn't owe anybody a cent and they can't starve. All part of the package. Now all he's got to do is produce. And I know damned well he can do that, because most of what BFK Associates sells was written by him—"

"So you think of everything. How many of these deals go sour?"

"Not enough of them."

"Eh?"

She shrugged. "A low failure rate means I'm not taking enough risks. I'm supposed to take risks. My failure rate is down to—Oh, DAMN YOU, Art Bonner! We're out of range and I can't remember and I don't like being cut off from my memory! What is going on?"

He sipped at his bourbon. "What did Tony want you to talk to his ex-wife about?"

She shook her head. "Art, I won't play games any longer. I want to know what's happening."

"Yeah. Hard to know where to start. You remember that reporter, Lunan? You and the PR people thought it would be a good idea to turn him loose—"

"Yes, and I don't think that documentary hurt us a bit."

"Me either," Bonner said. "But that wasn't what I was trying to say. He had an offer of his own. Information for interviews. I bought it."

Art paused and sipped at his drink. "The information was that a Fromate UCLA professor named Arnold Renn furnished the Planchet kid the data he needed to break into Todos Santos. Okay, so where did Renn get the data? We don't exactly advertise those codes."

She felt a tingle at the base of her spine. "Art, where does Tony fit into this?"

"I had Security watch Professor Renn. He spent yesterday night in Genevieve Rand's apartment."

"But—"

"Not the first time, either," Bonner said. "Genevieve and Renn go back a long way, to before Rand's divorce. She put in a year with an eco-freak outfit Renn was president of. That was back before there were any Fromates. Another interesting little item. Six years ago, Tony brought his son, Zach, to Todos Santos . . ."

"Well, of course he would."

"Yeah," Bonner said. "And he took the kid to Medical and had them take blood samples. Zach and himself. What he wanted was complete blood types. Rh factor, M & N factors, the whole damned works."

She frowned and started to frame a question in her mind, but there was no response.

"The only reason for that kind of test is to establish

paternity," Bonner said. "Which he did. Insignificant probability that the boy could be anyone's but his."

"But he did want to find out," Barbara said. "All right. Fine. But—Art, you don't really think Tony Rand is giving information to the Fromates."

"I don't know what to think. They'll be back, Barbara. With real bombs, as soon as they know enough about our new defenses."

"Yes, but Tony?"

"I'm scared to think. Barbara—suppose he is? He understands MILLIE better than we do! And MILLIE knows almost everything we know. So when you mentioned Genevieve just after Tony was acting crazy, all I could think of was to get the hell out and go where nobody could listen to us, not even MILLIE." He grinned. "Sorry I was so melodramatic about it, but I really was scared to think about it. I never felt that way before."

"I feel it too," Barbara said. "I think it's called panic. I don't blame you for wanting to run. But— Art, I thought no one could get at our files."

"Any security system is vulnerable. Especially to the one who set it up in the first place."

"Yeah, but come on, Art. I don't believe Tony is a traitor, and you don't either."

"No. And he's not usually a blabbermouth. But I imagine it's hard to keep secrets from your wife, even if you're not living with her. What did he want you to talk to her about, anyway?"

"She wants to live in Todos Santos. According to Tony, she's wanted to for a long time, but he won't let her. Now—" She repeated the conversation she'd had with Tony.

"She's putting the screws on, and Tony doesn't want to talk to her," Bonner said thoughtfully. "Which may not mean anything, and may mean—"

"I'm sure not. Certainly, she could be blackmailing him, but Tony wouldn't have told her about the security codes."

"Renn got them from somewhere," Bonner said. "And Tony's acting damned funny—"

"I'd act funny too if you told me to plan a jailbreak."

"Would you?" He was perfectly serious.

She had to think about that one. "No. I guess I wouldn't. Are we going to break Pres out?"

Art spread his hands. "Got any better ideas? Only—if Tony's compromised, so is the plan." He poured more drinks, for himself and for her.

"Should we be drinking any more?"

"Feeling it?"

"Some," she admitted.

"Good." He stood up, his eyes on hers.

So here it comes, she thought. Or not. It's all up to me. All I have to do is make some funny remark. Or say anything at all. He's scared to death! Of me? Why not? I've been a bit afraid of him myself.

She stood. Without her heels her head was just at the level of his chin and she had to tilt her head up to look into his eyes. They were very close in the narrow cabin. She stood, waiting, wondering what he was going to do. It was a funny situation, Art Bonner, decisive manager of Todos Santo, the man they all expected to be God, standing there trying to get up the nerve to touch his colleague. . .

Maybe we'd better leave. Things won't ever be the same between us if we—

He put his hand on her shoulder. His easy grin was back. "Damnation," he said. "I kept hoping for a wave or something to throw us together."

She giggled. "The boat's awfully steady—" Then, laughing, she threw herself at him. He caught her easily.

XV

extrasensory perception. *Abbr.* ESP Perception by supernatural or other extraordinary means.

—*American Heritage Dictionary*

SECRETS

It was long past noon, and Cheryl had started getting dressed, when she found the knife. Lunan was still in bed, a little too happy to move yet, watching her. She pulled his pants out of the tangle of their clothing and was ready to toss them to him, but she noticed the weight of his belt buckle.

First she studied the big, ornate steel buckle. Then she pulled on it, experimentally. She found the catch and it came out of the belt and became the handle on a five-inch blade.

"That's one you didn't show me," she said.

Lunan chuckled. "You were nervous enough."

She nodded. "It felt . . . dangerous. Walking all that way from the garage and *knowing* there were no guards watching. Why do you park that far away?"

"Well—"

"I know, you want the car safe, you told me. But

how can you feel safe, walking back? Is that what the knife is for? A *knife?*"

"I've never had to use it yet."

"Suppose the mugger has a gun?"

Lunan sat up grinning. "Does being nervous turn you on?"

Cheryl grinned back. *There's no way she could deny it,* Lunan thought. *No way at all. She was turned on last night, and that's what did it.*

"It felt . . . adventurous. I've never done anything like this before," she said. She shook her head, curls flowing. "Like something out of the past . . . something starring Clint Eastwood, with enemies on all sides of us and only one strong man to protect me."

I ain't Clint Eastwood, and I ain't all that strong, but I'll accept it—

They had arrived in late afternoon. He had showed her the locks on his doors, the cheap stereo equipment in plain sight, the good equipment all hidden, the shotgun behind the sofa, watching her reactions. He had assumed she would need soothing, but the opposite was true. It had excited her. They had made love at once. Twice. And they only pulled themselves out of bed to cook dinner.

That had fascinated her, watching him playing at impressing her by playing chef. She'd never cooked a meal in her life. He'd finished in time; they ate during the broadcast of Lunan's documentary on Todos Santos.

For I am your bold deceiver, thought Lunan. *Poor Miss Bailey, unfortunate Miss Bailey! Todos Santos had no place for the unabashed cocksman . . .*

She'd disagreed with some of what his television image was saying. They'd argued far into the night. He'd gleaned more than enough material to start another documentary. Dan Rather, watch out!

But her attitude was . . . suggestive. He was going to have to brace Bonner again, and soon. If the rest of the Saints felt the way she did, then Thomas

Lunan wanted in. The next step Todos Santos took could make Thomas Lunan famous. He watched her, a pretty but not beautiful girl, attractive but not irresistible, and totally unaware that she was the key to the riches of the Indies . . .

In that sense alone, Cheryl Drinkwater was the best thing that had ever happened to him.

When she tossed him his pants, he bowed to reality and began getting dressed.

She stopped in the doorway as they were leaving. "What?" he asked. She was studying him closely.

"I had a lovely time, Tom. But I don't think I'll be back."

Lunan had expected this. Sure. Not bloody likely you would. But we both got what we wanted . . . "You'd be very welcome."

She shook her head. "I know," Lunan said. "It was an adventure. You don't *have* to repeat an adventure. But maybe you'll change your mind." He knew that she wouldn't.

An angel had gone slumming. No more than that. But—how much variety could there be among the Todos Santos boys? Any Angelino was bound to be an interesting experience for Cheryl. She's cut off from the mainstream. One of us is . . .

Anyway, I tried to make it interesting for her. God knows it was for me, and I owed her that, maybe. But if I'm a little miffed, she's never going to know it—

• • •

Barbara woke in semi-darkness. The dock lights were on outside, and some of the yellow light filtered past the curtains on the cabin windows and fell on the cabin table, making strange patterns on her neatly folded tailored suit and striped panties. Her brassiere atop the pile didn't look like clothing at all. She moved lazily, snuggling closer to him, and felt his arm tighten around her.

"Your poor arm must be asleep," she whispered.

"It's all right—"

"Why didn't we think of this before?"

He chuckled softly. "I've thought about it for five years."

"Hmm. Me too. But not quite like this—"

The smile was still in his voice. "No. I wondered what—"

"Yes. Well, we'll just have to find out, won't we?" She giggled. "Here we are, both of us wondering what telepathic lovemaking would be like, and we still don't know."

"We can find out."

"Or not," she said. "Art—are you sure we want to continue this? We've stolen an afternoon. I'll bet they're going crazy back there, wondering where we are. But they're wondering, now. Do we want them to *know*?"

"Do you care?"

My darling, I don't care one damn bit, but then I'm a bitch with no reputation anyway. You're the one who's got to worry. "Do you?"

"Right now I don't even want to go back."

"Now just one minute, Mister! That's not even funny as a joke."

"Why not?" His voice was serious, and that was just a little frightening. "We're both rich. It's not as if we need our jobs—"

"The hell we don't," she said.

He was quiet for a moment. "Yeah. That's the part Grace could never understand. That I could love my job and still love her—"

"Now you've gone and said it."

"Said what?"

"That word. Love. Is this love, Art?"

"They call it making love."

"Damn you, don't make jokes. This is serious."

"Is it?"

"It could be."

He was quiet for a long time. "Do you mean that?"

"Yes."

"Good."

"I think we've been in love for years," she said. "If love is sharing and caring and respecting."

"Hmm. Love without intimacy."

"We haven't needed intimacy. We can get all of that we want, anytime we want," she said. "And have."

"Sure, but it's not the same, these affairs—"

"No." She nestled closer to him, then bit his nipple.

"Ouch. Turn about's fair play—"

"Not yet. Let's go back. They really will be worried about us. And you've got a jailbreak to plan."

"Sigh. I suppose you're right. One of us has to be sensible. You don't mind if I lose my head over you once in a while?"

"I want to move in with you. Would you feel crowded?"

"Um . . . we can make the next apartment over an adjoining one." A pause, and a scowl. "Maybe. Check on it when we get back."

"Good enough. We're at an age where we'll want *some* privacy. And that'll make it official." She swung her feet over the edge of the berth and began putting on her brassiere.

"What's the all-fired hurry?"

"Because, my darling, not only will they be worried about us, but—"

"But?"

"I blush to speak of it, but there does remain that unanswered question," she said. "And at our age, I doubt we could manage anything *three* times in one day—"

He locked his fingers in her bra strap; tugged gently. "You're kidding yourself. We're not going back to make love." She turned to look at him. "We're going back to face a dozen emergencies. I've got to check on Rand, and see if he's come up with anything . . ." His fingers loosened as he spoke. ". . . see how we're doing with the new defenses . . . the bastards could be breaking in with real bombs! And I should be checking on ways to get Pres out of California . . ." His hand dropped from the strap. "God knows what's come up since we left, but MILLIE'll tell us as soon as we're in range. Late tonight, if we're lucky."

She nodded solemnly. "Midnight. Your place. I can get myself moved in by then. *Damn!*"

"What?"

She laughed. "I tried to log it."

• • •

Bonner felt MILLIE return to him while the subway train was still aproaching Todos Santos.

MILLIE?

RECEIVING.

Summary.

Information flowed. Nothing urgent had happened. He glanced over at Barbara. She was staring at the ceiling, her eyes half closed.

Appointments?

NONE SCHEDULED. THOMAS LUNAN HAS REQUESTED ANOTHER APPOINTMENT AT EARLIEST CONVENIENCE. HE SAYS HE WILL WAIT IN THE MIDGARD BAR.

Screw him. Tell Delores I'll be in shortly.

ACKNOWLEDGED.

He waited until Barbara's eyes opened fully. "Anything interesting?"

"You rushed me off so fast I forgot an appointment," she said accusingly. "I haven't done that in years."

"Important?"

"Well, it could be. Sir George Reedy."

"Ah. Well, he wants to learn something. He won't be annoyed. Or at least he won't admit to it."

"I suppose. Ah. Here we are. With any luck I'll see you about midnight—"

"I'll keep an eye out for you."

• • •

Bonner's office staff had gone home, of course, leaving a thick stack of messages on his desk. Five were from Lunan, who seemed desperate to see him. Art thumbed through the stack, then dropped them into the wastebasket before settling into his big high-backed leather chair and putting his feet on the desk. He reached out to touch a button on the telephone console.

A pause, then Delores's voice came through. "Boss?"

"Here. How's Tony?"

"I fed him vitamin B-1 and a gallon of water. He'd never heard of that. Can you imagine? He's just been living through the hangovers."

"Is he in condition to talk?"

"Better than that. He sobers up as fast as he gets smashed. We've been making notes on the you-know-what. On paper. Tony's a little afraid of putting any of this in the computer."

"Good. Keep it that way. I'll drop in on you in an hour or so, if you don't mind."

A momentary hesitation, then, "Fine. Welcome. But keep it short. He has a dinner appointment with Reedy."

". . . Skip it. Send him to the sauna instead. 'Bye."

MILLIE.

HERE.

Locate Thomas Lunan.

MIDGARD.

Telephone link. Midgard headwaiter.

After a moment, the telephone said, "Yes, sir?"

"Find Thomas Lunan. He's a visitor, in the bar somewhere. Send him up here."

• • •

Art Bonner's outer office was dark, and Thomas Lunan stumbled twice as he made his way to the slightly ajar inner door. Shouldn't have had a fourth drink, Lunan thought. Hell with that.

Art Bonner was sprawled in a big leather chair. He

didn't get up when Lunan came in, but he waved toward an open sideboard. "Make yourself a drink."

Lunan poured a small Scotch and filled the glass with soda. He took a seat and lifted the glass. "Cheers."

"Cheers," Bonner said. There was a long silence. "All right, what is it?"

"I've been thinking of a diplomatic way to say this," Lunan said. "And there isn't one. Mister Bonner, are you planning a jailbreak?"

That threw him, Lunan thought. Got right to him.

"Why do you ask that?" Bonner demanded.

"Because you are," Lunan said. "And no, nobody told me. You don't have to worry about security leaks. I've talked to too many of your citizens. *They* expect you to get Preston Sanders out of jail."

"Who else knows? On the outside?" Bonner asked.

"Nobody I know of. Which doesn't mean someone else hasn't thought of it. But I haven't told anyone. Maybe I should have." Lunan waited for Bonner's response, and got an inquiring look. "I mean, you guys play that rough, you could make me disappear. I'm not one of your citizens. You don't figure you owe me a thing—"

"What's the point of this?" Bonner demanded.

"I want in," Lunan said. "I want an exclusive, on everything. In return, you get the story told the way I tell stories. Superbly. You saw my documentary?"

"Yes. It did us no harm—"

"It did you a lot of good, and you know it. Look, you want the story to get out. Not naming names, of course. But you want Los Angeles to get the message—"

Bonner looked thoughtful. "Perhaps."

"Perhaps, hell," Lunan insisted. "THINK OF IT AS EVOLUTION IN ACTION. Societies evolve too. That's the story you want out, and I'll see it gets out!"

"You'll also be in a position to blackmail us."

"I'm in it now," Lunan said. "One phone call and

you won't get Sanders out. Not easily, anyway. But
I'm not blackmailing you. I told you all about Renn,
didn't I? And I didn't even take any precautions,
because I'm not *going* to blackmail you. Not now,
and not later. I just want the story."

"And when the police ask you—"

"California has a very tough newsman's shield law,
Mister Bonner. It's protected me before."

"Maybe that's not quite enough," Bonner said.
"Maybe we'd want you to help out. Do something
yourself—"

Lunan gulped. Shit fire, of course he'd think of
that. "All right."

"Good. We'll let you know. Just stay available,
because you won't get much notice."

"I don't need much notice." Lunan lifted his drink
in salute. He wanted to jump up and sing heroic
arias. This would make his career! And it was the
only way to deal with these people. Level with them.
"Uh—you have thought about immunity," Lunan
said.

Bonner nodded. "The D.A. can certainly give you
immunity from prosecution by the State of
California."

"But not from you," Lunan said.

Bonner's smile widened slightly. "I knew you were
an intelligent man, Mr. Lunan. Cheers."

• • •

Tony Rand stepped out of the elevator, and leaped
back as shapes ran past him. He heard "Sorry!" and
saw two teenage boys and a laughing matron,
crouched low, moving toward the swings at a dead
run. They wore dark coveralls, and their faces were
striped dark as well.

The doors tried to close; Tony blocked them and
stepped out onto the roof, shaking his head. He was
still a little wobbly from the afternoon. Even so, he
knew he should be feeling much worse. B-1 and water
and a sauna . . . and never forget it, he told himself.

The restaurant was a fair walk from the elevators.
Tony passed gardens, a pocket-sized chaparral forest,
a football field. He might have been strolling through
any park; there were no visual cues to tell him that
he was a fifth of a mile in the air.

The lights along the walk had been dimmed to
twilight level. Tony noticed other human shapes
running or crouching in shadows. They too wore dark
coveralls and face paint, and there was a faint
glimmer of gemstones on their breasts. Tony kept his
hands half-raised as he passed them. *Noncombatant*.

He was nearly at the restaurant when there was a
ruby flash from behind him. The light-beam probed
into the bushes ahead and to his right. A young man,
no more than fifteen, stood, as his dark coveralls
flashed with bright light. He cursed horribly, then sat
heavily in the pathway and stared moodily ahead.
Tony nodded sympathy as he passed.

Schramm's was a glass bubble set at one corner of
the Todos Santos roof. Shallow steps led down from
the entrance; Los Angeles glowed through the unseen
wall, far below. It was no place for someone with
acrophobia. The headwaiter had seen Lunan's
broadcast, of course. "Welcome, O court magician!"
he chortled as he escorted Rand to the table where
Sir George Reedy waited.

"I'd like to push a Volkswagen into Thomas
Lunan's big mouth," Rand confided.

Sir George ignored that crypticism. "I had a scare
coming here. It was as if a street gang had taken over
the roof!"

"Nothing to worry about. It's a role-playing game.
MAN FROM UNCLE hunt club. Low-powered laser
pistols, and suits that light up when you're hit.
Fashion designer named Therri organizes them—it's
considered an honor to be invited." Aha, Tony
thought. He still doesn't catch on. "Of course
MILLIE and the Security force are monitoring it."

"But—I would have thought you'd call it off during
the emergency."

"Hmmm. I doubt anyone even considered that. It's been scheduled for months. Sir George, the stockholders don't like letting outsiders run our lives." Tony noticed a waiter at his elbow, and ordered a fruit daiquiri. Sir George's Pimm's Cup was empty; he ordered another.

"Have you been keeping busy, this past week?"

"Oh, certainly." Reedy's smile faded slightly. "Well, I'll admit time hangs a bit heavy while I wait out your war. The combatants haven't much time for a visiting tourist. When your Miss Churchward missed an appointment this afternoon, I thought I would . . . lose my aplomb. I needed that drink."

Tony nodded, feeling awkward.

"And yet it hasn't all been wasted time. What did cause the war, Mr. Rand? More to the point, if I build an arcology in Canada, how do I prevent conflicts with the outside?"

"Do you have Fromate groups in Canada?"

"They're not a large influence. They might become one, if we built something like Todos Santos."

"I wish I'd paid more attention to the bad feeling," Rand said. "I'm no good at politics. Damn it, should I have built this place to look less like a fort?"

"I see other possibilities."

"Good! Enlighten me."

Sir George smiled. "Actually I came to be enlightened. Still . . . should I put my giant building inside the borders of an already existing city? You weren't offered a choice there. I have one."

Tony's drink had arrived, and he sipped at it, cautiously. He'd blown his head off once today, and once was enough. "Yeah. You should be outside. You'll look less like competition. What else?"

"I've managed to see a good deal of Todos Santos. Your power system, food and water storage, Security—all tend to make you independent of outside supplies and outside forces. Are you aiming for economic independence too?"

"Sure. MILLIE would have told you that."

"Quite right. Is that wise? You'll end as a bubble of foreign matter inside the body of the city. Angelinos might well resent such a thing, and Los Angeles politicians would resent it most."

Tony looked at him. Practice for building a starship, he thought. Is that where I went wrong? But—"Wait a minute. Isolation isn't just a whim with us. It's what we're selling. People come to Todos Santos because they can get free of what's outside."

"The crime rate?"

"Not just that. Sir George, suppose you just didn't want to bother learning how to make out an income tax form? And deciding what's deductible every time you spend ten bucks, knowing some supercilious son of a bitch is being underpaid to second-guess you? And keeping little pieces of paper to prove it? It's a fun game, but why does everyone have to play? Sometimes it feels like the government wants to turn everyone on Earth into accountants." Sir George seemed about to interrupt, but Rand went on. "Accountants and lawyers. Half the government is lawyers, and when they make laws they don't write them in English. Nobody but a lawyer can tell legal from illegal, and the lawyers can't tell right from wrong anymore."

Sir George looked stunned. "I never felt that way at all."

"Plenty of our people do—at least that's what I hear in Commons. Independence is a lot of what we're selling."

Sir George nodded thoughtfully.

"Maybe you're right, though," Tony said. "Maybe we really shouldn't be inside anyone's borders. Build your arcology outside city limits . . . but get your subway built fast, because you'll need to be trading with the host city. Have you decided where to put the project?"

"I have half a dozen sites to choose from." Reedy smiled fleetingly. "I'll have to reject some. Toronto, for instance. Toronto has a superb underground shopping complex. Something like Todos Santos would be competing with that."

Menus arrived. Tony ordered without paying too much attention; he wanted to get back to the conversation. He noticed that Reedy, too, had barely glanced at his menu.

Reedy asked, "How would you build a Canadian arcology? Would you change the design?"

"Sure. I learned a lot, living here for all these years. Anyway, Todos Santos is the wrong shape for a cold country. You'll need more insulation, fewer balconies . . . more storage for food in the winter . . ."

Sir George had a sleepy look, as if he weren't quite paying attention. It was wasted on Tony Rand, who stared out at Los Angeles with unfocused eyes. "It doesn't have to be less open, and it doesn't have to look like a fort. Get yourself a mountain slope facing south. A quarter-sphere, hollow. In winter the low sun shines right into it. You can line it with apartments. Soleri designed it a long time ago, for Siberia, but it ought to work even better in your latitudes."

Reedy lifted an eyebrow and seemed thoughtful. "Thank you. But there are other decisions I must make. For example, am I selling independence, like you? And do I need such an elaborate security system?"

"I don't know," Tony said. "I'm an engineer, not a manager—" Ye gods. Is he trying to hire me? He sure sounds like it. Naw, he couldn't be. But—"Uh—would you give the top brass computer implants?"

Reedy frowned. "I hadn't thought of it. Implants are expensive."

"What's it like to have an implant? To know anything you want, just by thinking it? An arcology is terribly complex; it makes a Saturn-type moonship look like a tinker toy."

"I believe I see what you mean." Sir George smiled slowly. It wasn't his usual vague smile at all; it looked somehow predatory.

• • •

There was a new door in the east wall of Art Bonner's apartment. Bonner went through and found nobody home.

MILLIE. Time?

12:02:20.

Location Barbara Churchward.

MILLIE told him, and he relaxed. She was just coming out of the elevator, on her way. Moments later she opened the door and found him.

"Hello."

"Hi. How was Sir George?"

She shrugged. "As you predicted. Annoyed and pretending not to be. He really is grateful to us. With what he's learned he'll be able to get his Canadian arcology going in half the time it took us."

"Glad he wasn't too upset." He waved expansively. "It looks like you've lived here for years. How'd you find the time?"

"I had Services move me. I'll be weeks finding out where everything is. And how was your day?"

"Lunan's back."

"And?"

"He knows we're planning a jailbreak."

"Ye gods. How?"

"He's got a contact here. Cheryl Drinkwater. You saw her on the documentary. I think she told him more than she knew."

Barbara subvocalized. MILLIE. Data, Cheryl Drinkwater.

Bonner broke in. MILLIE, phone link with Barbara Churchward. "Love, I've started a file on Tom Lunan too."

Okay. MILLIE, data, Tom Lunan.

Information whispered into her mastoid bone. Updates—"He knows?"

"He's guessing. Cheryl can't possibly know, but she must have told him how the stockholders feel. The subway adjunct is common knowledge; he may have worked that in. Hell, maybe he's telepathic. Useful trait in an investigative reporter."

"How will you handle it?"

"Take him along. Make him an accomplice. I told him he'd be in at the kill . . . Dammit, sometimes we really do need some protection from our friends. This'll do it." He stretched. "Tired."

She nodded. "How's Tony?"

"Delores sobered him up and put him to work. I don't know whether he needs a keeper or not, but she's a good one. If she can stand it." MILLIE, file ILLICIT.

Barbara's jaw went slack as she listened to MILLIE's characterless voice describing Rand's updated plans. She backed into a chair and sat down. She began laughing.

Art grinned down at her. "I do admire subtlety."

"I'd have thought Tony would go for something more complicated. Delores must be keeping him honest. Hey, let's go to bed."

Art looked back at the new door in what had been a blank wall. They'd even remounted the pictures. "It all happened so fast—Yeah. Let's."

"Too fast?"

He was stripping off clothing and tossing it through the open door into his own apartment. They made a tight pattern on and around a reading chair. "I'm adaptable. Are there any special daydreams you'd like fulfilled?"

"I've been through that. Hell, I didn't mean to say that."

They moved into each other's arms. Eye to eye. Barbara wondered, "How do you feel?"

"Half—excited, half—apprehensive. It's been a long time."

"Why?"

"Complications. I get enough complications in real life . . . for years now . . ."

"This? Should we have waited?"

"Should have started earlier. Before those kids

got killed. Better late than never. What daydreams?"

"Rape. Once with a vampire. Costume number, masquerade at a con . . . science fiction convention . . . we kept the costumes on. I was in a white shroud. Tried not to move a muscle but . . . why am I telling you this?"

"It must be hard to lie subvocally."

"What do you daydream, Art?"

"Fast. Sudden seduction. No complications."

"Fast, right!" She swung out of his arms and yanked him toward the bed by one wrist. He found himself on his back, laughing, still bouncing, and she was sitting on his hips. "Fast enough?"

"And up against a wall. But I'm gettin' old, and it's been a long day—"

"We'll try it some morning."

She wriggled, and they were locked. Barbara bent toward him, and he thought, "No, stay upright. You'll pull loose."

"Thy servant." She swayed upright, and even leaned back, hands gripping and tickling the back of his knees.

He gasped. He thought, "Lovely. You shine by your own light." He held up his hands, and she took them, glowing at the compliment. His face altered as she moved up and down, slowly. The messages passing through MILLIE became incoherent.

And finally, breathing as if he'd run a marathon, Art sent, "I wonder what MILLIE thinks of all this."

• • •

Lunan found the tiny bar dead empty. He hoisted himself onto a stool and said, "Keep it simple. Um . . . Calvados. Soda on the side."

"Be right with you." The bartender finished pouring something pink and frothy out of a shaker, put that glass and a brandy snifter in the wells of a drink tray and set it in the dumbwaiter. He was grinning like a thief. He asked, "Insomnia?"

Lunan said, "Yah. Pure nerves." He took the snifter before Levoy could set it down; sniffed, sipped. "What's got you smiling like that at two in the morning?"

"I can't tell you," the bartender said happily.

"I just told thirty million people that there aren't any secrets in Todos Santos."

"Well . . . no offense, because you did a fine documentary on us, Mr. Lunan. But you're not a stockholder."

Lunan nodded. "I never asked you what you think about the Preston Sanders case."

The bartender's smile vanished. "I'm minded to brush up on my explosives. It's been years since I swore I was gonna be a law-and-order citizen, you know? But Sanders is a hero, and he's not being treated like one, and that's wrong."

Lunan nodded. No surprises. All the saints must feel that way . . . "Better make this a double."

"It's wrong. We can't let—" Levoy shook himself. He poured another generous ounce of Calvados into Lunan's snifter. "Okay, tell me what's got you so jumpy at two in the morning."

"That, too, is a secret. And if I knew all of it I wouldn't be so jumpy. Or maybe I would. Maybe I would."

• • •

"The Jacuzzi," Barbara thought suddenly. "We wouldn't have to be young. Better than a wall, love. There's no weight."

"No privacy either."

"Lunan says privacy's obsolete here. Art, there's the northeast-side Jacuzzi, on the roof. Reserved for adults. Lots of couples play games there. Regularly."

"Not really privacy."

"No. Security knows. Some of them use it too."

"You?"

"No. I've been invited. Twice." She spoke part of a name, and stopped. "I don't like this."

Art said, "We can cut MILLIE out of the circuit."

"Sure. I'm giving away too many secrets. But, Art, shouldn't we get to know each other?"

"Good question. Ancient question. I don't feel duty-bound, do you? We opted for some privacy in living arrangements. If the link is too uncomfortable—"

She nodded. "Asshole. Duty—bound! Are we still linked? Eek! Sorry, Art."

He chuckled. "Price of telepathy."

"With telepathy we could give each other pictures. Sensations. Memories."

"A great sunset? A Japanese bath?"

"The night four of us lucked into a Beef Wellington at Mon Grenier. It wasn't on the menu. It was for a private party and the chef made more than he needed. It was the best I've ever tasted, but part of it was just knowing we'd lucked into something."

"How would a machine transmit that? It's hardly a sensation at all. I wonder if we'll ever have real telepathy? Tony would know."

"Why did you and Delores . . .?"

She felt him tense against her. Tension slurred his subvocalized response. "I never knew. She just dropped me. Meant it, too."

"Skip it. What else do you daydream, love?"

"Orgies? Never been to one—"

"Too damn complicated."

"Oh?"

"It actually went like this . . . no, I only did it once. Fun while it was happening, but they weren't very bright people, and afterward two of the men kept bugging me. I'm sorry I did it. I was curious."

"With real telepathy you could show me."

"I'll show you. " She ran her fingers up his thigh, and he responded. "Just pretend I'm six different women."

"I think you probably are."

The table in the next room opened and sprouted a tray. Art went for the drinks. He handed a Pink Lady across the bed and said, "Now it's really official. The bartender knows."

They touched glasses. Art wondered, "You've never been married, have you? Why not?"

"Too . . . hmm. What kind of a man should I have married?"

"How would I know that?"

She spoke aloud. "I try to describe him and I get contradictions. A househusband? How would I respect him? An ambitious type, like me? But who runs our life? Who takes care of the kids and buys the groceries?"

"A houseful of servants. Or the service department of Todos Santos. No kid could be lonely or in danger in Todos Santos."

She nodded to herself, then suddenly looked him in the eye. "Shall we?"

He thought about it. Kids love it in Todos Santos . . . the way Cheryl Drinkwater talked about the day-care center . . . either of us could raise a kid, here, if we split up or one of us died . . . get him a link to MILLIE at eight or ten? "Yeah. One?"

"The only child usually has problems . . . nope, you're right. Here it's one big family. She'd be okay. I'm not so sure about the computer link. Age fifteen, maybe?"

"She? . . . We could choose the sex."

"We *could*, but let's not. Let's gamble. And I'll get my birth control implant taken out tomorrow."

"Hah. Then we're just wasting our time right now."

She rubbed up against him. "All I get is complaints."

"I've been wasting time, all right. Jesus, what I've been missing! No, don't stop. Do you like this?" Fingernails scratching lightly in a circular motion just above her buttocks.

"Like it."

Against their mastoid bones, a shrill buzzing.

And they were rolling in opposite directions. "Invaders," Art panted, running for the chair where he'd flung his clothes. "I knew it! Those kids were just a test run, and they didn't even know it."

"We'll have to speak to them about their timing."

"Harshly." He stopped with his pants in his fist. "Not too harshly. Damn, I don't want to kill anyone." MILLIE, phone link with Security. And tell Sandra I'll be at the worry desk in four minutes.

XVI

SAVE THE MINOTAUR!

"Let me in, dammit," Tony Rand shouted. "Who's the duty officer here?" This time. *This time.* It ticked through his head like the sound of a clock. He couldn't think what to do with his hands, and he stamped in impatience. *This time.* What was keeping them? This time nobody would die . . .

"This is Captain Vito Hamilton. My apologies, but you'll have to wait a moment—Ah. Positive identification. I'll open the door now, Mr. Rand."

The door opened. He dashed into the Security control room. The quiet calm of uniformed men at work calmed him too, a little . . . although there were signs that the guards took this seriously. Captain Hamilton was standing, not sprawled in an easy chair; and many of the peripheral screens had doubled crews.

One screen showed a map of the underground service areas of Todos Santos, with moving red blips in one of the tunnels. Below it was a screen entirely dark. Rand went over to it, glancing at the name of the guard lieutenant sitting there. He pointed to the screen. "What's this, Blake?"

Blake didn't turn around. "Paint. They spray-painted the camera before we even knew they were in the complex."

"How'd they get in?"

"Near as we can tell, they blew a hole through a wall separating the sewer lines from maintenance access Tunnel 4-B"

Rand pursed his lips silently. They should have been detected in that sewer, detected long before they got near 4-B. "I need a vacant console."

"Use this one," a guard said. He stood to give his chair to Tony.

Rand punched in file names. FILE NOT FOUND, the screen said. FILE NOT FOUND. FILE NOT FOUND. "Okay, that's one of the problems," Tony muttered. "Detection information never got filed. How many bandits?"

"Five, we think," the captain said from behind Rand. "MILLIE deduced that from the audio. Five, one definitely female, two carrying a heavy object."

"Sounds like they're serious. I take it you haven't seen them."

"Only one. They're screwing up most of our electronics again. And they seem to know exactly where the TV eyes are. Ah. There we go. Watch."

A screen showed an opening fire door. A shadowy figure came through. Bulky, rounded, snouted . . . Aliens aboard my starship! The figure came directly toward them, raised arm hiding snouted face, and aimed something at the camera. The screen went dark.

"Knew right where to go again," Hamilton said.

"Yeah," Rand muttered sourly. Right where to go. But this time . . . "Who's in charge of this operation?"

"I've been acting in command, with Sandra Wyatt

sitting in Mr. Bonner's office. Bonner is just getting to his station."

Tony picked up a phone. "Get Bonner for me—" He waited. "Art? Tony Rand. I'm down in Security. Let me handle this."

There was a significant pause. "Okay. You don't mind if I watch over your shoulder?"

"Would it stop you? Never mind. Thanks."

"Right. I'll tell Hamilton. If you need help, just holler." The phone went dead.

Rand smiled faintly, then turned back to the screen. "Retch gas. Use that in Tunnel 4, all chambers," he said. "And get some people down to—" he thought for a moment, calling up a picture of the tunnel complex—"5-C. Have them go west through 5 and north through 6 manually locking all the fire doors, and report on the phone as they get each one locked. On the phone, not through MILLIE. And I want one of your people to keep track of their progress on a paper map. Got that?"

"Yes, sir," Hamilton said crisply. "You think MILLIE's compromised?"

"I know damned well MILLIE's compromised," Tony said. He felt a tight knot in his stomach as he thought about what he'd seen. Camera locations known. The thickness of the wall between the sewer and 4-B had been known. And MILLIE couldn't remember that she was supposed to monitor traffic in that sewer. There weren't many people who could know all that and fiddle with MILLIE's programming. Somebody was a traitor—probably somebody on Tony's own staff.

He fished in his pants pockets. "Hamilton, I need a file folder. I left it at the guard desk in the Mall, one of the lockers. Here's the key. Send someone who can run."

Hamilton was doing something about those orders, but Tony ignored it. Nobody knew everything about the new defenses except Rand himself. He called up files, found them logged and working. The bandits hadn't chosen their route in; it had been forced on them by what they knew and what they didn't.

Back to the tracking programs. How were the bandits doing? Aha, Tony thought. "Let's try this." He began to type orders. The refrain grew in his mind. This time. This time.

Captain Hamilton was surprised to see that the chief engineer was grinning.

• • •

The five were sweating inside their wet suits. One reached for the zipper down his chest. The man next to him slapped at his hand, glaring behind the snout of his mask. They were all jogging, even the trailing two who were carrying a box between them. Those two stopped, reeling, panting; then began jogging again. Their breathing was stertorous, and they stumbled frequently.

• • •

"Sounds like Cheyne-Stokes breathing, doesn't it?" Rand was grinning like a wolf. "They'll start to fall over any minute."

"What did you do to them?" Blake asked.

"Well, I figured the next bunch of invaders would be in something like wet suits, in case we used VX again."

"We're not? We really did obey that court order?"

Rand nodded. This time. *This time* . . .

"But—sir, I got the impression that we still had war gasses."

Rand nodded happily. "So did a lot of people." And no wonder, since I spread that rumor myself. "So did the bandits. And the're coming in through the tunnels, and carrying gear to foul up our electronic detection systems, and carrying bombs or whatever . . . a lot to carry. I never heard of anyone carrying an air-conditioning unit to a burglary."

"Me neither," Blake said. He glanced at Captain Hamilton.

"So," Tony said, "I put some quartz radiant heaters along those tunnels to sort of enhance the effect. Now I'll bleed some air from the turbine heat exchangers into the ventilating system for the tunnels . . . Damn, I wish the cameras were working. I'd like to see if they open their suits." He grinned widely, plainly enjoying himself. This time! "At least I can talk to them. They're coming to another interesting area . . ."

• • •

"New construction," the leader said. "Look for new construction here."

"How the fuck do we do that?" Sherry demanded. She was a big, burly woman, even without her equipment; and she was panting, hard. "It's all new construction. Now what do we do?"

Then did the court magician's voice boom hollowly through the tunnel. "RETURN TO YOUR FORMER LIVES. NONE BUT THE IMMORTAL CTHULHU MAY PASS HERE."

The leader shook his head, the snout of his mask moving from side to side like an anteater's trunk. "Fuck off!" he shouted. To the others he said, "We hope this is it. Put some charges here and get back out of the way." He glanced at his watch. "We haven't got much time."

• • •

Rand listened to the aliens and muttered curses. "Just where are they planning to blast?" he demanded.

"I don't know, but I'm clearing my men out of all the adjacent areas," Hamilton said.

"Yeah, do that. We plastered new cement all over everything down there. With any luck they'll blow the wrong wall. Several wrong walls."

The explosion overloaded the microphones, which momentarily went silent. Then two screens lit.

"Nope. Northeast wall," Rand said. "They got some

power lines. MILLIE can compensate for most of that, but we better tell the residents . . ."

"Already done," Bonner's voice said from the speaker. "Now what?"

"We get to see where they're going," Rand said. He waited, then grinned mirthlessly. "Okay. Hamilton, I need your people to go down Tunnel 4 closing the fire doors. We can cut them off from their way in."

"Will they care?"

Rand shrugged. "You weren't supposed to ask that." He watched as another screen came active. A bulky figure advanced, spray can in hand, and the screen went dark, but a moment later the one beside it lit. It showed five shapes in profile: dull black, bulky, sexless, vaguely humanoid.

"By God," Bonner's voice said. "You have another pickup?"

"Sure," Tony said. In fact, boss, I have three more in there. Five's a critical area. This time . . . God, I wish I could remember which people know about which cameras. If I had an implant—

If I had an implant, Tony thought, I'd be getting false data from MILLIE, read directly into my mind. Just this once, I'm glad I don't. So try to remember: was it Alice who knew about camera 2, Tunnel 5?

The invaders went forward through the tunnels.

• • •

"Alma! Get your ass in gear, get moving!" the leader shouted.

There was no answer. Alma's face was tomato colored. Her eyelids were almost closed, showing white. Every gasping breath sounded like her last.

"Christ, she's had it," Sherry said. "Leave her!"

"You goddam bitch, she's one of us—"

"Shut up," the leader said. "Sherry's right. We have to keep moving. Get Alma's gear and come on."

Reese hesitated, then ran the zipper on her wet suit all the way down. Now she might live, if the saints didn't use war gas . . .

• • •

"They lost one," Hamilton said. "One's down."

"Right," Tony Rand said, with considerable triumph. "One down and four to go. Get that one and take it up to Mister Bonner. Ah, search it first, and we'll leave the camera on it till your men get there."

Hamilton said, "I'm not incompetent, Mr. Rand."

"And I'm not tactful. Can you live with it?"

No answer. Rand watched the invaders' progress through Tunnel 5. There were enough pickup cameras in the tunnel to track the four as they moved along, one ahead, two following with the heavy box, and one last who shouted orders.

The Security room door eased open. The entering guard was a woman, looking still in her teens, and lean as a snake. She must have made Olympic time down to the Mall and back, but she was barely panting as she handed a yellow manila envelope to Hamilton, who passed it to Rand. Tony spilled the contents across the desk in one smooth motion, then tried to sort them while watching three screens. It wasn't working; he had to look down. He fished out a page and said, "Hah."

Nobody commented. Tony shuffled through the notes—handwritten, barely legible—found another page and said, "Right. Get me Mr. Bonner." Dropped the papers and went back to watching.

• • •

"You go on," Sherry said. Her meaty face glowed in the orange light, reflections off water, as if she'd just stepped out of a very hot shower. "I can't go any farther."

"Get your ass up!" the leader shouted. "Put that mask back on!"

"Go to hell!" Sherry said; but she said it from the floor.

Gavin and Reese picked up her gear. The box was lighter now.

• • •

"That's two," Rand said with glee. This time! "A hundred eighty degrees in there. We'll get them all before it's over." And we'll get them alive, this time . . . He watched as the invaders moved across the screen, through fire doors, onward toward the central core of Todos Santos.

"You can't let them get much farther along that way," Bonner's voice said.

"Yeah, I know that," Rand answered. "Hang on." Hell. When will the others drop? He looked up to Hamilton. "Captain, give 'em more knockout gas. Those masks can't be comfortable."

"Yes, sir." The guard captain continued to stare at the screen.

"All right," Tony said. "I guess it wouldn't hurt if you put some of your armed people down there in Tunnels 5 and 6, sort of parallel to these yo-yos . . ."

Hamilton nodded eagerly, then began speaking orders into his headset microphone. "Bravo, go. Delta go."

Now they took one more turn, stopped, then went unerringly to the TV camera. The screen blanked momentarily, then came on from another angle as Tony activated the alternate pickup.

Damn, Tony muttered. Not much question about it now. "Art? Our mole is Alice Strahler. What do we do about her?"

"Don't know yet. You sure?"

"I mapped it. She knew about camera 2 in Tunnel 5. She didn't know about the radiants, and neither did the bandits, but she was supposed to enter a monitor program, and she didn't. And now they've knocked out a new camera she knew of, and didn't get one I never told her about. I've got another double check coming up, but it's her."

"Your assistant."

"Yeah. Art, she may not be guilty of anything but talking to the wrong person. She's a nice—"

"Okay, I'll deal with Alice," Bonner said quickly. Yeah, Tony thought. But she never blabbed innocently, not in that much detail. Hell.

Bonner's voice came on again. "Now just what are you going to do about those jokers down there? I hate to remind you, but they're getting close to the turbines and MHD systems."

"And if they zap one of those, we've had it. Yeah, I got the picture," Rand said, "but is that what they're after? Last time it was start a big fire."

"Uh-uh. Last time it was fake a big fire. Tony, it's the turbines. They don't really want to kill lots of people. Bad publicity. They want to make Todos Santos too expensive to run. Believe it, they're after the turbines."

On screen, the bandits were still moving toward the turbines. They were slow, in a turtle's race with heatstroke, and Tony had one more surprise for them before their route was clear, but after that—

What now? Wait? Send in Hamilton's SWAT teams? God knows he's got eager enough troops . . . Tony looked up, and saw that everyone in the room was staring at him. *Waiting for orders. My orders.*

O Pres! I never really realized what you went through. He looked up at the screens. The bandits had found the jog where he'd fiddled with a wall. Now they were moving on. On the next screen over, the second bandit to collapse had moved out of view. Damn! Two parties to keep track of now!

"Hamilton, send a squad through Tunnel 8. South of the turbines in 8, and keep them south of there."

"Yes, sir."

This time. Tony heard Hamilton murmuring orders. "Delta team to Tunnel 8. Automatic weapons. Full body armor as long as they can stand the heat."

"What happens in 8?" Art Bonner's voice asked from the speaker.

"I have another surprise for them," Tony said. He tried to sound confident. This time. *This time.*

• • •

The corridor had angled slightly left. Everything down here looked like new construction, but that jog wasn't on the map. But what could they do if they left the map? They went on, pacing off their distances, until Gavin said, "Here."

Reese and Lovin kept going, staggering with the bomb box. Gavin shrieked, "Here!" He could barely hear himself. Too many concussions.

They stopped, set the box down. A moment for heavy breathing, then they were setting up the plastique. Lovin inserted the wire, and they staggered back down the corridor.

The explosion slammed their eardrums. Gavin decided he was deaf. It wouldn't matter; none of them had really expected to live through this. They went back to where they had set off the blast. There was a shallow crater in the wall, but it still stood.

Reese screamed something inaudible. Gavin shook his head. They began to set another charge, bigger this time. Reese suddenly stopped, then pulled his zipper down to his groin in one convulsive motion. Gavin tried to shake him. Reese pulled away and ran, flinging his mask away, then the top of his wet suit

• • •

• • •

"That wall surprised them." Tony's grin showed sick fear behind it. "I didn't just beef up the wall, I put frangible disks in it and water behind to absorb the shock. And the other walls reflected the shock wave back at them."

The bandits were running back down the corridor. "I keep hoping they'll run out of explosives. Did you find the second bandit yet?"

"First one must have reached medical by now. Second one tried to go back the way they came.

Found himself blocked. No camera, but he doesn't seem to be moving. We'll have him in a minute."

The camera view was suddenly opaque with smoke and dust. It cleared gradually. Light from Corridor 8 glowed through a thigh-sized hole in four feet of wall.

"One more blast and they're through," Tony said. "Why are they doing this? Hamilton, I only see two of them."

"Do you have another camera back there, maybe?"

"If I can remember—" Tony tapped at keys, and a screen lit. The third bandit showed clear, curled up with his back to a wall, stripped naked, with face set in anguish and his hands over his ears. A gun lay a good distance away.

The remaining bandits ran into view, and one seemed shocked at his companion's condition. The other clicked something with his thumb while he tried to cover both ears with his other hand and arm. Dust blew toward them.

On the other screen, the hole in the wall was comfortably larger. "That's Tunnel 8," Tony said. No one commented. Everyone in the room knew 8 was the crucial area. "Have you got your squad in 8?"

"They're there," Hamilton said. "Dunhill, you ready? They're in place."

"Get them clear for a moment. I've got one last trick, but it's dangerous. Anaesthetic darts." *This time . . .* stoppit!

He typed rapidly.

FILE NOT FOUND. FILE NOT FOUND.

"Goddamn it!" he shouted. "Never mind, I can rewrite the program." Tony typed rapidly, watching two screens at once, thankful for the touch-typing course his father had made him take in high school.

One of the bandits eased through the hole in the wall. The two wrestled their box through, then the second followed.

"They're after the turbines," Lieutenant Blake said. "If they get those—"

"Blake," Hamilton said.

The guard lieutenant fell silent.

So what happens if they do get the turbines? Tony asked himself. Nobody gets killed. But the cost . . . And it would be a message to the saints. *Too many people hate you too fervently. You can't run Todos Santos economically because we'll keep ruining your expensive equipment. You'll go broke. You have to quit sooner or later. Why not now?*

Well? Would the money men in Zurich actually shut down Todos Santos if it became that expensive to run? They'd certainly not build any more arcologies. Nor would anyone else, not when it was clear the arcologies couldn't defend themselves. And, dammit, if Todos Santos goes broke then it can't run any longer, expenses, expenses, expenses, it's property rights against human rights, money against lives, Tony thought bleakly, and I'm defending the money.

I'm defending my city!

"Did Alice know about your darts?" Bonner's voice asked.

"I've been trying to remember." He recalled boasting about the darts. But to whom? Never mind. Nothing else to do anyway. He waited until they were both in Corridor 8, then hit the RETURN key on his console.

• • •

Lovin and Gavin straightened up with the mass of the explosives box pulling them down . . . and a dozen explosions burst from the walls.

Gavin found himself in fetal position, his cheek on hot concrete. It would be so easy to lie there, to wait, soon they'd come and take him where it was cool . . . No! He stood up, patting himself . . . and found himself bristling with darts. He sat up, laughing, entirely buzzed on fatigue poisons, adrenalin, and dehydration.

Lovin looked like a porcupine as he rolled over and stood up. They spent a minute pulling darts off each other in handfuls. The points might work through the

metal mesh imbedded between the thick layers of
their wet suits.

There wasn't a chance of their hearing each other.
Explosives had rendered them deaf, but even through
the deafness they could hear the roar of the Todos
Santos turbines. They picked up the box and
staggered toward the sound.

• • •

"Armor," Hamilton said. "I wonder just how good
that armor is?"

Tony leaned back in his chair. "I'm out of tricks,"
he said. "Damn Alice!" He turned to Hamilton. "Stop
them." But that wasn't enough, and he knew it. This
time ... But Tony was never happy with
euphemisms or imprecise language. "Don't let them
reach the turbines. Stop them even if you have to kill
them."

XVII

To us, heaven switches on daylight, or turns on the
showerbath. We little gods are gods of the machine
only. It is our highest. Our cosmos is a great engine.
And we die of ennui. A subtle dragon stings us in the
midst of plenty.

—D. H. Lawrence

(AFTERMATH)

"There's another one," Sergeant Gomez said. He
pointed to the Day-Glo sticker. "THINK OF IT AS
EVOLUTION IN ACTION," Gomez read aloud. "I
think I counted a dozen on the way here."

"Yeah," Hal Donovan said. "I'm getting a little
tired of them myself." He looked around the tunnel
complex. "Find anything?"

Gomez shrugged. It looked jerky. "Nothing the TS
cops didn't tell us we'd find."

"What's got you so nervous? You think it's a
setup?"

"Naw, that's not it. How are we going to find
anything if we keep getting lost? If the guards just
turned us loose in here I don't think we'd ever get
out. The Saints keep having to lead us around by the
hand."

Lieutenant Donovan nodded again. "I get a touch

of it myself. Well, tough it out. Keep stirring things around. I'll go get their official story."

* * *

There were only two men in the interview room. Donovan frowned. One was wearing the uniform of a captain of the Todos Santos guards. The other— Donovan had no trouble at all recognizing the youngish man in the thousand-dollar three-piece suit. He'd seen him often enough in court.

The man stood and extended his hand. "I'm John Shapiro," he said. "General Counsel for Todos Santos."

Of course they had their lawyer in the interview room. Donovan felt that he ought to resent that, but he couldn't really blame the Saints.

"I asked to see all the Todos Santos police involved in the shootout," Donovan said.

"Yes," the uniformed captain said. "But I was in charge, and I'd like to go over the story with you before letting you have at my men."

Donovan grimaced slightly. These goddam sensitive Saints! "Hell, Captain, we're all cops."

"I wish it were that simple," Shapiro said. "In any event, we are ready to cooperate with you as fully as possible." He sat down and opened a steno notebook.

Donovan chuckled and looked around the room. If Shapiro needed to take notes, Donovan was next in line to be Pope. He saw no point in saying so. "You're Captain Hamilton, then. You were in charge?"

"I was the senior officer of Todos Santos Security," Hamilton said.

"Which is not quite the same thing," Hal Donovan said. "Who was really running the show?"

"The police took my orders," Hamilton said. "No one else's."

No point in pushing that just now, Donovan decided. "All right, Captain. Suppose you tell me in your own words what happened."

"I'll do better than that," Hamilton said. He pointed to a TV screen imbedded in the far wall of the room. "I'll show you a lot of it."

The story went as Donovan expected. Intruders got into TS by blowing their way through a wall. The Saints used a variety of non-lethal weapons to try to stop them. Nothing worked, and finally the gadgets failed as they always did, and some cops had to put their arses on the line, and that always happened too.

The screen showed two policemen with rifles and a third with a bullhorn, crouched behind some kind of portable barricade (not a bad thing, Donovan thought; we ought to have something like that). They were in tunnels, and the sound track conveyed the rumble of machinery. The picture stopped, freezing that instant of time.

"They were approaching the turbines," Hamilton said. "We'd already tried the darts. They had armor. There was nothing to stop them from doing a hundred million dollars worth of damage—and after what we'd seen we knew damned well that's what they wanted to do. And we *knew* they had explosives."

"You sure did," Donovan agreed.

The TV drama came back to life. "YOU ARE UNDER ARREST," the bullhorn blared. "THROW DOWN YOUR WEAPONS AND FOR GOD'S SAKE LET'S GO WHERE IT'S COOL!"

The intruders came doggedly toward the camera. "Dunhill gave them another chance," Hamilton said.

The TS cop with the bullhorn stood. "SUR-RENDER," he shouted.

The leading intruder held out a revolver and fired. The two TS cops with rifles returned the fire at full automatic, a loud stutter of small-calibre high-velocity weaponry. The leading bandit began to fall, then there was an explosion.

"Dead man switch on his explosives, we think," Hamilton said.

"I see." The scene went on, showing messy details. Donovan sat down hard.

"There's a little more," Hamilton said.

The TV picture dissolved, then came up to show a burly woman, naked except for panties. She was holding a big Webley revolver in both hands, almost in a parody of the official police grip. The pistol waved back and forth.

"She was too tired to hold it steady," Hamilton said.

The woman fired, several times. The picture didn't show what she was shooting at.

"I had four guards in good body armor about thirty meters away from her," Hamilton said. "They didn't think she could hurt them, so they didn't shoot back."

Eventually the woman in the picture sat heavily on the ground. A half-dozen Saints in bulgy SWAT uniforms appeared. They grabbed her and handcuffs flashed.

"That's it," Hamilton said.

Donovan nodded. "The difference being that she didn't have any explosives."

"I suppose," Hamilton said.

"All right. I've seen it. Now can I talk to your men?"

Hamilton and Shapiro looked at each other. "Certainly," Shapiro said. "Of course you won't mind if Captain Hamilton and I stay here . . ."

I should mind, Donovan thought. But what would be the point? "Fine. Let's get this done."

After the interviews, Donovan went back to the tunnels and let Gomez lead him through the route the intruders had taken. They'd cleaned up some in the final tunnel, which was just as well. Even so,

Donovan didn't think he'd want any lunch. After an hour he had seen enough.

He left the Todos Santos underground complex, whistling again at the sight of the large holes blasted in one of the concrete walls. There were guards at every fire door in the tunnels, and the elevator door was opened for him by two more uniformed Todos Santos guards. They looked blankly at Donovan, but they didn't say anything. "Hell, it's not my fault," Donovan said. "It's homicide, and we have to investigate."

"Sure. Last time you jailed Mr. Sanders," the younger guard said. "Who this time? Officer Dunhill? Lieutenant Blake? Captain Hamilton? Or maybe somebody higher up—"

"Can it, Prentice," the older guard said. "The lieutenant's just doing a job. He can't help it if they put him in charge."

The younger guard's lips tightened. Donovan was glad when they reached the executive floor and he could get away from them.

In charge, he thought as he paced down the thickly carpeted corridor. It is to laugh, ho ho! The Mayor sends MacLean Stevens. Councilman Planchet has two field deputies here. The D.A. and the Coroner both come in person, and then they've got the goddam nerve to tell me I'm in charge. Hoo ha.

Donovan smiled at the receptionist and got an answering look that made him feel really welcome. Delores, Anthony Rand had called her. A nice name. Too bad I'll never get to meet her off duty.

She waved him into Arthur Bonner's office, and Donovan wondered about that for a moment before he realized that with the setup they had here, she'd known he was coming long before he got to her anteroom. She could have told Bonner while he was in the corridor. A good setup. Didn't have to keep people waiting.

Bonner was at his desk, and MacLean Stevens was pacing in front of it.

"Keep 'em at home, Mac," Bonner was saying. "Before we have to kill a lot more of them."

"Yeah. Great image. See Todos Santos and die. You don't have a city, you've got the anteroom to the morgue."

"That's about enough—"

"I surely agree," Stevens said. "If you mean enough dead kids—"

"Goddamn it, with all their gear, and a spy in my headquarters—"

"Dammit, Art, am I supposed to restrict the sale of wet suits?"

Donovan cleared his throat. Stevens turned, stared at him for a moment, and said, "Find anything new?"

"No, sir," Donovan said. "And we won't."

"That seems a strange attitude for a homicide investigation."

Donovan laughed. "Investigation. With all respect, Mr. Stevens, what's to investigate? We can look at the bodies, we can stick our fingers in the bullet holes, and we can talk to people. Then what? The Saints' Rent-a-cops say this bunch broke in. They shoota the guns, they banga the bombs. So the Saints shoot back, which God knows they're entitled to do, and the kids get hurt, and some get dead."

"You can make certain it really happened that way," Stevens said.

"Yes, sir."

"You doubt us, Mac?" Bonner asked. "It's really come to that?"

"Whether I doubt you or not, a lot of people will," Stevens said. "And they'll want proof one way or another."

"Which we can't get," Donovan said. "Mr. Stevens, we'll go over all the evidence. We'll interview all the witnesses. But no matter what we do, Mr. Bonner's people are as smart as we are, and they've had plenty of time to set the stage if that's what they wanted. So when it's all done it's going to come out the thing went down the way they said. They tried everything they could, and eventually they sent in their SWAT people. The bandits shot it out and lost."

"You have any reason to doubt that it happened that way, Lieutenant?" Art Bonner asked.

Donovan shook his head. "If I did, I wouldn't be talking like this. No, sir, I'm sure it all went as your people say it did."

"Good," Bonner said. "So why are your detectives poking into every corner of our defenses?"

Donovan shrugged. "You're charging the survivors, right? We have to gather evidence."

"Yeah," Bonner said. He gave Stevens a sour look. "Of course your cops have their normal share of curiosity. Speaking of prisoners, are you ready to take custody of them?"

"I can send for some troops."

Bonner's office was filled with police when Tony Rand came in. LAPD, D.A.'s men, deputy sheriffs, even a marshal from the federal district court, all waiting expectantly, until Colonel Cross and five Todos Santos guards brought in their prisoners.

They were both women. The male prisoner had collapsed from heat exhaustion, and would be taken by ambulance to the prison ward of County Hospital.

Tony Rand stared at the women unashamedly. It was the first time he'd seen them without their protective equipment and masks.

"Something wrong with me, fat boy?" one asked.

"Yes," Tony said. "You want to burn down my city."

"That's the court magician," the other woman said. "He designed this place. The chief technologist."

"So now he's here with the pigs."

"Enough." One of the policemen came forward. "You're under arrest. You have the right to remain silent. You have the right to consult an attorney. If you cannot afford an attorney—"

"Of course we gave them their rights earlier on,"

Colonel Cross announced. He seemed annoyed that anyone would doubt it.

"It never hurts to repeat it," a federal marshal said.

"Sounds just like TV, doesn't it, Sherry? Don't worry, officer, we'll go quietly. What are we charged with?"

"Suspicion of homicide," the policeman said.

"O, wow—"

"That's a heavy trip," Sherry said. "We didn't kill anybody. Their pigs killed our friends—"

"Your friends were killed during the commission of a felony," the Los Angeles policeman said. "That makes anyone involved in that felony an accomplice to homicide. You should discuss this with your attorney, not with me. Gomez, take them out."

"Yes sir." The uniformed policeman came forward and expertly handcuffed each of the women. Then with two policewomen and half a dozen other police he escorted them out of Bonner's office.

"There's one more," Bonner said. "But I thought you might want to keep them separated. Colonel—"

"Yes, sir," Colonel Cross said. He spoke into a microphone attached to his lapel, and a moment later a guard led Alice into the room.

Despite the police who had left with Sergeant Gomez, there were half a dozen left. Alice blinked as she looked at each face. When her eyes met Tony's, they fell quickly.

The LA officer came forward again. "Alice Strahler, you're under arrest. You have the right to remain silent. You have—"

Alice listened to the entire Miranda warning without comment.

Tony Rand couldn't stand it any longer. "Why?" he asked. "Alice, why?"

She shook her head.

"I trusted you—"

"Yes, sir," Alice said. "So did a lot of people."

"People who got killed!" Tony said. "You—damn

you, you made us kill people! You made Pres Sanders into a basket case, and—"

"That's not fair," Alice said. "You know I can't talk about any of that! Not here, with all these police—"

"Pres did," Tony said. "And I still don't understand you. You worked here. You *knew* what we were building, that people *like* it here, we don't pollute, we—"

"You don't live like humans, either," Alice said. "And even if you call this human life, it's not for very many people. Todos Santos is beautiful, Tony, but it uses too many resources to support too few people. The more successful Todos Santos is, the worse it will be for everyone else, don't you understand that? Don't you understand that technology is not the answer, that using technology to fix problems created by technology only puts you in an endless chain? That the more success you have, the more you make people believe that 'Progress' is possible, and Progress just leads to more technology and more waste and more doom—"

"Alice, you wear glasses," Tony said mildly. "You probably use tampons."

"One thing I do understand," Art Bonner said. "You gave us good reason to trust you. We believed you, and you betrayed us. I'm sorry your friends were killed, but I'm not sorry they can charge you with murder."

Murder. Damn, of course, she was in the conspiracy, and that led to murder and—

Conspiracy.

• • •

Eventually the outsiders left. Tony turned to go.

"A moment of your time," Bonner said.

"Yeah?"

"There are a lot of cops wandering around here," Bonner said. "Like a well-smoked beehive. And reporters. And everyone else, all looking at us."

Tony nodded. "Yeah. I've been meaning to catch some sleep, but it's interesting—"

"You won't get a chance to sleep," Bonner said. "I've been reviewing your plan to get Sanders out of jail. I like it."

Tony eyed him warily.

"It seems to me this is a good time," Bonner said. "While everyone's watching us. You did say weekend, and this is Saturday."

Oh shit oh dear, Tony thought. "But we don't *need* to. Not after this! Everybody will know we really need defenses . . ."

"What happened today won't change the fact that the kids Pres killed were carrying nothing more deadly than sand and paint. This may make it easier to get a jury to acquit him, but he'll still have put in a year in jail before it's over."

"And Pres? Have you asked him about this?" Tony demanded.

Bonner ignored the question. "Your plan needs some advance preparations," Bonner said. "As near as I can figure, if you start now, we can be ready tonight at lights-out. Any reason why you can't get to it?"

"Conspiracy," Tony said. "And if anyone's killed, it's homicide—"

"So don't kill anyone. You've already made up your mind, Tony. I don't have to wheedle you. So let's cut the crap and get at it. We both have work to do."

Tony nodded in submission.

XVIII

When we jumped into Sicily, the units became separated, and I couldn't find anyone. Eventually I stumbled across two colonels, a major, three captains, two lieutenants, and one rifleman, and we secured the bridge. Never in the history of war have so few been led by so many.

—General James Gavin

EXECUTIVE ACTION

George Harris had learned to disconnect his mind during heavy exercise. If he thought about the pain or the fatigue or the monotony, he'd stop. His body followed the routine while his mind daydreamed, or planned business strategy, or slept.

But on Saturdays and Sundays, shut away from his weights and machines and confined by concrete and iron bars, he had to improvise a routine. That took concentration. It took more concentration to ignore a distraction, the sad-eyed ghost in the upper bunk.

Twenty-nine . . . thirty. Harris rested for a few seconds, waiting until his breathing slowed before he spoke. A harmless vanity. Then, "I wish to hell you'd join me. You're in good shape. What were you doing on the outside, skiing? Surfing? You're not doing it now. In here I've never seen you do anything but lie there and eat your liver."

Preston Sanders didn't look up. His arms were behind his head, his eyes were on the ceiling.

"That raid last night has to help your case," Harris said. "They had real bombs, and the TV said there was a shootout. Guns and everything. This wasn't just kids out playing tricks."

Still nothing. "Now there's demonstrations all over the city. Fromates and a lot of outfits named Citizens for This and That want to burn Todos Santos to the ground and sow salt where it stood. Funny thing, though. There are counterdemonstrators. Nothing organized, but more than you'd expect." George went into his sit-ups. The patrolling guard stopped for a minute to watch, then moved on. On previous weekends he'd made witty comments . . . until George called him "Butterball" every time he passed, and then every felon in the block took it up, and now the guard generally didn't say anything.

. . . Thirty. George stood and went to the bunks. "You lie there long enough and you'll turn to butter," he told Sanders. "Jesus, you're younger than I am. Can you do thirty push-ups?"

"No."

"It'd take your mind off what's eating you. Sanders, it is impossible to think about what a jury will do to you when you're on your twenty-fifth push-up and going for thirty. Try it with me?"

Sanders shook his head.

He was the least troublesome cell-mate George Harris had ever had. More: He was a potential customer, even if he did turn off whenever George tried to swing the conversation around to new construction in Todos Santos. *I guess I brought it up too early,* George thought. *Too bad, but maybe that'll change. If I can get him to talk at all, and that's tough enough.*

"They didn't identify the raiders yet," Harris said. "But that commentator guy, Lunan, said they were an outfit calling itself the American Ecology Army. That's a splinter group that broke away from the

Fromates years ago, but Lunan says the two outfits still work together. He sounded real sure. I read everything I can about it, what with being in here with you. Besides, I knew the Planchet kid."

That got Sanders's attention. "I never did. What was he like?"

Harris shrugged. "Nice enough, I guess. Personable, maybe a little shy. I only met him twice. I could have liked him, except I heard about a stunt he pulled in high school. Never mind. The point is, he was a total damned fool and he died for it."

"He didn't die. He was killed."

"Yeah, sure, but he worked at it. Hey, you know you're a hero back in Todos Santos? Yeah, no kidding. I went to the Big Brothers lunch out there last week—"

"I always liked those."

"Yeah, I can see why. Quite a blast. I won a pocket computer in the raffle. Anyway, when they found out I was your cell-mate everybody wanted me to give you the same message. 'You done good.' "

"Who?" Sanders asked. "Art Bonner?"

"Yeah, he was one of them. Some others, too, I didn't get everybody's name. And Tony Rand." Harris looked sidewise at Sanders. "He's a strange one, isn't he?"

"He can be," Sanders said. "Tony's about the best friend I have out there."

"Oh, I can see how you could like that guy a lot. Once you got to know him. Anyway, they're all on your side. Sanders, it's dumb to lie there eating your liver. You got paid to do a job, and when the time came you earned your salary. You don't need to hear that from a jury. Think of it as evolution in action."

"What did you say?"

Harris laughed. "I saw it on—" He stopped. Listened. Then he said, "Get down from there. I mean it. Sit on the lower bunk. I think—" He listened again. "Feel that? I think there's a quake coming." He tugged at Sanders's arm, and Sanders came down. He wasn't that soft; he didn't drop, he lowered himself by the strength of his arms.

Harris said, "You feel it? Not a jolt, just shaking, like a preliminary temblor? Everything's vibrating—"

"I feel it."

"I hear something, too." It was right at the threshold of sound . . . but it went on, steadily.

"Machinery somewhere," Sanders said. "You're not from California, are you? Earthquakes can't be heard coming."

"Wha . . . ? Oh. Too bad." Harris considered going into deep knee bends; but by damn, he'd finally got Sanders talking, and he wasn't going to stop. "What I saw was a bumper sticker. 'RAISE THE SPEED LIMIT. THINK OF IT AS EVOLUTION IN ACTION.' "

Sanders smiled. "I can guess who said that first. It had to be Tony Rand."

"Really? I wouldn't have guessed that. I mean, I didn't get to talk to him very long, but I was impressed, meeting the guy that built the Nest." Aaargh. Wrong word, it had just slipped out. In haste, Harris continued, "What's he really like?"

"A good friend," Sanders said. "He didn't used to worry much about social relationships, politics, anything like that. Now he's . . . eating his liver, like you said. He's losing sleep because maybe he could have designed Todos Santos so I wouldn't have to do that." Sanders shuddered, and Harris was suddenly afraid there would be histrionics. But Sanders said quietly, "Maybe he's keeping me sane. Damn, I'd love to blame it all on Tony Rand. And I know he never thought of that. I know it. That's the nice part."

"Court magician," Harris said. "That's what they called him on the TV documentary, anyway." And I've got you talking now—

Only a miracle could have captured Harris's attention at that moment.

The miracle was a tiny hole that formed suddenly in the concrete floor, just where Harris's eyes rested.

George slid off the bunk and crouched to look. He poked at the hole with his finger. It was real.

Sanders asked, "What are you doing?"

"Damndest thing," Harris said. He thought he saw light through the hole, but when he bent closer to look, there was only darkness. And a trace of a strange, mustily sweet smell. "Orange blossoms? I saw this little tiny," he said, and fell over.

• • •

The vehicle Tony Rand was driving was longer than four Cadillacs, and shaped roughly like a .22 Long Rifle cartridge. Thick hoses in various colors, some as thick as Tony's torso, trailed away down the tunnel and out of sight. The visibility ahead was poor. The top speed was contemptible. The mileage would have horrified a Cadillac owner. It wasn't even quiet. Water poured through the blue hoses, live steam blasted back down the red hoses, hydrogen flame roared softly ahead of the cabin, heated rock snapped and crackled, and cool air hissed in the cabin.

For so large a vehicle the cabin was cramped, stuck onto the rear almost as an afterthought. It was cluttered with the extra gear Tony Rand had brought with him, so that Thomas Lunan had to sit straddling a large red-painted tank and regulator. There were far too many dials to watch. The best you could say for the Mole was that, unlike your ordinary automobile, it could drive through rock.

So we're driving through rock, Lunan thought, and giggled.

The blunt, rounded nose of the Mole was white hot. Rock melted and flowed around the nose, flowed back as lava until it reached the water-cooled collar, where it froze. The congealed rock was denser then, compressed into a fine tunnel wall with a flat floor.

Lunan was sweating. Why did I get into this? I can't get any pix, and I can't ever tell anybody I was here . . .

"Where are we?" Lunan asked. He had to shout.

"About ten feet to go," Rand said.

"How do you know?"

"Inertial guidance system," Rand said. He pointed to a blue screen, which showed a bright pathway that abruptly became a dotted line. "We're right here," Tony said. He pointed to the junction of dot and solid line.

"You trust that thing?"

"It's pretty good," Rand said. "Hell, it's superb. It has to be. You don't want to put a tunnel in the wrong place."

Lunan laughed. "Let's hope they want a tunnel here—"

"Yeah." Rand fell silent. After a while he adjusted a vent to increase the cool air flowing through the cabin.

Despite the air flow, and the cabin insulation, Lunan was sweating. There was no place to hide. None at all. If anyone suspected what they were doing, they had only to follow the hoses to the end of the blind tunnel.

"We're here," Rand said.

Noise levels fell as Rand turned down the hydrogen jets. He looked at his watch, then lifted the microphone dangling from the vehicle's dashboard. "Art?"

"Here."

"My computations tell me I'm either under Pres's cell or just offshore from Nome, Alaska—"

"You don't have to keep me entertained." The voice blurred and crackled. No eavesdropper could have sworn that Art Bonner was speaking to the soon-to-be-notorious felon, Anthony Rand. A nice touch, Lunan thought.

"No, sir," Tony said.

"As far as we can tell, you hit it just right," the radio said. "They're still at dinner. Or all the months of tunnel drilling around here got them used to the noise. Whatever. Anyway, we don't hear any signs of alert."

"Good," Rand said. He put down the microphone and turned to Lunan. "Now we wait four hours."

Lunan had carefully prepared for this moment. He took a pack of cards from his pocket and said, casually: "Gin?"

• • •

It was nine-thirty in the evening and Vinnie Thompson couldn't believe his good fortune. He'd been hoping for a decent score later, some guy coming back from winning a big bet on the hockey game at the Forum, or maybe a sailor with a month's pay. This early there probably wouldn't be much, but there might be somebody with bread, although most Angelinos were smart enough not to carry much into the subway system. Of course they'd carry money in the Todos Santos stations, but everybody in Vinnie's line of work learned early to stay away from there. The TS guards might or might not turn you in to the LA cops, but more important they might *hurt* you. A lot. They didn't like muggers at all.

Maybe tonight he'd get a break. He needed one. He hadn't hit a good score in two weeks.

Then he saw his vision. A man in a three-piece suit, an *expensive* suit with alligator shoes (like the ones Vinnie kept at home, you wouldn't catch him taking something valuable like that into the subway). The vision carried a briefcase, and he was not only alone, he'd gone through a door into a maintenance tunnel!

And there sure as hell wasn't anybody in that tunnel this time of night. What could Mr. Three-piece want? Take a pee? Meet somebody? While he was wondering about that, by God here she came! A hell of a looker, well dressed in an expensive pantsuit, and she was alone too! She went in the same door as Three-piece, and Vinnie snickered. She'd get a surprise . . . Once again he congratulated himself. Heaven couldn't offer more attractions.

She'd locked the door behind her, but it didn't take Vinnie's knife long to take care of that. He went through quickly and pulled the door closed. The corridor in front of him was empty, but he could hear rapid heel-clicks around the bend ahead of him.

He could also hear sounds of machinery coming from down the tunnel. Somebody was working overtime here. Well, that didn't matter, he'd just have to be quick, although that was a shame, the chick was a real looker and it'd be something to get into that. He could imagine her look of fear, and feel her writhing in his grasp, and he quickened his step to catch up to her. She'd be just around this bend in the tunnel—

He rounded the bend. There were half a dozen people there, all in expensive clothes. They looked up at him, first in surprise, then in annoyance.

Too many, Vinnie thought. But they looked like money, and he had his knife and a blackjack made of a leather bag of BB's and if he did this right—Feet scuffed behind him.

He was trying to turn, to run, when a bomb exploded under his jaw. Lights flared behind his eyes, but through the blaze he saw his vision again: fluffy razor-cut hair, and a broad, smooth-shaven face snarling with even white teeth, and a polished gold ring on a huge fist.

• • •

"Gin," Rand said. "That's thirty-five million dollars you owe me." He stared at his watch. "And now we go to work."

Lunan grimaced. So far they hadn't done anything. Well, nothing that would send you to prison. God knows what crime it might be to dig a tunnel under the County Jail (reckless driving?) but so far no harm done. Now, though . . .

Rand handed him a heavy tool and Lunan took it automatically. It was a large drill with a long, thin bit. Trickling sweat stung his eyes.

Rand was sweating too, and after a moment the

engineer removed his shirt. "*Damn* Delores," he muttered.

"Eh?"

"Oh. Nothing." Rand threw his shirt down the tunnel. Then he lifted the microphone. "We're starting in now," he said. "Everything all right at your end?"

"Yeah, barring three surprised muggers. Have at it."

"Roger." Rand hung up the mike and turned to Lunan. "Okay, let's get at it." He took a strip of computer readout from the console in front of him, then manipulated controls. A very bright spot of light appeared on the tunnel roof above them. "Drill right there," Rand said.

The ceiling was concrete, very rough. Lunan thought the drill bit too thin and weak for the job, but when he applied it and pulled the trigger, the drill ate in quickly. And quietly, Lunan noticed. After a while the bit went in all the way.

Rand took the drill and changed to a longer bit. "My turn," he said.

"What do I do?" Lunan asked.

"Just stand by." Rand drilled at the ceiling. When the bit was all the way in, he took out still another, this one a foot long, still very thin. He drilled cautiously, withdrawing the bit often. Then he saw light, and pointed.

"Mask time," Rand said. Lunan handed up a gas mask, then put on his own.

The hole in the ceiling was no more than a pinprick, which was what Rand had told Lunan to expect. When he had his mask on properly, Lunan went over to a large red tank. There was a hose attached to it, and Lunan handed up the hose and watched as Rand put it to the hole and sealed it in place with aluminized duct tape. "Crack the valve," Rand said, and Lunan turned the valve handle. There was a faint hissing. Rand pointed to the microphone.

"Phase two," Lunan said into the mike. "Hope we're in the right place—"

"All quiet here. Out," the radio answered.

Lunan replaced the mike. Quiet there, which was the tunnel entrance. Just one entrance, guarded by TS executives, which meant Lunan and Rand were safe. Of course it also meant there was only one exit. Unless they wanted to dig a new one, fleeing the law at a few dozen feet an hour . . .

Rand waved and made cutting motions, and Lunan shut off the sleepy gas. He worried about that gas. Rand said the stuff was the safest he could find, unlikely to harm anyone except possibly a heart patient; but there was no way they could control the dosages. This was the trickiest part of the maneuver—

Rand had removed the tube and widened the hole slightly. Now he was trying to insert the tiny, thin periscope, and cursing.

"What?" Lunan asked.

"Blocked," Rand said. Swearing terribly, he moved two feet away and tried the drill again. When light showed, he inserted his periscope and looked. He turned it this way and that, then chuckled and motioned for Lunan to come look.

Concrete floor, something overhead, all very dark. Tom Lunan adjusted the light amplification and rotated the periscope.

Aha. Foreground, a pair of feet showed under a very low ceiling. He was under a bunk. Beyond, a mouse's-eye view of a jail cell: concrete floor, toilet, sink, and a middle-aged felon in fine physical shape sleeping peacefully on Tony Rand's first periscope hole.

While Tom looked, Rand brought up the gas tube and put it to the new hole. "Body blocked the flow," Rand muttered, and went back to open the valve on the tank.

He let it run another minute, then disconnected the hose and brought up the periscope again. Meanwhile, Lunan had attached the electronic stethoscope to the floor. He put on the earphones. At highest sensitivity he could hear the sounds of breathing and a heartbeat. Otherwise nothing. He made the "OK" sign to Rand.

Rand nodded and turned to the control console. When he twisted dials, a large jack ascended from the top of the vehicle and rose until it touched the ceiling. Another control sent up a large saw and spray hoses. The saw began cutting in a circular pattern around the jack.

It wailed like a banshee. Lunan felt real terror. Surely someone would hear that, the horrible rasping sound that proclaimed "JAILBREAK!" Evidently it worried Rand too, because he rigged up the tank and sent more sleepy gas through the hole.

The saw cut on a bias, a concrete disk larger at the top than at the bottom. Eventually the cut was made, and Tony used the jack to lift the plug until it was two feet higher than the cell floor. Lunan helped him set up a newly bought aluminum stepladder. Rand scrambled up it and disappeared, while Lunan arranged Therm-A-Rest air mattresses on the flat top of the vehicle. Then he climbed up, squeezing under the concrete plug. There was a moment of terror when he dislodged his gas mask, but he got it back on without breathing.

Preston Sanders was on his side in the lower bunk, with his feet hanging over the edge. He'd lost weight since Lunan had seen him in a courtroom, but he was still heavy. They lifted him and Rand slid down through the hole again, leaving Lunan to lower Sanders down like a sack of potatoes, with Rand to catch him and let him down onto the mattresses.

Now they had to work fast. Rand smeared the concrete plug with epoxy and lowered it into place. Then he filled the periscope holes. While he did that, Lunan manhandled Sanders into the cabin of the machine, and thought about the origins of that picturesque verb. Man-handled. Yep.

"Got it," Rand said.

"Won't they be able to see the hole?"

"Yeah, sure, I couldn't make the join perfect, especially working from the bottom—but they'll never get that plug out without jackhammers and such. Let's get out of here."

"Get your shirt," Lunan said.

"Shit, oh dear. What else have we forgotten?"

"The ladder, and the mattresses, and—"

"That's okay," Rand said. "They can't be traced." He chuckled. "Well, not profitably, anyway."

"Hey, I'm supposed to get the whole story."

"You've got all the story," Rand said. "My instructions are to see you off before Pres wakes up. I make that to be about ten more minutes."

"Yeah. All right," Lunan said. So. The adventure was coming to an end. Ye gods, what he'd seen! The top brass—the TOP BRASS—of Todos Santos involved in felony jailbreak. Not that he could tell anyone, or even hint that he had certain knowledge. Rumor. All rumors . . . Lunan sighed. It was a hell of a story. Now all he had to do was figure out the best way to use it.

They drove away at the Mole's contemptible top speed.

• • •

Pres woke up twenty minutes later. He blinked and focused on Tony Rand, stared for a moment, and said, "We were just talking about you."

"Oh?"

"True. What's going on? Where am I?"

"We're roaring away in our trusty getaway vehicle, seconds ahead of The Law."

"Yeah, I can hear the roaring, anyway. It matches my head." Pres pushed himself up and looked back down the tunnel. "Good Lord. Tony? Is it the digging machine, the one that's making the subway under City Hall? Shit, are we really making our own tunnel?"

The Mole surged forward. Needles spun on the

panel, and the automatics cut off the hydrogen flow. Without melted rock to carry heat away from the nose, the nose itself would melt. Half-fused rubble slid past the cabin. Then the Mole lurched into the open night. Tony lifted the microphone from the console panel.

"We're loose." He put down the mike and turned to Sanders, grinning. "Most of the time you were asleep we were running back along an already-made tunnel. Then just before you woke up we started boring again. Now come on. You know, Pres, we might actually make it?"

Sanders was still groggy, but recovering. "Where are we now? Did you really break me out of jail?"

Tony led him out of the Mole and walked him through the night. Where was that stairway? "The OK Corral will never be the same. We've reached either the famed concrete banks of the Los Angeles River, or the equally famous Hoover Dam, depending." Ah. There were the stairs. "We go up, now."

"You gonna just leave the digger?"

"Jesus! Stay here." Tony sprinted back to the Mole and came back uphill more slowly, carrying his shirt and the gas cannister. "This could be traced. The rest of that garbage was all bought today, by credit-card number and telephone, delivered to a blind drop. It was charged to one Professor Arnold Renn. That might cause a bit of confusion."

"Renn? He's Fromate, isn't he?" Pres started to laugh.

"Art says he was the advisor to the Planchet kid," Rand said.

"Oh." Sanders was silent a moment, then laughed. "Hey, they'll think the Fromates got me!"

"Not for long they won't, but it might slow down the opposition."

Sanders stopped. "Tony, I don't like this much. I mean—you broke me out of jail. We're both wanted by the law. Where can we go?"

"We're going home, I hope."

"Yeah, but—look, Tony, Art must have put you up to this, and don't think I'm not grateful, but dammit, Art doesn't own Todos Santos! He can't hide me forever, the management council has to know, and some of them don't like me. Somebody'll turn me in, for sure . . ."

His voice trailed off when he realized that Rand was only half listening. Tony was trying to orient himself. Where the hell was the street? Where the hell was *anything?* They stumbled onward. Then, ahead, car lights flashed twice and went dark.

"Thank God," Tony said. "Come on, Pres, just a little farther. Ah. Good, they remembered to cut the fence. Here, through right here, and we go the rest of the way by taxi. Swallow your pride and climb in."

An ordinary Yellow Cab stood waiting for them. The driver didn't speak.

Sanders tumbled into the back seat, still rubber-limbed, and thrashed to right himself as Tony tumbled in beside him and the taxi took off. Pres complained, "Hey! The speed limit! My pride wouldn't take it if we got pulled in for reckless driving."

The cab slowed at once. Tony asked, "How do you feel?"

"Fine. No more headache. No hangover." Sanders settled back in his seat. "I feel great! Of course they'll find us—"

"Maybe not," Rand said.

The cabbie said, "Where to, sir?" and turned around.

"Mead? Frank Mead?"

"Did you think we'd leave you for the eaters? Welcome home. In a half hour you'll be wolfing a midnight snack and drinking genuine Scotch. No, brandy's your drink, right? Remy Martin, then."

"Frank Mead. Sheeit! I thought . . . never mind what I thought. Listen, Tony, if I'm awake now, so is anyone else you dosed, right?"

"It'll take them awhile to get their act together," Tony said. "They won't know how you got out or where you went. I sealed up the hole. It's a locked-room mystery, secret passage and all."

"That's all right, then." Sanders started laughing.

• • •

George Harris woke with a mild headache and a feeling that something was wrong. That was confirmed when he heard the guards running up and down the corridors. "Head count!" they were shouting. "Everybody stand by your bunks!"

"Pres, what the hell is all this?" George demanded. "Pres?"

When there was no answer he looked around the cell. "Jesus H. Christ!" he shouted. Now what? And how had it happened? He remembered the tiny hole he'd seen, and looked down at the floor, but in the dim light he couldn't see anything at all. Should he tell the guards? Tell them what, that his cell-mate was missing? To hell with those bastards! But if he didn't cooperate, they'd nail his arse to the wall.

George grinned faintly to himself and lay down on the lower bunk. It wasn't hard at all to go back to sleep.

"Uh?" George woke to bright lights and a dozen deputies in his cell.

"What? Where's Sanders? Where'd he go?" the fat jailer shouted over and over.

"Uh? Pres, tell these buzzards to buzz off—"

"Where is he?"

"That'll do, Winsome. Mr. Harris, I remind you that aiding an escape from lawful confinement is a felony. Now, are you willing to cooperate?"

"Sure," George said.

"Excellent. What can you tell us?"

It was hard to keep from giggling, but George managed a straight face. "Nothing. Not one thing. I went to sleep talking to Preston Sanders and I just woke up." He rolled out of his bunk and looked into the upper bunk. "Pres?" He lifted the blanket. Nothing. "Shit fire."

• • •

"Hal? Hal, it's the telephone."

Donovan came awake as from beneath a deep, stagnant pond, vaguely aware that Carol was speaking to him. Gradually he understood. "Okay, honey. Thanks." He took the phone and listened.

Carol watched from her bed. Her blue negligee fell open and Donovan winked at her. His pretense was that she *always* turned him on. She did, often enough.

When he put the phone down and reached for his pants, she looked resigned. She'd long since stopped asking questions. He'd either explain or he wouldn't.

"Not a new murder," Donovan said. "Maybe not even my case. But it was my prisoner." Even that didn't get a rise. She looked at him expectantly, even with interest, but she wasn't asking questions.

"Preston Sanders," Donovan said. "Technically my case and my prisoner. He's escaped from the County Jail."

"Escaped? Great heavens, Harry, how?" Carol Donovan demanded.

"Nobody seems to know, just at present," Donovan said. "I suppose they'll find out."

"So you're going down to the jail?"

"I'll start there. Just to see how they did it."

"How *they* did it?"

"Sure. I don't have to know what happened to know Todos Santos has made their move. I just hope it doesn't mean all-out war."

When Donovan arrived at the County Jail, a team of workmen were breaking through the floor with jackhammers. The officer in charge, Sheriff's Captain Oliver Matson, was an old friend. One of Matson's deputies handed Donovan Polaroids of the cell floor taken before the jackhammers started. There was a thin circular line showing clearly on the floor.

"He went out that way, all right," the deputy said.

"Here," a workman said. "Hey! Watch out!"

"What is it?" Matson asked.

"It's all hollow under there. A tunnel."

"Tunnel," Donovan said. Of course there had to be a tunnel. How else could Sanders have got away? But how had the tunnel got under the County Jail? "Holy shit!"

"What?" his friend demanded.

"The digging machine! The Mole!" Donovan shouted. "That's how they did it, they dug a subway tunnel with the Mole, that big damned digging machine of theirs—any minute now they'll report it stolen. Anybody want to bet they won't?"

"Oh, crap," Matson said. "Jesus. That's acting on the grand scale."

The workmen had the tunnel open. Deputies squeezed through and when they were out of the way Donovan and Matson followed.

"No doubt about it," Matson said. "A new subway tunnel—well, we won't need bloodhounds to follow *this* trail."

Donovan laughed, but he thought they might as well get out the bloodhounds. Nothing else was going to catch Sanders. Not just Sanders. He looked at the smooth-sided tunnel walls. "Just like magic," he said.

"Which?"

"We're looking for a magician. In this case a court magician."

It was highly irritating to Donovan that Oliver Matson hadn't seen the documentary. Donovan hated to explain jokes.

• • •

The meeting was in an apartment that showed on no maps of Todos Santos. It would have taken twenty people with excellent measuring instruments the better part of a day merely to prove there was an apartment there; finding the entrance and getting it open would take a lot longer.

Most of the Todos Santos brass was there, and Tony Rand basked in their approbation. Everything had gone well (and he could forget just how scared he'd been).

"What about the other guy?" Bonner asked. "Pres's cell-mate. Maybe you should have done him a favor."

"Whooo-ee," Sanders said. He bellowed laughter. "Jesus, no, Art. Harris is only in there on weekends! He'd have screamed bloody murder, to find out the cops are after him and—" He stopped laughing, and the general mood of euphoria faded. "So what happens now?"

"Several choices," Bonner said. "All of them reasonable. How would you like my job?"

"That's silly—"

"Not here," Bonner said. "And not an arcology. But Romulus has a lot of operations, and the top slot's open in one of them. How do you feel about going to Africa?"

Sanders lifted one eyebrow. "Seems a long way to run—"

Bonner spread his hands. "We'll talk about it in the morning. As I said, it's your choice. You wouldn't have to go too far—don't forget, at the moment the police have no proof that you escaped. You may be the victim of a kidnapping."

The grin, or part of it, returned to Sanders. "Do you really think we can pin it on the Fromates?"

Frank Mead snorted. "Wouldn't want to, would we? We saved one of our own, and I'd like it if everybody in the LA Basin knows it. As long as they can't prove it." He looked thoughtful. "We didn't actually put our autograph on anything, unless Tony—"

"Would Picasso refrain from signing his masterpiece?"

"Sign it or not, they'll guess," Art Bonner said. He giggled suddenly. "Speaking of signing your work—"

"What?" Barbara asked.

"The muggers. What should we do with the muggers?"

"Kill the sons of bitches," Frank Mead said.

"Hey, no," Sanders yelled. "Hey—"

"Don't worry, we won't," Bonner said. "Frank didn't mean that anyway."

Mead shrugged and massaged his fist. He had bruises under his large ring and on two knuckles, but there was a pensively happy smile on his face. "So what do we do with the meat heads? Where are they, anyway?"

"In a dark room off Medical," Bonner said. "I believe the technical term is 'under heavy sedation'. Of course we'll have to let them go, eventually."

"They were bad dudes," Mead said.

"Hard on Los Angeles," Delores said.

"Nothing Los Angeles doesn't deserve. But I had an idea—"

"Should we be making decisions now?" Barbara asked. "We're all pretty soused."

"Good point, sweetheart," Bonner said. He went to her and took her hand. "Let's go home. Oh. Tony—"

"Yeah?"

"The LA cops will want you for questioning. I'd as soon they didn't find you."

Delores came up and put her arm through Tony's. "That answers one question," she said.

Tony frowned the question at her.

"My place or yours? We can't go to yours," she said. "Mine will be safe enough. For a while." She marched him out of the room.

XIX

They [corporations] cannot commit treason, nor be
outlawed nor excommunicated, for they have no souls.
—Sir Edward Coke, Lord Chief Justice of England
Sutton's Hospital Case, 10 *Report* 32, 1628

RETRIBUTION

Her position was odd, and she was cold. The sheets
and blankets were twisted all to hell. Delores
untangled them enough to pull them over her head.

Feeling nice . . . feeling sleepy. Would she be able
to get back to sleep? They hadn't slept much last
night.

Where was Tony?

She heard the *ting* of room service delivery, and
smelled coffee. Coffee and unidentifiable breakfast
smells. Suddenly her hunger was like teeth gnashing
in her belly.

Shorted on sleep, they'd burned considerable energy
last night. The court magician had never before
shown any such tendency toward satyriasis. Being a
hero must make a man horny, Delores thought.

She sat up and called, "What have we got?"

"All kinds of things." Tony sounded cheerful, and

well he might. "Melon. Blinis. Eggs Benedict. Coffee and hot milk. Vodka right out of a freezer."

She came to see. *So little time, so much to do*—She tore into a thick wedge of honey-dew melon, and for a time there was silence. Tony seemed as hungry as she was. Even so—*"Hombre,* we'll never eat all this! Which are blinis? The pancakes?"

"Right. Beluga caviar, sour cream and a splash of hot butter between two buckwheat pancakes. The iced vodka goes with the blinis, if you've a mind. Who's gonna question my expense account on a day like today?"

Her spoon stopped moving. *Your last day.* She looked up. Had he guessed?

He had. "Lunan gave me too much publicity. The Angelino cops are sure to guess who did it. Where do you think they'll send me?"

She cut into a blini while she considered. Art might send Tony out with Pres Sanders. They got along. Or . . . it hit her as she raised the fork to her mouth. The appointment with Sir George Reedy. Art would try to sell him Tony's contract. Canada!

Then she tasted the magic of a blini. "Tony, it's *wonderful!*"

"Yeah. You'd have to own Todos Santos to eat like this every day. I'm glad the Soviets are finally cleaning up their rivers. Hey, Delores, I don't really care where they send me—"

She couldn't tell him. Art wouldn't like her jumping the gun.

"—I just want to know you're coming with me."

In that moment she knew the answer. Guarding her boss's secrets from her lover, automatically, reflexively, told her where her loyalty lay. She said, "I'm not."

Tony said nothing, but the life went out of his face. He swallowed, with difficulty. He started to say something, stopped.

She *couldn't* let him beg. In haste she said, "Tony,

I've got power and respect here. I'm the General Manager's secretary. It's an important job—"

"I'd probably be moving to another arcology. Or building one."

"And I'd be the court magician's old lady. Tony, I didn't even settle for General Manager's mistress! That's an interchangeable slot—no pun intended—"

Tony's laugh was more of a bark, and Delores didn't smile. "I want something permanent. I've got it here."

Now he looked up. "You know, the whole city wondered why you and Art broke it up."

"No privacy in this place."

He poured a thimbleful of vodka into a chilled liqueur glass. "You gave me one classic hero's welcome," he said. "I won't ever forget."

"Pour me one too."

• • •

"You've gone insane," John Shapiro said. "Absolutely bonkers."

Lieutenant Donovan nodded to himself. Right enough by me, he thought. They've all gone nuts.

They stood at the main surface entrance to Todos Santos. An enormous banner fluttered overhead: THINK OF IT AS EVOLUTION IN ACTION.

They were surrounded by police and lawyers. Donovan could see: uniformed Todos Santos guards to the rank of major; three FBI men; federal marshals; *scads* of Los Angeles County Sheriff's deputies, some in uniform and others in plain clothes; his own three LAPD cops; two United States Attorneys; and four Los Angeles County Deputy District Attorneys, one of whom had just served a paper on the Todos Santos General Manager.

Plus five Todos Santos attorneys including John Shapiro, who had insisted on reading the warrant, aloud, from beginning to end. Eventually he finished.

"You can't search an entire city," Shapiro said. "Even if that were possible, you can't do it with a single warrant! If you want to look somewhere, you have to get a warrant for that particular place—"

"Impossible!" the Deputy D.A. said. "There are too many places—"

"About a hundred thousand private apartments," Shapiro agreed. "And each one a separate dwelling. '. . . and no warrants shall issue, but upon probable cause, supported by oath or affirmation, and particularly describing the place to be searched, and the persons or things to be seized.' Sixth Amendment."

"I know that."

"I wondered," Shapiro said. "Because it doesn't look as if you've read it lately. You've got some of the second part. Persons to be seized, Preston Sanders and Anthony Rand—although I challenge your proper cause for wanting to arrest Mr. Rand. But the rest of this document is ridiculous. How ever did you get a judge to sign it?"

"It's signed," a sheriff's deputy said. "Now let us in."

"And another thing. You name MILLIE as a 'place to be searched.' Just how do you propose to search a computer?"

They were interrupted by a burst of laughter from the Todos Santos manager. "He looks like he's got canary feathers in his whiskers," Donovan muttered to his assistant.

"These papers are in order," the D.A.'s spokesman said. "Now are you going to let us in or do we have to break in?"

Shapiro shrugged and looked to the General Manager. "Mr. Bonner?"

"Admit them under protest. Get their names and badge numbers. We'll want to sue." Bonner turned and stamped away.

Shapiro stood aside, and Donovan followed the horde of police through the entryway and into the broad corridor.

"Where the hell do we start?" Sergeant Ortiz asked.

Donovan shrugged. "Thank God I'm not in charge of this farce. Cops sure can be stupid sometimes. I don't know what those guys will do, but what we do is nothing. We're not going to find anything, and we all know it. Why go through the motions?" He paused in thought. "For that matter, I'm not so sure I *want* to find this Rand character. Next time they might take away the whole damned jail."

"Or City Hall."

• • •

"In there," Guard Lieutenant Blake said. He indicated a low door. "I'll be here in the service tunnel, and Security is watching all the corridors. If the Angelino cops get close, we'll hold them up."

"Right," Tony Rand said. "Thanks."

The access door from the service corridor was low, and Tony had to duck to get through into Art Bonner's temporary office. It nearly matched the real thing. The desk and viewscreens were almost identical, though the shelves were empty of the sailing memorabilia and other clutter that Bonner kept.

The door outside claimed the suite was an apartment occupied by a retired Marine colonel. Inside were Bonner, Barbara Churchward, and Sir George Reedy.

"Come in, Tony," Bonner said. "We're just putting the finishing touches on our agreement—"

Sir George didn't look very happy. Tony regarded the Canadian's expression and asked, "How much are you getting for my contract?"

"Oh, we're being quite reasonable," Barbara said cheerfully.

"It's too much," Reedy protested. "He's a wanted man. They'll extradite him and we'll have nothing for all that money."

"No, you can give him political asylum," Bonner said. "If it comes to that, which I doubt. I doubt they'll even try on a federal level. If they do, Shapiro can keep the State Department tied in knots for years.

It isn't as if they had any real *evidence* that Tony was involved in their jailbreak. Our problem is that they can keep him in courtrooms forever."

"Do I get a say in this?" Tony asked.

"Sure, Tony," Bonner said. "It's this way. You have a contract with Romulus Corporation. Romulus is negotiating consultation fees for helping the Canadians build their new arcology. They want a lot of engineering help. If you like, you'll be in charge of the engineering team. That's one of your alternatives—I would have thought the most attractive one."

"What are the others?"

"You can go to Zimbabwe with Pres—"

Tony Rand frowned. "Zimbabwe? Where the devil is that?"

"It used to be called 'Rhodesia,'" Barbara said.

"Why would Pres want to go to Rhodesia?" Tony demanded.

Sir George's eyebrows lifted.

Barbara laughed. "He really doesn't know, Sir George. He never pays attention to anything outside Todos Santos. Tony, Zimbabwe was a colony run by whites until a few years ago. Now it has a black government. A fairly good one, as such things go in Africa. Romulus has had its eye on Pres as honcho of corporate operations there for a long time; now's a very good chance. We put the idea to Pres, and he likes it."

Tony nodded. Pres would like it. A good promotion, with a chance to run his own show. Would he resent getting this promotion because he was black? Or find that amusing? Have to ask him . . .

"So you could go with him," Bonner was saying. "You work well with Sanders, and Romulus has some extensive civil engineering operations in Zimbabwe. It would be a good place to stash you until we need you on the orbital construction shack—"

Rand looked from Bonner to Reedy. "Umh huh. That last part sounds pretty good," he said.

Reedy chuckled. "You needn't bring out the sandbags." He looked thoughtful. "But there's the general strike that Councilman Planchet has called against Todos Santos. I'm not certain I want economic reprisals taken against me—and there would be for hiring Mr. Rand."

"Well, they might try it, but what can they really do to you?" Bonner asked. "They're too far away."

They're too far from Canada, Tony Rand thought. But not too far from us! A general strike! That's got to have Art worried out of his mind. He doesn't show it, but it's got to be hurting us—

"Perhaps you're right," Sir George said. He stared pensively at the ceiling for a moment, then said, "I'd want it clearly understood that we have you two on call. I'll want you by hologram for at least ten hours a month, and two weeks a year actually in residence."

"Both of us?" Barbara asked.

"Certainly," Reedy said.

Bonner looked thoughtful. So did Churchward and Reedy.

Now they're doing it again, Tony thought. Consulting. From the look on Sir George's face, they've cut him out—now they've let him overhear something—damn, what must that be like? I've *got* to find out. And maybe—

Tony cleared his throat. "I've never been to Africa," he said. "It sounds good."

Nobody paid any attention to him for a moment. Then Barbara smiled, slightly. "Oh, come on, Tony."

"We can at least consider it."

Bonner shook his head. His look was decisive. All right, Tony thought. I'll shut up. But just for now. You've not heard the last of this!

There was more silence. Then all three, Bonner, Churchward, and Reedy, were smiling. "Eight hours a month and ten days a year," Art Bonner said. "Excellent."

"Agreed," Sir George said. He extended his hand, then withdrew it slightly. "Mind you, I'll not aid in helping either of them escape."

"No need," Bonner said. "You'll take care of sending Sanders on to Salisbury. We'll get them both to Canada."

"Quite. Very well." He extended his hand again. Bonner took it, and after a moment Barbara put hers atop the other two.

Leaving me out, Tony thought. Taking me for granted. We'll show them, we will—

Bonner stood. "A moment." He stood silently for a moment. Sir George joined him in the pose. They waited nearly a minute, then Bonner opened the outer office door. A uniformed Todos Santos guard stood outside.

"Sir George will be leaving this afternoon," Bonner said. "I expect he'd like to pack now."

"Right," the guard said. He led Reedy away.

Bonner came back and closed the door.

"OK, sweets, what does Tony think he's doing?"

"O come on, Art, It's obvious what he wants."

"?"

"Tee hee. You'll see it in a second. I'm surprised at you."

THE POLICE HAVE REQUESTED ALL FILES UNDER DIRECTORY TITLE RAND.

"Dump it for them at 300 baud."

"Art! Are you sure?"

"We cleaned Rand's directory first thing. Took out everything not routine, then we added a few files. Old engineering catalogues. Maintenance schedules. Ratings of TV shows. Makes a pretty big file—" MILLIE, what is the total stored in Rand's directory?

23,567,892 BYTES

"Good Lord. Art, that will take hours to print out—"

"Yeah, that gives the cops a hobby. Now what is it Rand wants? Delores? He's got her—"

"No, no, Delores won't go. But that's not his primary want anyway. Come on, use your head."

"Oh! " Bonner grinned. "All right, Tony, why the sudden interest in trips to Africa?" He watched, amused, as Rand tried to keep a poker face.

"Well, I always did get along with Pres, and—"

"But you could be talked into going to Canada?"

"Well, yes, but it would be expensive. I want—"

"Oh, never mind, Tony," Bonner said wickedly. He made his voice sound resigned. "We'll lose money on the Canadian deal, but if you really want to go to Africa, well, we owe you, and—"

"Uh—"

Whatever Rand was going to say was drowned out by Barbara's laughter.

"Art, you are really cruel."

"Maybe once in a while." "Tony, it's going to cost you."

Rand looked wary. "What's going to cost me?"

"The implant. That's what you're holding out for, isn't it? Jesus, I never saw a worse negotiator. Fortunately, your interest is our interest . . ."

Rand looked more wary than ever.

"Of course we'll want an exclusive contract for your services, with veto power over any outside jobs and the right to reassign you at our convenience—"

"Yipe. That's slavery!" Rand protested.

"Yup. We'll also want you here part of the time. Not in person, of course, but we'll let you roam around Todos Santos by robot, and set up regular holographic conferences, with us and with your replacement."

"What do you intend to do, work me to death?"

"Not quite. Of course you always have the option of quitting on half pay—you won't be able to work for anyone else, but half what we pay you is plenty."

"So what's to keep me from taking your implant and your money and going off to grow petunias?"

"We'll chance it." "About as much chance of that as I have of turning into a werewolf. Keep him idle for six months and he'd be a raving maniac."

"There are those who say he—skip it." "That's settled, then," Barbara said. "Smile, Tony, you win. You'll get your implant." She paused. "You don't look very happy about it."

"No, no, that's fine." But Tony still wasn't smiling.

"For a man who's about to go off alone, he really is putting a good face on disaster."

"Yeah. Too good. I don't like it."

"There is a problem with this," Barbara said. "You won't be able to come back to the States. Not for a while, anyway. You might have difficulty seeing your son."

"It isn't Zach he's going to miss, it's getting laid regularly."

"Both, I'd say. And don't be narsty." "Is there a chance Genevieve might be persuaded to go with you?"

Rand shook his head violently. "Why would she do that? There won't be any high-status place like Todos Santos in Canada. Not till I build it!"

"Which is just the point," Barbara said. "If she'd come with you, you'd know it's because she believes in you. It wouldn't be just for the status. She'd earn her way, just as you will—"

"Aren't you laying it on thick?"

"With Rand? You can't lay it on too thick. Look at his face. We've got him."

"But will Genevieve believe any of that?"

"Who cares? So long as she'll go. And I think she will. From everything I've heard, she's pretty sharp."

"Why do you want Genevieve to go with him anyway, pet?"

"Come on, haven't you seen him when he talks about her? He's still in love with her. Delores knows, everyone else knows, except maybe Tony."

"I liked seeing Tony happy, and he was for the few days he had Delores."

"He'd be happy with Genevieve. Believe me."

"She'd never do it," Tony said.

"You'll never know until you ask her."

"*How* do I ask her? The cops will be watching her all the time. Probably have her phone tapped."

Barbara nodded. "That's true. But I can talk to her for you, Tony. Find out what she thinks. If it sounds good I'll bring her here. They'll never be able to follow *me* inside Todos Santos!"

I AM PRINTING THE REQUESTED FILES.

You will not answer any other requests from the police until that printout is completed.

ACKNOWLEDGED. THE POLICE ARE NOW ENTERING YOUR MAIN OFFICE. SANDRA WYATT IS WITH THEM.

"I'd appreciate that, Barbara," Tony said. "I—I guess I really would like it if Djinn came with me. Not that I think she will."

"We'll see."

"BOSS THIS IS SANDRA. I'M TALKING INTO A HUSH PHONE. THERE'S NO WAY YOU CAN ANSWER ME. THE COPS HAVE BROUGHT ALICE STRAHLER UP HERE. THEY'RE TRYING TO TALK HER INTO GUIDING THEIR SEARCH. THEY'RE PROMISING HER IMMUNITY. HAVE MILLIE BLINK YOUR OFFICE LIGHTS IF YOU UNDERSTAND."

"Holy shit," Bonner said aloud. "MILLIE, blink my office lights. Tony, they've brought Alice here. Can she help them find anything in MILLIE that we don't want them to know?"

"Maybe," Rand said. "We did all the obvious things—"

"I did a few that weren't so obvious," Bonner said. "Such as erasing your access logs, and taking your name off all the accession records for the City Hall and County Jail plans and such."

"But we still could have missed something," Rand said.

"What?"

"If we knew, we wouldn't have missed it," Barbara said impatiently.

"And we probably did miss something," Rand said. "No way we could be sure. And—well, Alice could have hidden a few files herself."

"She didn't know about anything illegal, did she?" Bonner demanded.

"No, but she might embarrass us."

"Meanwhile, the economic harassments continue," Barbara said. "That strike can hurt us—"

"It's already hurting us," Bonner said.

"Right. So." Barbara stood suddenly. "Art, it's time to call off this war. I think we should have a peace conference."

"Think we're ready?"

"We can get ready."

More data whispered against his mastoid bone. "Holy cow. Sweetheart, you're a mean broad."

"Economic warfare is my specialty." "So," she said. "You call MacLean Stevens and invite him to bring Councilman Planchet out. Tony, we'll have an hour or so to talk. How would Todos Santos go about putting pressure on Los Angeles?"

• • •

Art Bonner looked at the wreckage of his office and cursed. The place was a mess, with holes in the wall, chipped plaster, ripped upholstery; there were books scattered everywhere.

"I tried to get it cleaned up," Delores said. She spat. "Cops! I can get the worst taken care of before your appointment—"

"Leave it," Bonner said. "The main thing is to be sure their bugs are gone and our cameras are working."

"We did that first off," Delores said. "Of course that made some of the mess—"

"It's all right." Art sat behind his desk and looked at the readout screens. "Tony, you there?"

SURE AM. The letters flowed across one desk

console screen. VISUAL AND AUDIO PICKUPS WORKING FINE.

"Good."

MACLEAN STEVENS AND COUNCILMAN PLANCHET HAVE ARRIVED AT THE SOUTHEAST HELIPORT.

Thank you. Link to Barbara Churchward. "You there, sweetheart?"

"Right here. Tony had some ideas too."

"This is it, kids. Payoff time."

• • •

Big Jim Planchet held his lips to a tight line as he entered the big office. It was here, he thought. Right here. They gave the orders and my boy died. Right here.

He followed MacLean Stevens in, not really hearing the introductions and greetings, not seeing anything at first. Then he looked around, seeing the destruction. Holes in the walls and ceiling. Books thrown to the floor, covered with plaster dust, then walked on. Some of them looked to be expensive books, art volumes. Furniture had been ripped open, rugs slashed.

"Your cops were thorough enough," Bonner said. "They didn't find anything, but then I doubt they expected to."

"Not my cops," Stevens answered. "Sheriff's people, not mine."

"Balls. You could call them off anytime you wanted," Bonner said.

"You lost an office. I lost a son," Planchet said coldly.

"I'm sorry about your son," Bonner said. "If we'd known any way to save him, we would have, but he was just too damned convincing! We were betrayed ourselves. Alice Strahler—the one who told Renn how to get your kid in here? The Sheriff's men were talking about giving her immunity."

Planchet started to say something, but held back.

"If you'd been a bit more cooperative, I doubt the deputies would have trashed your office," Stevens said.

"Cooperative how?"

"That goddam computer, printing out page after page of TV show ratings!"

"They asked for it," Bonner said. "I can't help it if you've got a bunch of stupid cops trying to talk to a smart computer."

"Look, Bonner, this isn't a game," Planchet said.

"I couldn't agree more," Bonner said. "So. Shall we be serious? If you want a drink I can send for anything you'd like. My delivery system got broken this afternoon when one of your cretins thought he'd found the secret compartment we hide engineers in."

"That's serious?" Stevens asked.

Bonner couldn't help it. He laughed. "The cop sure thought it was. You should have seen him, with his head stuck in the conveyor, which picked just that time to deliver a royal gin fizz . . ."

That got a grin from Stevens. "We'll pass the drinks for the moment. All right, you called the conference. Your turn."

"Sure," Bonner said. "I want to negotiate a peace settlement."

"No deal without Sanders and Rand," Planchet said.

"Then no deals at all," Bonner said. "Sorry to have wasted your time, gentlemen." He stood up. "I'll get you an escort back to your helicopter."

"Hell, we just got here," Stevens said. He looked at Planchet. "You know damned well they're not going to turn Sanders over to us."

"Then we hurt them until they do," Planchet said. "You think the strike hurts now? Wait till we have a *real* strike. Nothing will go in or out of this building. Nothing."

"Sure," Bonner said. "And we counter with a boycott. Miss Churchward starts making purchases from San Francisco. We bring it by ship and land it in Long Beach. It will be the best thing that ever happened to the west coast merchant marine, but Los Angeles won't make much out of it.

"Then there are our waldo operators. They've elected a spokesman." Bonner touched a switch on his desk console.

Armand Drinkwater's apartment appeared on the screen. Drinkwater sat idly, his tools neatly stowed away. "Just can't work this way," he said. "How can I work when an Angelino cop could break in my door anytime he wants to? I'm used to *knowing* who's going to visit me. The rest of us all feel the same way."

Stevens nodded grimly, and he and Planchet exchanged glances.

Aha, Bonner thought. They've already heard about that one. Wonder who called? Might be the Secretary of State. Those medical gizmos Drinkwater was making were pretty important, and the orbital work even more so. So let's rub it in . . . He touched buttons.

Rachael Lief came onto the screen. Behind her, in *her* screen, was a lunar landscape complete with irate astronaut. "I can't tell you when I can get back to work," Rachael said. "When things are settled here. You could get someone else—"

The astronaut cursed again. Bonner cut him off and looked expectantly at Planchet. Your move, Bonner's look said.

"How are shipments going to get here from Long Beach?" Planchet demanded. "I told you, we'll see that nothing comes in or out—"

"Not even food?" Bonner asked innocently. "I'm not certain, but I think the Constitution prevents U.S. cities from making war on each other. If you let people starve to death in here, it will get on national television. Are you going to stop food from coming in?"

"Don't be silly," Stevens said.

"Me, silly? Come on, now, who was it threatened to

leave us besieged in the castle? You're more medieval than we are. Private wars, yet."

"Damn you, this is no joke!" Planchet shouted.

"And just to be *sure* you understand that—" Bonner's hand hesitated above the keyboard, then withdrew. "Councilman, I've already told you we regret what happened. You can't possibly believe we wanted to kill innocent kids—and you've seen all the warnings we gave, the signs those kids went past, the locked doors they went through. You're an intelligent man. You know damned well there wasn't another thing we could have done. And either you or Stevens would have done the same thing if you'd been sitting in Preston Sanders's chair, too!"

Bonner paused for a moment. "You don't have to respond to that. But think about it. While you're thinking, let me show you another one."

The TV screen showed the iceberg resting in Santa Monica Bay. "This goes with it," Bonner said. He took a Xerox from his desk and handed it to Stevens. "That gives me operational control of all Romulus assets in the southwest. Including the power plants in Baja. Also the iceberg. Now watch closely. Are you watching?" MILLIE: are the skiers all evacuated from the iceberg?

YES.

Have Rand do Phase One of Fimbulwinter.

Nothing happened for a moment. Then the floating plastic liner which trapped melted icewater and kept it separated from the salt water of the Bay rippled along its entire length. The iceberg itself seemed to move, slowly, majestically. On the windward side of the berg, thousands of gallons of salt water slopped in.

"Hey, for God's sake!" Planchet protested.

"So far your constituents can drink brackish water," Bonner said. "I don't expect they'll like it much, but it won't hurt them. Would you like to try for straight salt water?"

"You need that water as much as we do," Stevens said.

"Watch again," Bonner said.

The TV screen shifted to a personable young lady. The legend underneath said "Sandra Wyatt, Deputy General Manager." A male voice-over said "We interrupt regularly scheduled programming for an important announcement."

"This is a Stage Two water conservation notice," Wyatt said. "We have reason to believe that the city of Los Angeles may interfere with our water supplies. As you all know, we have large internal storage systems, all of which are full. It will be inconvenient, but we shouldn't have any real problems if everyone does their share. The Stage Two water conservation plan imposes the following restrictions. All residents will immediately—"

The screen went back to a view of the iceberg, which was still in motion but no longer shipping water into the plastic liner. "Want to bet your people will conserve better than mine?" Bonner asked. "You won't run out of drinking water, but you'll shut down more industries than I will . . ."

"I can get an injunction," Planchet protested.

Bonner laughed. "Go ahead. There's the phone. With luck you might get a court order in the next hour. We won't even oppose it—"

MILLIE, I want about half that much water sloppage again.

"Are you watching? Incidentally, my chief engineer tells—uh, excuse me, *told* me that it takes three full days to flush the system once it's been thoroughly contaminated with salt. That's assuming our people do it. Doing it without the computer and using outside work crews can take from two weeks to forever, depending. Just thought you'd like to know."

That got to them, Bonner thought. "Of course, you could go back to pumping water from the Owens Valley and the Sacramento Delta," Art said. "You might have some trouble from the Fromates though. Didn't they dynamite your aqueduct once?"

Still no answer.

Data rippled into his mind. He grinned. "Now here's something interesting. There's a large shipload of cement about to leave Portland, Oregon. Romulus bought it to send up to Prudhoe Bay, but Barbara has authority to divert it for our use. We were just about to put in an order with a local outfit, but if we're under local siege I'll want to assure my supplies."

"That'll cost you a lot," Stevens observed.

"Not so very much. We got the cement at a good price." He cocked his head to one side and looked thoughtful. "Actually, we might even *save* money."

Planchet turned to Stevens. "Do you believe that?" Stevens shrugged.

"I could let your investigators find that file," Bonner said. "Or show it to you here. Want to see for yourself?"

"All right, I'll just call that bluff," Planchet said. "How much—"

He stopped because MacLean Stevens was laughing so hard it was hard to hear anyone else speak. "He really got you," Stevens said. "What difference does it make whether he tells you a story or has MILLIE tell you? You think the computer won't lie for him?"

"He can't have made up that many stories in advance—"

"He doesn't have to make up *anything* in advance," Stevens said. "Don't you understand, he's talking to that goddam computer every second. The computer's in his *head,* Councilman!"

"Christ. And that's what my kid was up against . . ."

"He almost beat us," Art Bonner said. "If that makes you feel any better."

"It doesn't."

"He did beat us," Art said almost musingly. "Our goal was a capture . . . Mr. Planchet, what *can* I say? Nothing we do will bring Jimmy back. But you,

you're helping the people who *really* killed him! The Fromates. And I can't believe you're actually on their side."

Planchet sat heavily. "I thought about that already," he said carefully. "I thought about it a lot. Damn it, I don't know what to do." He pounded his big fist into a bigger hand. "All right, Bonner, what is it you want?"

"I want this strike ended," Bonner said. "I want your cops out of my city, and my people back to work. I want things the way they were before—"

"Before," Planchet said. "We can't do that. But I guess we can stop hurting each other. Anyone tries that, it'll be political suicide. But Sanders and Rand are wanted, and they'll stay wanted."

"Done. You'll never see either one of them again. Mac, take your police and go. Mr. Planchet, call off your strike and I'll start flushing the iceberg tub. And put my people back to work. All right?"

Planchet's lips tightened. He looked from Bonner to Stevens, then at the iceberg on the screen; and slowly he nodded.

Done. Break out the champagne.

XX

Successful and fortunate crime is called virtue.

—Seneca

PERSUASIONS

"Sure you don't want a driver, Miss Churchward?"

"Thank you, no, Sergeant. I don't have far to go."
She smiled warmly and climbed into the roadster.
Like all cars in Todos Santos, it was company
property; individually owned cars didn't make sense.
It was cheaper to keep a fleet and lend them to
residents.

In theory, no car was reserved for any particular
person. In practice, certain specially equipped cars
were used by a very few top executives, and Barbara
considered the little Alfa Romeo "hers." She got in
and adjusted the seats and mirrors carefully, then
touched a switch inside the glove compartment.
Testing relay. MILLIE?

ACKNOWLEDGED. RELAY OPERATIVE.

Her implanted transceiver's range was fairly short,
but the car had a powerful relay system, good
anywhere in line of sight to the large antenna on top

of Todos Santos. She nodded in satisfaction, then checked each gauge. She started the car and listened attentively to the engine. Eventually she felt ready to face Los Angeles traffic and put the car in gear.

She spiraled up and up to the top of the ramp and out into the greensward around Todos Santos, choosing a route that led through a wild area. It wasn't actually wilderness: the native chaparral of Southern California is ugly brown most of the year, and the Todos Santos residents didn't want to look down on that; after some experimenting, the company's agronomists developed shrubs that stayed green with minimum artificial irrigation. The resulting greensward was pleasant to drive through, and the deer and rabbits and coyotes seemed to like it a lot.

The city's walls towered high above her. When she reached the edge of the park, she saw that the picketing Angelinos were gone. Stevens and Planchet had acted swiftly once they made the basic agreement. Up above, though, the Todos Santos residents hadn't removed their banners. THINK OF IT AS EVOLUTION IN ACTION.

Link to Bonner.

"Here I am. Pretty busy."

"Just a note. That banner has to go. It can't be helping our relations with the Angelinos."

"Guess you're right. I'll take care of it. Anything else?"

"Not right now. Bye."

The apartment building was modern Spanish, mostly concrete and tile, built over an underground parking structure and around a bricked patio. There was a parking place right in front, sparing her the drive down a narrow ramp.

A thick arched passage led to the interior court. Unlike most such apartment buildings, the swimming pool was in a separate area so that the brick-floored inside patio seemed cool and inviting, rather than being a glare of concrete deck and chlorined water. Genevieve Rand's apartment was on the second floor, up a flight of stairs and along an iron-railed balcony.

Barbara rang the bell, and was annoyed when there was no answer. Confirm time of appointment.

MILLIE didn't answer either.

Blast. Out of range. Too much concrete between me and the car. Oh, well. I'll keep ringing, I know—

The door opened. Barbara and Genevieve eyed each other appraisingly. She's not bad at all, Barbara thought. Kept her looks and figure. Maybe just a touch plump, but so is Delores. Tony must like them that way. "Barbara Churchward. We had an appointment—"

"Yes. I—I'm not sure we have much to talk about."

"I've come this far. You may as well hear what I have to say." She's certainly nervous. Because Tony's wanted? Are the police inside? That could be it, better watch what I say—

"Yes, won't you come in?" Genevieve stood out of the way, then closed the door behind when they were inside.

The apartment was neat. Expensive furniture. Plants. Little touches of color here and there, all very tasteful. A door was open to a hallway and at the end of that was another room, larger but not so trimly kept, with books and toys and a sewing basket visible on a big smooth-topped table. "Very nice," Barbara said.

"Would you like anything? Sherry? Coffee?"

"Nothing, thank you."

Genevieve indicated a chair. She hovered nervously until Barbara sat. "What can I do for you?"

Barbara made a snap decision. She couldn't talk here; not until she knew what was wrong. "I'd like to take you out to Todos Santos."

"Oh. Is—is Tony there?"

"I couldn't say. But just before he disappeared, he made an appointment with you—"

"Yes, that's right."

"Actually, he wanted me to keep it for him, even before the big flap with the police."

"Oh. Then you're—"

Barbara laughed. "Great heavens no! Oh, I like Tony, but no, we're not involved. No, Mrs. Rand, it's just that he asked me to, well, to negotiate with you. It seems he didn't trust himself."

"Negotiate? But to do—"

"For you to join Tony, if that's what you want. Of course there are problems just now. We could discuss all this better out there—"

Genevieve didn't say anything.

Ha, Barbara thought, you still want to live with Tony if I'm any judge of expressions. I'm also certain we're not alone. If we're going to talk, we'll have to get out of here. "I really wish you'd come with me. We could be back in an hour, and there's a lot to talk about." Barbara stood and went toward the door. "Please—"

"That'll do it."

It was a man's voice. He was just stepping out of a closet. Barbara turned toward him. "My, officer, wasn't it uncomfortable in there?"

Genevieve laughed hysterically. "Officer! He's no policeman, he's—"

"Shut up."

The bubble of Barbara's amusement popped and was gone. Not police?

There were more people now. A not unattractive but certainly large woman came out of the playroom. Another man came from a side door in the same hallway. This one carried some kind of two-handed firearm with a fat barrel. Barbara had seen one like it before, but couldn't remember where. One of Colonel Cross's men? It didn't matter. It was a submachine gun, and that made these desperate people indeed.

MILLIE!

Nothing.

Damn these concrete walls! "What do you want?"

"We want you, Mizz Churchward."

"Miss," she said automatically.

"Traitor," the woman said. She came over to stand very close to Barbara. "Pig."

"Leona," the first man said. "That's enough."

"Just how am I a traitor?" Barbara asked. *If I can keep them talking—*

The woman hit her hard across the mouth. Barbara stepped back gasping. The woman hit her again, first with her fist, then slapped her, forehand, backhand. "Now do you understand?" Leona demanded. "You're nothing, pig. Nothing. You'll do what we want, and you'll talk when we want you to, and you'll be polite. Understand?"

Barbara spat out pieces of a broken tooth, and felt bloody saliva run down her chin.

The hard hand struck her again. "I asked you a question, pig."

"I understand."

"All right. Let's get them both out of here," one of the men ordered.

Leona was holding a black cloth hood. She put it over Barbara's head, then took her arm and began pulling her. Barbara stumbled along somehow. The whole side of her face throbbed, and it was hard to breathe inside the bag. Her nose was stopped up, and she continually swallowed salt blood.

"And keep quiet, understand?"

"I understand."

Something siezed her left breast and squeezed horribly. Barbara gasped with pain.

"I didn't say you could talk. Now shut up and come on." The hand squeezed again. Barbara stumbled and nearly fell. The woman lifted her by her breast, and Barbara felt faint from the pain. She was half dragged until she could recover her balance.

MILLIE? MILLIE . . . MILLIE . . . God where are you? MILLIE—

ACKNOWLEDGED.

O thank God. Record. Security alert. Link with Bonner.

"What is it?"

"I'm being kidnapped. Present location Genevieve Rand apartment."

"! We're on our way."

"Going down some stairs now. Blindfolded. The stairs face north, we're turning right, right again—I'm turned around, I don't know which way I'm going. We're going down again, I suppose into the garage under the apartment. Art, I'm scared."

Nothing.

"Art!"

"Get in the car and lie on the floor. That's it. Right there."

MILLIE—Art—someone—

Nothing. O boy. Hang on, no panic, they'll find me. Art will take care of that. And then it'll be my turn with that sadistic bitch. She's probably a Lesbian. Wonder what she's afraid of most? Maybe rats. I can have her put in with a whole cage full of rats. Spiders, too. Whatever she doesn't like. MILLIE—

She heard the car motor start. The car began to move. It seemed to be going slowly, turning slowly, moving slowly. It tilted sharply and continued to move.

Up the parking ramp. MILLIE

ACKNOWLEDGED. "You faded on us, sweetheart. Look, you keep trying."

"They have me in a car. We'll be driving away. Away from my car. Away from the relay."

"Keep telling us which way you're going. Don't stop transmitting."

"I'm scared . . . We turned left at the top of the ramp. Now we're moving, faster. There's no gear shift. Electric automobile. Running smoothly. Good springs and shocks I think. We're turning right—are you still there?"

"Still hear you. Keep telling us."

"Now we're going again. Turning right. Uphill. Uphill and turning. A freeway ramp! Leveling off. Accelerating. We're on a freeway. Art—"

Nothing.

O Lord.

MILLIE. MILLIE. MILLIE . . .

• • •

"The Montana Street entrance," Bonner said.

"Only one on ramp there, and it goes south," Colonel Cross said. "They're headed toward us on I-5."

"We've got to find them," Bonner said.

Cross nodded crisply. "I want every car with an implant relay out on that freeway. Cruise up and down and keep on Miss Churchward's frequency. MILLIE will tell you if she gets anything."

"Right," Lieutenant Blake said. He spoke softly into a telephone handset.

Bonner lifted his own telephone. "Sandra, locate every portable transceiver we have and get them into cars that don't have relay units. I want to blanket this city with relays. Let Security know when you've got them ready to roll. If we get enough cars out there, one of them has to hear her—"

"I already thought of that, Art," Wyatt said. "It's being done. Anything else?"

"No, I have Colonel Cross with me and he's handling it. We're taking a lot of your cops. You'd better cancel leaves and call in some off-duty guards."

"Already on that, too, chief. Leave the routine to me. I'll run the city. You find your lady."

"Yeah. Thanks." Bonner put down the telephone. MILLIE.

ACKNOWLEDGED.

Anything from Miss Churchward?

NO NEW COMMUNICATION WITH CHURCHWARD.

Listen hard.

INSTRUCTION NOT UNDERSTOOD.

• • •

Tony Rand hurried past Delores without seeing he

and without waiting to be announced. He charged into Bonner's office. "Art, I just heard—"

It hit him, then. Before he'd only been worried. Now he felt a cold hand in his guts as he saw Bonner and Colonel Cross and Lieutenant Blake sitting grim-faced, not doing anything.

Not doing anything. Which meant there was nothing to do. They'd have thought of all the obvious stuff—"Is it certain they took Djinn?" Tony demanded.

Colonel Cross glanced at Bonner, then nodded. "Yes. We have our people in Mrs. Rand's apartment now, and neither she nor the boy are there."

"Zach's with his grandmother," Tony said. "I talked to him on the telephone before the jailbreak and he said his mother was sending him off for two weeks."

"That accounts for him, then," Cross said. "And of course Mrs. Rand *could* have gone voluntarily with the kidnappers—"

"Batshit," Tony said.

Cross shrugged.

"They got Barbara at Genevieve Rand's place," Bonner said. "They were obviously waiting for her. And Genevieve has been fairly chummy with Professor Arnold Renn—"

"She wouldn't have helped them kidnap Barbara," Tony said. "She can be a screwball, but she's not *that* screwy."

Bonner spread his hands. "Makes no difference anyway," he said. "Join the club. Sit down and wait."

"We should be doing something—"

"Agreed. What?" Bonner demanded. "Let me tell you what we're doing now. Maybe you will think of something."

Rand felt a quick surge of hope, but when Bonner finished talking, Tony couldn't think of a thing to add.

• • •

"Central, this is One Zed Niner. We have a weak transmission from Sweetheart. I say again, we have a weak transmission from Sweetheart. Our location is 18400 block of Staunton Avenue. We have no directional antenna, but we can cruise until signal peaks. Instructions?"

"Stay out of sight, One Zed Niner. Do not let Playmates see you. We do not wish Playmates to know we have means of locating them. I say again, get your vehicle out of sight and stay there. Continue to monitor transmissions from Sweetheart. We will attempt to focus an antenna on your vehicle so that Sweetheart will be able to communicate directly with us. Do you understand?"

"Understood. Will comply. One Zed Niner out."

• • •

"What the hell are your troops doing?" Bonner demanded.

"Take it easy," Colonel Cross said. "And stop snapping at us. We're sending the cars out there, including hers. We had contact with her, and she wasn't moving, and it's only a matter of time before we get through to her again. For God's sake, boss, keep your shirt on."

"Yeah. All right. I'll try."

"Now about that other matter. Do I call in help?"

"No, Colonel. Not unless you think you have to. I'd rather we did this ourselves," Art Bonner said.

Amos Cross grinned. "So would I. But I do warn you, the LAPD SWAT team is one of the best in the world. They haven't lost a victim yet."

"And you don't think our people can do it?"

"If I thought that, I'd insist we call in LAPD," Cross said. "We've got sharp troops. But of course they don't have the kind of experience regular SWAT outfits get."

How could they? There hadn't been a barricaded-with-hostages case in the history of Todos Santos. Am I right to take chances? With Barbara and Genevieve?

"Tony, you get a voice in this decision. Should we call in LAPD?"

Rand looked helpless. "Colonel Cross is the expert, not me. I'll go along with whatever you two decide."

Putting it square on me as usual, Bonner thought. So be it.

"Art! MILLIE answered me! Art!"

"Thank God. I'm here, babe. Are you all right?"

"Not too bad. They're a little rough, but I can take it now. But I don't know where we are—"

"We almost have you located. That's how you hear us, we have a relay unit near you. Soon as I get a couple more cars there we'll triangulate and locate you. One question. Should we call LAPD SWAT or take care of it ourselves?"

"Just us. Please. I've stayed sane thinking what I can do to those—uh—O God—"

"Barbara!"

"Whew. They do get—I'll try to control that. You need me to keep transmitting so you can locate me, don't you? I'll try. One. Two. Three. Four . . ."

"Colonel, get our troops ready. That's a bad situation there."

"What's happening?" Rand demanded. "Did you hear something? Is Djinn all right?"

"Don't know, Tony," Bonner said. He help up his hand, palm outward. "Don't distract me. Colonel, let me know when your people are in position. They'll have to go in fast . . ."

● ● ●

"Lie down, bitch."

O God, not again. "You hurt me last time. I—"

"Shut up, or I'll give you to Leona."

Could that be worse? MILLIE. Have you located me? Uh. Thank God it's not my fertile time. Do they all do this? They raped Patty Hearst. Maybe they think it will convert me. Oh Lord that hurts—

"It's the revolution. It's coming, and nothing you can do about it. We'll end the Corporate State. It'll just die, when people find out they don't have to knuckle under, they don't have to put up with big companies to get enough to eat . . ." The lecture dissolved as his arms went around her and he squeezed her, his hips moved faster and faster—

"Where are they now? Can you locate all of them?"

"There are four men and one female. One of the men is in the closet with me. I don't think there are any weapons in here with us. I can take care of him if the others won't interfere. I don't know where they have Genevieve."

"You're sure Genevieve is not one of them."

"Yes. Very sure. They—they hurt her. And I don't know where she is, or where the others are. I—"

"What is he doing in a closet with you?"

"Art, what in hell do you think?"

"I'm sorry. Stand by. We're about ready—"

Think of something else. Anything else. She remembered her friend Jeanine who studied Zen. You handle pain by accepting it, attending to it, thinking about it, make it a part of yourself until it's commonplace and nothing special and then it isn't pain at all, only it's not working—

"Ha, you get interested too, don't you, honey? We can do this a lot—"

There was a splintering sound from the next room.

"What in hell was that?"

"HOLD IT RIGHT THERE. MOVE ONE INCH AND I'LL BLOW YOUR BALLS OFF."

"Shit—what is this?" He tried to scramble up.

Barbara reached up and seized his testicles. She clenched her fist hard, pulled, twisted. He shrieked and flailed helplessly in the dark. It was his screaming that brought the guards.

XXI

No one is fit to be trusted with power. . . . No one.
. . . Any man who has lived at all knows the follies
and wickedness he's capable of. . . . And if he does
know it, he knows also that neither he nor any man
ought to be allowed to decide a single human fate.

—C. P. Snow, *The Light and the Dark*

DILEMMAS

"Are you all right?"

"Yes. No. I've got a broken tooth, and a cut on
my face. But mostly I feel dirty. Sticky–dirty . . . Art, I
HATE them—Dr. Finder wants to give me a shot. I
think I'll let him."

"She says she's all right," Bonner said.

"Is Djinn all right?" Tony demanded.

Bonner looked helpless. "Barbara hasn't said. Damn
it, Colonel, why can't you talk to your people—"

"I'm getting through now," Cross said. He spoke
into the telephone. "All right, Captain, I've got you
on the speaker. You're talking to Mr. Bonner, Mr.
Rand, and myself. Report."

"Yes, sir. We are in complete control of the house.
Mrs. Rand is hysterical but otherwise physically
unharmed. She may have been sexually abused, but
that isn't certain. Miss Churchward had a nosebleed
and has a cut on her left cheek which will require

medical attention. She was—a man was in the—" The
guard stammered for a moment, then resumed in a
dry professional voice.

"Can you hear the policeman reporting to us?"

"Yes."

"We have four prisoners, three male and one
female. One male prisoner was apprehended while
committing rape. Miss Churchward greatly assisted in
his apprehension."

"You needn't put any of that in your report,"
Bonner said. "We'll edit that considerably."

"Thank you. I'm going to sleep now, Dr. Finder
gave me a shot . . . I love you."

"Love you."

"That's about all, sir. We broke in clean. The Los
Angeles police have not been called and no one is
likely to call them. We're waiting for instructions."

Cross looked expectantly at Art Bonner.

"Bring them all here. And the fewer people who
know about this, the better."

"Right. What are you going to do with them?"

"That, Colonel, is one hell of a good question."

• • •

Genevieve Rand found the situation thoroughly
ambiguous. On the one hand, the Todos Santos
guards had rescued her, and they couldn't have been
more polite. On the other—she didn't know where
she was, and the polite guards wouldn't let her leave.

She was in a comfortable room, the living room to
a large apartment somewhere in Todos Santos. She
had use of a bathroom. All the other doors were
locked, and there were no windows. They'd left her a
box that looked like a radio; someone always
answered if she talked into it. They'd had a physician
talk to her. And now they ignored her—but they
wouldn't let her go.

At least I'm safe, she thought, and shuddered. She'd
always been a little afraid of Ron Wolfe, even when
he'd been an above-ground member of the movement.

He was one of the intense ones, ready to sacrifice
everything—and everyone!—to the Cause. Including
himself, except that his objective assessment was that
he was far too valuable to be sacrificed lightly.

That had been her first thought, once she knew that
they intended to kidnap Churchward: Ron Wolfe
thinks he's too valuable to be sacrificed, and I'm
going to see him commit a capital crime.

She'd even tried to play along with them, pretend to
join them, but they weren't having any. Arnold Renn
had told them all about her attitudes and wants and
wishes and desires, and they weren't about to trust
her; and when they'd taken her as well as
Churchward she'd felt relieved that they hadn't killed
her on the spot, but she didn't think she had very
long to live. She remembered her terror when Wolfe
blindfolded Churchward—and didn't bother doing it
to her.

So. Thanks to the Todos Santos people, I'm safe;
but now what? I'm still a witness, she thought. I
wonder what that means?

The door opened and Tony came in.

Her first impulse was to run to him, but she was
seated in a deep, soft chair and she couldn't get up
easily; by the time she could stand, that moment had
been lost.

But he looks worried, and relieved, and glad to see
me, so maybe it's right after all—"Hello, Tony. I
thought you'd be out of the country by now, what
with the police after you and everything." And wow
do I sound calm and cool and collected, and is that
the right way to handle this? Competent. He likes
competence. Not having to worry about people. So
yes, it is the right way if I can just keep it up . . .

"I was just leaving when they told me," Tony said.
"Are you all right?"

She tried to shrug, and flinched; it felt like she'd
been kicked under the shoulder blade. She'd hit a
corner of something when the big woman threw her

across a room. "Some interesting bruises. Nothing permanent."

"Good." He was looking into her eyes, as if he really thought you could read minds that way. "I—uh—Miss Churchward was going to talk to you. Did she tell you what—I mean, did she explain what she wanted to see you about?"

"Some. We got interrupted."

He waved his hands around nervously. "Hell, I used to be able to talk to you, why can't I now? Djinn, do you want to come to Canada with me? It'll mean starting over, on a new arcology, one I can build *right*—"

"Ah. She never got that far. Oh, sure, I should have realized: you've *got* to leave, don't you?"

"Yeah. But Sir George Reedy has me signed up for another ten years of inspired drudgery, thank God. Do you want in, you and Zach?"

Genevieve almost laughed. What she wanted was *out*. *Out* of Los Angeles, *out* of the Fromates, *away* from anyone who knew her. She pictured a snowy wilderness, and a gigantic, formless building with thousands of glowing windows, isolated on the ice. All her mistakes left behind.

She wanted that. Now how best to bargain with Tony?

"Uh—Djinn, I want to be honest with you. This is a big job. My contract looks like they've reinvented slavery! And it isn't something I can do by rote, either. This one won't be anything like Todos Santos. I need a different design, it's a colder climate . . . there are new materials I'd like to . . . Djinn, what I'm trying to say is, I won't have a lot of time for family life, not at first—"

"I'll come." Jesus, he was about to talk himself out if it! "We'll come. It's all right, Tony. I'm a big girl, and I'm used to taking care of myself. I'll find plenty to do." Out of here, in a place where nobody knows me.

"Then it's settled? You'll come with me?"

She remembered that TV documentary. Safety. You're safe in Todos Santos. We can do that again, Tony and I. She nodded, and hugged him, carefully. Feeling fragile.

There were five people at the conference table. They had just taken their seats when Tony Rand brought Genevieve in. Art Bonner half stood and bowed perfunctorily. "Art Bonner," he said. "And Frank Mead, our comptroller. Colonel Cross of Security. John Shapiro, corporate counsel. Preston Sanders, formerly my deputy. You already know Barbara Churchward. I presume Tony told you why we're all here?"

"No." Genevieve seemed calm enough.

"Well, it's simple enough, and we thought you ought to have a voice in the discussion. We're trying to decide what to do with the kidnappers."

"But—" Genevieve looked puzzled. "But surely you'll turn them over to the police . . ."

"If we do that, you and I will both spend months in a courtroom," Barbara said. Her voice was slurred, and a thick bandage covered the left side of her face. "Which would mean that you could not go to Canada with Tony, and I certainly have better things to do than watch trials."

"Yes, but what can we do with them?" Genevieve demanded. "I mean, you can't just kill them—"

"I could," Barbara said. "Two of them, anyway. Except that I'd want to do it slowly."

"If you really mean that, I'll arrange it."

"I don't know. It just popped out."

"So what do we do with them?"

"Don't know. I don't want to sit in courtrooms. But I'm damned if I'll just let them go!"

Genevieve Rand looked shocked, then thoughtful; then she looked disgusted with herself.

"Barbara, be serious," Preston Sanders said. "You

don't want blood on your hands. Believe me you don't!"

"Pres, I understand how you meant that—but I am serious," Barbara said.

"Then there's Professor Renn," Bonner said. "Mrs. Rand, are you certain he arranged this kidnapping?"

"I'm certain he tapped my telephone," Genevieve said. "I saw him doing it—he said he'd dropped the phone and took it apart to check it. And Ron Wolfe and those other people are Arnold's friends, and they knew when Miss Churchward was coming."

"I'd say that's pretty certain," Barbara said.

"Certain enough for us. Not certain at all for the D.A." Shapiro said. "For that matter, the way we've violated their rights, we couldn't get *any* of them convicted now. Be more likely that we'd go to jail."

"Another good reason to put them out the airlock," Tony Rand said.

"No." Sanders's voice was low and determined. "Tony, think how hard you tried not to kill anyone in the last break-in. How hard I tried the first time. Did no good. We were forced to it. But this time, *this time* we have them alive, we haven't had to kill anyone, and dammit, we *can't* do it in cold blood. They're human beings too, just like us, and nobody appointed us judge and jury."

"I point out that the cost of putting them before a proper judge and jury is unreasonably high for the victims," Bonner said. "And we don't have jails and prisons here. But I just don't know what to do." He looked around helplessly. "I suppose I should start by asking the victims. Genevieve?"

"There's got to be a better way than murder."

"Barbara?"

She shrugged. "Three hours ago, I'd have cut their throats myself. Now, I'm not so sure." She shook her head. "I pass."

"Tony?"

"Put them out the airlock."

Bonner was surprised at how vicious Rand sounded.

So were several others, judging from their expressions. "I mean, what are the alternatives?" Rand asked. "If we let them go, they can get us in plenty of trouble—"

"Could any of them prove that we've held them?" Art asked.

"What do you mean by proof?" Shapiro said. "They might or might not recognize the guards who captured them. Otherwise—what proof could there be?"

"And we can see that our guards have a hundred witnesses each to swear blind they were on duty here," Bonner said. "So. They can't complain to the LA cops . . . not that they'd dare anyway, since they'd have to say what they were doing when our guards grabbed them."

"So. You've proved that we can turn them loose," Frank Mead said. "I'm not sure I care much for that. They'd be right back again, costing us—"

"With your permission," Amos Cross said. "With your consent, I'll talk to each of them. I think I can get it across that if we ever see or hear of any one of them again, we will declare open season on them— and that if we have the slightest doubt about our own ability to finish them, we can afford high-priced open contracts . . ."

"Is that your recommendation, Colonel?" Bonner asked. "That we turn them loose with a warning?"

Cross shook his head. "I pass on giving an opinion, Mr. Bonner. When the police become judges, your society is in real trouble."

"All right," Bonner said. "We've got three muggers we apprehended in the subway, and four kidnappers. We may as well take the easy case first. I gather everyone is for letting the muggers loose?"

No one said anything.

"We've kept them fairly heavily drugged," Amos Cross said. "And one of them babbled a lot. Enough to convince our guards that he's a murderer."

"And you're going to turn them loose on Los Angeles?" Genevieve Rand asked.

Frank Mead shrugged. "Who the hell cares about Angelinos, as long as *we're* not bothered by them again?"

"Angelino laws left them loose to hurt our people," Rand said. "If the Angelinos don't like the situation, let them change it. We did."

"So. We've got three muggers, four kidnappers—and Professor Renn."

"We don't have Renn."

"We can acquire him," Bonner said. "And the question before the house is a simple one. What do we do with them?"

"Think of it as evolution in action," Barbara Churchward said. There was no humor in her voice at all.

XXII

LAWS AND PROPHETS

Professor Arnold Renn threw clothes into an Air Force B-4 bag. He worked clumsily, with almost frantic haste. From time to time he glanced at the ornately engraved card that lay on his bedroom table. "THINK OF IT AS EVOLUTION IN ACTION."

Get out. Get away. It'll blow over. They can't really hurt me. But—

There had been a dozen of those cards. In his box at UCLA. At the faculty club. Under the windshield wiper of his car, and another on the car seat although there was no sign that the lock had been forced. In the refrigerator, and now in the bedroom, and Tina had no idea how they had got into the house.

The threat seemed unmistakable. Best not ignore it, not with the headlines about the jailbreak following the unsuccessful attack. And worse. There wasn't *anything* in the papers, or on TV, about a Todos Santos official being kidnapped, and there wasn't any answer at Genevieve's apartment, or at the Fromate headquarters, or—

Best get out of town. Take a leave of absence until things blow over. Let a graduate assistant meet the classes for a while. Get away. Let Tina follow later, if she wanted to. But get away, get out, go now.

He finished packing and took the suitcase out to the garage.

"Good afternoon."

Renn looked up, startled. The man stood lazily against the garage door. He smiled slightly, but there wasn't anything pleasant about the short-barreled shotgun he held. "Uh—"

"No need to say anything at all. I have a message for you."

"What—"

"It's simple. Goodbye."

Renn had just enough time to understand before the buckshot tore his chest apart.

• • •

Vague sensations shaped themselves into a pattern. Cold. Grass tickling cheek. A distant moaning nearby. Slowly Vinnie came to awareness of them all, and more. Pain, sharpening, until it felt like the left side of his face and neck had been smashed to bloody mush.

Like the long-faced creep with the empty pockets who'd cursed them in the subway, several weeks ago. He'd looked like Vinnie felt, when Vinnie got through with him. But Vinnie remembered his face, long and sullen and hating . . . and another face flashed vivid in his brain.

Styled curly blond hair; broad, smooth clean-shaven face; new dark blue suit and vest, bas-relief tie in scarlet and dark brown; gold at both wrists, gold ring . . . walking money. Seen only for an instant, with a look on his face such as Vinnie had never seen on a mark: unearthly joy, as the mark cocked his fist for another blow. The big fist with its big gold ring had just blasted Vinnie's neck to pulp, and was set to do it again.

They hated him. Vinnie had never *felt* that before. They cringed, they tried to reason with him, they handed him wallet or watch or purse, they ran . . . but they hated him. They would kill him if they could.

He reached for another face, seen later through a haze of some drug. A face out of a nightmare. Seen in close-up, a woman with impossibly huge eyes, hair exploding around her head, fiendish grin . . . and a tool in her hand, a needle tearing curves across his belly. He tried to scream and another needle jabbed his arm and it all went away.

Vinnie tried to curl himself tighter; he moaned, and the moan became a yell as it tore his throat open.

He was sitting upright, naked as a peeled egg. There were others around him, all naked, painted like so many Easter eggs. Six plus Vinnie. Some still sleeping; some staring about them in terror.

Where are we? He sat up and looked around. Green shrubbery to one side. On the other—

On the other, Todos Santos was a wall across the sky. The windows blazed like tens of thousands of eyes.

Run. He had to run. He sprang to his feet and everything went blurry; he hardly felt the jar as he fell back. "How was I to know?" he shouted. "How did I know it was you people in the subway?"

A voice from the distance mocked him. "THINK OF IT AS EVOLUTION IN ACTION," the voice called.

He looked behind him. There, across the field, over at the city street that bounded the Todos Santos greensward, was a large TV truck, with a cameraman standing on top. The camera, and other instruments, were pointed at Vinnie.

What am I doing here? But there was no place to go. Not really. And he wasn't alone.

Strangers . . . no. That was Runner Carlos,

clutching himself tight to make himself smaller. A small, hard man who sometimes raided the subways, whom Vinnie avoided when he could . . . very hard to recognize with no hair, no moustache, his whole body painted bluish-white. The great bulk of a man painted leaf green, sleeping peacefully on his side, would be Gadge, who ran with the Runner and took his orders. Vinnie had never seen him undressed. What he had taken for muscle on Gadge seemed to be mostly fat.

But who were the other four? And what did it say across their chests? He strained to focus his eyes. THINK OF IT AS EVOLUTION IN ACTION.

Vinnie fought back a laugh. It would tear his throat, and annoy Gadge and Runner Carlos . . . and Vinnie himself had been painted deep rose. His belly bore the same cartoon as the rest. Like a trade mark. He rubbed it, not understanding, and found a slight ridge, and understood.

Tattoo, just healing. Vinnie remembered the woman with the needle—and, instantly, the man with the gold ring. He understood, then, that he would never see his belly in a mirror without remembering both: the huge-eyed woman with the needle, and the mark cocking his gold-decorated fist, ready to pound him to death.

• • •

Maclean Stevens drove up to Lunan's camera truck. "What's going on?" he demanded.

Thomas Lunan grinned. "Some sad people out there. All dressed up and no place to go."

"Who are they?"

"I think you'll find three of them are from the American Ecology Army. Underground types, wanted by the FBI. Three more are common crooks your cops will recognize."

"You seem to know a lot—"

"Shield law," Lunan chanted. "Shield law, shield law, shield law. No sources. But it's all true, and you really will want to arrest the three Ecology Army types. I doubt if you can charge the others."

"But—why?" Stevens demanded. "Why are they there?"

"If I had to guess," Lunan said, "I'd guess they annoyed Todos Santos."

Stevens set his lips in a grim line. In the field across the street, the sleepers were stirring. They kept glancing nervously toward Stevens and Lunan. Mac waved to the police who'd come out with him. "Round them up. Indecent exposure will do to get them to the station house."

The police sergeant laughed. "Right. Okay, troops, let's go . . ."

"So it finally happened," Stevens said.

"What happened?" Lunan asked.

"Todos Santos cut itself loose. Now they're completely above the law. They're judge and jury and executioner."

"But they're not," Lunan said. "Don't you see, that's the whole message here." He lowered his voice. "I'm prepared to deny I ever said this. Mr. Stevens, some of those people did more than *annoy* the Saints. They kidnapped and abused one of their highest officials. They had her for several hours before the Todos Santos guards rescued her."

Stevens frowned.

Lunan nodded. "Exactly. They really could have been judge and jury and executioner. Who'd know? Instead, they've chosen to stay part of the human race. Oh sure, they're also protesting your brand of justice. They want to see it changed. But they haven't cut loose from humanity."

"You can say that. You haven't just come from looking at Professor Renn's body."

Lunan looked up sharply. "What?"

"Somebody blew him away with a shotgun. You didn't know *that*, huh?"

"No. But it wasn't Todos Santos."

"Why is that, Lunan? Would they have used a death ray?"

Lunan laughed. "They just didn't. Mac, you may want to be careful investigating Renn's murder. You might find your favorite City Councilman wasn't as sharp as he thinks he was."

"Planchet? Planchet . . . yeah. God knows he had motive. Lunan, do you *know* this?"

"No. Sounds like a hired kill, though, doesn't it? That could be Planchet, or Diana Lauder's parents, or someone connected to the Ecology Army types Renn sent in to die. But I know what Todos Santos had in mind for Renn, and that wasn't it. They wanted to scare him out of the country."

Stevens mulled that.

The LAPD officers had just finished rounding up the gaily colored nudies. Stevens watched the last one loaded into a black and white. Then he looked past the greensward, past the orange grove, on to the enormous building beyond. Free society or termite hill? Or both?

Is this really the wave of the future? "For now," he told Lunan. "Just for now and for this moment they haven't quite cut loose from the human race. But can you live in that and stay human forever?" His arm swept expressively to indicate the enormous city/building, its windows glaring orange-white in sunsetlight.

The great orange banner was still there. "THINK OF IT AS EVOLUTION IN ACTION." As they watched, it rippled and moved. Someone was lowering it.

"*You* could live there, Lunan. You'd be welcome," Stevens said. "When are you planning to move in?"

"No," said Lunan, and then he bellowed. "Arbry, get a camera sweep of those windows!" His voice dropped again. "That'll go nice. A hundred thousand eyes, but they're all looking inward. No privacy at all, and no interest in what goes on out here. No, that's not *my* life style."

"Not mine either—"

"Why does it have to be? A Venice boatman would go crazy in there. So would a Maori tribesman, but that doesn't make him *right*. What would a Roman Legionnaire think of *your* life style? What would Thomas Jefferson think of me? There are a lot of ways to be human."

"Maybe." Stevens turned, in time to see the great banner flutter down from the battlements and settle gently to the ground.